monsoonbooks

BAMBOO HEART

Ann Bennett was born in a small village in Northamptonshire, UK. She read Law at Cambridge and qualified and practised as a solicitor. During a career break, to have children, she started to write. Her father had been a prisoner of war on the Thailand–Burma Railway and the idea for *Bamboo Heart* came from researching his wartime experiences. The research took her to Southeast Asia, a place she loves and has returned to many times. She lives in Surrey with her husband and three sons and works in London as a lawyer.

Bamboo Heart is volume one in a Southeast Asian WWII trilogy that includes *Bamboo Island* and *Bamboo Road*. Learn more about the author at: *www.bambooheart.co.uk*.

BAMBOO HEART

ANN BENNETT

monsoon

monsoonbooks

Published in 2014
by Monsoon Books Pte Ltd
71 Ayer Rajah Crescent #01-01, Singapore 139951
www.monsoonbooks.com.sg

First edition.

ISBN (paperback): 978-981-4423-73-1
ISBN (ebook): 978-981-4423-74-8

Cover design by Cover Kitchen.

Backcover illustration of a hospital ward on the Burma Railway by
Murray Griffin, 1946 (pen and brush and brown ink, pencil, white gouache
on paper). Image copyright©Australian War Memorial.

National Library Board, Singapore Cataloguing-in-Publication Data
Bennett, Ann.
Bamboo heart / Ann Bennett. – First edition. – Singapore : Monsoon Books
Pte Ltd, 2014.
pages cm
ISBN : 978-981-4423-73-1 (paperback)

1. World War, 1939-1945 – Prisoners and prisons, Japanese – Fiction.
2. Burma-Siam Railroad – Fiction. 3. Prisoners of war – England – Fiction.
4. Prisoners of war – Thailand – Fiction. 5. Fathers and daughters – Fiction.
I. Title.

PR6102
823.92 -- dc23   OCN871636245

Printed in Singapore
16 15 14   1 2 3 4 5

In memory of my father, Dick Bennett

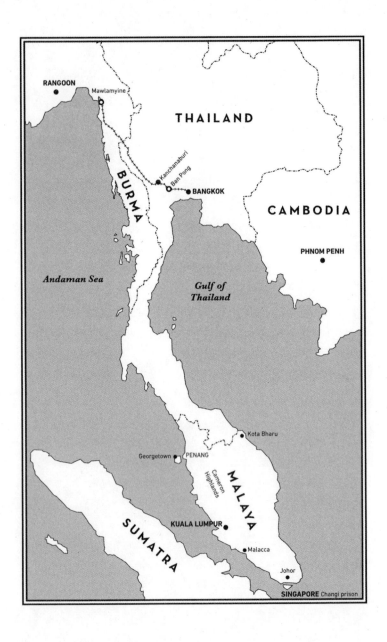

DEATH RAILWAY

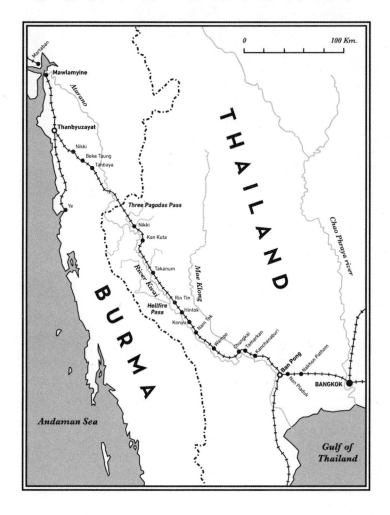

Martaban
Mawlamyine
Ataran
Thanbyuzayat
Nikki
Beke Taung
Tahbaya
Ye
Three Pagodas Pass
Nikki
Kon Kuta
Takanum
River Kwai
Mae Klong
Rin Tin
Hintok
Hellfire Pass
Konyu
Nam Tok
Wampo
Chungkai
Tamarkan
Kanchanaburi
Ban Pong
Nakhon Pathom
Non Pladuk
BANGKOK
Chao Phraya river

THAILAND
BURMA

Andaman Sea

Gulf of Thailand

0   100 Km.

Prologue

Thailand, May 1943

'Hey!' Tom shouted. 'I need some more. You've spilled half of this.'

The guard bent over to stare at him, breathing heavily, his narrow eyes slits of hatred and derision.

'What you say?'

'I said this has spilled. I need some more food.'

The guard leaned over further and slapped Tom's face. Then he straightened up and spat down at him. Tom felt the warm glob of the guard's phlegm settle in his hair. His stomach turned in revulsion, but he did not reach up to wipe it away.

'You not ask!' screeched the guard, his voice hysterical. 'You must be punish.' He aimed his boot at the side of Tom's head, catching him above his left ear. Everything around spun and reeled from the blow.

'You bastard! I'm starving in here. I'm going to die.'

But the metal roof was already being slammed shut above his head, and he was left there, reeling from this new pain, his stomach taut with starvation.

He stood, slightly stooped, in this narrow earth prison that was already putrid and festering from the wastes of its former inhabitants. Tom's whole body cried out in pain. The ache in his back, welded into this awkward position, was excruciating, and his legs had turned numb, were close to collapse. Mosquitoes and flies buzzed around his open wounds and settled everywhere on his sweating body, covering him in bites that swelled and itched. His face was swollen from the kicks and punches of the guards, and his limbs and torso were turning blue with bruises. His ribs cracked sickeningly with every breath he took.

Tom watched as the sun slipped behind the jungle-covered hills in the distance, leaving the sky shot through with streaks of red and pink. Sunset was swift in the tropics, and within a few minutes everything he could see through the bamboo bars above his prison pit would be enveloped in darkness. He welcomed the night. It meant that, if only for a few hours, it would feel a little cooler inside the pit. It also meant that by some miracle he had survived another day.

Each morning, as the sun came up he listened out for the sound of the bugle. This would summon the camp to roll call. He would watch the other prisoners stumble out of their huts onto the open space in front of the guardhouse and assemble there in unsteady lines. They hardly looked like soldiers anymore. Most of their uniforms were filthy and ragged. Some no longer had shirts and wore only loin cloths, exposing their skeletal bodies to the full glare of the sun. Some of them would cast furtive glances in the direction of the punishment pits, no doubt looking out for any sign of life from him, wondering if Tom was still alive, probably thanking God that it was him and not them in the pit. Tom, in turn, would look out for the men he knew, recognising them from the way they walked, the shape of their bodies, the rips on their uniforms.

Roll call and inspection consisted of the Japanese officers marching up and down the lines of men, slapping or shoving with rifle butts any man who did not bow correctly or show proper respect. Tom would watch from the pit, holding his breath, praying that it would be over quickly and the beatings would not be too severe.

When they were released, the men would cross the ground to the tool sheds and collect what they needed for their day's work on the railway cutting: crowbars, sledge-hammers and pickaxes, shovels and baskets to dispose of the waste. They would then begin their weary march up the jungle track to the cutting. Tom knew what faced them on the day ahead. Endless hours of back-breaking work, chipping away at the granite rock, or shovelling and hauling the waste rock to tip away at the edge of the cutting. All the time they would be bullied and abused by the guards who would slap or prod anyone they thought to be slacking.

But here in his earth prison, shivering in pain and misery, and standing barefoot in his own urine, his shorts covered in excrement, Tom longed to be setting off up the jungle path alongside those men. Each day was plagued with the fear that at any moment he might hear the clatter of the metal lid being thrown aside, might feel the force of rough hands dragging him out of the pit and across the clearing, that he would be made to stand up in front of a tree and mown down in a hail of bullets.

The prisoners would return after dark and queue up at the cookhouse for another meagre meal of rice and stewed vegetables. Tom would then see the dark shape of one of the guards approaching his corner of the camp. The metal roof would be thrown aside, and a tin plate and mug would be shoved towards him. If he did manage to grab the plate and lower it to his trembling lips, he found it difficult to force the food down his throat. His stomach, weak with starvation and sickness would rebel, and if he did manage to swallow any of the dirty, barely cooked rice, he would often vomit it up again, down the front of his ragged shirt, already stained with his own sweat and blood from the beatings. It was at moments like that, covered in vomit and drowning in his own filth, racked with pain and delirious with fever, when he felt like giving up, like simply collapsing here and surrendering to his fate.

It was at moments like that when he needed to distract himself with memories. He would focus on those years before the war, the people he had known, the good times he had once had. It was an effort, but with shaking fingers he would sometimes take out the photograph that still sat in the top pocket of his shirt, pressing against his chest. He would gaze at the image of the woman he loved, at her perfect features, at her glossy black hair drawn back from her face. But tears would prick his eyes as he looked at her. Those almond-shaped eyes and soft lips seemed to belong to another lifetime.

It was only after nightfall, when the darkness and silence of the camp blotted out his dreadful reality that he would be able to close his eyes and conjure the image of her face properly. She would then come to him, as if in a vision, and those soft brown eyes would caress his face, easing the burning and throbbing of his wounds, if only for a moment. Then he would reach out a trembling hand to touch her cool smooth skin, and she would smile. She would open those perfect lips to say something to him. But no matter how hard he tried, how much he strained his ears, he could never quite catch her words.

1

Hurrying out of the tube station on to Highbury Corner, Laura shivered in the chill drizzle of the winter afternoon. She glanced at the darkening sky and pulled her coat tightly around her. Hovering on the edge of the pavement, she scanned the lanes of stationary traffic for a cab, but seeing none, stepped onto the road, and nimbly threaded her way through the cars.

Her ankle turned as her left heel snagged between two uneven paving stones, and she cursed her tight work skirt and high heels. A goods lorry splashed past with a hiss of air brakes, spattering her legs and the hem of her skirt with filthy water.

'Bloody hell!' Ducking her head against the rain, she carried on, past the assortment of dusty charity shops, ethnic grocers and empty cafés, towards St. Paul's Road. Soon she was away from the heavy traffic, hurrying along the broad pavements of Highbury New Park in the grey-green light filtering through the plane trees

As she rounded the final sweep in the road, and the old house came into view, she quickened her pace. There it was, still stately despite its shabby paint work. In years gone by it had not looked out of place, but now it stooped apologetically between its two smarter, recently gentrified neighbours with their white windows and scrubbed brickwork.

Laura saw that someone was standing in front of the house. She slowed down, panting from the effort of running. It was an old man. Dressed in a battered hat and grey overcoat, he was almost indistinguishable from the tree under which he sheltered. He seemed to be watching the house. Laura hesitated, puzzled. Then, taking a deep breath to steady her thumping heart, she ventured a few steps towards him. He turned and began to move away from her, shuffling rather than walking.

'Hey,' she called out, but he didn't turn.

She watched his retreating form for a second then shrugged. He was probably one of the tramps who slept rough around Finsbury Park Station and was straying from his normal patch.

She paused before lifting the latch to the front gate. How overgrown the garden was. The scent of damp grass conjured a memory of pottering around behind Dad as a toddler, watching him weed the flowerbeds and prune the honeysuckle that smothered the front wall. She glanced up at the house. The curtains on the second floor sagged across the windows. A few greying socks hung from a clothes horse on the balcony, soaking in the rain. Ken, the lodger, would be fast asleep in the studio, amongst his paint pallets and whisky bottles, where he had been staying since he turned up for a brief visit in the summer of 1962.

There were no curtains on the top floor. It had been empty since the Chaudhry family had moved out. A couple of pigeons nested under the broken guttering, their white droppings streaking the front wall.

The windows of Dad's study were shut today. Normally he would have them open to let out the smoke as he sat puffing away on roll-ups, reading or working at his desk.

Letting the gate slam behind her, Laura rushed up the path. As she clattered up the front steps, the door to the basement clicked open.

'Is that you Laura, love?'

She hesitated. She'd wanted to avoid this.

'Marge?'

The old woman appeared beneath the parapet; her hair was hennaed but grey roots were showing through. She was dressed in the same nylon overall and slippers she'd been wearing for decades. A tabby cat rubbed itself against her legs. Laura caught the bitter tang of cat-piss wafting up from the basement.

'Thank goodness you've come, my love! Your dad's in the back sitting-room. Ken brought his bed down for him when he came home from hospital.'

'How is he? You really freaked me when you phoned this morning.'

The old lady's gaze slid away from Laura's. Her lips quivered.

'Not so good, my love. He's had an awful shock. Poor old Tom.'

'I'd better see how he is,' Laura took another step. Why didn't the old bat just go back to her cats and let her get out of the rain?

'Coming down for a cuppa later, love?'

'Yes, sure,' Laura answered automatically, fumbling in her bag for the key.

She let herself in through the front door. She stood still for a second, taking in the atmosphere and silence of the old house, its familiar smells of tobacco and stale cooking.

Then she kicked off her shoes and threw her coat on the hall table. The door to the back sitting room was shut. She pressed her ear to the panel. There was no sound, so she opened the door. The curtains were closed and she had to pause to let her eyes adjust to the gloom. The room's furniture had been shoved together to make space for Dad's bed. His portable radio chattered softly from the corner of the room.

'Laura?'

She crossed the room and knelt down beside her father.

'Dad.'

He raised himself onto one elbow. His blue striped pyjamas sagged from his bony shoulders. A crepe bandage was wrapped around his forehead.

'Come here. I wasn't expecting to see you. I thought you were in Paris.'

He held out his arms. He was smiling, but his face was pale and drawn with pain. She leaned forward to hug him. She put her arms around him, but sensing the fragility of the bones in his arms and ribs was afraid to hug him too tightly.

'Marge called me this morning,' she said. 'I came straight away.'

'You shouldn't have come all that way. What a fuss about nothing. What on earth did they say at work?'

'Nothing much. They couldn't object really, could they? Anyway, what happened to you?'

'Fell down the damned steps to the library. That ridiculous sodding stick gave way. The rubber bottom had worn down so it slipped—'

He paused for a coughing fit.

'Ruddy leg broken in two places. Not that it was up to much anyway. Banged my head too.'

'I hope they dosed you up with painkillers.'

'Of course. Morphine, codeine, the works. I'm rattling like a tube of Smarties.'

She straightened up and smiled down fondly at him.

'Why don't you go and change?' he asked. 'You don't want to spoil that lovely suit.'

'Don't fuss over me, Dad. I'll go up and change in a bit.'

'I'll tell you what then,' he looked up at her craftily. 'I could do with a beer.'

'You sure? It's a bit early.'

'Nonsense. It's nearly dark. There is some in the fridge in the study.'

She padded through to his study at the front of the house. Her feet were still wet from the walk.

'Can I turn on the heating?' she called. 'It's a bit bloody cold in here, Dad.'

'Boiler's broken down. I've been meaning to get it fixed.'

'Jesus. What a state …'

She stopped in the doorway to the study. Towering piles of books, newspapers and journals crowded every surface, the desk, the sideboard and even the floor. On the desk, ringed with coffee stains, were dirty cups and glasses, an ash tray overflowing with cigarette ends. She walked in, glancing briefly at the portrait of her mother and herself as a baby placed on the mantelpiece. Then holding her breath to avoid taking in the study's smells, she pulled up both the sash windows and began to collect the dirty crockery. There was a book open on the desk. She flipped through the pages. What had Dad been reading? *A History of the British Empire.* Just the usual stuff.

She was about to move away when she saw something poking out from between the book's pages. It looked like a photograph.

She slipped it out and stared at it. A faded sepia portrait, battered and creased. One of its corners had been torn away. It was someone she'd never seen before. It was a young woman. Although her complexion was pale, she had oriental features: dark eyes the shape of almonds, slightly tilted at the edges, a full mouth, a sheen of black hair drawn back severely from her face. She had a serious, demure expression, betraying a trace of surprise at the flash of the camera bulb. Laura turned over the photograph. The ink was so faded it was almost colourless. It looked as though it had been in water, but she could just make out the words written neatly in flowing script: 'To my dear Thomas. Good luck. Joy de Souza. Penang, November 1941.'

She stared at the photograph, confused. Then, with a pang of guilt she remembered the day she had found the letter with the Penang post mark, the one that had been scuffed by the letter box. She must have been fourteen or fifteen at the time. The exotic stamp had caught her eye, and when she pulled the letter free from the box, she'd noticed that she could read part of the letter through the torn envelope. It was but a small step to tear it a little further and ease out the letter. She'd heard Dad come in through the front door before she had read beyond the first few lines. She had panicked. Shame washed over her now as she remembered how she'd thrown the letter into the sitting-room fire and watched the flames devour it.

'Laura. You still there?' Dad called from the other room.

She slipped the photo back inside the book and went to the fridge.

'Won't be a minute,' she called, steadying her voice.

In the small kitchen at the back of the house, she rinsed one of the dirty glasses and filled it with beer. Dad was coughing and wheezing again when she came into the room. He held out his hand for the glass. After a few sips the cough subsided, and he dabbed his eyes with a crumpled handkerchief.

'Roll up a cigarette for me, will you? There's a good girl.'

'Your cough sounds dreadful, Dad. You should really give it a rest.'

'I don't think it's going to make that much difference at this stage, do you?' He winked at her. 'An old man deserves some pleasures in life.'

Sighing, she went to the sideboard and found the green tin of Golden Virginia; the cigarette papers and matches were in the desk drawer. Folding the paper and measuring just the right amount of tobacco, she packed it into the fold and rolled him a cigarette, just as he had taught her to do as a child.

After he had taken a couple of puffs, he lay back on the pillows.

'Pull that chair up, there's a good girl. Come and sit with me. I've been so damned bored.' She dragged an armchair over to the bed and sat down beside him.

'I didn't notice at first,' he said, peering at her. 'You've had your hair cut.'

She pushed her hands back through her damp hair. She felt colour creeping into her cheeks.

'It must look frightful. I forgot to bring an umbrella. I came straight from the office. It wasn't raining in Paris when I set off.'

'It suits you short like that. Very gamine, I think they say. What brought that on?'

She hesitated, glancing away, hoping he wouldn't notice her blushing. Was this the opportunity she'd been waiting for to tell him about Luke?

'Nothing really,' she replied. 'I just fancied a change.'

'How's it all going in Paris?'

'Fine, Dad. I told you on the phone last week. It's all going really well.'

'When is it you're coming back to London?'

'Next month. The posting ends then. I told you on the phone.'

'Met anyone out there?'

'Anyone? What do you mean?' But she knew what he meant.

She avoided his eyes. She wasn't going to get into all that now.

'And the work? Enjoying it still?'

'Of course. Who wouldn't? It's a fantastic opportunity.' It was the answer she knew he wanted.

He reached out and squeezed her hand. 'I'm so proud of you, Laura. You know that, don't you?' She smiled weakly and looked away. If only he knew how much she loathed her job.

'Marge asked me down for a cup of tea later,' she said, to change the subject.

He let out a wheezy laugh, which ended in another bout of coughing.

'Her old ginger cat's had another litter, you know. There must be at least ten of them down there now. The basement steps stink. So does the flat, probably.'

'I noticed. She's battier than ever, Dad. Why don't you do something about it?'

'After all these years? You've forgotten how good she was to us when you were little.'

She hadn't forgotten. The endless hours she'd spent in that gloomy basement, staring up from the window at the front gate, waiting for the moment when her father's shoes and legs would appear and he would be home from the office. The portable TV flickering in the corner, showing *Peyton Place*, *Crown Court*, *The Flowerpot Men*. Marge would make her peanut butter sandwiches on Mother's Pride, would serve them along with milky tea in chipped mugs.

'Of course, I haven't.' She felt her irritation rise, but tried to hide it in her voice. 'I'll go down later.'

The pips on the radio struck the hour, and they both fell silent, listened to the news headlines.

'Today saw the worst rioting and violence at the News International Plant in Wapping, East London since demonstrations began about a month ago. Eight policemen were injured and over fifty protesters were arrested. Around five-thousand demonstrators were estimated to have assembled at the scene ...'

Luke would be there, she realised with a shock.

'Mounted police and riot shields were used for the first time to control the pickets and demonstrators ...'

'Bloody government. Over-stepping the mark again,' Dad murmured. 'First it was the miners, now the print-workers. When on earth will it stop?'

Her mind was racing. Was Luke one of the people arrested? Had he been hurt? She could hear his voice now, his mocking laugh, teasing her for being anxious.

'It's got to be done, Loz. Those bastards. They're out to break the workers. We've got to fight back,' Luke would say.

'Laura?'

The news had finished and the announcer was introducing a new programme.

'Today, in 1942, Singapore fell to the Japanese. This was a turning point in the war for Britain and for the British Empire ...'

'Laura! Could you switch off the radio?'

She fiddled with the dial. There was silence. Dad was watching her face. His clear blue eyes missed nothing.

'Are you OK? You look miles away.'

'I'm fine.'

'You sure?'

'Look, Dad, I came here to see how you are. Could you stop worrying about me?'

'Well, you can see how I am. On my last legs. Or leg I should say.' He smiled at the feeble joke, displaying his missing teeth.

'Has anyone else been to see you?' she asked.

'Only Marge and Ken. No-one else knows I've had a fall. Why do you ask?'

'No reason. It's just that there was someone standing outside the house when I arrived.'

He frowned.

'An old guy,' she went on. 'Looked like a tramp. Grey hat and coat.'

His expression changed. The humour and twinkle vanished. His face drained of colour. For a moment she didn't recognise him.

'Are you all right, Dad?'

He looked away. He took some deep breaths and drew deeply on his cigarette. Then he turned back towards her, still pale but his features now composed.

'Was it someone you know?'

Slowly, he nodded his head.

'Leech,' he almost spat the word.

He took the cigarette out of his mouth. Laura could see that he was shaking. He turned to her, gripped her hand and looked her in the eyes.

'He's been pestering me. If he comes to the door, don't let him in. Promise me this.'

'You're frightening me now. How do you know him? Was he … one of your criminals?'

He loosened his grip on her hand.

'No. No, he wasn't a client.'

She waited for him to go on, but he seemed lost in his own thoughts again. The clock on the mantelpiece chimed a quarter past the hour.

'I knew him in the war, Laura,' he said at last. 'He was ...'

Then he whispered something. His voice was so hoarse that she had to lean forward to catch the words.

'In my camp.'

His fist was cold and clenched so hard that she could feel the bones of his knuckles under the stretched flesh. A chill went through her. In her twenty-six years she had never heard him speak seriously of what he had endured during the war. He would often make joking reference to his lame leg – 'My old war wound,' he would say. And after a few beers he would break into the bawdy songs he had learned as a soldier. But she had never heard him speak seriously about the war.

They sat in silence, listening to the ticking clock, to the sounds of the drills in the house opposite theirs, to the rumble of a tube train passing them deep beneath the house.

Finally, she asked in a small voice, 'You've never really talked about it, Dad.'

He shook his head.

'No. I've never talked about it.'

The words were said with an air of finality. She had the urge to ask him to tell her. She opened her mouth to speak, but he patted her hand and smiled.

'Roll me another one, there's a good girl.'

2

Tom straightened up to ease the burning pain in his back. He looked around him. Night was falling in the jungle. The red sun was slipping slowly beneath the ragged horizon. Kerosene lamps had been lit so work on the railway cutting could continue by their flickering light. All around him, living skeletons laboured, hacking away at the rock with pickaxes, hammering spikes into the granite, clearing rubble into bamboo baskets and passing them down the long chain of waiting men to the edge of the cutting, to be tipped over the precipice.

The light from the lamps and the rapidly setting sun glinted on their sweating bodies. The men were barefoot and almost naked, wearing only ragged shorts or tattered loin cloths, and were so thin that their eyes bulged out from hollow cheeks, their ribs clearly visible beneath the skin. The scene was one of constant movement as men swung sledgehammers above their heads in a rhythmic action and brought them down on the thick metal spikes. The air rang with the continuous sound of chipping and tapping, metal upon metal, metal upon rock.

A sharp prod between his shoulder blades made him lurch forward, and he nearly fell to the ground. He turned to see the Korean guard they had nicknamed 'Fat-so' standing behind him, wielding a bamboo cane.

'Speedo, Speedo,' squawked the Korean, sweat standing out in droplets on his brow.

The man leaned forward and prodded him again, harder. Tom took a deep breath and raised the heavy sledgehammer above his head, bringing it down hard on the head of the spike. Pain ripped across his shoulders and down his arms and spine, from the motion he had been repeating for over twelve hours now. He winced, blinking away sweat. His eyes met Harry's solemn stare.

'Not long now, lad. Nearly the end of the shift. Don't let 'em grind you down,' Harry said, crouched on the ground, holding the spike in position.

'Speedo, Speedo!' yelled the guard again, suspicious. He brought the cane down again, this time on Harry's shoulders, leaving another livid stripe alongside the others he'd inflicted that day.

A shout went up at the end of the cutting, where the track emerged onto a rocky ledge. Tom looked round to see that a prisoner had collapsed on the ground, and was being beaten by a guard. His heart lurched with shock when he saw it was his friend Archie. He had gone down with malaria the day before but had been dragged out from the hospital hut to join the work party that morning, despite the protests of the doctors.

The guard lashed Archie's body with a length of wire again and again, yelling furiously in Japanese. The rest of the men had stopped work and were watching, mute, helpless. It was a familiar scene. Tom looked around. Where the hell were the officers? They should be intervening to stop this. They were probably further down the cutting. With each blow Tom felt his anger boiling. His fists clenched with rage, and he tried to restrain himself. But after a few minutes he could no longer bear to watch in silence. He threw his hammer aside and ran over to the guard. Seizing the man's wrist, he stopped him before he could inflict another blow.

'Stop it, you bastard! He's sick,' Tom had his fist tight around the guard's wrist.

The guard turned. He was bald, skinny, his eyes narrow with contempt. He dropped the wire whip and pushed Tom backwards. Tom stumbled and fell sprawling on the ground. Sharp stones dug into his back. The guard began kicking him in the ribs, and searing pain ripped through him at every blow. The guard then turned away to focus his attention again on Archie, who was crawling away, squirming towards the edge of the track on his belly. Fat-so had joined in now. He aimed a kick between Archie›s legs. Archie stopped moving and lay still in the rubble. The Korean seized one of his hands and dragged him to the edge. He heaved Archie over the top where the waste was tipped, giving him a final contemptuous kick as he slid down.

'You work, work!' screamed the Korean turning back to Tom, pointing to where Harry was still crouching with the spike. Tom dragged himself to his feet, picked up the hammer and swung it above his head. Pain tore through his ribcage, but he bit his lips and stayed silent. He wasn't going to show them how much it hurt.

'You don't learn, mate,' Harry said. 'You got off light that time. It only makes things worse in the long run. Haven't you learnt anything about how they operate?'

'What about Archie?' Tom muttered through his teeth.

Harry shrugged. 'We'll carry him back to camp and see what the docs can do.'

As he worked on, trying to ignore his pain, Tom kept his eyes fixed on the edge of the precipice, willing Archie to appear. But there was no sign of him.

After another hour or so a small party of Japanese engineers appeared at the end of the cutting. One of the guards blew a whistle and work stopped immediately. Tom and the others stood watching, leaning wearily on their tools, as the engineers strutted around the site, inspecting the day's progress, conferring intensely, gesticulating, pointing. The air grew thick with anticipation; it was not unknown for engineers to pronounce that progress was insufficient and that more work must be done before the prisoners were released and could trek back to camp. But tonight one of the group nodded sharply to the guards, and the prisoners were allowed to form a column and march out of the cutting to begin the three-mile long trek through the jungle back to the camp.

Before the guards could prod them into line with the others, Tom and Harry rushed to the edge of the track. They could see Archie, a few feet down, his body wrapped around a tree trunk. The two men scrambled down to him and began to haul him up to the path. They slipped and struggled on the loose rubble. Archie's body was limp and lifeless.

'You'll be alright, Archie old mate,' Harry kept saying as he panted with the effort of carrying him. 'Stay with us, lad.'

Tom looked at Archie's face anxiously. Behind the cuts and bruises it was deathly pale. But he could tell from the way Archie's eyes flickered that he was still alive.

The walk back to camp was a laborious struggle for Tom and Harry. Archie was like a dead-weight between them. They each held an arm and dragged him along. His body was heavy, slippery with sweat. He was virtually unconscious and unable to support his own weight or help them in any way. In their exhaustion, it was an almost impossible task for Tom and Harry. Occasionally, Archie would open his lips and utter a low moan.

'Do you think he's going to make it?' Tom asked Harry.

'I hope so. But he's in a terrible state. We'll take him straight to the hospital hut. The docs can work miracles sometimes. And at least he's young.'

The prisoners made their way down the dusty track, barefoot and treading earth still hot from the sun, some limping from tropical ulcers, some so weak from illness or starvation that they had to be supported by others. The jungle was teeming with life, even louder now that darkness had fallen; the trees and bushes came alive at night with the squawking and chattering of insects and birds.

Camp was a muddy clearing in the jungle, with rows of long bamboo huts thatched with palm leaves standing beside the wide fast-flowing river. Most of the men made straight for the water and splashed off the dust and sweat of the day from their bodies. Tom and Harry made their painful way with Archie dragging between them, straight along the bank to the last hut in the clearing – the hospital hut.

The smell of rotting flesh and the sight of hollow-eyed men, sick with dysentery or malaria, recovering from an amputation, or their stomachs bloated with beri-beri, made Tom's stomach turn. It also struck icy fear into him. Fear that it would soon be him. That like so many of these men he would not recover. That he would end up in the fast-growing cemetery at the edge of the camp.

The camp doctor, Colonel Bell, and two orderlies rushed to help them lay Archie out on one of the bamboo platforms at the far end of the hut.

Colonel Bell leaned over and examined him, shaking his head. Then he called for some boiled water and began to clean and dress Archie's wounds. The orderlies assisted him. One passed him old rags to use as dressings, and the other held a lamp overhead. Tom avoided their eyes. He'd often seen the short one, Leech, trading the possessions of dead patients in the camp.

They had soon cleaned the blood and dirt from Archie's face, but his eyes were two swollen puffballs and his nose still cut and bloody. Tom shivered at the grey pallor on his features.

'He's unconscious, and in a bad way,' said the doctor, picking gravel out of the wounds on Archie's stomach with a pair of tweezers.

'Do you think he's going to pull through, Doc?' asked Tom.

The doctor looked up. His face was lined with exhaustion. In it Tom saw the weariness and resignation brought on by months of seeing men die, of not having the equipment or drugs to be able to save them.

'God knows, Ellis. He was bad enough this morning, before he was beaten up by those savages. Now, I just can't say. It all depends on his will to live.'

Tom flinched. Archie was a fragile lad, vulnerable and easily daunted, prone to despair. It would be easy for him to just give up the fight.

'Is there anything we can do?' asked Harry.

'No,' the doctor said wearily. 'Why don't you come back tomorrow morning and see if he's come round?'

Tom and Harry left the hut, trying not to look at all the other broken men lying there on bamboo struts, waiting for death. Then they made for the river. Tom gasped as he entered the cold water, but felt instant relief as it soothed his wounds and bathed his aching muscles. He lay on his back and stared at the dark sky with its sprinkling of stars, listening to the gentle lapping of the water and the distant hum of the jungle around him. For a few exquisite moments he emptied his mind of the horrors of the day.

Soon his hunger forced him out of the water. He flicked the droplets off his skin and joined the men forming an untidy queue outside the cookhouse. When Tom's turn came he held out his tin, and the cook ladled a spoonful of watery rice into it, weevils floating amongst the soggy grains.

'Steak and caviar tonight, Ellis,' joked the cook, adding a spoonful of stew, consisting of a few plant leaves and a couple of lumps of fatty meat. Tom forced a smile.

Someone had lit a small fire outside one of the huts to keep the mosquitoes at bay, and despite the steamy heat of the evening, men were drawn to it. Subdued groups of men sat around it, smoking and eating. Tom took his place amongst them and began eating his rations as slowly as he could, chewing each mouthful many times despite the hunger that gnawed away inside him. Over the months of starvation, he'd trained himself to do this. He hardly tasted the food. He simply knew that if he didn't eat what he was given, everything, no matter how his stomach turned at the sight of it, he would not survive.

Harry eased himself down beside Tom, and soon Ian Ryan joined them. Ian, naturally tall and thin, looked even more emaciated now.

Settling himself on his bony haunches, he glanced quickly at Tom then produced something from under his shirt. It was round and hard, a fruit. It looked a bit like a bright green grapefruit.

'What the hell's that?' asked Tom.

'I got it from the kampong. There's a little wood next to where we have to load up the trucks. There are three or four trees there, but only one of them has any fruit. This was just lying on the ground. One of the Thais said it is a pomelo. It's OK to eat.'

'What are we waiting for then?' Harry took out a blunt knife and hacked greedily at the skin, slicing the fruit skilfully, then handing Ian and Tom a slice each.

'Mmm …' smiled Harry, the pomelo's juice oozing from the sides of his mouth. 'It's good alright.'

'It's good …' said Ian. But he didn't smile. He seldom did, and today he seemed even more preoccupied than usual. He stared into the fire, his face tense.

'I heard about what happened at the cutting today. You shouldn't have challenged the guard, Tom,' Ian said in a low voice, his eyes darting around cautiously.

Tom shrugged. 'I'm sorry. I just snapped.'

'You don't want to draw attention to yourself, or we're stuffed. You know what I mean, don't you?'

'Yes. I know. I realise that. I'm sorry. It won't happen again.'

There was a long silence. Ian was staring into the fire, waiting until the men sitting closest to them had finished eating and moved away towards the huts.

'I managed to speak to the Thai again today about … About the plan,' he said at last, his voice a whisper.

'Really?' Tom stiffened. The hairs on the back of his neck stood up.

'Yes. He took me aside while we were loading the truck. He's found a village down the valley where we can stay the first night. If … if we make it that is. Then we won't have to do the whole ten miles through the jungle in one day. He's all set for the day after tomorrow. I've got to let him know tomorrow if we're on for it.'

Harry leaned forward. 'Can we trust him?'

'Sonchai is rock solid … It's our only hope. We'll have to pay them, of course. But we knew that.'

'I've got thirty dollars saved, stuffed in me bed poles,' said Harry.

'I've got twenty,' said Tom.

They stopped talking as another man drew up and squatted close by.

'Word has it that the weather in the mountains is improving,' the man said.

They knew the code. The man meant that the Allied effort on the frontier in Burma was holding out. Someone had an illegal radio in one of the huts. No-one knew who it was, but when the radio picked up the BBC news, it was broadcast by whispers throughout camp. It was one of the things that got them through each dismal, back-breaking day.

'Any other weather reports tonight?' asked Tom.

'No – not tonight. That's all. Maybe tomorrow.'

When he'd moved on to the next group of men, Tom said, 'But what about Archie?'

'What about him?' asked Ian.

'Well, he won't be able to come. He's going to be laid up for days, maybe weeks. He might not even pull through.'

Ian hesitated. Then he said slowly and deliberately, 'We've said from the start that if one of us was ill, the others would go on. We've been planning this for weeks. Now is the right time. The monsoon will break very soon, and if we don't go in the next day or two, then it will be impossible to try at all.'

'Couldn't we just wait a few days and see how he does? We owe it to him.'

'No.' Ian was vehement. 'The time is right now. If we leave him behind and he survives, he'll understand.'

'I'm not sure.' Tom hesitated. It seemed wrong. They had all been in it together, the four of them. They had depended on each other almost from the first. Without the others Tom knew that he would have given up the struggle to survive months ago. Without them, perhaps Archie would give up.

'What's the matter with you, man? You getting cold feet?' asked Harry.

'No. It's just that … Well, you know how he is. How do you think he'll cope without us?'

Harry and Ian looked away. They knew as well as he did that Archie needed them. That he was younger than his nineteen years and vulnerable. That he was prone to days of blackness, when he would crawl onto his bunk and refuse to speak to anyone. That losing his pack and spare clothes had almost finished him, and that losing his friends and his reason to carry on *would* finish him.

They heard a sound behind them suddenly, and the men stiffened. The medical orderly, Leech, appeared from the shadows. A dapper little man, he always managed to dress neatly in clean clothes whilst the rest of them wore filthy rags. He moved towards them purposefully and squatted down beside them.

'Any of you gentlemen interested in doing a trade? Rice now for rice and soup tomorrow? Or two fags in return for tomorrow's rice?'

'Shove off, Leech. You should be ashamed of yourself,' muttered Harry.

'I'm only helping men get what they want. Any of you fancy a smoke? A dollar for twenty. Or some duck-eggs? Fresh in from the village today.'

'I said shove off. You deaf or something?'

'You might regret speaking to me like that, Baines,' growled Leech, his jovial manner gone. 'One day you might need my services.'

'Stuff it, Leech. You're living off others' misery! Like I said, you should be ashamed of yourself,' Harry snapped, although he was looking wistfully at Leech's pack.

'Come on, Baines. Look at you, ogling my grub, I know you want some.'

'I said beat it.'

Leech spat on the ground beside them and moved on, grumbling.

'Look, we'll talk later,' said Ian, watching him go. 'It's not safe here. We'll meet at the latrines at ten. We can decide what to do then.'

3

Tom lay on his bunk, listening. The grunts and sighs of the weary men tossing and turning on their beds of bamboo mingled with the sounds of the jungle: the calls and cries of the night creatures, the drone of insects, the whine of mosquitoes. These nocturnal sounds reminded him that there was life outside the horror of his daily routine, and that the vast jungle surrounding and enveloping them was seething and pulsating with life, vibrant with colour and sound. Life that never ceased, and carried on oblivious to the ordeal that was being played out in its midst. This thought, as he lay awake on the bare bamboo at night and listened for the whoop of monkeys or the cry of a jungle cat, kept him alive.

That, and the thought of her face. He didn't need to get her photograph out of his top pocket. He could feel it there, cool and flat against his chest. If he shut his eyes and concentrated for a long time he still had a perfect picture of her face the last time they had met. The time they had said goodbye at the docks in Georgetown. She'd looked up at him, a question in her eyes.

Perhaps she had wanted Tom to ask her to marry him, and not leave her wondering what their future held. How he wished now that he had seized the moment when he had the chance, that he had not left the question hanging in the air like that. But he would ask her, if he got out of all this. The thought of being with her kept him going. If all else deserted him he could return to that thought, and it would not fail him. He would get back to Penang one day and find her, and then he would marry her.

His mind wandered back to the day that had changed his life, had set in train the chain of events that had taken him to the tropical island he would make his home, would grow to love. That momentous day in 1938 when he had walked out of work and slammed out of his parents' house. He remembered wandering the streets aimlessly for a while. It had been a perfect autumn day, the air cool and refreshing. The trees in the squares of Bloomsbury were turning all the shades of red and gold. He sat on a bench in Russell Square for a while, eating an ice cream, watching the nannies play with their charges on the grass.

He had wondered about what he was going to do. He supposed he would have to find another job. But who would give him one without a reference? Finishing the ice cream, he carried on walking aimlessly in the direction of the river. He strolled through Covent Garden Market where there was much clattering and shouting as the stalls were being put away for the day, and then found himself on the Strand. He was just thinking that he would make for Embankment Gardens and sit there for a while, when he walked past the office of an employment agency.

It was almost five o'clock then, and a man in overalls was moving a portable sign from the pavement. Tom could just read the words on the sign through the man's legs. He'd often wondered subsequently what direction his life would have taken if he had arrived on the Strand five minutes later.

'Strong fit young men wanted for outdoor work in Malaya.' The words were written in a typeface that made them look like handwriting, placed against a backdrop of palm trees and a white beach bordering a glittering sea.

Tom went into the office. The young man behind the counter looked up wearily and took down his details. He obviously wanted to head home for the day. He took the papers through a door into the back of the office and came back almost instantly.

'It's your lucky day. Mr. Andrews has just got time to see you before he leaves.'

Tom was ushered into a stuffy little office, more of a cabin really. It was furnished with just a desk and two chairs. Mr. Andrews was a large thick-set Scot with a handlebar moustache and patches of sweat under his arms.

He explained that he worked for the United Rubber Company, which was recruiting young men to manage workers on the rubber estates all over Malaya. There was a particular vacancy that they still needed to fill – the job of overseer for a small plantation on the island of Penang.

'There isn't much rubber production on the island itself. Most plantations are on the mainland,' Andrews said, 'but Georgetown is an important centre for the rubber industry. The Trade Association is based there and there are several import-export companies in the town. So that plantation is a bit of a showcase for us. We need someone trustworthy and presentable to manage it for us. You look as though you might fit the bill.'

He then asked Tom a series of routine questions, and finally enquired about who would be able to give him an employment reference.

Tom looked down awkwardly.

'Well, I'm not sure about that. It's a bit difficult. You see, as a matter of fact, I walked out this morning. We had a bit of a difference of opinion.'

Andrews glanced at his watch.

'Look, Mr. Ellis. You are just the sort of material we are looking for. You seem a genuine sort of chap. We are not going to make too many difficulties about this problem with your last employer. I wouldn't like it to become a stumbling block. Is there anyone, anyone at all who could vouch for you, who could simply write a letter to say that you worked at this firm for five years?'

Tom instantly thought of Gerry Buttle, the chipper court clerk at Arbuthnot and Boodle. Gerry was always coming up with new money-making schemes. Tom was sure that Gerry would be prepared to write him a reference if he made it worth his while.

'If you can bring it back tomorrow, you can sail on Monday. As I said, a simple letter would be more than adequate.'

Gerry was quite amenable to writing a most glowing reference, especially after being treated to several pints at the Queen's Head on Cheapside and pocketing the five pound note that Tom slipped him. He even entered into the spirit of the agreement and suggested writing it on the firm's notepaper.

Tom sailed for Malaya the following Monday in the company of a group of other young single men, each with his own reason for heading East. He spent most of the voyage lying on his bunk in the tiny cabin, or on the deck, reading. He had the occasional drink, but managed to resist the temptation to fritter away all his savings drinking at the bar or gambling at blackjack in the games room.

As the ship headed east and the weather grew warmer, the atmosphere on board began to change. People grew more relaxed and sociable. Tom relaxed too, and his spirits rose. He began to forget the boredom and frustrations of the last few years. He began to look forward to his new existence.

Six weeks later they docked at Georgetown on Penang Island. As Tom walked down the gangplank onto the shore he could see instantly why they called Penang the 'Pearl of the Orient'. He was enchanted.

Georgetown was a gleaming colonial town with white stuccoed buildings set around spacious squares and greens. It oozed oriental charm. Tom was taken to the offices of United Rubber by rickshaw; his luggage followed behind on another one. He sat back on the leather seat and absorbed the sights. The rickshaw took him through the Chinese quarter. The streets were teeming with people and lined with shop-houses, their shutters painted in pastel shades. They were filled with every imaginable thing for sale, the goods flowing out onto the pavements. The rickshaw trundled past ornate Chinese temples, English churches and exotic mosques with towering minarets.

After signing his contracts at the offices, he was taken back to the waterfront to spend his first night at the Eastern and Oriental Hotel. That evening he had a taste of the good life that was to be his for the next three years. He had a butler and a valet to look after him in his room. He took cocktails on the terrace, overlooking the harbour, and then ate a three-course meal in the sumptuous dining room, surrounded by potted palms and cooled by fluttering ceiling fans.

The next morning he was met by the company agent and taken by pony trap up into the hills to the plantation. He was shown his bungalow, complete with three servants: a houseboy, a garden boy and a cook. The bungalow was built on a hillside, with a view over the tops of the rubber trees and towards the distant hills and the sea.

The very next day he started work. His job was to oversee the production of rubber on a four-hundred-acre plantation of trees. The work was undemanding and the rewards grossly disproportionate to the effort required of him. Most of the workers under him were Hokkien Chinese, some Tamil. Over the next few months he quickly learned the rudiments of both languages, and as a result increased production on his patch considerably.

His days passed in a fairly predictable routine. He would rise early, bathe in the water brought to him by the houseboy, and have a simple breakfast on the veranda. He would then walk down to the headquarters of the estate, meet his gang of workers and discuss with them about which trees were to be tapped that day. As they got on with the work, he would walk around the plantation and ensure that everything was going to plan.

In the afternoon the workers would bring back buckets full of latex to the plantation headquarters to be measured into the vats. Tom's job was simply to record what each worker had brought so that they could be paid the correct sum at the end of the week.

It had been pure bliss for Tom. To sit on the veranda once work was done for the day, watching the sun go down over the rubber plantation, sipping a gin sling that the house boy had mixed for him, listening to the cicadas in the frangipani trees behind the bungalow, gazing at the distant blue-grey hills. Or to spend the evenings dancing at the club to a jazz orchestra, or to run off to his chaste meetings with Joy, so laden with unspoken desire.

He lay there now on the bare bunk, his stomach still grumbling after the meagre evening meal, the bamboo slats digging into his bony spine. It seemed scarcely believable that he had been that carefree man lazing on the veranda in Penang, that he had ever led that life of simple pleasure and luxury.

He thought back to the shock he had experienced the first time he had endured hard labour when they arrived at camp. The men had been ordered to clear a section of jungle for the railway track and were given only the most basic of tools to chop down great thickets of bamboo and towering trees, to drag them out by fixing ropes around them and pulling them in teams. He remembered how his whole body had ached painfully after the first day, how blisters had formed on his feet and hands, how his muscles had seized up in protest.

The months wore on. From clearing the jungle for the railway, they were building it, moving stones and earth by hand in wicker baskets, handful by handful, to build embankments, chipping through solid rock with rudimentary tools to make cuttings through the hillsides, constructing bridges from logs of wood they had felled. And all the time, they were forced on by the guards, who lashed them and shoved them and screamed at them to work faster: 'Work, work! Speedo, speedo!'

Tom, Harry and Ian faced each day with resignation. They did what they had to do to get through. But Archie did not have their resources or maturity. Each day when he woke up, it was clear from his expression that he would rather be dead than face another back-breaking day of shifting gravel or chiselling rock. He would barely greet the others or respond to their banter. He went about avoiding anyone's eyes, sinking deeper into his own morose world.

They had been working there for a few months, and had been moved to the second camp along the line, when Ian was chosen to go on a work party to the nearby town to collect food supplies for the camp. He was chosen for his height and strength. He could lift sacks of rice and swing them onto the back of a lorry with ease, despite the fact that he had become pitifully thin. Ian started to bring back small items of food to supplement their diet, and gradually Archie's spirits seemed to lift a little. His skin improved, and at last he began to talk to the others. Occasionally, his face would light up in a smile.

One day when Ian came back with the truck, he had seemed uncharacteristically excited. He waited until after the evening meal, when most men had gone to their bunks, before speaking to them.

'I met someone who can help us,' he had told them in a hoarse whisper. 'If we manage to get out of the camp and make it downriver for ten miles, he's got a truck. He'll drive us to Bangkok.'

'Why?' asked Harry, instantly suspicious. 'Why would he do that?'

'He goes down to Bangkok twice a week to collect supplies for the camps,' Ian explained. 'We'd have to pay him, of course. His child is sick. He's desperate for money.'

'But why would he risk it? He works for the Japs, doesn't he? It must be a set up,' said Tom.

'No. No, it's not a set up. There's a whole group of Thais who want to help. They're a sort of unofficial resistance movement. Didn't you know? They've been smuggling medicines into the hospital, and they've sent extra food into the cookhouse loads of times.'

Tom and the others still looked doubtful.

'Look,' Ian went on, 'all we need to do is to creep out at night. Maybe on a Saturday, because there's normally no work on a Sunday, so we wouldn't be missed. We'd have to get to his house somehow. As I said, it's about ten miles downstream.'

'Ten miles? It's bloody jungle all the way,' said Harry.

'He can't risk coming any closer. The roads are all patrolled by Japs near the camps.'

'But how are we going to get through?' Tom asked.

'There are paths only the locals know about. He's going to give me a map, if we're on for it.'

'But won't there be Jap patrols in the jungle around the camp?'

'We'll just have to be careful. No-one's saying it's going to be easy. Are you up for it?' He looked around eagerly. Tom and the others didn't say anything.

'Let's face it. We're not going to survive this anyway. We'll either die of starvation or disease, or they'll kill us when they don't need us anymore. Look how many poor bastards have bitten the dust already. I can tell you this – I'd rather die trying to escape than in that filthy hospital hut of some disgusting disease.'

There was a pause as they all exchanged looks. Harry was the first to speak.

'You're right. We've nothing to lose. What about you, Tom?'

Tom hesitated, then he voiced a concern that had been bothering him since Ian first began speaking. 'But when they discover we've gone, they'll take it out on the others, won't they? Remember what happened in Changi when someone tried to escape?'

They all fell silent as they remembered the day a man had escaped from a work party. He had been mown down in a hail of bullets. To discourage the others from trying to flee, six men had been selected from the parade at random, lined up along the perimeter fence and bayoneted to death in front of the rest of the prisoners.

'Christ, I hadn't thought of that. How bloody stupid of me,' said Ian slowly, burying his face in his hands. 'You're absolutely right. We couldn't risk that. We'll have to do some thinking.'

For days they had carried on with their routine of hard labour, trying to put the idea of escape out of their minds. It was unthinkable to put the other prisoners at risk. They had all witnessed the brutality of the Japanese and Korean guards at first hand. Men had been beaten to death for working too slowly or for stealing food from the Japanese cookhouse. They didn't want to contemplate what reprisals would be exacted if someone tried to escape.

However, now that the idea of getting out of the camp had been sown in their minds, they found it difficult to drop it. Harry began to talk incessantly about his hometown; Archie visibly brightened;

Tom's own dreams about Joy became more frequent and more vivid. Her face would swim before his eyes without warning at all times of the day and night. Even whilst sweating and toiling on the railway, as he swung the pickaxe down on the black rock of the cutting, her face would be before him, her gentle eyes searching for his, a smile on her lips.

He knew it was useless, and that even if he managed to escape he could never get back to Penang, which was occupied by the Japanese. But the mere thought of getting away from here, of regaining his freedom, somehow made the idea of being with her again more of a reality.

A few days after they had first spoken about their escape, Ian brought it up again during their evening meal.

'I've had an idea,' he said staring into the fire. 'I'm going to talk to Colonel Scott about … Well, about you-know-what.'

'What on earth for? You must be mad!' said Harry.

'All officers should support escape attempts. It's in the King's Rules and Regulations. Don't you remember?'

'But we all had to sign that thing they made us sign in Singapore, saying that we promise not to escape.'

'That was signed under duress. Everyone knows that. We were all crammed into those filthy barracks at Selarang and told we couldn't leave until we signed that paper. Nobody's going to take any notice of that. I'm going to speak to him. He might be able to think of something … Some way to help us. I'm going right now.'

'Hey, be careful,' warned Tom, but Ian was already striding across the camp towards the officers' hut.

When he came back, about an hour later, Ian could not hide the grin that was spreading across his face.

'It's fine. He said to go ahead when we're ready,' he said, settling himself down on the ground beside the others.

'You're joking. What did he say?' Harry was smiling too.

'He said he would cover for us the first few days. Make up something about extra men in the hospital hut. When they finally discover that we've gone, though, he's prepared to say that it was on his orders.'

The others' mouths dropped open in unison.

'What the hell?' began Tom.

'Well, he thinks that they would never touch him. He's the only English bloke at camp who speaks fluent Japanese. He's the interpreter, isn't he? Without him, they wouldn't be able to explain what work needs to be done. It would be chaos. No work would get done. The Japs wouldn't risk that for their precious bloody railway. What about the glory of the Emperor and whatever?'

'I suppose that's right, isn't it? He's the only one they wouldn't dare to touch,' said Harry slowly.

'Yes. He's going to see if he can get us some extra rations to take with us.'

They all looked at each other, amazed that their dream might after all come true at last. But their elation was tinged with fear, of what would happen if they were caught, of what lay ahead and beyond the camp, of the dense jungle with its teeming life of dangerous creatures and poisonous plants.

Lying on his bunk of bare bamboo now, Tom thought about what answer he would give Ian. He was torn. Should he leave the camp with Harry and Ian, and give himself a chance to get away from all this, a chance for freedom and a future? Or should he do what he knew was the right thing to do, stay behind with Archie and make sure the boy made it through his illness and through his captivity?

4

Laura sat beside the bed and watched her father drift off to sleep. The daylight gradually faded and soon the only light in the room was from the gas fire. Very gently, so as not to wake him, she leaned forward and eased the cigarette end from between his fingers, scattering ash onto the blanket. She stubbed it out in the grate.

Then she crept across to the door, cursing each creaking floorboard, glancing back to check he wasn't stirring, and left the room. Shivering in the hall, she grabbed her coat and pulled it around her shoulders. Then tiptoeing to the table she lifted the telephone receiver. She glanced at her face in the hall mirror. She looked pale and tense, and her hair was still damp from the rain.

She dialled the number to her apartment. It rang and rang, then the answer-phone clicked in, and her own voice spoke to her, gratingly cheerful: 'Hi, this is Laura. I can't come to the phone right now. Please leave a message.'

'Luke,' she whispered. 'It's me. If you're there could you please pick up? I've been trying to get hold of you for a couple of days. I'm in London. Dad's had a fall. I need to talk to you. Are you there?' She waited, holding her breath until there was a bleep at the other end signalling the end of the tape. She hung up.

'Damn.'

She picked up the phone again, dialled the number to the office in Paris, asked to be put through to Adam.

'Hi, Laura. You OK?' came his bright tone. She could picture him working at his antique desk in the vaulted office, the lights of the Trocadero twinkling through the tall windows behind him.

'How's your dad doing?' he asked.

'Well, he's pretty down, I'm afraid. He's had a really bad fall. I think I'll probably need to stay in London for a couple of days.'

'Don't worry about the work, Laura. It shouldn't be a problem. Jeremy can cover for you at the Banque-de-Clichy completion meeting tomorrow. All the documents are drafted thanks to your hard work. You take as long as you need.'

'Thanks. I'll give you a call tomorrow.' She was about to ring off when he cut in again.

'Oh, and when you come back we can have that dinner I promised you. I was going to book the Trianon for Friday evening.'

'I'm not sure ...' she hesitated, pulling a face at herself in the mirror.

'No strings attached, Laura. I just want to thank you for everything you've done on the Clichy takeover.'

She shivered as she remembered that drunken moment at the New Year's party. She could hear the thumping music, could feel his hands on her breasts, could taste the red wine on his tongue.

'Let's talk about it when I get back, shall we?' she said.

'Sure.' Was there a trace of hurt in his voice?

'Give my very best wishes to your dad. I hope he gets better soon.'

She put the phone down and caught sight of herself in the mirror again. Her cheeks were flushed. She frowned at her reflection.

'You bloody idiot,' she said out loud.

She heard a cough from the top of the stairs and looked up to see Ken standing there in a striped dressing gown. He was red in the face and swaying slightly on the top step. How much had he heard?

'Laura,' he said, 'when did you get here?'

'About an hour ago. Marge called me this morning. Dad's just gone off to sleep.'

'Well, the rest'll do him good. Come on up to the studio for a cuppa. I don't think there's much in your Da's fridge.'

She hesitated. She thought about Luke again. If she slipped out now and got a taxi on St. Paul's Road, she could be at the Barbican in fifteen minutes.

As if reading her thoughts, Ken said, 'You're not thinking of rushing off again, are you?'

'I just thought I might pop down to my flat while he's asleep,' she said, trying to sound casual. 'You know? Check if there's any post, see if everything's OK.'

'Can't that wait? I haven't seen you for months.'

Disguising her reluctance, she began up the stairs towards him.

'Anyway, I thought you were going to get tenants while you were in Paris,' he said.

'Oh, it didn't seem worth it in the end. All that hassle. It's only a few months.'

'Lucky to have the choice,' he said. 'Your Da tells me you're earning a massive salary now. Plus bonuses, he says.'

'He does exaggerate,' she protested, laughing. 'I'm always overdrawn anyway, whatever I earn.'

He winked and pecked her on the cheek as she reached the top of the stairs.

'Only joking, lassie. I've no interest in material wealth as you well know. Only it would help if you could introduce me to some of your well-heeled clients or yuppie friends. Someone who might have a passion for modern art? I could do with a patron. Or perhaps *you* could buy one of my pieces?'

'I don't need to, do I?' she joked back. 'I can always come up here to look at your art.'

They reached the next landing and Ken held open the door to his studio. She walked into the familiar smells of oil paint and turpentine, mingled with that of the town gas from the leaky fire that flickered on the far wall. The big room was as untidy as ever; discarded tubes of paint, crumpled clothes, newspapers and books littered the floor. The walls were randomly decorated with posters and newspaper cuttings.

Between the windows leaned an enormous canvas, a giant nude crudely executed in brush strokes.

'Oh, that's just Betty,' Ken said, following her gaze. 'Don't mind her. She's nearly finished. Have a seat.'

Laura moved a pile of dirty washing and sunk onto a battered chaise longue. She could feel the broken springs through the worn fabric. She watched Ken boil a kettle on the little gas stove in the corner. He made her a cup of tea in a tin mug and poured a generous measure of whisky into his own cup.

'It must have been dreadful when Dad had his fall,' she said. 'You were with him, weren't you?'

'Well, I was just coming up the road. We'd arranged to meet at the library in Hackney, and I was a few minutes late. We were going to go for a pint. But when I came along he was standing at the top of the steps talking to someone. As I got closer I realised they were arguing.'

'Arguing? Who was it?' Laura sat forward in her chair.

'It was some shabby old guy. Could have been a tramp. Your Da was shaking his fist at him and got so agitated he picked up his stick and started waving it at the man. Then he lost his balance and went crashing down the steps. I rushed to help him. He'd bashed his head and I couldn't get any sense out of him. When I looked round for the old guy, he'd buggered off.'

'Did you ask Dad who it was?'

'I tried when he was at the hospital. But he was so confused and in so much pain that I just decided to leave it. I figured that he'd tell me sometime if he wanted to.'

'There was an old man watching the house when I got here today, Ken,' she said. 'He looked like a tramp as well. I asked Dad about it, and he went as white as a sheet. It was really weird. I've never seen him like that. Eventually he admitted that it was someone he'd known in the war. Someone from his camp.'

'That's very odd,' Ken frowned. 'After all these years. Did he say what the man wanted?'

'No. He wouldn't talk about it. Completely clammed up.'

'Well, he's never spoken to me about the war. And I've known him for nearly thirty years.'

Laura fell silent, staring into her cup. The image of the young woman in the photograph came back to her. Something must have prompted Dad to dig it out after all these years. Was it the encounter with Leech that had brought back her father's memories?

She toyed with these thoughts, turning them over and over in her mind, searching for answers, but after a while her niggling worries about Luke resurfaced. Was he in a hospital somewhere, or in a police cell? If she went to the flat, she would be able to use the phone to make enquiries.

'I'll have to go in a minute, Ken,' she said. 'I really do need to go to the flat.'

'I should be careful. There are a lot of undesirables out there on the streets this evening. Rent-a-mob militants. Violent bunch.'

'It's OK. I'll get a taxi.'

'Well, finish your tea first. Tell me what you've been up to in *gaie* Paris.'

'Oh, nothing much. I have to work really long hours. It's just like London really.'

'No time for art galleries?'

'Well, sometimes. I went to the *Jeu de Paume* last weekend.'

'And what about boyfriends? It's a while since you split up with that banker chappie, isn't it? What was his name? I forget.'

'Matthew. Yes, we split up a few months ago, just before I went to Paris. You're being quite nosey, Ken.'

'What about that guy I saw you with last time you were home? In the Island Queen.'

She stared.

'I don't remember that,' she said, playing for time.

'Oh, I don't think you saw me. You were sat at a table in the corner. You looked quite engrossed, the pair of you, so I didn't disturb you. He didn't look your usual type at all. Quite the hippy. Long hair, five o'clock shadow, leather jacket.'

'Oh,' she said frowning, as if trying to remember. 'You must mean Luke Goddard. He's just a friend of a friend. I brought him here once actually. He met Dad. Didn't you meet him then?'

'No. I'm sure I'd have remembered. What did Tom make of him? Not exactly ideal husband material, is he?'

'Ken! Luke's just a friend. As a matter of fact Dad and he hit it off really well. They got talking politics. Luke's really left wing. He supports loads of really worthwhile causes.'

She stopped herself. She was sounding too enthusiastic.

'And?' Ken was watching her face, a teasing smile on his lips.

'Like I said, he's just a friend,' she said looking down, studying the dregs of tea. 'There's nothing in it.'

Ken raised an eyebrow.

'If you say so.'

* * *

The streets were surprisingly quiet as the taxi hurtled through Islington and Clerkenwell. Laura saw a few people standing outside the pubs drinking, and little groups of men walking quickly together as the cab rattled through Smithfield Market and headed up Cheapside. As the cab neared the Bank district, it passed a row of buildings that were under construction. Workers and cranes operated by floodlight.

The taxi drew up outside the hi-tech apartment block next to the Barbican. Laura paid the driver and took the lift to the tenth floor. The flat was smelt unfamiliar as she let herself in, of stale cigarette smoke and alcohol.

'Luke?' she said tentatively.

She switched on the light. There were dirty cups and half-finished pizzas in cardboard boxes on the coffee table. Newspapers were scattered around. She noticed a week-old copy of the *Socialist Worker*. She glanced at the headline: 'Police Use Heavy Tactics on Innocent Protesters.' An overflowing ash tray and several lager cans were on the floor, spilling their contents onto the white carpet. A grubby duvet and pillows lay on one of her leather sofas, as if someone had been sleeping there.

'What the hell?' Luke really was the limit. She'd said he could stay here if he needed to, but this was a bit much.

In the galley kitchen dirty plates were piled on the side while the tap dripped into scummy water in the sink.

She went through to the bedroom. Perhaps he was asleep in there. She switched on the light.

There was a shape under the bedcovers. Laura felt a wave of relief and a shiver of excitement, despite the state of her flat. She would surprise him. She kicked off her shoes and rushed forward, realising how much she had missed his touch in the weeks they'd been apart.

'Luke,' she pulled back the covers.

'My God!' She jumped back in shock.

It wasn't Luke in her bed, but a younger man. His thin face was pale, and purple bruises ringed the flesh beneath his eyes. His blond hair was matted and dry. He was snoring gently through half-open lips that were crusted with sores. Grunting at the intrusion he rolled over and his eyes flickered open for a second. He raised a bony arm to shield his eyes from the light. On the inside of his wrists, Laura saw red needle punctures lining his veins.

'Who the hell are you?' she asked.

He stared back at her vacantly through bloodshot eyes.

5

Tom glanced at his watch. It was almost ten o'clock. It was nearly time for him to meet Harry and Ian at the latrines and give them his answer. Miraculously, he still had the watch that his father had given him when he first set off for Malaya in 1938. Each time he glanced at it he was reminded of the look on his father's face, severe behind his dark-rimmed glasses, as he had given the watch to him.

'I sincerely hope that this next episode in your life will be rather more successful than the last, Thomas,' he'd said drily.

'Thank you, Father,' was all Tom had said in response.

What would Father be doing now? His routine had probably changed little. He would still be taking the tram each morning from Gordon Square to his office in the city, dressed in a pin-striped suit and bowler hat, carrying his umbrella, briefcase and rolled up copy of *The Times*. There had been no letters from home since Tom had been captured. Had the house in Bloomsbury suffered in the Blitz?

It was hard to imagine, here in the jungle, that life still went on in grey London. Despite the hardships of his incarceration, he did not miss the city. He merely thought about it sometimes, in a detached way.

He had a clear image of when he had taken the decision to leave home. And it was more than just a decision to leave, it was a decision to go a long way away from there and never return. It had been building up for years, had been working up to that point ever since his father had called him into his study that evening a few months after he had left school.

He had spent that summer of 1933 with a bunch of school friends. They were all delighted to be free of the constraints and tedium of their public school, where countless hours were spent reciting Latin verbs and poring over the poems of Tennyson and Wordsworth, or shivering on the playing field. Schooldays had been unremarkable and uneventful for Tom, except for his friendship with David Lambert, and his hatred of one master, Doctor Sharp, who took sadistic delight in the physical punishment of boys who misbehaved. Sharp would have made an excellent Japanese soldier, Tom thought now.

During those months after he left school, Tom had nothing particular to do. He spent endless lazy summer days in the company of David and a group of others, including David's older sister Elsie, whom Tom found himself attracted to. They all used to take trains out to the home-counties or to the coast, to walk in the country or to picnic by the sea. They talked idly of going to Europe together, to visit the museums and art galleries of Paris and Florence, to experience the splendours of Venice and Athens. But they had done nothing concrete towards achieving this.

That particular day they had put their bicycles on the train to Tunbridge Wells and cycled through the Kent countryside, stopping at a pub for lunch. Tom got back to London late, sunburned and feeling a little heady from the lunchtime beer. He was ready to go up to his room and take a nap, but as he had passed the study on the first floor his father had called him in.

Father was sitting behind his desk. He was red in the face, and his eyes had that bleary look, seemed a little out of focus. He had already started on the whisky. There was a bottle on his desk, and a half empty glass.

'Have you given any thought to what you are going to do, my boy?' he asked, leaning back on his chair. 'To do, Father?'

'With your life, for God's sake,' his father said, his impatience already surfacing. 'Have you thought about what you are going to do with your life?'

Tom considered the question carefully, trying to focus. It was not something that had troubled him unduly.

'Why, Father?' he asked, stalling for time. His mind went back to Elsie, and the kiss they had shared in the garden of the country pub when David had gone in for the beers.

'Why? Because I am not prepared to finance your dissolute ways forever.'

Tom remembered that particular word. It still made him smile for some inexplicable reason.

'Dissolute?'

'Yes! Lazy, lax, self-indulgent. Call it what you will. You know exactly what I mean.'

His father was becoming angry now. Tom recognised the signs of his shortening temper. His face turned a purplish red, and he began to breathe quickly. He topped up his whisky glass.

'Those days are coming to an end, my boy. I've arranged a position for you. Starting next Monday.'

'A position?'

'Yes. It is not well-paid, but it is respectable, and if you work hard it will lead to a professional qualification.'

Tom frowned, the seriousness of the situation dawning on him.

'But, Father!'

'Don't Father me! I have been more than generous to you. You can't seriously expect me to pay for you any longer. You are a grown man, for God's sake.'

Tom stared at him, uncomprehending. He could not imagine the end to his heady days of freedom.

'So, this position, Father. What is it exactly?' he asked at last.

'Well, it is in a law firm, in the city. You will be a clerk, articled to an acquaintance of mine, Mr. Arbuthnot. He is a solicitor.'

'I'm not interested in the law.' He was beginning to panic. His mind returned to Elsie and how she'd promised to spend a day with him the following week. Just the two of them. They'd planned to slip off to Brighton together. How could he do that, stuck in a miserable office?

'Well, what are you interested in?'

'Oh, in art and literature, philosophy, ideas.'

His father leaned back and laughed a cruel, humourless laugh.

'Well, I can't see you making a living out of any of those things.'

'I hadn't really thought about it like that.'

'Well, perhaps you had better start thinking about it then, my boy. You've been spoilt. I blame your mother. All that is coming to an end.'

Tom knew it was useless to argue. As he left the study, his mother was waiting in the passage. She was dressed, as she always was in the evening, for her appearance on stage at the opera. Her dark hair was swept up and off her face, and she wore a black lace evening gown. She was wringing her hands.

'I'm so sorry, Tom,' she said gently, but he pushed past her without responding.

So the following Monday Tom put on a suit and left the house with his father to catch a tram from Gordon Square to Threadneedle Street in the city.

Number Fifty was a monolithic stone structure with porticos

and an elaborate coat of arms above the door, located opposite the Bank of England. Tom mounted the stone steps to the building with a feeling of dread. The reception hall was panelled in dark oak and furnished with leather chairs, just like a gentleman's club. He had the feeling that no sunlight ever penetrated here. His employer came to meet him. He was a greasy little man, who walked with a stoop and wore thick glasses. He greeted Tom with a damp handshake and put him to work immediately, listing an enormous pile of files to be archived.

The work was not at all as Tom had imagined. If he had ever considered it at all, he had thought of the job of a lawyer as being concerned with standing up in court, strutting about, giving eloquent and persuasive speeches in defence of his client. But this was not like that at all. It was all about paperwork: drawing up commercial contracts, memoranda and articles of association of companies, company accounts, shareholder agreements. All to be copied and listed, and filed and entered into records.

There were five partners in the firm, who were all interchangeably dull. But the sprightly court clerk from the East End, Gerry Buttle, with his bawdy sense of humour, provided the only chink of light in the otherwise endless grey days. From the first day to the last, Tom found the work unbelievably boring. But the weeks turned to months, the months into years. It wasn't how he'd planned to spend his youth, but he felt powerless to break free. It was if he was trapped into an endless routine by the will of his father. As if he had no choice.

The tedium was only broken by the evenings he spent out with David, who had also succumbed to parental pressure and taken a position as a clerk in a huge insurance company in Holborn. Elsie had faded from the scene. After a brief but passionate interlude she had announced that she had no intention of getting stuck with a solicitor's clerk, and she was off to see the delights of Europe with a female friend.

He still lived at home with his parents. He didn't earn enough to move out. Life at home never changed. His father, and now he, too, rose at seven in the morning, dressed in a suit for the city, and took breakfast in the breakfast room overlooking Gordon Square, served by the kitchen maid. The meal was taken in silence. His father read *The Times*, while Tom stared out the window at the passing trams and buses.

In the evenings his father retired to his study with his bottle of whisky. His mother would spend long hours in front of the mirror before setting off in a taxi for the Coliseum, where she sang in the chorus. She usually returned after they were in bed, and was never up for breakfast. Even on the evenings she was not working, she rarely spent time at home. It was an unspoken rule in the household that she was not questioned about her whereabouts.

Every six months, Tom went along to the Horticultural Halls in Victoria to take the next paper in the endless examinations it was necessary to pass in order to qualify as a solicitor. After five years he duly qualified. But he felt no joy at this achievement. What he felt instead was fear, an uneasiness, as if he had taken a wrong turning, and that his true life, the life that he should have been living, was somehow being played out in another dimension. He developed a dread of the passing years, of going to and from the city every day for the rest of his life like his father. He examined his face in the mirror daily, looking for signs of ageing, worrying that the years were creeping up on him while his proper life had not yet started. He felt stifled by his existence, but unable to step off this endless treadmill.

Then one day, in 1938, everything changed.

He was working at his desk one morning, when Arbuthnot called him into his office.

'One of the clients has made a formal complaint, I'm afraid, Ellis,' Arbuthnot began.

'Formal complaint? About what?'

'About the warranties in the share transfer document, in the takeover of Hills and Noble. You know, we did that transfer last year. Apparently the warranties misrepresented the situation, and the clients are now being sued.'

'Yes, I remember the takeover, but I didn't draw up the document. I didn't draft that one. You did, sir.'

Arbuthnot shook his head vehemently.

'Oh, no, no. I haven't drafted one of those things for years, my boy. It must have been you, Ellis. You do them all nowadays.'

'But I remember this takeover specifically. You drafted it as a special favour to Mr. Noble, because he is a friend of yours. You said that you wanted to deal with it personally.'

Arbuthnot shook his head stubbornly. It became clear to Tom that Arbuthnot was not going to take the blame. Tom was going to be the scapegoat, no matter what he said or how many years of faithful service he'd given the firm.

Tom stared at the man, at his little sweaty face that had smug satisfaction etched upon its every line. Something snapped inside him.

'You know what, Arbuthnot? You're a coward. That's what you are. You would prefer to see me take the rap for this than stand up and admit you got it wrong. You're a pathetic, grovelling little coward.'

Arbuthnot sat up straight. His eyes were snapping open and

shut. He blushed.

'How dare you insult me like that? I've never been spoken to like that in all my life. I'm afraid you're going to have to be reprimanded, Ellis.'

'Oh, reprimand me all you like. It won't make a jot of difference. I'm sick of this damned place, and I'm sick of the mind-numbing activity that passes for work around here. And I'm sick of you and your self-satisfied partners. You can shove your job. I'm out of here.'

He collected his brief case and umbrella, and left the building. The last memory he had of the place was of Gerry's startled face as he had swept out of the office.

Tom had headed straight home. When he had let himself in through the front door, he had found his house unnaturally quiet. He went through the hall towards the sitting room, but something made him stop before entering. He heard his mother laugh. She laughed as he had never heard her laugh before. It was a low intimate laugh, full of playful suggestion.

He opened the door, and she had jumped and looked round, startled. A flush began on her neck and quickly spread to her cheeks. She had been leaning forward and talking to a man in the other chair. They had been holding hands. Tom caught sight of his mother snatch her hand away as she turned towards him. The man was young. He could not have been more than thirty-five, but he had the appearance of a dandy, with his toothbrush moustache and his perfectly cut suit. After an imperceptible pause, the man carried the moment off perfectly, sat back in his chair as if completely at his ease.

'Oh, this is Mr. Terry. He's the stage manager at the theatre. Mr. Terry, this is Thomas, my son.'

Without a word Tom turned on his heel and left the room. In

that moment what he had suspected for years became clear to him. He knew now why his father hid away in his study and took comfort in his whisky. He knew why his parents rarely spoke and why they slept in separate rooms. And in that same moment of revelation, came the realisation that he must leave. He must leave as soon as he could and start a new life somewhere else. The stifled, unhappy lives of his parents sickened him. He could not stay there, now that he knew.

He realised now that, even if he were to make it out of the camp alive, he wouldn't go back to London. The city held nothing for him anymore. He had once been content there. But now the city just represented boredom and frustration.

What he pined for was Penang. He longed to have back his life on the rubber plantation. His daily routine of strolling amongst the rubber trees and inspecting the tappers at their work had provided him with just the right amount of exercise, had kept him lithe and tanned then and full of energy. He looked down at his pitiful body now, bony and skinny from hard labour and malnourishment, his sallow skin covered in insect bites and cuts and bruises.

He slipped off his bunk. His father's watch showed that it was ten o'clock. He'd finally made up his mind about what to do.

Tom tiptoed out of the hut and across the dark compound to the latrines. If he didn't already know the way, his nose would have guided him there. The wooden *benjos* were set over putrid stinking pits, heaving with maggots, despite the best efforts of the officers to ensure that they were constantly dug over.

Harry and Ian were already there, lingering beside the end hut, casting nervous glances in the direction of the guards on night watch, who were busy playing a noisy game of cards outside the guardhouse.

'Well?' asked Ian in a whisper as Tom approached. 'Have you made up your mind?'

'Yes, I have.'

'And?'

Tom hesitated. His friends were waiting for his answer, their anxious eyes fixed on his face.

'Look, I'm sorry, but I can't come with you,' Tom finally managed to say. 'I've thought it over and it always comes back to the same thing – I just can't leave Archie alone. He would be destroyed without us here. He's in a bloody awful way as it is and I just couldn't let him down … If you could just wait until he's better?'

'You know that's impossible,' Ian said, sighing.

'I know. I know. I understand. So when are you going to go for it?'

'Tomorrow evening, when we get back from work. We'll just slip away after the meal.'

'What about the map?'

'Sonchai's bringing it tomorrow when we go for the delivery. He's getting us some hunting knives too, for cutting through the undergrowth.'

'Well, then …'

There was nothing left to say. Except for goodbye. Tom felt a surge of emotion.

'Shall we say our goodbyes now?' he asked. 'We might not have a proper chance tomorrow.'

He held out his hand. What an inadequate gesture shaking hands was, Tom thought. If only he could forget his Englishness and give them both a hearty hug. But he knew that Ian and Harry would recoil from such a display of affection.

A lump rose in his throat as they both shook his hand.

'Good luck,' Tom said. 'And for God's sake be careful.'

'Shhh,' Ian suddenly whispered. There was a movement from the other end of the latrines; someone slipped out and crossed the dark compound.

'Who the hell was that? I thought you'd checked, Harry?'

'I did. When we first got here, but someone must have slid in while we were talking.'

'I hope to God he didn't hear anything.'

'Of course, not,' said Harry. 'We were whispering.'

'Well, let's split now, before anyone else turns up,' said Ian, nerves giving his voice a hard edge.

As Tom crossed the compound to his hut, the pain of parting with his mates struck him like a physical blow. Ian and Harry and their friendship had got him through this far. How was he going to cope without them? Archie would be no help to him. The support would be all one way. He would be the one helping and cajoling the other along, finding extra rations, trying to sustain the fragile morale. Tom already felt the heavy weight of responsibility pressing down on him.

6

The next day the men were forced out at dawn to work on the cutting as usual. This time it was Harry's turn to hammer first while Tom held the spike. His friend looked pale under his sunburn and for the first time since Tom had met him, he wasn't talking.

A couple of times, Tom tried to make conversation, but Harry hardly responded. At last, when the guard who'd been hovering around them was out of earshot, Tom asked him in a low voice, 'Thinking about tomorrow, mate?'

''Course I am. Can't think about anything else,' Harry muttered, straightening up.

'Worried?'

'A bit.' Harry glanced over his shoulder.

'Just think. This time tomorrow you'll be at the village.'

'No stop!' The guard was returning, yelling at them.

Harry lifted the hammer and smashed it down on the spike, avoiding Tom's gaze. Tom didn't try to speak to him again, and Harry was silent for the rest of the shift. Tom saw the faraway look in his eyes. In his mind, Harry was probably halfway down the jungle trail already, cutting through the forest, making for freedom.

When they got back to the camp at the end of the day, Harry turned to Tom.

'I've got something for you. A keepsake,' he said, rummaging in the pocket of his shorts. He handed Tom a battered military badge. Tom peered at it in the darkness. It was hard to make out the inscription on it.

'It's the badge of the Northumberland Fusiliers. That's St. George killing the dragon. It's a bit dirty though. I've kept it under the bed.'

'Thank you, Harry,' Tom said, touched. He slipped the badge into his pocket.

'Oh, and there's something from Ian too.'

He passed Tom a ring. Tom had often seen it dangling on a string around Ian's neck.

'It's got his initials on it. In case you need some extra cash, you could trade it.'

'Thank you. I'll try not to.'

Then on a whim he took the watch his father had given him out of his pocket and handed it to Harry. 'Look, why don't you take this in return? It could be useful, and if things get tough you could always sell it.'

Harry took it reluctantly. 'Are you sure, lad? This must be worth a packet!'

'Your need will be greater than mine.'

Tom held out his hand once again.

'Good bye, Harry.'

Harry took his hand. Tom could feel the nervous sweat on his friend's palm.

After he'd eaten his evening rations, Tom went back to his hut to lie down. He didn't want to see Harry and Ian slip behind the cookhouse and out into the jungle. It all seemed so final. He tried not to think about what they were doing, but his mind returned to them constantly. It could have been him, hacking through the undergrowth, following the little-used path along the river bank, making for the native village, leaving the camp and all its horrors behind him. Eventually he drifted off into an uneasy sleep, but kept jolting awake, sweating and breathing hard. Could he be going down with malaria like Archie? Towards morning he realised it was simply his nerves.

The next day was Sunday, an official rest-day for the prisoners. Nevertheless, roll call was still held at dawn, and everyone was forced to come out of their huts and line up on the parade ground. Tom dragged himself up and out, keeping his eyes fixed on the ground in front of him, trying to appear normal.

The men were counted and at the end the Japanese commanding officer, nicknamed 'The Ripper' by the prisoners, turned angrily to Colonel Scott.

'Two men short,' he barked.

The colonel gave a relaxed smile.

'Oh, yes,' he said, almost too nonchalantly, scratching his head. 'That will be the two men taken into the hospital yesterday evening. Malaria again, I'm afraid.'

The Ripper looked at him suspiciously, then gabbled something in Japanese and pushed Scott backwards with his cane. He strutted up and down the lines a few more times, peering at each man with narrowed, suspicious eyes. Unable to find anything else wrong, he dismissed them.

As they walked back to the hut, a man next to Tom nudged him in the ribs with a sharp elbow.

'Oi, where are your two mates?'

'Mates?' Tom frowned.

'Yes. You know who I mean. You're always with 'em.'

Tom shrugged, feigning ignorance. He wished the man would pipe down; a group of guards was watching them.

'I've no idea,' he said. 'Probably on the other side of the ground. They'll be about somewhere.'

The man eyed him sceptically then moved away to talk to another group. Tom clenched his fists when he heard the man saying, 'Have you seen those two fusiliers? You know, the tall, skinny one and his little mate?'

Tom spent the rest of the morning lying uneasily on his bunk, trying to read an old copy of *War and Peace*, one of the few books circulating in the camp. This version had been passed from man to man, was thumbed and filthy, its pages soft with use. Normally he would have spent the time with Harry and Ian, playing cards or chess, or just sitting around chatting. He could not help wondering how they were getting along, how far they had gone down the trail, whether they were safe.

Later in the morning, parade was called again. This was unusual. Tom watched as the Ripper held an animated conversation in Japanese with Scott. Both men were speaking in raised voices. Other British officers gathered around anxiously. Once, when Scott turned away from the Ripper, Tom caught sight of his face and saw the look of naked fear on it.

The men were kept standing to attention in the baking sun for over an hour. At last they were released, but as they walked away, Tom saw Scott being pushed into the guardhouse by a group of Japanese soldiers.

'Dear God.' Tom looked away.

He went to the hospital hut to visit Archie. Archie was still lying on the same bunk at the very end of the hut. As Tom went down the line of sick men, he caught sight of Leech tending to one of the patients. Leech looked up and stared hard at Tom as he walked past. Tom stared back.

Archie was awake now. His breathing was uneven and quick. Droplets of sweat stood on his forehead, and his pale face was a mass of bruises and cuts. His eyes were sunken and sallow. He fixed Tom with a fevered look, and reached up and grabbed Tom's shirt, pulling him close. 'They've gone, haven't they?' he asked.

Tom was so close he got a mouthful of Archie's hot breath, rotten with fever. He looked around anxiously then put a finger to his lips.

'How do you know?' he asked in a whisper.

'The men have been talking about it. Two missing from today's parade. I guessed it was them.'

Tom nodded. 'They went yesterday.'

'But why?' asked Archie. 'Why did they go without us?'

'They couldn't wait. The monsoon will be here any day. Then it will be impossible to get through.'

'They could have waited. I'll be better soon.'

'Well, they had to go, Archie.'

'Bastards!' said Archie, lifting his head and putting all his energy into the word.

Other patients turned to look at him.

'Keep your voice down, for God's sake. You don't want to drop us in it,' Tom admonished the boy.

When parade was called again at dawn the next day, Tom could tell straight away that something was very wrong. He saw that there were far more Japanese soldiers standing outside the guardhouse than usual. With a chill, he noticed that some of them wore the uniform and white armbands of the *Kempeitai*, the Japanese Military Police. Tom kept his eyes to the ground, but his heart was pounding beneath his ribs. He could hardly keep his knees from shaking.

The Ripper addressed the parade in pidgin English. 'Prisoners, something very serious happen here. Two men missing from camp. Two of your comrade violate the Emperor name by daring to escape. But nobody can escape Imperial Japanese Army. We know who these men are … We know where they go.'

Fear sliced through Tom. Had Scott talked? Had they beaten him down until he broke and had told them everything? It was unlikely. They would never have dared to torture the only Japanese speaker amongst the English soldiers, and Scott would never speak voluntarily. The Ripper must be bluffing, Tom told himself. But he still felt weak with dread. His head was swimming. He could hardly stand.

The Ripper's speech went on, denigrating anyone who shirked the sacred work of the railway. Eventually the Ripper concluded by saying, 'Make no mistake! Whole camp pay for this!'

Then he gestured to a group of guards. They ran over to the hospital hut. There was a commotion inside, and after a few minutes the sick men from the hut were brought out to the parade ground. They came slowly, one by one, hobbling on crutches or supported by others. They were poked forward by the rifle butts or bayonets of the guards. Some were so weak they couldn't stand, and had to be carried by other men. Archie came last of all, Colonel Bell supporting him on one side and Leech on the other. They were all made to stand in the middle of the clearing in the full glare of the sun. Tom turned away from the pitiful sight.

All day long the entire camp stood to attention on the parade ground. There was no let up from the heat of the sun. The guards gave them no food or water.

Tom's tongue became dry and hard as if it were swelling in his mouth. His throat was so parched that he could no longer swallow. Several men collapsed to the ground, where they were left. The guards slapped and kicked anyone who bent down to help them.

Half way through the morning the sky darkened suddenly, and it began to rain. Sheets of water hit the camp, blown horizontal by a strong wind. The palms were almost bent to the ground by the force of the storm.

Still they stood there. Men lifted their faces to the sky and opened their mouths to take in a few drops of rain and ease their thirst. Then the rain stopped as suddenly as it had started. The sun came out again, and steam began to rise from the ground.

It was afternoon when the Ripper marched out of the guardhouse and abruptly dismissed the men. Tom began to walk towards his hut, eyes to the ground. Perhaps everything would be alright after all. Then, he felt a hand grip his shoulder. He turned and opened his mouth to protest, but the words froze on his lips. The Ripper himself was standing behind him, staring at him with narrowed eyes.

'Not you. You stay. We need talk to you.'

A shove from a rifle butt between his shoulder blades sent Tom stumbling along on quivering legs. A few paces away, he noticed Archie, staggering along towards the guardhouse as well, a group of Japanese soldiers with bayonets prodding him forward.

The guards pushed Tom across the parade ground until he reached the steps of the guardhouse. Then they shoved him forward. The force of the push sent him sprawling onto the wooden veranda. Two of the guards then seized his elbows and dragged him up roughly through the door of the hut.

He'd never been inside the guardhouse before. Bizarrely, it was set out like an ordinary office. The Ripper sat behind a wooden desk stacked with files and papers. There was even a filing cabinet in the corner.

'You bow,' the Ripper said. Two *Kempeitai* officers were

standing behind him, staring impassively at Tom.

A defiant voice in Tom's head made him hesitate.

'Bow!' This time the Ripper shouted the word, and Tom felt the hands of the guards forcing him forwards. They then grabbed him by the arms and dragged him to a hard chair in front of the Ripper's desk.

The Ripper stared at Tom. He could have looked an imposing and handsome man. He was slim and well-built and had regular features, but the constant look of venomous disdain on his face made him look ugly.

'You know why you here, Private Ellis?' he said at last

Tom shook his head.

'No ... Sir.'

'I think you *do* know why you here.' The Ripper raised his voice. 'I sure you do.'

When Tom shook his head again, the Ripper leapt to his feet, knocking his chair backwards.

'You do know!' he screamed. The guards shoved Tom forward so he almost fell out of the chair. Tom knew that to show his fear would be the worst thing to do. He lifted his head and met the Ripper's eyes.

'I tell you why,' the Ripper went on. 'You are here, you and the red-hair, because you friends with escape men.'

He rested his hands on the desk and leaned forward with a triumphant smile, an evil gleam in his black eyes.

Tom swallowed. His mouth went dry. How the devil had they found out so quickly? He was sure they hadn't gone through the camp checking men against the register. But how could they have worked out their names without doing that? He shivered at the thought of how much they knew, and how quickly they'd managed to find out. His mind turned to Scott again. Had he squealed?

'But I not need you to talk, Private Ellis,' the Ripper said with a sly smile. 'I not need you to talk. We have information. But you will be *punish* for this. Punish hard.'

'But why, sir?' Tom protested, knowing it was useless. 'I didn't escape. I'm still here, aren't I?'

'You not answer back,' said the Ripper grimly, and one of the guards slapped Tom's face, catching the cheekbone with his metal ring.

'You to be punish so other men not try escape.'

The chill of dread gripped Tom. He had seen their punishments. Water torture, beatings, beheadings.

The Ripper nodded to the guards. They dragged Tom out of his chair, bundling him across the room and out through the door. They shoved him down the steps. Once again he fell, sprawling onto the parade ground.

Then rough hands were on his arms, jolting him to his feet. They slapped and punched him. His face was already burning from the slapping he'd received inside the hut, and now the slaps came harder, again and again. Then they started to punch his body too. Tom put his fists up to try to ward them off. This seemed to make the guards even angrier, so they hit him harder. His eyelids were swelling, and blood was dribbling into his eyes, and then everything he saw was through a film of red. His eyes closed almost completely. He kept his teeth clamped together. He wasn't going to give them the satisfaction of crying out. Would they ever stop?

Two more guards joined in, punching and kicking him. The blows came from all directions, winding him, making him stagger. They went on and on, jerking him this way and that. The force of one kick made him bite his tongue. A fist in the stomach made him double over with pain. Then a kick from behind buckled his knees, and he fell to the ground.

He was face down in the dirt, and they were all kicking him at once. He heard a voice screaming. It took him a few moments to realise it was his own. They kicked him harder. How long was this going on? He prised open his eyelids and caught sight of the Ripper standing at the top of the guardhouse steps, watching him, cold pleasure in his narrow eyes. Tom hoped that he would pass out.

When he could endure the pain no longer, the beating suddenly stopped. He looked up. The parade yard and surrounding trees were spinning round him. As they gradually slowed, he saw that the Ripper was holding his right hand up, motioning the guards to stop. ·

They jerked Tom to his feet. His legs were collapsing beneath him. Dizzy and swooning, every bone and muscle in his body cried out in pain. He tasted the nauseating sweet blood that filled his mouth, retched then spat it on the ground. Two of his teeth came out along with the blood. What the hell were they going to do next? He couldn't take any more of this.

'That enough. For now,' said the Ripper. 'We have something to show you,' he looked at Tom. 'Something that interest you very much.'

The rough bamboo gates that separated the camp from the road were dragged back by some guards, and a truck was driven through. It was one of the lorries used to collect supplies for the camp.

It stopped outside the guardhouse.

'Get in!' shouted the Ripper.

The guards pushed Tom up the rear ladder and onto the back of the truck. They shoved him down on a bench that ran along the side. The truck reeked of rotting vegetables, although it was empty except for a few shovels and some other tools lying on the floor.

Then, from behind the guardhouse, they brought Archie. Tom sat up. My God, what had the bastards done to him? Archie was unable to walk, and was being dragged by two guards, his feet and legs bending under him like those of a rubber doll. He was almost unconscious. His head was lolling on one side, his face and body a mass of cuts and grazes. His eyes were open, but his pupils were disappearing up under the lids.

They dragged Archie up to the lorry, and threw him bodily over the tailgate. He lay on the floor of the truck, motionless.

Tom crouched down beside him. He shook his arm.

'Archie, Archie! It's me, Tom. Are you OK mate? Talk to me, please.'

There was a flicker of recognition in Archie's eyes. He raised his head a fraction and the ghost of a smile passed his lips. Then he let his head drop down on the floor again, and although Tom shook him again, he did not respond any more.

The lorry started up. It had a chugging, throaty engine. Four guards with rifles jumped on the back. The Ripper got up beside the driver. As they swept out of the gates and down the road towards the town, a group of prisoners gathered round to watch them go, consternation on their faces. As the truck rattled through the gates, Tom saw one man cross himself. A chill went through Tom. He looked away, trying to dismiss the image from his mind.

The truck drove slowly through the town of Kanchanaburi. Its progress was constantly interrupted by bicycles, rickshaws and pony carts. Tom had never seen the town before. They'd been brought to the camp by river, on flat-bottomed barges. The town seemed a poor and ragged place. They passed through narrow streets of ramshackle houses built of bamboo and rattan. Stalls selling fruit and vegetables lined the dirt road. Everywhere the frightened eyes of the locals stared back at him. They appeared cowed and afraid, but too curious not to look.

Where were they were being taken? Perhaps they were going to be executed. The man who had crossed himself had clearly thought that.

The truck soon left the town behind, and they were driving along an open road that ran alongside the river. On one side was thick undergrowth and the river bank was fringed with palm trees. Beyond the river jungle-clad hills stretched towards the blue horizon. Where the hell were they going? But it was useless to speculate, and he had to concentrate on keeping still. Each jolt and bounce of the lorry jarred his fractured bones.

A few miles along the valley, the truck turned off the road and bumped down a rutted track, which wound its way through dense undergrowth and past native huts with chickens and pigs rooting about. Villagers watched nervously from their dusty compounds.

The truck finally came to a halt beside a wooden hut at the foot of a small hill. The hill was covered in jungle growth, luxuriant bushes and creepers. Near the road there were a few trees smothered with delicate white flowers. On the grass under the trees was a scattering of green fruits, the same ones that Ian had brought to camp the other evening.

'Pomelos,' Tom muttered, remembering the name. The word sounded odd in the silence. The guards bristled, startled by the sound of his voice. They stiffened and pointed their rifles at him.

The Ripper turned and barked to them in Japanese. They relaxed, letting the guns drop.

Tom waited to be dragged off the lorry, but they left him sitting on the bench as they jumped down and stood to attention beside the vehicle.

It was then that he saw Harry and Ian. They were being pushed at gunpoint out of the wooden hut. They were almost unrecognisable from the men who had set off into the jungle just two days before, full of hope. They were both shackled at the ankles, chains between their legs. Ian stooped as he walked. There were so many cuts on his face that his features were obscured. His eyes were swollen and red, and his nose looked as though it was broken. He wore only a loincloth, and his torso, too, was a mass of wheals. He walked as if in a dream, staggering and swaying.

Harry looked even worse. There was a huge gash on one side of his head, oozing blood. Blood had seeped down his neck and shoulders and had dried there in a dark brown mess. Like Ian, he was covered in bloody gashes. He was limping as if he were lame. Shock and fear cut through Tom. What had these poor devils been through? And what did the Japs have in mind for them now. There was an idea in the back of his mind, but it was so dreadful he could not bring himself to acknowledge it.

The Ripper jumped down from the driver's cab. He screamed something to one of the guards, who jumped on the back of the lorry and dragged out the two shovels. It was now clear why they had brought along the shovels.

Tom watched in horror as the guard pushed the shovels towards Harry and Ian. The Ripper strutted in front of them and pointed to the ground under the pomelo trees.

'Dig!' he yelled at them. 'You dig!'

They both began to dig. They made slow and painful progress. It was obvious that neither man had any strength left. But this did not seem to bother their captors. They sat down on the ground to watch, as if it was street entertainment. They lit cigarettes and lounged there, laughing at the struggle of the two prisoners. Harry and Ian collapsed several times. When this happened, one of the guards would leap up and pull him to his feet, shoving the spade back into his hand and yelling, 'Dig! Dig!'

Tom watched, transfixed, as two oblong trenches were slowly and painfully made on the ground before Harry and Ian.

On an impulse he stood up. 'Ian! Harry!' he yelled in a cracked voice. 'I'm here. You're not on your own. We'll get out of this.' He knew his words were pointless, but he needed to let them know he was there.

At first he thought they hadn't heard him, but then Ian slowly turned his head in Tom's direction. He was frowning, searching with swollen eyes, looking for Tom but unable to see where he was. Then the Ripper screamed, 'Shut up! Sit down!' and one of the guards leapt onto the lorry and pushed Tom down with the rifle butt. Another guard gave Ian a kick, and slowly Ian turned back to his gruesome task.

Helpless, Tom watched, while the guard held a rifle to his head. After Harry and Ian had been digging for some time, the sky darkened and there was a sudden clap of thunder. He felt the warm rain drench him as he stared at his friends. Ian and Harry slowed down, almost to a standstill.

The Ripper scrambled to his feet. 'Work! Work! No stop!'

They worked on, but the earth had turned to mud and sludge, and the trenches had filled with water.

But by the time the two shallow graves had been dug, the rain had stopped and the tropical sun was once more streaming through the branches.

Then the Ripper stepped forward and pushed Harry and Ian against the trunks of the trees. He yelled his orders to the guards, who lined up in front of the truck, their rifles drawn.

The Ripper proceeded to put blindfolds on the men. However, Ian and Harry both pushed the blindfolds off their eyes. The Ripper shrugged and stepped away, and it was then that Ian lifted his head and saw Tom. Their eyes met. And Ian did a strange thing. He lifted his right arm and saluted Tom with sharp military precision. Tom, in turn, pushed the rifle aside and stood up in the truck, clicked his heels together and saluted back. He fixed his eyes on Ian's face. He owed it to him to be strong. He would show these bastards he wasn't scared. He held the salute, unaware that his face was contorted, that tears were streaming through the drying blood and dirt on his cheeks.

The Ripper screamed his final orders in Japanese, and the guards opened up their rifles. The sound of gunfire ripped through the clearing.

7

Laura stared at the stranger in her bed. She reached out a tentative hand to touch his arm, but the needle marks on his arms brought to mind the advertising hoardings she had seen on every street corner, showing granite gravestones engraved with 'RIP' and warning of AIDS. Instead, she grabbed his bony shoulder through the covers and shook him. He rubbed his eyes. His fingernails were lined with dirt and bitten raw.

'Hey! Cool it, will you?'

'Who the hell are you? This is my bloody flat.'

'I'm Rory, Luke's mate,' he said groggily. 'You're Laura, right? We met at the squat. Don't you remember me?'

She stared at him. It was coming back to her. The day Luke had first taken her to the 'commune', as he called it, in a boarded-up terraced house in Stoke Newington Church Street. He'd introduced her to a couple of girls there, dressed in caftans and smoking dope at the kitchen table; they had eyed Laura with suspicion. Then she had met Ray, a West-Indian with an Afro, who'd leapt up to shake her hand and had greeted her with a public school accent. She had also met a fresh-faced boy there, who had sat cross-legged next to a rucksack in the corner of the gloomy room. He had looked as though he was dressed in clothes that his mother had bought him.

'Rory here's just back from Spain, Loz,' Luke had told her, winking conspiratorially.

'That's nice. Did you have a good holiday?' Laura asked, automatically polite.

Luke burst out laughing.

'You're so naive, Loz. That's what I love about you! It wasn't a bleeding holiday. He was hanging out with the Basque Separatists. Thought he was being cool. He didn't realise they were fucking terrorists until he got back and I put him straight about it.'

Rory coloured and shrugged, but stayed silent.

'Yeah. Well, you've got a lot of ground to make up for that particular fuck-up, mate,' Luke said, ruffling the boy's hair.

The wasted face she was looking at now scarcely bore any resemblance to the boy she'd met less than a year ago.

'Luke said it was OK to stay,' he mumbled. 'We got chucked out of the squat a couple of weeks ago. They're going to redevelop it. The landlord got a court order.'

'That doesn't give you the right—'

'Luke didn't think you'd mind. He said you'd be cool, that you were right behind the protesters at Wapping and you wouldn't mind us using your place to sleep. We've been really quiet.'

'He could have asked me,' she muttered. 'Anyway, where is he now?'

'The bastards have got him in Wapping nick. They arrested loads of people this afternoon. I came back here to sleep. I've been on the night shift.'

'Arrested? Why?'

'For nothing. They just rounded guys up and put them in pig wagons. They were lashing out with truncheons. Loads of people were beaten up. You should have seen the blood. They had riot shields, the works.'

'I'd better go and see him,' she said.

'You might be able to get him off. You're a lawyer, right?'

'Not that sort of lawyer,' she said grimly, walking to the door.

She turned. 'I'll be coming back. I suggest you get up and get this place cleared up before I do.'

On the way to Wapping, Laura kept checking her watch. Dad would be awake by now. How could she have left him? He'd be expecting her to be there when he woke up. What excuse could she make? She'd have to admit that she'd gone to look for Luke, and that she was involved with him. She bit her nails and stared out of the window as the dark streets flashed past.

Ever since she'd taken Luke back to the house in Highbury the previous autumn and introduced the two of them, she'd had a feeling that Dad would disapprove of Luke. She could just tell by the way Dad had behaved that afternoon. Even though he'd been superficially polite and chatted amiably to Luke about politics, she'd known from the twinkle in her father's eyes that he was mocking Luke. And the fact that he'd not said anything at all about Luke afterwards had proved that he'd been unimpressed.

She realised now that it had been a mistake to take Luke to the house while she was still supposed to be going out with Matthew. Dad had always liked Matthew. He might have teased him for driving a sports car and wearing a Rolex, but he'd often hinted that he'd be happy to have him as part of the family.

The taxi driver couldn't get close to the police station. The road was blocked with riot vans parked bumper to bumper. Groups of angry people milled about.

'I'll have to drop you here, darling. You going to be alright? It looks a bit rough out there.'

'I'll be fine.'

She shouldered her way through the restless crowd, up the front steps and into the lobby of the station. People were shouting and pushing. The two officers at the desk were sweating, trying to keep control. Laura, taking advantage of being short and slight, ducked her way through the press of bodies and emerged at the desk in front of the officers.

'I need to see Luke Goddard,' she had to shout. The policeman smiled. It wasn't a pleasant smile. He held a hammy hand to his ear.

'You'll have to speak up, love.'

She repeated Luke's name. The officer scanned his list. He took his time.

'Ah, yes. Pretty boy Goddard. He's one of our guests. You family, love?'

'Not exactly. Please don't call me love.'

'Ah, I see. You must be his bit of skirt.'

He narrowed his eyes, leering at her. She stared back at him.

'I would ask you to take a seat, love,' he said with mock politeness, 'but we seem to be quite busy tonight. I'll see what I can do.'

Scowling at him, she moved away from the desk. She spotted a payphone on the far wall and pushed her way towards it. She dialled the number to her father's house. The phone rang for a long time before she heard Ken's voice.

'It's me. Laura,' she said with relief, pushing a ten pence coin into the slot. 'I'm really sorry, but something's come up. I might be a bit longer than I thought. Is Dad OK?'

'He's still asleep. Are you in a pub? There's a hell of a din over there.'

'No. I'll explain later. When he wakes up, please tell Dad I won't be long. Could you get him something to eat?'

'I'll ask Marge.' The bleeps cut in, and she had to hang up.

Laura leaned against the wall and waited. She watched as people were brought in, handcuffed between two officers, most of them kicking and shouting. Some had bloody faces. She felt a wave of nausea and realised she hadn't eaten anything since the tasteless sandwich she had been served on the flight from Paris.

Occasionally, a policeman appeared through a door in the opposite corner and shouted out a visitor's name. Each time the door opened she looked up eagerly. It seemed like an age had passed before he came through and called, 'Visitor for Goddard?'

She made her way across the room and followed the policeman down a dingy corridor lined with grubby grey doors. At the end he opened one and held it open to let her through.

Luke was sitting at a table in the middle of the room. He looked up as she entered. She noticed a bruise on his right cheek. He was smoking, blowing white rings towards the ceiling. As she crossed the bare room towards him, she realised that she was feeling nervous.

'Loz,' he said, standing up and breaking into a broad grin. 'How fantastic to see you! They said there was a young lady to see me. I didn't realise it was you. What are you doing here?'

She went to put her arms around him, but noticed the police officer standing at the end of the room, glowering. She drew back and sat down opposite Luke.

'I had to come back to London,' she said. 'Dad's had a fall. Why are you in here? Why haven't you phoned me?'

'Yeah. Sorry about that. I meant to, but it's just that I've been on the picket line every day.'

'And what about that boy in my flat? Rory.'

Luke leaned forward and stubbed out his cigarette. He looked her in the eyes.

'The guy was homeless. I knew you wouldn't mind. You said I

could stay, Loz. One more person hardly made any difference.'

'You could have asked me. The guy's an addict. I saw the marks on his wrists.'

Luke leaned back and began to laugh.

'He's a diabetic, Laura. Give the poor guy a chance.'

She felt the blood rush to her cheeks. How naive she must look to him.

'I'm sorry. I just assumed …'

'Well, you assumed wrong. All those AIDS posters have got to you. Have terrified you stupid, just like they're meant to.'

'You haven't told me what you're doing in here,' she said, changing the subject. Luke lit another cigarette.

'They've charged me with GBH. I'm up before the magistrates in the morning.'

'GBH?'

'Yeah. I'm supposed to have thrown a brick through the window of a TNT lorry. The driver's in the hospital, apparently.'

'That's a serious charge.'

He shrugged. 'The paperboys will trump up anything to get at legitimate protesters. It's OK for them to beat up innocent civilians though.'

'Paperboys?'

'Murdoch's lackeys. The boys in blue. They've got instructions from the top. They don't care if the charges are bogus, Laura. Any bad publicity for the workers is good for Maggie, good for Murdoch.'

'Now, now, Goddard. Take it easy,' the policeman in the corner piped up. Luke glanced at him and narrowed his eyes. He looked as though he was about to say something but obviously thought better of it, and looked back at Laura.

'So what are you going to do?' asked Laura. 'Did you have legal advice?'

'No. No point. It wouldn't have made any difference. I know my rights.'

'But if you didn't do it?'

He gripped her hand, suddenly serious.

'Of course, I didn't do it, Laura. Peaceful protest – that's what I've always stood for. You know that.'

She looked back into his eyes. She knew those eyes so well, hazel with dark flecks, and she knew all the little lines around them too. Looking at him she was reminded about why she loved him. There was an intensity in his look that made everything around her melt away. It was as if nothing in that moment except the two of them mattered.

'It would have been different if you'd been here earlier,' he said. 'You could have helped me.'

She frowned. Where was this leading?

'Now that you're here, you could represent me tomorrow morning, couldn't you?'

'Me?' she said, beginning to panic. 'I don't do criminal law.'

'I'm sure you could do it. Wasn't your old man a legal aid lawyer? A champion of the oppressed? It must run in the blood. Or perhaps *he* could come down and do it.' He was smiling his mocking smile.

'You don't need to be unkind. He's ill now, Luke. And he's seventy-one years old. He doesn't practice anymore.'

'I was only kidding. But you could do it. You're always saying how you missed your vocation, how you hate your work. You could do something really good for once, instead of just lining the pockets of the fat cats.'

'I wouldn't be the best person for you. You'd be better off with someone from the law centre. You know, where Dad used to work. He still keeps in touch with them, goes down there to help out sometimes. I could phone them for you.

'No. I don't want anyone from the law centre. I want you.'

'But I haven't stood up in court for years. And even then it was only for simple stuff. I really think …'

'You can do it. If you love me like you say you do, you wouldn't hesitate.'

'Of course, I love you. You know that,' she lowered her voice, acutely aware of the hostile presence of the policeman rocking to and fro against the wall.

'Have faith in yourself, Loz.'

His eyes were on her face. She knew he was testing her.

'OK, I'll do it,' she said finally, meeting his look of challenge. 'I've got some textbooks at Dad's. I'll also speak to someone at work tomorrow morning and see if they can help me. What time's the hearing?'

She saw triumph flash in his eyes.

'I knew you'd do it, Loz. Two o'clock. Thames Magistrates.'

It was almost midnight by the time she returned to Highbury. One of Marge's cats was howling in the side passage. She crept up the front steps and let herself into the chilly hall. Silently, she opened the door to the back living room. She heard her dad snoring in his corner of the room. The reassuring sound brought a smile to her lips. The lamp beside the bed was switched on; a tray with dirty dishes lay on the floor.

Relieved, she left him sleeping and tiptoed upstairs to her old bedroom at the front of the house. She shut the door behind her and kicked off her painful shoes. She realised she hadn't stayed the night in her room since she'd bought the flat in the city two years before.

But Dad always kept the room ready for her in case she should want to stay.

The room was still furnished with the cream-painted matching set he had bought for her fourteenth birthday. She remembered her delight when it had been fitted, and how special she'd felt sitting down at the dressing table for the first time. It looked like something out of a doll's house. On the walls hung the posters she had stuck up of David Bowie and the Stones, and photographs of her and her school friends. A few of her law books stood on the shelves, gathering dust.

On the dressing table, encased in a silver frame, was the last picture taken of her mother: she was standing in the front garden, before a rambling white rosebush, holding Laura's hand in her own. When her mother had died, Dad had hacked down the rosebush to its roots with an axe, wincing as if with each fall of the axe he was cutting himself. She had stood and watched, dumb with shock. It was only years later she'd understood that he didn't want to see the roses bloom without her mother there.

The picture was fading badly, the features on the two faces melting away. How she'd studied her mother's face in this picture as a teenager. How she'd envied her mother's natural blonde hair and perfect features, comparing them unfavourably with her own straight dark hair and quirky looks.

She picked up the photo now and stared at it as she had done so many times before, as if doing so would give her some connection to the woman she could barely remember. Only by screwing up her eyes and concentrating hard could she recall the details of her mother's face, the tone of her voice, the comfort of sitting on her warm lap and snuggling in her arms and playing with the silver cross her mother wore round her neck.

She wondered how different her own life would have been if her mother had lived. It was a pointless train of thought, as she had learned years ago. She didn't want to return to that emptiness and frustration she'd often experienced while growing up.

She put the photo back on the dressing table and drew the floral curtains, then undressed quickly, shivering in the unheated room. Rummaging in a drawer she found an old pair of pyjamas. But as she slid between the sheets and stretched to switch off the lamp she noticed a book on criminal procedure on the bookcase. She remembered her promise to Luke. She got out of bed to fetch the book. Then, fighting back the urge to fall sleep, she turned to the chapter on committal proceedings.

8

'You've got your smart suit on again. Are you off somewhere?' Dad looked up as she walked into his room. Weak winter sun filtered through the dusty window, making him look faded and pale.

'Yes.' She hovered by the door. 'Would you like me to bring you anything before I go? I didn't wake you before. You looked so peaceful.'

'Where did you go last night? Ken said you had to rush off.'

'I'm sorry. I nipped back to the flat while you were asleep.'

She looked down at the threadbare carpet. She had to tell him now.

'And I needed to see someone.'

He turned to look at her. His eyes were watery, the skin underneath them smudged with dark shadows.

'No need to explain,' he said.

'It was Luke.'

For a moment he looked confused, then he blinked and his face cleared. He smiled mischievously.

'Ah, yes. Our militant friend.'

'No need to be sarcastic, Dad,' she said sharply. 'I thought you agreed with his views anyway.'

'There's no need for you to be so defensive, Laura. What was it you said he did for a living?'

'Nothing at the moment. He's out of work. Does that matter?'

'You're entitled to see whom you like,' he said, shrugging and turning away. 'I knew you liked the fellow when you brought him round.'

'Well *I* knew, too, that you didn't approve of him. I could just tell.'

'Don't let's argue, Laura. I'm tired. I haven't got the strength.'

'The thing about Luke is,' she went on, 'he's got the bottle to stand up for what he believes in. That's what I admire about him. He's not like other people.'

Her father didn't reply.

'I'll get you some breakfast, and then I'll have to go out,' she said stiffly. She wasn't going to tell him about where she was headed or what she was going to do. Not now.

'Don't worry about the breakfast. I don't feel like anything at the moment,' he said.

She hesitated at the door. It was just like him to be stubborn.

'It's up to you. I'll see you later.'

*　*　*

The court lobby was thronging with people. She approached an usher with a clipboard. He turned to her and nodded officiously.

'You here to represent one of them?' He cast a disapproving eye in the direction of a group of men wearing 'Don't buy the Sun' stickers.

'No. My client was charged yesterday and remanded in custody. He should have been brought to the cells by the police.'

The usher scanned the list on the clipboard, taking his time.

'Only two. Let me guess. Is it Goddard?'

She smiled. 'How did you know?'

'Instinct, my dear.'

As the usher turned round to lead her to the cells, she noticed that a 'Don't buy the Sun' sticker was stuck to the back of his jacket. As he passed the group of men, they nudged each other and sniggered.

'Do you want to see your client first or talk to the prosecuting solicitor?' the usher asked.

What the hell should she do? She was considering his question carefully when the usher turned around and said, 'Oh, here's Mr. Talbot now. He's prosecuting today.'

She looked up to see a familiar figure bearing down on them.

'Neil.' She had not seen him since the graduation ball, when he had got boorishly drunk and vomited in the bushes.

'Laura Ellis!' A blush was deepening his already florid complexion. He had put on weight. 'Fancy seeing you here. I heard a rumour you were a high flyer in the city.'

'And I thought you had gone off to Australia in pursuit of … What was her name?'

'Ah, yes … That was a long time ago. That all ended in rather an unfortunate manner. So, are you here to defend someone? Hardly your usual line of work, I'd have thought.'

'I'm here to defend Luke Goddard.'

Neil raised his bushy eyebrows.

'Pretty clear-cut case of GBH. We've got all the witness statements from the police officers. We also have eye-witness accounts of him lobbing a breeze block at the windscreen of a lorry. Today will just be committal proceedings. The police are opposing bail.'

'Now wait a minute. Before you steam ahead, I need to see the statements and discuss the position with my client.'

'I've got copies for you,' he said dismissively, handing her some papers. 'I don't think you'll find anything to dispute here. Between you and me, the guy's a scumbag.'

'This is my client you're talking about,' she said, eyeing him coldly.

Laura strode away. She scanned the witness statements. Three policemen. Almost identical accounts. They could have been cut and pasted onto each other. She turned to the usher.

'Could I see my client now, please?'

Luke was in a tiny low room lit by a strip light. When the usher left they were alone.

'Done some homework?' he asked.

'I did a bit of swotting up last night and spoke on the phone to someone in the office this morning. He only defends the occasional businessman who's up for speeding offences, but he knew the gist of things.'

She handed him the witness statements.

'This is bullshit, Laura,' he said when he'd finished reading them. 'Can't you see that?'

'They all say the same thing as far as I can see.'

'That's my point. Hang on a minute … This one here – Foster. I know him. He's a violent bastard. I saw him beating up a protester behind one of the vans. His boss had to step in and stop it getting out of hand. Last I saw of him they were putting him in the back of one of their own vans. He couldn't have seen what happened because he wasn't there.'

'How do you know it was him?'

'I know, Laura. When you've been on the picket line for a month, you know their faces pretty well. They're a hard bunch, believe me.'

'But it will be your word against theirs. It will be difficult to prove he's lying when three of them say the same thing.'

'Whose side are you on for God's sake?'

'Well, we've got to be realistic. Why don't you tell me what exactly happened there?'

'Yeah, well, I was on the picket line with the other guys. We'd been there for a few hours. There was a lot of tension. There were more police than ever before. They had riot shields. They were determined to break the protest. A few scuffles broke out here and there, and they tried to arrest a couple of people. But we managed to fight back and get them away. This had been going on for a couple of hours when the lorries started to come out of the plant to deliver the evening editions of *The Sun*. Those drivers are psychos, I tell you. One of them, driving an articulated lorry, mounted the pavement and drove at some of the protesters. Everyone scattered about, but someone lobbed a breezeblock through the windscreen, and the lorry went out of control and hit a wall on the other side of the street.'

'So who was it?'

'I don't know. There was so much going on, it was impossible to see properly. Someone punched me in the face, and I could hardly see out of one eye.'

'Tell me some more about the policemen you saw beating up a protester.'

'This guy had been taunting a line of police. He was swearing at them, shouting, calling them "paperboys". All of a sudden, they all went for him, about five of them. They hit him with truncheons. He fell over and then they started really laying into him. This guy, Foster, he was the worst.'

'OK. I'll talk to the prosecuting solicitor. Let me see what I can do.'

She went back up to the lobby. She found Neil Talbot in a corner, chatting to a police officer.

'Can I have a moment?'

She saw him exchange glances with the policeman before he left him.

'You can't use these statements,' she said. 'One of your witnesses, Foster, is lying. He wasn't at the scene. He was already inside a police van. He'd had to be restrained from beating up a protester. I'm surprised you don't know that already. Or perhaps you do?'

'Is that what Goddard says?'

'We have other eyewitnesses who say the same thing,' she said.

'That's a surprise, when you've only just spoken to your client.'

Laura stared at his sweating, florid face.

'How do you know what I've done or how many people I've spoken to about this? Rest assured, if you persist with this charge, I'll bring witness after witness forward to testify to witnessing PC Foster being restrained by his superior officers. Don't you think it looks a bit strange that they've put him forward as a witness in those circumstances? A bit of a slip, don't you think? And while I'm on the subject, it also seems a bit odd that all the police statements are almost identical. As if written by the same person, one might think. It is going to look very bad for the police if they are shown to have been falsifying their statements, on top of beating up innocent protesters. Don't you agree?'

'I'd like to know which witnesses you're going to bring forward to testify to this.'

Her mind was racing. Who could she call? If it was just Luke saying this, it wouldn't be enough. She turned to go.

'I'll let you have the list straight away.'

She turned and walked up to the bunch of men by the door.

'Were any of you present when Luke Goddard was arrested,' she asked, stepping into the circle.

'Sure. We were there.' One of the men said.

'Did any of you see a group of police officers attack a protester?'

'Yes, I saw it,' a young lad piped up.

'And did you see a police officer being restrained?'

'Yes, I did. They had to bundle him into the police van.'

'Would you be able to pick him out?'

'I think so, yes. Tall chap. Hard looking. Pock-marked face.'

'Would you be prepared to give evidence about that?'

'Yes. Anything to discredit those pigs. Anything.'

'Thanks. Anyone else see it?'

They all murmured that they hadn't, but they were prepared to give evidence anyway.

She went to the payphone in the corner and dialled the number to her flat. It rang for a long time. Then, she heard Rory's voice.

'It's Laura. I've got to be quick. Were you there when Luke got arrested?'

'Yes.'

'Did you see some police officers beating up a protester?'

'Yes. But that happens all the time.'

'Did you see one of the officers being restrained from going too far?'

'Yes. The big bastard, Foster.'

'Would you be prepared to come to court and swear it was him?'

'Of course. Do you want me to come now?'

'I'll call you back if I do.'

'But Laura …'

She put down the phone and strode back to Neil.

'I have at least two eyewitnesses, who are prepared to stand up in court and swear. Your case is non-existent. The evidence is fabricated. That much is obvious to anyone reading the statements.'

Neil walked away angrily to speak to the officer by the window.

In a minute or two he returned.

'OK. We're prepared to drop the charge of GBH, as long as your client will plead guilty to a charge of breach of the peace and agree to keep the peace for a month from now.'

They went into court, and the magistrates' clerk read out the charge of breach of the peace. Laura got up to say her client pleaded guilty, and the magistrate read out the sentence. Luke would be unable to approach the News International plant or go anywhere near the Highway or Wapping High Street for a month.

'You're free to go, Mr. Goddard,' the magistrate then said, and a cheer went up from the gallery.

She joined Luke in the lobby afterwards. He was surrounded by people slapping his back, shaking his hand. He was jubilant. She saw in his eyes the same infectious joy that drew people to him, that had first attracted her to him.

'You're a gem, Loz. You've got hidden talents,' he said, kissing her on the lips. 'Coming for a drink to celebrate? All these guys are on for a pint at the Jolly Sailor.'

'I'd best get back to Dad. He's not well at all.'

'He can't be that bad, surely? We could go back to your place afterwards.'

He pulled her towards him, and she felt a shiver of desire at the touch of his hand on her waist. But she pulled away.

'Look, I'll meet you later. You go to the pub with the others, and I'll see you at the flat this evening.'

'You always were your daddy's girl, weren't you?'

He kissed her again.

She took a taxi back to Highbury. As it turned into the road and moved towards her father's house, she saw that a light was revolving around the trees, bathing the house fronts in blue. An ambulance was parked outside the house. A few onlookers were hanging around on the pavement.

A group of people moved slowly through the front garden. She recognised the dark uniforms of paramedics and realised they were stooping with the weight of a stretcher.

'Dad!' She thrust some notes through the partition of the taxi and jumped out before it came to a stop. She ran down the pavement.

Ken and Marge were standing beside the stretcher, white-faced. A paramedic was adjusting an oxygen mask over her father's mouth. Another held a bottle with a drip above him as they manoeuvred the stretcher into the back of the ambulance. She couldn't see Dad's face.

She turned to Ken. Her mouth was dry with shock. He shook his head. Tears were standing in his eyes.

'Heart attack,' he said.

9

Harry was hit instantly and fell, slumped in front of the tree trunk. Ian was still saluting when he was hit, his body jerked about by the force of the shots. When he finally fell he was still holding the salute, his eyes staring ahead in bold defiance. Tom, shaking all over, sunk down on the bench. After a few agonising seconds, the guns finally fell silent.

Tom jumped up from his seat on the back of the truck.

'You murdering bastards!' he yelled at the firing squad.

The guards turned towards him, screaming in Japanese, but he took no notice of them. He leapt down from the truck and ran to where Ian and Harry had fallen. He knelt between them, sobbing, staring at their bodies in horror. The sickly smell of fresh blood oozing out from their punctured flesh caught the back of his throat. It made his stomach turn.

His friends lay there half covered in earth, their bodies scattered with white flowers from the pomelo trees. On an impulse, Tom picked up a twig laden with flowers and shoved it into his pocket.

With trembling fingers, he then reached out and closed each of their eyelids in turn. Their skin was warm. He shut his own eyes and uttered a small prayer for each of them. He had never been religious. He knew that if there was a God, he had not been there to protect Harry and Ian, or to stop the horror that was unfolding in this jungle. But he knew that Harry and Ian had both been religious;

they had both attended the services on Sundays that the padre held on the edge of the camp. Inadequate as it might be, saying a prayer for them seemed the right thing to do now.

'Goodbye my friends,' he said softly. 'I will never forget you.'

The guards were still yelling at him in Japanese. They surrounded him, rifles pointed.

'Here.' The Ripper thrust a shovel towards him. 'Bury them.'

The Ripper clicked his fingers, and the guards leapt forward and kicked the bodies into the shallow graves. They fell in awkwardly, their limbs at odd angles. Tom wanted to get down into the graves to rearrange their arms and legs so that they were at least lying properly. He moved forward but two guards pulled him back.

'Bury them,' repeated the Ripper, impatient now. He drew a pistol and pointed it at Tom.

So Tom began the grim task of burying his dead friends. Slowly, he began to shovel earth over them. He could hardly bear to look at where the earth was landing. His own body was racked with pain and the smallest movement made him wince. Tears streamed down his face.

He had buried countless bodies in Singapore. Many of them rotting and mutilated, disembowelled or headless. He had not known any of those poor people. This was different. Every shovel of earth that he threw into the graves, that he heard landing on the flesh of his friends reinforced the horror.

When it was over, he leaned on the shovel handle, sweat pouring from him. The guards pushed him on to the back of the lorry. Archie was still sprawled out on the floor, unconscious. Tom was relieved that Archie hadn't witnessed what had happened. It would have destroyed him.

The engine of the truck roared into action, and it turned round in the clearing. As they rattled past the native hamlet, an old Thai woman emerged from one of the huts. In her arms she carried a bunch of jungle flowers. He watched her cross the track and waddle towards the graves. She must be going to put the flowers there. The simple act of kindness brought a lump to his throat.

As they drove back to the camp, Tom could not stop thinking of Harry and Ian, of the cruelty and pointlessness of their deaths.

The light faded quickly, and it was dark by the time the lorry swung through the camp gates and rattled to a halt beside the guardhouse. It was supper time. The men were lining up patiently beside the cookhouse with their mess tins and mugs. Tom's own stomach was taut with hunger, but he had no desire for food.

The guards pushed him off the lorry, and he stood unsteadily in front of the guardhouse. The Ripper jumped down from the front of the truck and strutted towards him. From the look in his eyes, Tom realised that the Ripper had not finished punishing him.

'You and your friends disgrace the name of Imperial Japanese Army,' he barked. 'We have to give punishment. We have to show men what happen to men who try escape. They must know harsh punishment follow to him and to his friends.'

He snapped his fingers at the guards, who jumped to attention and surrounded Tom. They seized his arms and dragged him across the clearing, towards the other side of the camp. With every step, they wrenched his arms as if to pull them out of the sockets. The pain was excruciating, but Tom did not cry out.

As they crossed the clearing, Tom's heart filled with dread. He realised where the guards were taking him. Behind the hut where the tools were kept and opposite the guardhouse were two punishment pits. These were narrow holes dug in the earth. In them a man could stoop with only his head and shoulders held above the ground.

Around the top of the hole, thick bamboo canes had been driven into the earth to form a cage so that the occupant could not escape, or even see very much from within. There was little light or ventilation to begin with, and corrugated iron sheets were put on top of the bamboo struts during the day to amplify the heat of the sun.

Since Tom had been brought to the camp, he had seen only two men being sent to the pits before. They had been caught stealing tools and trying to sell them to the Thais outside the camp. One of the men had died in the pit after three days; the other had been released eventually, but he had never recovered. He still went about camp muttering nonsense, a faraway look in his haunted eyes, alternating between raging at others and crumbling into tearful self-pity.

Tom glanced behind him. They were dragging Archie along too. The boy's head lolled to one side, and his limbs were limp.

He'll never survive this, Tom thought. And perhaps I won't either.

He stared ahead. Colonel Scott was pleading with the Ripper outside the guard house, gesticulating, bowing. The Ripper was shaking his head firmly.

They reached the first pit, and the guards lifted Tom then dropped him into the hole. He landed feet first. There was barely enough room to kneel. He had to stand stooped, his knees and back bent into the available space.

The hole already stunk of faeces. The smell was putrid, suffocating, unbearable. Through the bamboo bars that surrounded the top of the pit, there was just enough space for Tom to see across the parade ground. He pressed his forehead against the bars and peered through. Colonel Scott was still there outside the guardhouse pleading with the Ripper. Other officers stood around helplessly. One of the guards came back and shoved a tin of water and a bowl of rice at him, then slammed the corrugated iron lid down over Tom's head. Most of the food and water had spilled onto Tom's head and dribbled into the ground before he could reach up for it.

He ate and drank what was still left then sank down in despair. He closed his eyes, trying to shut out the horror of his situation. The image of Joy swam before his eyes. She was looking up at him, smiling her shy smile, with tears in her eyes. She was giving him something. A photograph. Automatically he touched the breast pocket of the shabby shirt he had worn every day for months. He could feel the reassuring shape of the photograph, still there next to his breast.

'Joy,' he breathed. 'I'll come back. One day I'll come back.'

Then he remembered the flowers he'd taken from the graves. He pulled them out of the pocket of his shorts and, putting them up to his nose, took a deep breath of their scent. Immediately he was back under the pomelo trees, shovelling earth that fell with a dull thud onto the bodies of his friends. The smell of the flowers brought back the smell of their blood, fresh, rapidly congealing in the tropical sun. He began to retch. He brought up the water and his rice meal, vomiting it onto the sides of the hole and onto his shirt. He was sweating and gasping, his body racked with pain. Afterwards he sank back against the earth of his prison, weak and exhausted.

'How the hell am I going to get through this?' he asked out loud.

For a long time he crouched there in despair. His thoughts were out of control. They were like scattered jigsaw pieces, sometimes fragmented, sometimes fitting together in a coherent whole. The images of Harry and Ian appeared before him, of their bodies covered in blood and dancing before his eyes as bullets hit and sliced through them. Then suddenly those images faded and Joy was running towards him, emerging from the smoke of the guns. At least it was Joy's face, but she had the body of a lithe and graceful puma. He tried to stretch out his hand towards her, but the pit prevented him from touching her, and as he struggled to reach her, she melted away into nothingness. She was instantly replaced by the image of his father, who had taken the shape of a lion, and had a tattered mane and rheumy drunken eyes. The lion was crouching, about to spring. Tom again tried to put out his arms, this time to shield himself from the lion's pounce, but again found his movement constricted. He tried to cry out in fear, but as he did so the lion spun away into darkness, and then emerged again. But now, it had turned into a feral dog, and it was coming to him, and Tom saw that it was injured and limping, dragging one leg behind it. He struggled to remember where he had seen it before. It was moving towards some trees just out of his vision when it stopped and turned towards him. He saw then that it was Archie, his face swollen and livid from his beatings. Tom opened his mouth to speak to Archie, to reassure him that he would help him, but no words would come.

Tom crouched there sweating and panting, trying to get a grip on himself. He knew he had to take control of his mind if he was ever going to get through this. He needed to get hold of something tangible. Sweating and shaking, he tried to focus his mind. He knew he must think about something other than his predicament. But all he could think about were Harry and Ian, and the great emptiness he felt at losing them. How was he going to survive without them? He had depended on their company for everything until now. They had helped him get through each day in the camp. Without Harry's cheerful banter and Ian's quiet good sense, he would have given up the will to make it through this hell months ago. His mind kept returning to the image of their bloody corpses lying under the pomelo trees, inside those inadequate shallow graves. How was he ever going to get over losing them?

The four of them – Tom, Ian, Harry and Archie – had been in it together from the start. Or almost from the start at least. Most of Tom's platoon from the Straits Settlements Volunteer Force had been killed on Singapore Island in the final battle. Poorly trained and unprepared, with inadequate equipment, they had been overwhelmed by fire from Japanese tanks. One by one they had fallen in the muddy storm drain, where the Volunteers had been waiting for the Japs to march into the city. Except for Tom. He had managed to stay alive.

When the order to surrender came and the defeated troops were rounded up and marched through the ruined streets of Singapore to the barracks at Changi, Tom fell in with a platoon from the Northumberland Fusiliers. He noticed Ian on that first march. Ian marched tall and proud, swinging his arms freely, his back ramrod straight, staring defiantly ahead of him. Many of the men were distracted by the crowds of Asians lining the route, waving Japanese flags, throwing vegetables at the Allied soldiers, booing and jeering at them. Tom had observed the bewildered faces of many of the soldiers, humiliated by this display. But Ian had marched on, unperturbed.

Tom had also noticed Harry. Harry had been injured in the battle. His arm was crushed and bloody. Yet, like Ian, he marched with pride, head held high, jaw fixed against the pain, a look of proud determination on his face.

Tom didn't get to know them, or even speak to them, for several weeks though. He rarely spoke to anyone in those first few weeks. He was still in shock at losing his platoon, at losing all the men he had trained and fought with and had grown close to. The terror of the battle and the horror of seeing his friends massacred in cold blood had filled him with fear, had left him reeling with shock. He found he could not speak of it, but speaking about anything else either seemed impossible after what he had witnessed. Shutting himself off, he gradually came to terms with the loss of his friends, the privations of the camp and the horrors of the work parties.

He fell into the routine of the prison camp at Changi, sleeping in a cramped and foetid hut by night, and by day carrying out tasks that the officer in charge of the hut allocated him. The soldiers had quickly learned that if they didn't grow their own food to supplement the starvation rations dealt out by the Japanese, and that if they didn't clean and take care of the camp, they would become sick and die.

Sometimes Tom was detailed to tend the vegetable patch, sometimes to dig the latrines, sometimes to clean the huts. However, on the days he was chosen to go out of the camp on a work party, he had found himself filled with dread. Men were picked out at random from the parade in the morning, loaded with others on the back of a crowded truck, and taken to a piece of waste ground or a beach outside the city. There they were given shovels and ordered to bury the bloated and mutilated bodies of the Chinese who had been massacred as collaborators with the *Kuomintang*.

On these days, Tom learned to switch himself off, to blank his emotions against whatever he saw. He watched grown men crack after a day of this gruelling work, break down and cry like frightened children. He decided that he would not give in like that.

After a few days, he was struck down with dysentery. His stomach was gripped with searing gripes, and he had to rush to the latrines several times an hour, often not making it in time. He began to lose weight; none of the food he ate would stay in his stomach. He became weak, shaky, was in constant pain.

One afternoon when he was sweating on the latrine, doubled

up with agony, the Japanese guards called a parade. Everyone had to come out to the parade ground, stand in line and be counted. The guards often did this on a whim, for no better reason than to amuse themselves. Paralysed by spasms, Tom found he could not move. He tried to get up, but swooned with pain, collapsing back on the makeshift seat. So he stayed where he was, praying that no-one would notice he was not in the line-up.

A stab of fear went through him as he heard the Japanese officer shouting, barking orders to his men. He listened helplessly as they searched the huts, banging the doors back and pulling out bunks. Then they came to the latrines. He heard them search every one of them, getting closer and closer to where he sat, frozen with fear. He was shaking when they pulled him from the seat, his trousers down, brown liquid oozing down his legs. The guards propelled him forward onto the parade area, laughing and jeering. They threw him on the ground and kicked him. Someone stamped on his head, grinding his face into the dirt.

After that they dragged him to his feet and pushed him into the centre of the ground. The guards dismissed the rest of the men and allowed them back to their huts, but Tom was forced to stand there in the baking sun, holding a plank of wood above his head. Each time his strength failed him and he had to lower it, one of the guards would punch him in the stomach and shove his arms up again. After a couple of hours of this, Tom collapsed to his knees, unable to stand. He no longer cared what they did to him. A guard came and kicked him repeatedly until he blanked out with the pain.

He woke up in a strange hut. It must have been the nearest one to where he had collapsed. He was lying on one of the bunks, and someone was bathing his face with a damp cloth. Several men were standing over him, anxious expressions on their faces.

'He's coming round now. Let's get him over to the hospital hut.' Tom recognised the speaker as the tall proud soldier from the march. 'Come on, Harry, give me a hand. We can do it together,' the soldier said to his friend.

The two of them hoisted Tom to his feet, put his arms over their shoulders, then half carried, half dragged him along the line of huts to the one set up as a makeshift hospital.

The officer in charge looked up in surprise as they entered: 'Good God! Is that the poor chap who was given a beating on the parade ground earlier? I thought he was dead.'

Tom stayed in the hospital hut for four days, unable to move, drifting in and out of consciousness. Harry and Ian came to see him several times a day, bringing him things they had saved from their own rations, or had managed to purloin somehow: a boiled egg, an orange, a cup of thin soup. And gradually he started to recover. The dysentery passed and his wounds began to heal. Tom found himself looking forward to their visits. He began to appreciate Ian's laconic humour and Harry's sharp observations, and the two of them seemed to enjoy Tom's company as well.

After that they all looked out for one another. It was an unspoken contract that they would share their rations between them; if someone was short one day, the others would make it up for him. If one of them happened to be out on a work party and managed to buy or pilfer some food and smuggle it back to camp, he would share it with the two others. If one was ill, the others would look after him and make sure he had enough to eat and drink. And when food was really short, one of them would try and sell one of their last treasured items – a pen, a watch, a ring – to provide food for all three.

Harry and Ian came from the same small northern town. They

had signed up for the Northumberland Fusiliers on the same day, although they had not known each other before that. Harry was a tough little man, with a tanned face lined like a walnut. He had been a store manager in a clothing factory, and he was fond of telling anecdotes about his workmates or his boss. He had a jovial manner and a quick sense of humour. Harry had a wife and a young son back in Lancashire, but he rarely spoke of them.

Ian was different. He was younger, and quieter than Harry, but he had a steely edge. He had been a draftsman in an engineering firm. Tom quickly saw that he had adopted a few ground rules to get through his ordeal. He never let anything get him down, and took every situation as it came without complaint. He was resilient and resourceful, taking the opportunity to bargain for food with the locals whenever it arose. Under his slow, deliberate manner lurked a deep, thoughtful intelligence.

They had been in Changi for over six months when one day, after the morning parade, several hundred men were selected to leave the camp. They were to be sent up-country to work. Rumours had been circulating that the Japanese had started to use prisoners to build a railway through the jungle in Thailand, in order to supply to their troops fighting the Allies in Burma. The three of them had discussed it before and wondered what it might mean for them if they were selected. Perhaps conditions would be better there? They could hardly imagine that they would be worse. But when they were selected, there was little time to further discuss this development. They were ordered to leave straight away.

The guards herded the men, like cattle, into steel railway trucks. The heat inside was unbearable, as hot as ovens; thirty men crammed into each truck, with barely enough room even to sit on the floor. Sweat had poured from Tom's body; he had struggled for air. No buckets were provided, so when someone wanted to relieve himself, the others had to hold him out of the steel door, so that he could go over the edge of the track and spare the floor.

The journey lasted for four days. The train only stopped once each day for food, when a bucket of rice and soup was passed around, and each man had to dip his mess tin into it and eat what he could. The hunger that had plagued them at Changi became far worse. At night it became bitterly cold, and they found themselves shivering. Then everyone had to take turns to lie on the floor to sleep as there was not enough room for everyone. Tom, Harry and Ian had shared a corner, changing positions wearily every few hours.

It was not until they arrived at the end of the line that they had met Archie. On that long exhausting tramp through the jungle from the final sidings at Ban Pong to the base camp where work on the railway was to begin, a boy with ginger hair and pale skin, red-raw from the sun, was stumbling along in front of Tom. He was clearly suffering from exhaustion and fell down repeatedly. The guard in charge of their section kept yelling at him and prodding him with a bayonet. In the end Tom and Ian had picked him up and helped him along.

'Thank you,' he whispered through cracked lips, barely looking at them. Tom saw that the boy's face was a mass of sores and inflamed insect bites. There was even one on his right eyelid, so swollen that the eye would not open properly.

When, after hours of marching, they had finally arrived at their destination, they were drained from the march, weak from hunger. The guards ushered them into a clearing, where a few small huts had been constructed from tree trunks and thatched with palm leaves. The boy had flung himself down beside his pack under the trees at the edge of the clearing.

'You can't stay there,' said Tom. 'You'll have to come inside the hut. It's not safe out here.'

'I'm not going in there,' said the boy with sudden spirit, looking at him in the eye for the first time. 'I can't stand it, lying so close to everyone, people coughing and puking. It's disgusting. I'd prefer to be out in the open.'

'But you haven't got anything to lie on. You'll get sick.'

'I'm already sick. We all are. Anyway, I've got my kit bag to lie on, and I've got a shirt for a blanket.'

Tom had hesitated. For some reason he felt responsible for the boy. He seemed so vulnerable and lonely. But, he reasoned, he couldn't force him to sleep inside the hut.

'It's your choice.' He had reluctantly left the boy where he was.

The next morning, as they queued impatiently for breakfast beside the temporary cookhouse, the boy joined the queue and it looked as though he had been crying. His swollen eyes were bloodshot, and he seemed even more miserable than the day before.

'What's up?' asked Harry.

The boy just shrugged his shoulders and looked away. Tom had the impression that he was struggling to keep back the tears.

'Come on, lad,' coaxed Harry gently, 'you might as well tell us what's wrong.'

'My kit bag and shirt are gone,' he muttered at last. 'I woke up and found they'd vanished. Some bastard must have had them.'

'What was in there?'

'Everything. Everything I had. My spare shorts, my mess tin and fork, my penknife. And my pictures … My photographs of Mum and Dad.'

Ian patted him on the back.

'Don't worry, lad. We'll sort you out. We can rustle up a spare mess tin and other stuff for you. You won't go short.'

From then on, Harry, Ian and Tom had helped the boy face each gruelling, dismal day at camp.

Now, the thought that Harry and Ian were no longer there was almost too much for Tom to bear. The four of them had looked out for each other. They had shared rations, cared for each other if they got sick and provided the support they all needed to get through each day's labour. How was he going to get through this without them? And if he ever did get out of this god-forsaken pit, how was he going to make sure that Archie remained strong through this ordeal, without the reinforcements of Harry and Ian? How was he going to make sure that Archie did not give up the fight? How was he going to do this alone?

10

Laura balanced herself precariously on the pull-down seat of the ambulance. She clung with slippery hands to a metal bar, lurching from side to side as they raced through the dark streets. She could hear the wail of the siren. It sounded as if it came from a long way away.

She watched in anguish as the paramedics worked on her father.

Don't leave me, Dad, she pleaded silently. For God's sake don't leave me.

The ambulance slowed down. She glanced out of the window. They were moving along a narrow residential street, manoeuvring between badly parked cars.

'We're getting near the hospital now,' one of the men informed her, looking up. He had an Irish accent. His eyes were bloodshot and exhausted. He must see this all the time, Laura thought.

'Try not to worry,' he said. 'We'll be there soon.'

She swallowed.

'Is he going to be alright?'

'We're taking good care of him. As soon as we arrive we're going to take him straight into the trauma room. Someone will tell you where to wait. Try to keep calm.'

When the ambulance drew up under the hospital canopy, they opened the back doors, and bright lights from the entrance flooded in. Hospital staff surrounded the stretcher and carried it swiftly from the ambulance, placed it onto a trolley and wheeled it inside. Once through the doors, more people in white coats joined the convoy and rushed the trolley down a long corridor. Laura had to jog to keep up with them. Everything around her was a blur.

Suddenly the little crowd disappeared through a pair of swing doors marked 'Intensive Care. Medical Staff Only'. She was alone in the dingy passage; it was not unlike the corridor in the police station, except this one smelled of disinfectant, the other of sweat and despair.

She sunk onto a plastic chair and put her face in her hands. Nobody had told her where or how long she would have to wait.

Unable to sit still, she got up and paced about. She strode to the end of the corridor and stared out of the window onto an empty car park lit by the harsh glare of floodlights. She didn't want to go any further or turn the corner, in case someone came through the double doors with news. She turned round to see that the corridor was deserted. Would they forget she was there? She had an impulse to run back to the doors and push them open. How could they be taking so long? Why didn't someone come and tell her what was going on?

She wondered what life would be like without her father. She shuddered. It was impossible to contemplate such a thing. He'd always seemed so healthy, making light of his constant cough and his bad leg.

The doors opened and a doctor came through. He was shorter than Laura. He had oriental looks and was probably Chinese. She walked towards him and he looked up at her and smiled briskly.

'Your father is stable now. You can see him. He won't want to talk much. Better not to tire him.'

'Is he going to be OK?' she faltered.

'He has a very weak heart. It has been weakened … He may have suffered from malnutrition in the past.'

'Malnutrition?'

'Yes. Was he short of food when he was young? For a sustained period perhaps?'

'He was a prisoner of war … Of the Japanese. I know that.'

'I thought so. I have seen it before. There is even a name for the condition – bamboo heart. It means that the heart has been permanently weakened by starvation. He needs to be very careful.'

She swallowed and stared at him, trying to take in what he had just told her. Bamboo heart? It sounded incredible. Starvation? Dad had never even hinted at that.

How little she really knew about his life, of his time in Malaya before the war, the woman in the photograph, his time as a prisoner. She knew nothing of the horrors he might have suffered. How could I have taken you so much for granted all these years? And by the selfish act of a teenager, throwing the letter from Penang into the flames, she had probably denied him contact with someone he had once loved.

How can I ever make it up to you? How can I make up for being selfish and callous, of always putting myself first?

'Can I see him now please?'

'Of course,' the doctor pulled open the door for her.

Dad was lying on a high bed on the other side of the room, surrounded by tubes and monitors. Laura rushed over to him. His face was grey, but he parted his lips in a weak smile. She kissed his cold cheek.

'Sorry,' he said in a whisper.

'Sorry? I'm sorry. I wasn't there. And I left in a bad mood this morning. How could I have done that to you?'

He clasped her hand. 'It was my fault.'

She shook her head, feeling that if she said any more she would break down in tears.

'How are you feeling?' she managed to say feebly.

'I've felt better.' His lips moved slowly, and he attempted a smile.

'You must have been terrified.'

He shook his head. 'No. Not by that …'

He fell silent, and she wondered what he meant. She sat down beside the bed. She couldn't bear to have secrets from him anymore. She knew she must tell him about the letter. She opened her mouth to speak, but then hesitated.

He was watching her face, waiting for her to speak.

'I'm so glad you're …'

'Still alive?' He said the words she couldn't bring herself to say.

Her eyes filled with tears, but before she could speak again, a West Indian nurse with an ample frame and smiling eyes came in and began fiddling with one of the monitors above her father's bed.

'I'm sorry, my dear, but we need our rest now,' she said to Laura. 'Could you come back again tomorrow?

Laura got up quickly. 'Of course. Yes. I'll come back in the morning. What time?

'Visiting hours is between ten and eleven.'

She leaned forward and kissed Dad, screwing her face up to hold back the tears.

'See you tomorrow, she whispered.

Outside the room the doctor was bustling past with a clipboard, hurrying to see another patient.

'Is he going to be OK?'

The doctor stopped. He looked at Laura as if he didn't remember who she was. Then he glanced at his board and said, 'Ah, yes …

Mr. Ellis. He'll be in intensive care for a couple of days. The first two days are the most critical. After that we'll move him into the main ward. He's done well today. It was touch and go for a while though.'

* * *

When she let herself in to the house, she found Ken and Marge waiting anxiously in the back kitchen. They were sitting at the table. Marge clasped a mug of tea in her hands with fingerless gloves. Ken had a tumbler of whisky in front of him.

'He's going to be OK,' she said, sitting down at the table, taking a grateful gulp of whisky when Ken pushed the tumbler towards her.

'Thank God.' Marge burst into tears of relief.

Laura couldn't face going back to the flat that night. She hated to admit it to herself, but she was not sure if Luke would share her concern about Dad being in hospital, and it was best to avoid having that suspicion confirmed.

The telephone rang as she was going up to her room to bed. It was Luke. He sounded as though he'd been drinking.

'I thought you were coming to the flat?' he said blearily. 'Where are you? I've been waiting.'

'Dad's had a heart attack, Luke. I've been at the hospital.'

There was a long silence. Then he said gently, 'Are you OK? Do you want me to come over?'

Tears of relief sprung to her eyes.

'No. I'm fine. I'll be better on my own. I'll have to go back to the hospital in the morning.'

'If you need me, just give me a call. Anytime. And, Laura, thanks for what you did for me today.'

It seemed so long ago she'd almost forgotten.

'It was nothing. Anyone could have done that,' she said.

* * *

The next morning she was outside her father's hospital room at ten o'clock sharp. She saw that had more colour in his cheeks but his eyes were still ringed with exhaustion.

'I'm sorry I was difficult about Luke,' was the first thing he said to her as she walked in. 'I had no right, and it was very foolish of me.'

'I'm sorry I reacted the way I did.'

'All I want is for you to be happy, Laura. That's all I've ever wanted. And if he makes you happy, that's all that matters.'

She looked away. Could she answer truthfully that Luke made her happy?

'I wanted to ask you …' she began once she had regained her composure. 'It might seem a strange thing to ask, but I've been wondering about when you were young. Did you have other girlfriends? Before Mum I mean?'

'What a strange question. Dozens of course,' he answered with a smile.

'No, seriously. What about in Penang? Was there somebody special there?'

She thought she saw him flinch at the words, but he recovered himself quickly.

'Why do you ask?'

'We received a letter once,' she began carefully, 'with a Penang postmark.'

'Oh, it would have been from the Volunteers' charity. They used to write sometimes, asking for contributions. Why?'

'It got lost. I mean … I lost it.'

'Don't worry about it. Like I said, must have been just the Volunteers. Nothing important.'

She opened her mouth to protest. She knew it wasn't from the Volunteers. They wouldn't have opened the letter with 'My Dearest Tom'. But she hadn't the courage to tell him. Perhaps she could try to approach it in another way.

'When you're better, do you think you might tell me about what happened to you back then?'

He frowned. 'Then?'

'In the war, I mean. I'd like to know. I've never asked before, but I've begun to realise that I ought to know about it.'

'You wouldn't understand,' he said wearily. 'No-one who wasn't there would understand.'

'I could try. I am grown up now, Dad.'

'I always kept it from you. And your mother, as well. I wanted to protect you both from it.'

'Protect?'

'Things happened then that … aren't easy to talk about.'

'Couldn't you try?'

He shook his head. 'I did it once. That was enough.'

His voice was beginning to falter. His eyelids were drooping.

'Who? Did you talk to someone about this?'

'Alfred, I think his name was. Arthur or Alfred … Stone. Yes, that was it. You can ask him if you want to know.'

'But who is he?'

'Oh, just someone I met after the war. Look, I'm tired now, Laura. Please.'

She felt miserable. She had meant to tell him about burning the letter, but had failed, and she'd now exhausted him with her questions.

The doctor Laura had met the day before walked into the room. Her father looked up and made an effort to smile at him. '*Cha*,' he said in a weak voice.

'*Loo hoe bo?*'

Tom replied, '*Wah hoe.*'

'What language is that?' Laura stared at the both of them.

'It is Hokkien Chinese,' said the doctor. 'My family comes from Malaysia, and I gather your father learned the language when he lived there before the war.'

'Really? I had no idea. Dad, you never told me you could speak Chinese.'

'Well, it was a very long time ago. Besides, I've almost completely forgotten it, I'm afraid. I haven't spoken a word of Hokkien for years.'

'Your father is just being modest. He has an excellent accent,' said the doctor with a warm smile. He turned to Laura. 'Look, I'm very sorry, Miss Ellis, but I'm going to have to ask you to leave now. I have some checks to do on your father, and then I must continue on my rounds.'

'Could you just give me a couple of minutes?' Laura pleaded.

'I'm very sorry, but he will really need to rest after the tests. We mustn't tire him. You can come back tomorrow.'

As she trudged down the long echoing corridors towards the exit, Laura berated herself for having lost the courage to tell him the truth. Why hadn't she insisted that the letter wasn't from the Volunteers? Pure cowardice. But did it really matter anymore? Whoever had written the letter had never written again. If she had been that concerned about getting in touch, she would surely have done so. And what difference would it make to her father to know about this now anyway? It would just make him angry about something she had done such a long time ago.

Why, though, was he so reluctant to tell her about the war? She would try again tomorrow. She thought with regret about all the times she could have asked him: night after night through the years, when they had sat in companionable silence over the evening meal. Or afterwards, as they had sat in his study together, she working on her schoolwork, he reading at his desk or on his old settee. She could have asked him about the war anytime, but she hadn't. She hadn't even stopped to consider him at all. All their conversations had focused on her: her education, her friends, her career. She had simply assumed that Dad was perfectly content with his life, going to his job at the law centre each morning and spending his evenings with friends, drinking with Ken or playing darts at the pub at the end of the road.

She was nearing the hospital entrance now, and the corridor was widening out. There were more people about: doctors and nurses hurrying to and from shifts; anxious visitors, like herself, carrying bunches of flowers wrapped in cellophane; the occasional patient, marked out by a feeble and pasty look, wandering about in pyjamas, dragging drips on wheels or propelling themselves in wheelchairs.

Laura began to feel claustrophobic. She needed to escape and started to speed up, but as she passed the front desk she noticed a familiar figure talking to one of the receptionists.

'Luke?'

He turned. 'Ah, there you are, Loz. I came to look for you. I called your dad's house, but the old Scottish guy said you were here. You look washed out, babe. Come here.'

She let him take her in his arms. She buried her face in his hair. She recognised the scent of her own Vidal Sassoon shampoo.

'I've missed you so much,' she said.

'I'm so sorry I haven't been around. You must have been through hell. How's your dad?'

'So so. He's very tired. He really looks ill.'

'Come on, let's get out of here. Hospitals are so depressing. Shall we go to the flat?'

'What about Rory?'

Luke laughed. 'His mum and dad turned up this morning and whisked him away in the family Jag. His dad's some sort of big-shot banker or something. Gave me a right bollocking.'

They walked across the car park towards the bus stop on the main road.

'It's hardly my fault the guy couldn't stick university, is it? People like them make me vomit.'

'Have they taken him home?'

'Yeah, back to stockbroker belt. He phoned them last night. He was acting a bit strange at the pub with the guys from the protest. I know he's been ill, but he was really anti-social. A few of the guys started ribbing him for being a toff. I guess they were a bit unfair.'

'Well, perhaps it's for the best that he's gone.'

'True. We can have the place to ourselves.'

Back at the flat he pulled her to him, and kissed her. She returned his kiss, but when she felt his hands on her breasts, she froze, and then pushed him away.

'I'm sorry, Luke. I just can't. Not today.'

'It's just been so long, that's all. I've missed you so much.'

'I know. I've missed you too. I just feel so bad about Dad and everything. I need a bit of time, that's all.'

'OK, I understand.'

'Look. Why don't we go down to the café in the Barbican and

get something to eat? There's no food here. It'll be my treat. Then, would you mind very much if I had a rest? I hardly slept at all last night. I feel drained.'

'Of course not,' he said. 'Let's do that, then.' But she saw from his expression that the rejection had irritated him.

After lunch, Luke made an excuse about having to meet somebody in Hackney and left. Laura returned to the flat alone. She did not have the energy to try to persuade him to stay. She drifted off into a deep dreamless sleep, but was awoken by the distant repeated ringing of a bell. As she surfaced, she realised it was the telephone. She forced herself to wake up and picked it up.

'Laura?' It was Ken's voice. 'The hospital has been trying to get in touch with you. You need to go back there straight away. Tom's had another heart attack. It sounds serious.'

11

Tom knew he must have drifted off to sleep, because when he woke up, jolted up by the tinny notes of the bugle announcing the morning roll call, he found that he had slipped deeper into the pit and his forehead was resting on its muddy wall. The pain that seized his body was enough to remind him of where he was and what had happened to him. Every muscle and bone was aching, and now the sores on his face and body from the beating were running with pus and throbbing.

Even though the sun was only just rising, the temperature in the punishment pit was already uncomfortable. Trickles of sweat were running down his forehead and into his eyes. Every time he drew breath he almost retched from the acrid smell of vomit and faeces.

He peered through the bamboo slats of the cage around the top of the hole and watched the familiar routine of men standing in line and being counted by the guards. If anyone was not standing to attention correctly he was punished with a slap or a kick.

Tom noticed a few of the men glancing in his direction. Colonel Scott and Captain Strang were both pleading again with the Ripper in front of the guardhouse, gesticulating and pointing in Tom's direction. The Ripper just dismissed them harshly. They wandered away, shaking their heads.

When the men queued at the cookhouse for breakfast, Tom waited for his plate of rice and cup of water; a guard shoved them into Tom's pit through the bamboo slats. Once again, most of it spilled down the sides of the hole.

'How is my friend?' said Tom. The guard hesitated, eyeing him suspiciously.

Tom nodded towards the pit where they had put Archie. The guard stared at him for a moment, his face expressionless. Then he said, 'No talk … No talk,' then gestured running a knife across his throat. He slammed the corrugated iron back down on top of the bamboo and stomped away.

Tom tried to force himself to eat the food, but the rice was full of weevils and little stones, and was barely cooked. He gagged repeatedly whilst forcing it down his throat.

He watched the other men collect their tools from the sheds and set off on the long march to the railway cutting. And then, he heard a clap of thunder and the sudden sound of rain hitting the tin roof above him. It was deafening. The water began to seep through the top of the pit and trickle down the sides. The pit began to fill up with filthy stinking water. Soon Tom was standing up to his ankles in it.

He thought about the men struggling towards the cutting, slipping in the mud, soaked to the skin. He remembered how much worse the conditions at work became when it rained, and how, despite the tropical heat, it was impossible to get dry. The thatched roofs of the atap huts leaked at night as men lay shivering on their bunks.

The rain reached a crescendo and then eased off. Steam began to rise from the clearing. Tom wondered how Archie was bearing up. He glanced around and, seeing that there were no guards nearby, he called Archie's name. He waited for a response, but there was none. He tried a few more times, and still heard no sound from the direction of Archie's hole. Tom did not want to contemplate what might have happened to him.

'Perhaps he's asleep,' he said to himself, not really believing his own words.

He knew he needed to put Archie out of his mind. He would go mad with worry otherwise. He forced himself to think about something else.

His mind wandered back to Joy. To the day when the two of them had gone to the beach together. Joy had carried her shoes and clung onto his arm, shrieking with a mixture of fear and pleasure, urging him to come out as the waves had lapped at her skirt.

'Next time we should bring our bathing costumes and swim,' he said as they walked back up the beach. She fell silent for a few moments.

'I'm afraid I can't swim,' she finally admitted with woeful eyes.

'Never mind, you can still splash around in the waves ... And I could try teaching you. Would you like that?'

She brightened straight away and beamed up at him. 'I'd like that very much.'

So the following weekend they had driven out towards one of the deserted beaches near Gertak Sanggul on the southern side of the island, stopping at a roadside food-stall on the way to pick up a lunch of fried rice wrapped in banana leaves and some bottles of soft drink.

When they reached the beach, Tom slipped into his trunks and spread out the towels as Joy got changed behind the bushes. She seemed to take a long time, and as she emerged she was tugging at the shorts of the old-fashioned bathing suit, pulling them over her legs modestly. Tom couldn't resist a quick glance, taking in her slim brown thighs and the way the costume clung to her firm skin. He looked away quickly though, not wanting to embarrass her further.

He took her hand, and they walked together into the gently lapping waves and were soon wading deeper, pushing through the water with their thighs. But Joy began to pull back.

'It's cold!'

'Believe me, Joy. It's not really cold at all,' he said laughing, 'You'll soon get used to it. This is nothing.' He remembered shivering in his trunks as he had swum in the rain on Brighton beach one English summer's day.

He held her hand tightly and she followed him deeper until the water swirled and eddied around their waists.

'Now,' he said. 'Let's try. You need to bob down so your shoulders are underwater. Then put your hands together in front of you like this, and push forwards through the water. Look. I'll show you,' and letting go of her hand he had demonstrated pushing off and taking a first stroke. Hesitantly at first, Joy did the same, her teeth chattering, a look of profound concentration fixed on her face. She crouched down and pushed forwards through the waves. For a few seconds her body was suspended there, floating on the surface, before she began to panic, beating around, arms and legs flailing.

Tom leapt forward and put his arms around her waist, lifting her out of the water and holding her close as she clung to him.

'You did it! That was brilliant!' he said.

'I thought I was going to drown!' she gasped, laughing, the joy of her achievement shining in her eyes.

'Come on, you're nearly there. Try again. You push forward, and I'll hold you up.'

Time and time again they tried, until Joy took her first tentative strokes alone while Tom hovered beside her.

As they walked back up the beach, exhausted, she slid her arm around his waist and said, 'Thank you, Tom. Thank you so much.

You were so patient. Do you know, I've lived my whole life beside the sea but I never thought I would ever be able to swim in it?'

He had held her to him and kissed her on the lips. Her lips were soft and tasted of salt. She seemed surprised and stiffened momentarily, drawing away, but then she yielded, pressing her body against his, returning the kiss with equal passion.

They lay down on the towels under the shade of the coconut palms and watched the sunlight play on the waves making the sea glitter and shimmer. Joy stretched out, luxuriating in the warmth, and again Tom admired the smooth lines of her slim body. He watched, fascinated, as droplets of water gathered and ran in rivulets down her thighs, leaving salty tide-marks on her skin. He noticed how the white sand sticking to her feet and calves contrasted with the smooth olive-brown of her skin.

'This is absolute bliss,' he said lying back and watching the bright blue sky through the moving fronds of the palm tree above. 'I could live here forever.'

'Don't you want to go back to England?' she asked.

'No, never,' he said. 'I really don't care if I never see the place again. There's nothing there for me.'

He smiled and took his hand. 'And there's everything here for me.'

'It means so much to me, being here with you,' Joy said shyly.

Tom propped himself on his elbow and reached out to tuck a stray lock of hair behind her ear. 'I just want it to go on forever, Joy. Just like this. Just the two of us.'

She turned to look into his eyes and smiled.

'Me too, Tom.'

* * *

Later, as they packed their belongings into the car, he asked Joy if she would like to come back to his bungalow for tiffin. 'You haven't been there yet,' he said. 'I'd really love you to see it.'

She hesitated. 'I'm not sure. Mother is expecting me back,' and a troubled look crossed her face.

Perhaps it was too soon. He knew how strict and conventional her upbringing had been, how important religion and tradition were to her.

'We could always drop in and let her know where we're going,' he said.

'No. It's probably alright. As long as I'm back by around eight o'clock, I'm sure she won't mind.'

The sun was going down as they drove along the coast road and by the time they had turned inland towards the rubber plantations it was dark. Tom pressed the accelerator down, and the old Morris spluttered and surged forward. He wanted to reach the bungalow quickly so that they had some time there together before he had to take her home.

They entered the plantation and began to drive along the straight road, past the regimented lines of rubber trees. They passed the little settlement of wooden huts where the tappers lived with their families. They were outside, cooking over open stoves, by lamplight, or sitting on the front porches of their huts, smoking, enjoying the cool of the evening.

A hundred yards or so beyond the hamlet, a dark shape emerged suddenly from between the trees and hurtled straight into the car. Tom heard Joy scream, and he slammed his foot on the break. Although the car squealed to a halt in a cloud of dust, the front tyres slammed into the creature with a sickening crunch. It had all happened in a flash. They sat there for a moment in stunned silence.

The smell of burning rubber from the tyres filled the car.

Tom's mouth was dry with shock. He glanced at Joy and saw that she was sobbing quietly.

'Are you alright?' he asked. 'Did you hit your head on the dashboard?'

She turned to him and nodded, tears glistening in her eyes. He reached out and felt her forehead. A lump was already forming above her eyebrows.

'I'm so sorry, Joy,' he said. He switched on the inside light and looked at her tear-stained face.

'Don't be sorry for me,' she said. 'What about that poor animal. What was it anyway?'

'I don't know. A dog, maybe?'

She began to open the passenger door. 'Let's go and find it. Do you have a torch?'

He fumbled in the glove compartment and found a small hand torch.

'You stay here, Joy. It's not safe. I'll go.'

He got out, crossed the road and jumped over the storm drain that separated the plantation from the road and began to walk through the trees. He flashed the torch around. It felt desolate and lonely here between these lines of grey trees. But he didn't have to go far. The shape was slumped under a tree. He shone the torch at it and realised that it was a dog, a feral one, yellow and mangy, lying there taking frantic shallow pants. These wild dogs usually hunted in packs, but this one was clearly sick and had been left to fend for itself. It was pitifully thin. Its chest and one leg were crushed and bloody. Ribs poked through the fur.

He knelt down beside the animal and then heard footsteps in the leaves beside him.

'Is it alright?' came Joy's voice.

'No, I'm afraid it's going to die.'

She dropped down next to him.

'I can't bear to see an animal in pain,' she said, beginning to sob again.

He put his arm around her and drew her to him. 'It won't suffer for long, Joy. Look. It's hardly breathing now.'

Joy covered her eyes, but Tom watched as the animal closed its eyes and its shallow breathing finally stopped with one last great shudder.

'It won't suffer any more, Joy,' he said gently. 'Come on. Let's go back to the car.'

He held her close and helped her back through the trees, across the storm ditch and into the passenger seat. He got in beside her and turned to her. She was still crying quietly, sobs shaking her body.

'My poor love,' he said, taking her in his arms again, and kissing the salty tears from her face. 'I'm sorry, Joy. I'm so sorry,' he murmured, with a lump in his own throat, covering her face with tiny kisses. She responded for a moment and kissed him back before turning away.

'Let's get to the bungalow,' he said, starting the engine.

'No,' she said. 'If you don't mind, I'd prefer to go home now.'

He turned the car round in the road and headed back towards Georgetown, his spirits dashed. The day that had been so full of happiness and promise was now ruined. They drove in silence until they reached the outskirts of the town.

'Will you promise me something, Tom?' she asked suddenly, turning to him.

'Of course. Whatever you want.'

'Will you go back tomorrow morning and bury that poor

animal? I just can't bear the thought of it lying all alone out there. It should be buried properly.'

'Of course. I'll do that if it will make you feel better.'

'Thank you, Tom,' she said. 'You're a really good man.'

And in the darkness he felt her move towards him and slide her arm around his shoulder, felt the warmth of her fingers as they caressed the back of his neck.

Joy was still silent as they entered the outskirts of Georgetown, turned off the Burmah Road and drove through Pulau Tikus, the Eurasian district. As Tom drew up in front of her house and turned to kiss her goodbye, he was surprised when she said, 'Why don't you come in? Meet my family. It would be nice. They are always asking about you.'

'Are you sure?'

'I'm quite sure,' she said laughing, and he realised she was making an effort to put the unsettling incident with the stray dog behind her.

He felt apprehensive as he followed her up the wooden steps to the front door. As they crossed the veranda he noticed pots of flowering geraniums arranged around the front door, their red petals bright against the white-painted wood of the little house.

Inside, the tiny hallway was neat and tidy and crowded with polished furniture. Surfaces were covered in crocheted white cloths, on which china and glass ornaments were arranged. It didn't feel like a house where several children lived.

'Is that you back, Joy?' came a woman's voice from the back of the house. Aromas of frying food and exotic spices wafted towards them from the same direction.

'Yes, Mother, and I've brought along a friend,' said Joy, smiling at Tom conspiratorially. Joy's mother emerged from the kitchen, wiping her hands on the apron she wore over her sari, her face flushed and sweating from cooking. She was a stout woman with a careworn face, her wispy grey hair escaping from an untidy bun.

'Oh, is this Mr. Ellis at last?' Her face lit up in a smile. 'How wonderful to meet you! Father! Father! Come and see who's here!'

While she pumped Tom's hand up and down in an enthusiastic greeting, a short grey-haired man wearing thick glasses emerged from another room, carrying a newspaper. Like the mother, he also had a slight air of defeat about him. He was wearing a pair of threadbare suit trousers and a shirt and tie despite it being a Saturday. Tom suddenly felt self-conscious about his appearance, his shirt crumpled from the beach, his hair tousled from swimming and probably full of sand.

The father shook hands with Tom, too, but his handshake was formal.

'Very pleased to meet you, Mr. Ellis. We have heard a lot about you. Please, do come inside.'

He beckoned Tom into the living room, which was also crammed with heavy furniture and crowded with ornaments. Tom noticed a large gilt-framed painting of Christ on the cross on the wall. A colourful statue of the Virgin Mary took the pride of place on the sideboard.

'So, where have you two youngsters been today?'

'We went to the beach, Father. Tom taught me how to swim!' said Joy, her eyes shining.

'Well I never …' said her father, shaking his head. He tailed off, clearly lost for words.

'Would you like to stay to supper, Mr. Ellis?' said the mother from the doorway. 'I am just about to dish up.'

Tom hesitated, conscious that every penny must count in this household. Would they have enough for him? But he quickly realised it would be rude to refuse.

'I'd love to,' he said, smiling. 'It smells delicious.'

'Children! Supper,' shouted Joy's mother, and at once there was a banging of doors and a clattering of feet as all of Joy's brothers and sisters emerged from other rooms or from the garden. They were all talking and shouting at once, excited at the sight of a stranger. It amazed Tom how they all fitted into this tiny space, and he thought back to his own childhood spent in that large silent house, with no brothers or sisters for company.

'Be quiet, everyone!' said Joy, laughing and holding up her hands. 'I would like you all to meet my friend, Mr. Tom Ellis. Tom, this is Grace, this is Hope, this is Paul, this is Luke and this is Elijah.' The last child was tiny. He couldn't have been more than three or four. Tom bent to shake his hand and everyone laughed in delight.

All the other children shook hands excitedly with Tom, jostling for position, grinning at him and saying 'How-do-you-do?'. Looking back now, years later, although he could not remember their names nor conjure up all their faces, he had an impression of a group of lively, inquisitive children, full of fun and mischief and energy.

Their mother clapped her hands. 'Now, all of you, go and wash your hands in the kitchen. Then sit down at the table. Quickly, quickly, or the food will get cold.'

For a moment Tom wondered if her orders included him, but the father took his arm and said, 'Come on through to the dining room, Mr. Ellis. Sit down at the table. You can be the first,' and guided him with a firm hand across the passage into another room, where a large table that filled virtually all the available space was set for dinner.

Joy quickly moved the places along and set another one as Tom and her father sat down. She sat down beside Tom.

'It is very nice that Joy has made a new friend,' began her father. 'She is a very special girl, you know. She lives up to her name. She is truly our pride and joy.'

Tom smiled at him, wondering if this was going to develop into some sort of lecture or warning.

'Oh, Father, really,' said Joy, and Tom saw that she was blushing, but her smile betrayed her pleasure at his words.

'No, I mean it. You are a treasure. You are a gifted teacher and were a very talented student.'

'I'm sure,' said Tom. 'You must be very proud of her. And I'm very proud to count her as my friend.'

By now the children had sat themselves down with much noisy chatter and the scraping of chairs. Joy and her mother brought out two enormous bowls from the kitchen, one containing steaming chicken curry, the other rice. They began doling out portions onto plates and passing them around. Tom found himself feeling inexplicably nervous. It reminded him of the times he had been invited to the homes of school friends and had to sit through formal mealtimes and be subjected to scrutiny and questioning from their parents. He knew that he was under scrutiny here too.

'Let us say grace,' said Joy's father. This was a surprise to Tom, but he realised straight away that it shouldn't have been. The family instantly bowed their heads, and Tom followed suit. Tom had not said any sort of prayer since his schooldays. He opened one eye and looked around the table. The whole family was deep in prayer. It struck him then how important their faith was to them, and how central it was to Joy's world, although she rarely spoke to him about it.

'Bless us, O Lord, and these your gifts, which we are about to receive from your bounty, through Christ our Lord. Amen.'

They all opened their eyes instantly and began to eat and talk at once. The room was filled with the chatter of voices and the squeaks of forks on plates. The food was delicious, highly spiced and fresh-tasting, the tastes bursting on the tongue. Tom wished his cook at home would make curry sometimes instead of persisting in his pale imitations of English dishes.

'You're a soldier, aren't you?' said one of the boys to Tom, leaning forward eagerly.

'Oh, I'm not a proper soldier, I'm afraid. I'm just a Volunteer.'

'But if there's a war, you'll be in it won't you?' asked the boy. 'You'll be able to fight and fire a gun?'

'Oh, but I'm not sure that will happen ...'

'Stop it with those silly questions, Paul!' ordered the father. 'There is not going to be a war. The British are very well equipped. They will defend their colonies to the hilt. It says so in *The Straits Times*. The Japanese are just ... What do you say ... rattling sabres. The Empire is very well defended. We have a very good army indeed.'

'So why are they calling up the Volunteers then?' the child persisted.

'I said stop. Didn't you hear me?'

Tom felt awkward that he had caused this disagreement within the family. He realised that Joy must have felt his discomfort because, to his surprise, he felt her hand on top of his on the table, giving it a gentle squeeze of reassurance. He turned towards her, and her smiling eyes met his. Then, she removed her hand and resumed eating as if nothing had passed between them. But Tom noticed that her father and mother had observed this brief exchange. He saw the mother's secret look of knowing pleasure before she looked down at her plate again. He also saw the father draw himself up in his chair, frowning and clearing his throat loudly in disapproval.

There was silence around the table for a few moments, until Joy's mother broke it by speaking to Tom. 'Joy tells me you were once a solicitor in London, Mr. Ellis. Is that correct?'

'Oh, please call me "Tom". Yes, I was. I worked in the city for a while.'

The father turned to him.

'And why did you give it up, may I ask?'

'Well, it didn't suit me, I'm afraid,' said Tom. 'I … I needed a change.'

The elderly man peered at him through his pebble glasses, a puzzled expression on his face. Tom caught sight of Joy across the table, looking down at her plate, her fork poised.

'But I don't understand, Mr. Ellis. It was a good job, was it not?'

'Oh, yes. Yes, it was a very good job. I was lucky to have it. But …' He was struggling for words. He realised that a blush was creeping up his cheeks. How could he explain his decision to this man, who had probably spent a lifetime trudging daily to a dismal office on the docks, who had spent his days at a soul-sapping clerical job? It must appear highly frivolous to him to throw up the chance of a legal career in the city.

'I wanted to travel. And I had the chance to come out here,' Tom finally managed to say. It wasn't quite the truth, but it would do. Again he caught sight of Joy. She was looking at him, a smile of sympathy on her face.

'I must say I do find this very strange,' went on her father shaking his head. 'You had the chance of a well-paid and professional career ahead of you, and you throw it all away just to travel?'

'Oh, Father, please!' Joy burst out suddenly. 'Leave Tom alone! He is our guest here after all. Please don't cross-examine him. He has his reasons. You should respect that.'

Tom was surprised by the look of passion in her eyes. Her cheeks were flushed. It was the first time he had ever seen her angry, and despite his embarrassment, a warm feeling crept over him at the strength of her defence.

'Joy! Please don't speak to me like that. I apologise if I was rude. I had no intention to be in the slightest.'

Again there was an uncomfortable silence. All that could be heard was the sound of cutlery on china and enthusiastic chewing. But gradually the children resumed their chatter, as if the incident had never occurred.

Later, when the meal was over and Tom had said his goodbyes to the children and thanked Joy's parents for their hospitality, Joy came out to the car with him.

As he got into the driver's seat, he said, 'I'm sorry that your father doesn't approve of me, Joy.'

'Oh, you mustn't mind him. He can be a bit abrupt at times. He has rather fixed views about some things, I'm afraid. But he has a heart of gold really.'

'He obviously thinks I'm a bit of a waster, throwing up my career to come out here. I'm sorry I let you down, Joy.'

She gripped his hand and looked him in the eyes. 'Please don't say that, or even think it. You didn't let me down. You've never let me down.'

She leaned in through the car window and kissed him.

That night, when Tom was asleep in bed, Joy returned to him in his dreams. They were back on the beach, running in the waves, hand in hand, leaping over the tiny breakers, laughing and splashing. Joy tripped and fell over in the water. She was still holding his hand, and she tugged at it, looking up at him, wordlessly urging him down beside her. He looked into her eyes, and he saw that they were deep pools of infinite promise. She was drawing him closer and closer. She kissed him, and he felt her hot, salty lips on his. It was a kiss of pure love. An overwhelming feeling of happiness spread through his whole being.

Then she was drawing him down on top of her, still holding his gaze. He covered her neck and shoulders with kisses and took deep breaths of the sweet heady scent of her skin. Then with gentle hands he began to explore the curves of her body, firm and soft, wet and slippery from the water that lapped around them. Then he felt her hands slip around his waist and the pressure of them on his back, hot against his skin. She pulled him down, further and further, deeper and deeper, until they melted together, moving as one in the shallow waves until there was no going back.

He awoke with a jolt, sweating and breathing heavily. The dream had been so vivid that he was disappointed when he turned to find that Joy wasn't beside him. He thought back over the events of the day and realised that they had cemented his feelings for Joy. He had not felt this way before, about any other woman. He knew it wasn't simply that he longed for her physically. He loved her. He loved her for her simple generous nature, her sweet smile and the way she filled him with an all-consuming feeling of happiness and peace. And he knew now, from the way she had kissed him today, and the way she had behaved towards him during supper, that she felt the same way about him.

12

It rained the day they buried him. Abney Park Cemetery was shrouded in a soft mist. As a child, Laura had been afraid to even walk past the gates, but as a teenager she'd overcome her fears and ventured into the derelict church to smoke with her friends. It was a forlorn place. The ornate graves and elaborate tombs built by wealthy Victorians, neglected for years, were now crumbling. Tombstones had toppled over and graves had caved in, stones tumbling into the void.

Dad hadn't been a religious man, but Marge had insisted on a church service.

'You need to give your poor old dad a proper send-off. Your mum would have wanted it, and he certainly deserves it,' Marge had said, lips pursed obstinately. Laura had gone along with it, too numb with grief to object.

The service was over now, and the mourners stood around the freshly dug grave while the priest conducted the burial service. Laura stared straight ahead, dry eyed, her shoulder touching Luke's. She looked around at the assembled faces. So many people. People who'd worked with Dad over the years at the law centre. People he'd helped in various ways, had represented in court and helped fight the authorities to solve their immigration problems. There was the Chaudhry family with their six children, all immaculately dressed; they had lived on the top floor of the house until they were able to afford a home of their own. There were friends and neighbours.

There were people from Highbury Social Club, where her father had played darts. There was Ken, standing alone, sober for once, and there was Marge, flanked by her two grown-up sons.

Laura's eyes wandered to the other side of the cemetery. With a start she noticed someone standing there, away from the crowd. It was the man she'd seen watching the house the day she had come home from Paris. Now, as then, the old man was sheltering under a tree. This one was an old oak beside a derelict grave. He held a black umbrella above his head; he wore the same grey coat and battered hat as he had the other day.

She watched him closely, making sure it was the same man. Then, suddenly, she saw him turn and look at her. She could still hear Dad's voice: 'Jim Leech. I knew him in the war. He was in my camp. If he comes to the door, don't let him in.'

She looked away and tried to focus on the priest's words: 'Ashes to ashes, dust to dust ...'

When she glanced back at the old man, she saw that he was staring at her, his eyes never leaving her face.

Eventually the service ended and her father's coffin was lowered into the grave. Ken was the first to step forward and throw earth onto the coffin. Fighting back tears, Laura picked up a handful of earth and threw it into the pit. As she did so she closed her eyes and breathed a last thank you to her father.

At last the burial was over and people stood around in awkward little knots, talking. Laura looked at the old man again. He was still standing there under the tree. It had stopped raining now, and he'd lowered his umbrella.

She took a deep breath and strode towards him.

'I'm Laura Ellis. Can I help you?'

He dropped his gaze. He seemed nervous, pushing his hands into his pockets and taking them out again.' I knew Tom,' he mumbled. 'Were you related?' He spoke with a cockney accent.

'I'm his daughter.'

'Of course.' He grew silent.

'Is there anything I can do for you?'

'He was a good man, Tom. A very good man,' he muttered.

'He certainly was.'

'You know, I knew him back then. In the war,' the old man said, suddenly looking into Laura's eyes. His eyes were sharp, blue. Startled by their intensity, she looked away.

'Yes,' she said. 'He told me. You are Jim, aren't you? Jim Leech?'

'That's right.'

'I saw you standing outside the house one day.'

'He wouldn't talk to me. He would never talk to me. I've tried to speak to him many times over the years, but he never would.'

'Do you know why?'

'Yes. It's a long story. A very long story, indeed. I just wanted to thank him. To pay him back. He saved my life.'

'Really?'

'In the war, yes. He saved my life. He didn't have to, but he did. And if it wasn't for him, I wouldn't be here now.'

'Laura, love?' Marge was calling for her. 'We're going back to the house. The car's waiting. Are you coming?'

'I have to go.' Laura held out her hand.

He took it and, gripping it hard, pulled her close to him. She realised now how thin he was. His face was gaunt and bore the lines of age, his cheeks hollow, pallid.

'Can I come and see you one day, Miss Ellis? There's a lot I need to explain.'

She hesitated, remembering her father's plea. 'I'm not sure …'

'Laura?' Luke was calling her now.

'Why don't you come and see me then? There's things I need to tell you.'

He thrust a small card into her hand. But he was still gripping her arm. She began to pull away.

'I have to go now,' she said. 'They're waiting for me.'

'You will come, won't you? It would mean so much to me.'

She hesitated, glancing at the card. 'Perhaps.'

'Mr. James Leech, Albert Mansions, Kensington Gore,' she read aloud. He was watching her, waiting for a reply.

Yes. All right, I'll come. I'll come and see you next week,' she said reluctantly.

She pulled away from him. She saw that everyone was hovering by the cemetery gates, waiting for her. She began to move towards them. She saw Luke detach himself from the group and walk towards her. He put a protective arm around her shoulders when he reached her.

'Who the hell was that?' he asked.

'Some old guy Dad knew in the war.'

She could feel the old man's eyes on her back as she walked away with Luke.

* * *

'What are you going to do with the house?' Luke suddenly asked. They were tidying the study, sorting through Dad's books and putting aside a pile to take to the charity shop.

Laura looked up, surprised, not sure why he was asking her this.

She had asked Luke to come back with her to the house in Highbury on the dreadful day Dad had died. They'd hastily packed a couple of suitcases of things from her flat and brought them over in a taxi. He'd stayed with her ever since.

She'd gone through those first few days like a sleepwalker. She barely remembered most of what had happened or what she'd done or said. Luke had been with her all the time, comforting her when she needed to cry, making sure she remembered to eat and drink. On the second day she had spoken to Adam on the phone and told him she couldn't come back to work for a while.

'Take as long as you need, Laura,' he had told her. 'Perhaps you should take a few weeks off. You sound really shaken up. You've got some leave due anyway. I'll talk to the other partners and smooth things over with them. If you need to talk any time, you know where I am.'

Having Luke there had helped her through those dark days. But now, a few days after the funeral, he seemed to be getting restless.

'I've no idea,' she answered. 'I haven't really thought about it.'

'Have you thought about putting it on the market? It's probably worth a fortune.'

She put down the book she'd been flicking through and straightened up. Her knees ached from kneeling on the wooden boards.

'Marge and Ken live here,' she said. 'If I sold it, I'd have to ask them to leave. I'm not sure I could do that.'

Luke laughed. 'You used to say how soft your dad was on them. It's your chance to do something about it.'

She turned on him.

'I can't believe I'm hearing this from you! I thought you were a socialist. Now you're talking about making a couple of pensioners homeless.'

He held up his hands. 'Steady on, Loz. It was just a suggestion.

146

You used to go on and on about the smell of cat piss from the basement. I was just thinking about what's best for you.'

'Well, I used to moan about it, but things are different now. Dad's not here. Marge has been here since before my mum died. She looked after me when I was little. Dad gave her the place downstairs when she was homeless. She had two little boys and left her husband because he was a drunk and beat her up. I can't just turn her out. She wouldn't have anywhere to go.'

'What about Ken?'

'Oh, he was a mate of Dad's. They met at the social club when I was tiny. He's a struggling artist. I don't think he makes any money at all.'

Luke shrugged. 'It's your call, Loz. But if I were you, I'd give it some consideration. You've got to think of yourself.'

She bit her lip and turned back to the bookcase. But as she took the books from the shelves and sorted them into piles, she sensed resentment bubbling up inside her.

'I still can't believe you said that,' she burst out, unable to contain herself. 'You've always been dead against landlords who try to get rid of squatters.'

'Calm down, won't you? He moved towards her and slipped his arms around her waist. She felt his lips on her neck. Her skin tingled at his touch.

'I'm sorry,' he said.' It's none of my business, I know. I shouldn't have said anything.'

She felt his hands on her breasts, and her whole body weakened. Reluctantly, she turned to kiss him back.

'Forgive me?' Luke said, when they pulled apart. 'I'll make it up to you later, I promise. Look, shall I go and make you a cuppa? Perhaps we could order a takeaway again.'

He went into the kitchen, and she could hear him putting the kettle on the stove. Now that he was out of the room, she went to her father's desk and pulled open one of the drawers. She'd been meaning to empty them out for days. There might be some important papers in there, but she'd felt strange about doing it with Luke in the room. She eased the bottom drawer open. It felt wrong to trespass on Dad's space like this. These drawers had been out of bounds when she was little. As she pulled the drawer open, instead of piles of paperwork, she found an old wooden box wedged inside it. She pulled it out and put it on top of the desk. The lid was stiff, closed with a rusting lock, which she prised open with a paper knife.

Laura stared at the odd assortment of grimy items inside. At first glance they looked like bric-a-brac from a jumble sale. She fished them out, one by one.

She peered at a rusty medallion on a chain, blackened with age and dirt. It was engraved with a coat of arms; it looked like Saint George on a rearing horse, plunging a stake into a dragon that was cowering on the ground. Laura looked closely. Around the edge were engraved the words 'Northumberland Fusiliers.

Then there was an old brass signet ring. It looked cheap and, like the medallion, had become dull with age. Three initials were inscribed on it. Laura could just about make them out by holding it up to the light: 'I. F. R.'

She picked a small coloured badge out of the box and turned it over in her hand. The sound of Luke's footsteps behind her made her close her fist around it.

'What's all that stuff?' he asked, putting the tea on the desk, and then nuzzling her shoulder.

'This is the badge of Dad's regiment from the war, I think. He was in the Straits Settlements Volunteer Force.'

Luke took the badge and looked at it.

'Pretty rusty, isn't it?'

'I could polish it up. I'm sure he kept it for a reason,' Laura said.

'Alternatively, he might have just chucked a load of old junk in a box and forgotten all about it,' Luke said. 'You're not going to keep all that stuff, are you?'

She looked back in the box. At the bottom were two sheets of fragile tracing paper; pressed between them lay a twig of flowers, brown with age. They were not like any flowers she'd seen before. Under them were a few spent bullet cases.

'Shall I just take that lot out to the bonfire?' said Luke. 'It's all filthy.'

'No. All these things must have had some significance for Dad. I think I should keep them.'

'Do you have any idea where it all comes from?'

'Not really, but I could ask that old guy.'

'Old guy?'

'You know. The one from the funeral. Jim Leech. They knew each other from the war. I said I'd go and visit him. I was thinking about going over tomorrow morning.'

Luke stared at her. 'Why do you want to do that? It could be risky.'

'Risky? He's an old man, Luke.' When he didn't reply, she couldn't resist adding, 'It was a hell of a lot riskier for me to go to the police station after the riots, that night you were arrested. Don't you think so?'

He pulled away from her and sat down on the sofa.

'I didn't ask you to come to the bloody nick.'

'Well, it's good for you that I did come. You'd have still been in there now if I hadn't.'

'Oh, get over it Laura. OK, you helped me. But I would have got off anyway.'

'I like the way you say that now. I remember you being pretty grateful for my help at the time.'

'Yes, I was grateful. I am grateful. But look at me now. I can't do anything. I can't go to the picket line or anywhere near it. I'm just kicking around in this house doing nothing. I feel useless.'

'You've not been doing nothing. You've been helping me.'

'Yeah, but that's not doing anything positive for the cause, is it?'

'Well, that's not my fault. I had to agree to those conditions, and you were happy to accept them at the time.'

Luke stood up and grabbed his leather jacket from the back of the chair.

'I'm going out,' he muttered. 'I'm sick of hanging around here. I need some air.'

'Where are you going?' she asked, alarmed at this sudden change of mood.

He marched out of the room, slamming the door behind him. She went to the window and saw him walking down the path, without looking back.

'You bastard.'

She sat down on the saggy sofa and buried her face in her hands. Here, amongst her father's old books and clutter, in the room that still smelled of his cigarettes and bore his imprint more than any other in the house, her loss came home to her and was almost too much to bear.

13

Albert Hall Mansions was a rambling red-brick Victorian building. As its name suggested, it was next door to the Albert Hall. Approaching it from the bus stop on Hyde Park Corner, Laura was surprised to see how grand it was. From her brief conversation at the funeral with Jim Leech, and judging by his shabby appearance, she had expected him to live somewhere down-at-heel.

Jim's apartment was on the ground floor. He showed Laura through a panelled hall and into a cavernous drawing room, crowded with heavy antique furniture and gloomy paintings. Buses rumbled past, rattling the dusty windows. The old man asked her to sit down. She sunk into a large sofa with sagging springs. Jim brought her a stewed cup of tea and handed it to her with shaking hands, spilling some of it onto the saucer.

Looking even more frail without his hat and coat, Jim was painfully thin, his face pale and drawn. He wore a baggy white shirt, and his trousers were held up by old-fashioned braces. On his feet was a pair of brown leather carpet slippers. It was the first time Laura had seen him without his hat. What was left of his hair was pure white.

'This is a very nice flat,' she said, looking around at the huge room with its high ceiling.

'Yes. I've lived here for about thirty years. It's served me well.'

'And what did you do for a living?' She could not resist the question.

Jim smiled. 'I expect you're wondering how someone like me managed to fork out for this place, aren't you?' he asked. Laura felt herself colouring.

'Well, I don't mind telling you. I built up me own small hotel chain. Started it up from nothing. After the war I got a job as a porter at the Savoy. I was clever all right, and I worked out how the hotel business works and how to make money out of it. I scrimped and saved enough to buy a bomb-damaged building in Kensington. Did it up gradually on a shoe string. Managed to do a lot of the work myself in me spare time. Then, when it opened, and started to make a profit, I looked around for another one. I've got five of them now, dotted about central London. They are called Leech's Hotel. They're not the Savoy, but they're cheap and cheerful, popular with commercial travellers and the like. They always turn in a tidy profit.'

'Amazing. That you built it all up from scratch like that,' said Laura.

'Well, I made me own luck.' There was a silence, and Laura sensed that he had something to tell her. From the way he was staring at the carpet and breathing hard, it seemed as if he was gathering up courage to do so.

'I did that in the camps too, you know,' he said at last, lifting his eyes and looking straight at her. 'In the war. I was a sort of, well, an entrepreneur. I suppose you can call it that. I regret all that now though. Bitterly regret it.'

'Why?' she asked gently. In his face, haggard and pained, she glimpsed the same look she had seen on her father's face when he had spoken about Jim Leech and the war.

'Because I cheated starving men. I bought things from them dirt cheap and sold them on for a profit. I took advantage of their weakness and the fact they were hungry. I sometimes gave them money for giving up their rations the next day, and sold those rations to another man for a profit. I bought things from the villagers outside the camp whenever I could, and then sold them at a profit. I lied and I cheated … And there was worse, much worse.'

Laura watched his face, waiting for him to go on, but he seemed to falter.

'I wasn't the only one, mind you. There was a little group of us businessmen operating the black market. But I was the lynchpin, the head of operations, always.'

'But why? What made you do it?'

Jim shrugged his shoulders.

'I'd always been poor. I was a teenager during the Depression, was living in the East End. Me dad was a labourer. He was often out of work. I knew what it meant to be hungry. So when I spotted ways of making things better for myself, even if they wasn't legit, I did them. It was the survival instinct kicking in, I suppose.'

'You mustn't blame yourself. The circumstances were extraordinary. None of us knows how we'll react until something dreadful happens.'

'But I do blame myself. I blame myself every day. I torture myself with the memories. I try to make amends.' There were tears in his eyes now. 'When I think of all those poor lads who never came back …' Jim trailed off, shaking his head.

Laura bit her lip. 'What was it you wanted to tell me, Mr. Leech? Why did you want me to come and see you?' she asked when he looked as though he had recovered his composure a little.

Jim looked at her vaguely.

'Ellis would never talk to me,' he said at last.

'He seemed to be angry with you. He wouldn't say why though.'

Jim shook his head again.

'He had good cause,' he said. 'But he saved my life, you know.'

'Yes, you said. How did that happen?'

'Yes, he saved my life. It's only because of him that I'm here.'

Laura felt awkward. She wasn't getting anywhere with her questions. It seemed as if she and Jim were stuck in a loop. He gave the impression of being unwilling or perhaps unable to divulge anything further.

'He didn't need to do it,' Jim went on. 'Could have left me for dead. He was a good man. Tom Ellis. The best.'

After a pause, Laura asked, 'Have you ever heard of anyone called Arthur, or Alfred, Stone?'

'Stone? Arthur Stone?' Jim went into deep thought. 'Can't say I have. There were a few Arthurs in the camp, of course, but I don't remember anyone called Stone. I'm sorry. Why do you ask?'

'It's just that Dad said that if I wanted to find out about his story, I should ask this Mr. Stone. But he didn't say who it was.'

'Well, why don't you look in the records of the regiment. Your father was in the Straits Settlements Volunteer Force, if I remember correctly. There might be a list, or a register of POWs at Imperial War Museum. They've got lots of records there. Old diaries, all sorts of stuff.'

'Thank you. That's a very good idea. I'll go there tomorrow if I can.'

She got to her feet.

'I should be going, I'm afraid. I've got lots to do at home.'

'Tom was very lucky with his family. I didn't have any children … Couldn't, I should say. My wife died very young. You married?'

'No,' said Laura.

'But you were with someone at the funeral, weren't you? That long-haired fellow.'

'Yes. He's a friend.'

She thought about how she'd spent last night in her childhood bedroom, alone, listening for the sound of the front door, waiting for Luke's footsteps on the path. He hadn't even phoned to say where he was.

She followed Jim through the dim hallway to the front door.

'You know, I always kept tabs on Tom Ellis. I always knew where he was, what he was doing. I know he did a lot of good work in that law centre he founded, didn't he? Helped out immigrants and poor people who couldn't afford a solicitor.'

'Yes. He did.'

'It was only lately that I tried to talk to him though.'

'Why was that?'

'Oh, because I had some bad news a couple of months back. I've been ill for a while. Went for all sorts of tests. Finally found out that I've got cancer of the bowel. To tell you the truth, I don't have very long to live. I wanted to make my peace with Tom before I went. But, sadly, he went before I managed to do that.'

Laura felt a rush of pity for this frail old man.

'Oh, I'm so sorry to hear that. How dreadful. Look, would you like me to come and see you again?'

'No. That's very kind of you, except I'm going into hospital for treatment tomorrow. They're not sure how successful it's going to be.'

'Would you like me to visit you in the hospital?'

'No, no. I probably won't be feeling up to much. I'm so glad you came to see me, though. I feel as though I have made my peace with Tom. Well, partly anyway. You do remind me of him. You have his dark hair, and that sort of knowing expression he used to have.'

Laura shook his bony hand as she left. As she went down the steps, she turned and smiled. Jim was raising his right hand in an unsteady wave; he looked so vulnerable standing on the doorstep in his baggy clothes, his face strained and grey with pain. As she walked away, her eyes filled with tears.

* * *

The next day Laura set off for Imperial War Museum, as Jim Leech had suggested. She needed to distract herself, having spent another restless night at her father's house, listening out for Luke, alternating feverishly between worrying about where he was and being angry at him for having walked out on her. She wondered if he'd broken the injunction and gone back to the picket line. Or if he'd gone to the latest squat to sleep with one of the hippy girls. How could he leave her at a time like this?

Part of her wished she'd never met him, or become involved with him, and that she'd stuck to the straightforward men she'd always dated. Like Matt. She had always known where she had stood with Matt, even if he was sometimes boring and predicable. He would never have left her alone like this, after leading her to believe that he would be there to support her. Why did Luke do that? If he'd just walked away and never shown her any kindness after Dad had died, it would have been easier to take. Perhaps she would have been better with another safe bet, like Adam, after all.

She tried to put Luke out of her mind as she took the tube to Lambeth and walked to the museum. She told the receptionist that she was looking for records from the war in the Far East. She was taken upstairs in an antiquated lift by a very young assistant librarian, to the reading room.

'I'm afraid my colleague is off sick today. He's the real expert on the Far East, but I'll do what I can to help,' the girl said nervously. She looked as though she was just out of college. In an effort to look the part, she had tied back her hair severely and wore heavy horn-rimmed glasses.

The girl led Laura to the records of the Straits Settlements Volunteer Force, which were stored in a leather-bound volume high up on a dark shelf, just under the vaulted roof.

Laura opened the volume, her hands shaking, and scanned the list. She was shocked to see 'killed in action' or 'POW in Japanese hands. Died in captivity' printed beside so many of the soldier's names.

Her heart leapt when she turned a page and came across her father's name:

'Thomas Charles Ellis, Private. Captured Singapore, February 15, 1942; Discharged Penang, September 1945.'

There was no Arthur or Alfred Stone on the list, and only two Arthurs altogether.

She closed the dusty book with a sigh. The assistant was hovering close by.

'Do you think it's possible that my father left an account of his experiences, and it is lodged here?' Laura asked her.

'There are several first-hand accounts by prisoners of war. Most of them are transcribed from original diaries. Would you like to look at the list of names on the microfiche?'

Laura sat at the machine and looked through the microfiche records, which listed the names and other details of prisoners of war who had written down their accounts. There was no Thomas Ellis on the list, and no Arthur or Alfred Stone.

'I'm so sorry,' said the girl. 'When my colleague gets back, he might be able to help you further. He's been here for years. He's a real expert. Would you like to read any of the first-hand accounts while you are here?'

Laura glanced at the clock. She had plenty of time. Why not spend the afternoon in the peace and anonymity of the library, instead of languishing at home, feeling sorry for herself?

The girl brought her a pile of cardboard files.

'Please be careful with them – they're getting old. Some of the paper is very thin.'

She sat down at the huge polished table and opened one of the files at random. It was typed on an old-fashioned typewriter, on wafer thin yellowing paper. It was by Private George Stringer of the Royal Norfolk Regiment.

'The three years I spent on the Thai-Burma railroad were hell on earth. We were beaten on a daily basis. Beaten by the Japanese guards and by the Koreans who were worse in their own way. Because the Japs were cruel to them, they wanted their own back on the prisoners. I remember my best mate, Sam Jones, being beaten for not working hard enough. He was ill with dysentery and so weak he could hardly move. Only, they didn't care about that. When he collapsed by the side of the railway, they set on him with bamboos and sticks.'

'Food was really short in the camps,' another soldier had written, 'and consisted mainly of rice and watered-down stew with the occasional bit of gristly meat in it. Often we would find flies and other insects floating in there too. We were permanently hungry, especially with the physical exertion of labouring all day and with walking to and from the railway. We exchanged anything and everything we owned with the Thai villagers outside the camps, for a few duck eggs or pieces of fruit. One man made the mistake of trying to steal food from the Jap quarters. He was caught, and his punishment was to kneel in front of the guardhouse on sharpened sticks of bamboo buried into the ground. He knelt there for two days, and when he was finally released he had to be carried away by his mates. He couldn't walk for days and was left with permanent scars on his knees.'

In another soldier's account, she read, 'The Japs insisted that we should bow to them whenever they passed, no matter what we were doing or where we happened to be. This rule was applied even when we were working on the railway. One morning we were at work with pickaxes and hammers when a Jap officer happened to come and inspect our section of the railway. One of the men in my platoon was a bit slow in putting down his tools and did not bow to the officer immediately. The Japs dragged him away and tied him to the trunk of a nearby tree with a length of barbed wire. We could hear his screams as the sharp metal pierced his skin. He was there for three days. We weren't allowed to give him food or even water. When they finally cut him loose the skin on his arms and belly was ripped to shreds and already infected. The men carried him down to the camp on a stretcher, but he died in the camp hospital a few days later of septicaemia.'

Laura felt a lump in her throat as she read on, stunned by the horror of what she read. Account after account of beatings, starvation, illness, of heroic acts, camaraderie and friendship.

The light faded in the skylights in the vaulted roof, and the lamps were switched on above the tables. She read on. After a while, the librarian approached her.

'I'm sorry, but we're closing in a few minutes. Could I please take back the files?'

'Thank you. This is all so interesting. Astonishing. I had no idea.

Have you read these?'

'Some of them. But, as I said, my colleague is the expert. He's done lots of research in Thailand. He's been to see the bridge and what's left of the railway. There's a museum there, you know, by the River Kwai.'

As Laura made her way back to Highbury, she hardly noticed the other people on the tube, or those who passed her by on the street. Her mind was full of the jungle, visualising bone-thin men sweating as they laboured away, moving logs, heaving rocks. How could Dad have kept all this to himself all those years? How could he have been through something like that and never mentioned it to his only child? She thought of how he must have starved and suffered, and the doctor's words came back to her: 'bamboo heart'.

Back at home, she stood on the threshold of Dad's bedroom, staring in. She hadn't been able to face clearing out the drawers or even changing the sheets since he had died. She wondered if he had anything hidden in his room, any relics of his past. She stepped inside and ran her fingers along the dust that covered the top of Mum's dressing table. He'd never moved it from the corner of the room where Mum used to sit, brushing her hair or putting on her makeup in the mornings. The old musical box was still there. It had belonged to Grandma Louise, her dad's mother. Laura remembered opening it breathlessly as a child, and watching in wonder as the miniature ballerinas sprang to life and jerked across the mirrored surface to a tinny rendition of 'The Nutcracker Suite'. Now the box looked shabby and dusty. She tried to lift the lid and realised it was stuck. A lump formed in her throat at the thought that the box, once polished and prized, was now forgotten.

She opened the top drawer of Dad's chest and found several pairs of his socks: some in pairs, others odd, most of them full of holes. For some reason, the sight of them lying there in the drawer, the intimate reminder of his lack of care for material things, brought tears to her eyes. She slammed the drawer shut and sat down on the bed sobbing.

She looked up to see Ken in the doorway.

'I'm so sorry, lassie,' he said, sitting beside her, his own lips quivering. 'Perhaps you're not ready to sort through your Da's things yet.'

'I wasn't sorting through his things. I was … looking for something. I've just been to the War Museum. I read some of the accounts of men who'd been on the railway with Dad. Oh, Ken, what he must have been through. I was just looking to see if he'd saved anything, you know, from that time.'

'I don't suppose he kept anything. He didn't want to remember it.'

'There were a few odd things in a drawer in the study. A couple of old badges and a ring. I wondered if he'd kept anything else.'

'You don't need to torture yourself with all this.'

She shrugged. 'It's the least I can do, after what he went through.'

'But not now, lassie. Why don't you wait a while? What's happened to laughing boy, by the way?'

She couldn't help but smile at the nickname. She dried her eyes.

'I'm not sure. He's gone away for a few days. I think he found it a bit claustrophobic here.'

'He shouldn't leave you at a time like this.'

'It's not his fault …' she began, but stopped. It was useless to argue. Ken was right.

He'd been right all along about Luke.

'Ah, well. It's not my place to say anything,' he went on.

'Like "I told you so"?'

'An artist's intuition, perhaps,' he said with a wry smile.

'Can you think of anywhere that Dad might have kept stuff?' she said after a short silence.

'Hmm,' Ken thought for a moment. 'There was an old trunk of Tom's in the corner of the loft. I remember seeing it when I put some old paintings up there years ago.'

'Shall we go up and have a look?' She got up from the bed with a tingle of anticipation.

Ken found an old step-ladder in the back yard and carried it up to the top floor. It wobbled as he mounted it and pushed open the loft door. She watched from the landing as he hauled his bony frame through the trap door.

'Can you see anything?'

'There used to be a light up here somewhere. Ah, here it is.'

The trapdoor space filled with yellow light. This was followed by a few thumps and crashes as he moved the old pictures aside. Then came the sound of him dragging something heavy across the loft floor, and the sight of his bare feet dangling down through the hole.

'Hold onto the ladder, lassie. I'm coming down.'

Ken held the ladder for her when she climbed it. She tried not to look down at the gap between the banisters, through which she glimpsed dizzying views of the hall, three flights below. She crawled into the filthy loft full of bird droppings and dirt. In front of her was an old leather trunk covered in dust. She stood up and wiped away the dust on the lid. She saw that a torn luggage label was glued onto it: 'Mr. and Mrs. Edward Ellis, 15 Gordon Square, London'. Beside the address was a faded date stamp. Peering closely, she could just make out the words: 'Georgetown, November 1941.'

14

Tom lost track of how long he'd been festering in the pit. His whole body was in constant pain. His muscles and bones still throbbed and ached from the beating. The stinging and itching from the cuts on his skin, now swollen and suppurating with infection, was intolerable. He was forced into a constant stoop, his spine bent to fit the shape of the pit. Would he ever be able to stand straight again? Not that it mattered. He would probably die in here, or be dragged out and shot like Ian and Harry.

Often he was deafened by the tropical rain drumming on the tin roof, gushing down the sides of the pit, collecting in the bottom, so he was up to his knees in filth. He remained there shivering uncontrollably, his teeth clamped together, overwhelmed with hatred for his captors, willing the time to pass and his ordeal to be over. At other times the sun would beat down on the metal, heating up the pit to oven temperature. Steam would rise from the putrid puddle, and his body would run with sweat. Barely able to breathe, he would slip into a heady, delirious state, his mind clouded with bitterness and confusion.

Every day was the same. Before the sun rose, he would be jolted from his semi-conscious state by the clatter of the tin roof being ripped off above his head. One of the guards, jabbering at him in Japanese, would shove a plate of semi-cooked rice against his face, before slamming the tin roof back over him. With trembling hands he would try to force the food down his throat, gagging and retching out most of it.

Through the bamboo bars he would then watch the camp assemble for roll call as the sun rose over the jungle. Row upon row of emaciated men dressed in rags would line up, their heads bowed, bodies reluctant, but shoulders drooping in resignation to the inevitable routine.

How he longed to be back in the relative anonymity of that line up, to be amongst them as they collected the tools from behind the guardhouse and began the weary march out of the gates and into the jungle for the day's work to begin.

When the last of the stragglers had left, the interminable daylight hours, sweltering under the metal roof, would begin. When it wasn't raining, the officers would sit outside their hut playing bridge or chess. In the afternoons some of the officers, along with the medical orderlies and recovering men from the hospital hut, would take tools and spend a couple of hours digging the latrines.

Once a day a shout would go up, and the camp gates would be dragged aside for the lorry to rumble through, carrying rice and vegetables for the evening meal. The sight of that lorry always sent a shiver through Tom. Ian had been replaced on the truck with another tall prisoner. Tom noticed that he didn't haul the rice sacks with as much strength or vigour as Ian had done.

In the evening, after the sun had dipped behind the far-off hills, the men would return from the railway, staggering with exhaustion from the day's work. Tom would watch them make straight for the river to bathe, and he would long to feel the cool water on his own skin, to lie on his back watching the stars, even for a few moments.

A few times, as men queued outside the cookhouse, one or two of them would detach themselves from the crowd and head across the clearing towards the punishment pits. Tom's heart would leap with anticipation and gratitude each time, and his mouth would water at the thought of the rations they would be bringing him. But each time the guards would rush to surround the men and drag them away, screaming at them and punching them to the ground.

Several times each day Tom would shout out Archie's name, but there was never any response. On the third day, Tom saw that the guards didn't bring any food for Archie. A stab of dread went through him.

'What's happened to him?' he asked when a guard pushed a bowl of rice into his own pit. The guard stared at him, frowning. 'Why aren't you feeding him?' Tom pointed in Archie's direction. The guard yelled something in Japanese and slammed the metal lid down on him.

Tom had no idea how Archie was doing in his pit. Despair threatened to overcome him.

He knew he had to fight it. He forced his mind away from the present and tried to think about something else. About anything else. He had to stop himself from worrying and from going crazy in this hole of hell.

His mind ran back to Penang, and to the leisurely days spent in paradise.

One evening, Tom had been sitting on his porch, pleasantly tired after the day's work. He had written home and received a terse letter back from his father, telling him that there was little news on their side, but wishing him well. The letter also spoke of the worrying political situation in Germany, of Hitler's threats against Czechoslovakia and Poland, and the rumblings of war. It all seemed too far away to concern himself about, here on this enchanted island.

As he had been sipping his first gin sling, a burly man in his thirties appeared on the veranda.

'I'm Henry Martin,' the man said, holding out his hand. 'I live at the bungalow just down the hill. I'm probably your nearest neighbour.' Tom stood up and shook his hand.

'Very nice to meet you, Henry. Haven't I seen you at the plantation headquarters?'

'Yes, that's right. I work for Penang Rubber Association in Georgetown. It's a trade association. I often have to visit the estates to discuss business.'

'Can I offer you a drink?'

'That's kind of you, but I really came to see if you'd like to come to the club for a game of tennis.'

'Well, I haven't played since school, so I won't be able to give you much of a game, I'm afraid.'

'Never mind that. It's just a bit of fun. And I'll show you round the club at the same time.'

'The club?'

'The Penang Club. It's in Georgetown. I'll sort out your membership. You must join up. All the Europeans are members. It's where everything happens. Without it, I think we'd all die of boredom here.'

That evening Henry drove him down the winding road through the hills into the town. The Penang Club was in an elegant white building overlooking the sea, with marbled interiors and surrounded by immaculately kept lawns. The club had Malay bearers to open the door for you, to pass you a towel whilst you played tennis, and to help you get dressed after a shower.

As Tom predicted, he was not much of an opponent, and Henry beat him in straight sets. Afterwards, they went into the bar for a drink.

Although still early evening, the bar was already packed. A jazz band was playing on a small stage.

'Everyone drops in for a sundowner at this time,' explained Henry, seeing Tom's surprise. 'It's a very sociable place, you'll see.'

They sat out on the terrace, overlooking the harbour as the huge red sun slipped behind the hills at the back of the town. A boy brought them gin slings and cashew nuts. Henry began to tell Tom anecdotes about some of the people in the bar: planters, civil servants, businessmen.

At the next table sat a group of women, fashionably dressed and smoking slim cigarettes from holders. They were drinking cocktails at an alarming rate, constantly asking for their glasses to be refreshed. One of them, a woman wearing a lot of eye makeup and deep red lipstick, and her dark hair cut in a stylish bob, kept glancing in Tom's direction.

'Oh no,' Henry whispered, grinning. 'You've attracted the attention of Millie. God help you.'

'Who is she?' Tom asked, looking at the woman, feeling a flush creeping up his cheeks.

'Oh, she's the wife of Sir James Atherton, the senior judge on the island. I have to warn you about her, Tom – she eats young men for breakfast.'

Tom watched as the woman pushed back her chair and languidly wandered over to their table. He could not help noticing that her black cocktail dress was cut very low and clung tightly to her curves. She stood, eyeing the men with unconcealed amusement, blowing smoke rings towards them.

'So, who have we here, Henry? A new recruit to our little band of merrymakers?'

'Yes, Millie. Allow me to introduce you to Tom. Tom Ellis. He joined us this week at the estate. He's moved into the bungalow next to mine. Tom, this is Millie. Millicent Atherton.'

Tom stood up, feeling self-conscious, and held out his hand to the woman. She took it and raised it to her lips, all the time watching him, an amused look dancing in her grey eyes.

'Enchanted to meet you, Tom,' she said, 'We don't often get good looking young men coming our way nowadays. We'll certainly have to make the most of you.'

On the drive back to the estate, Henry had given him some advice: 'I saw the way Millie looked at you, Tom. She won't be able to keep away. But a word of warning, old man … Don't let her get to you. She's as hard as nails under all that superficial charm. A couple of unfortunates made the mistake of falling in love with her, and they regret it. She's heartless, believe me. She sees love as a sign of weakness.'

Tom stared ahead at the road and the rubber trees that lined it, grey and ghostly in the arc of the headlights. He wondered fleetingly if Henry was speaking from experience.

One evening, not long after that first trip to the Penang Club, Tom heard the roar of an engine outside his house, the crunching of tyres on the gravel drive leading into his bungalow. He wondered briefly if it was Henry, but it would be unusual for him to drive. Henry normally walked the couple of hundred yards between their bungalows.

The houseboy showed the visitor through to the veranda.

'Lady Atherton, Tuan,' he said, beaming broadly at being able to introduce a guest at last.

Tom got to his feet and shook her hand, feeling self-conscious.

'Lady Atherton. What a pleasant surprise. Would you like a drink?'

'Very much so.' She sat down. The boy served them drinks, and they made small talk for a while. She asked him how he was settling in, and told him some trivial news of other expatriates on the island. She had a clever and entertaining way of telling anecdotes, and when she listened to him, she made him feel as if she found him irresistible, as if his words were truly enthralling. He wondered why she had come over to see him.

At last she put down her glass and said, 'Well, I must be pushing along now, but I came here to ask you something. My husband and I are having a small dinner party next Saturday evening. I would very much like you to come. Oh, here's an invitation. That makes it official.' She fumbled in her bag and handed him a large white envelope.

He drew out a card embossed with silver writing: 'Sir James and Lady Millicent Atherton request the pleasure of your company at High Tops …'

Tom could think of no reason to refuse. He had very little to do in the evenings and, if he was honest with himself, was beginning to tire of spending them alone on the veranda, however beautiful the view.

As Millicent said goodbye, she held his hand to her lips. She said, looking at him through lowered lashes, 'I must say, I am very much looking forward to making your acquaintance properly, Mr. Ellis.'

She kissed his hand, and after she had gone he had noticed the deep red stain of her lipstick on the back of his hand. It gave him an odd thrill to see it there. That evening, when he took his shower in the bath house under the bungalow, he was careful not to wash the stain off his hand.

The dinner party was a sumptuous occasion. The Athertons lived in a gracious colonial mansion on the outskirts of Georgetown. As Tom drew into the drive, he saw that the whole house was lit up with strings of fairy lights. A procession of motor cars was drawing up at the front steps, disgorging the passengers and moving on; the guests then mounted the steps to the glittering colonnaded porch and were greeted by their hosts. In the panelled library, bearers in starched white uniforms carried about trays of drinks and canapés. The guests were of all shapes and sizes, from the richest plantation owners down to the humblest nurses and civil servants. Tom found himself chatting with an earnest young woman with ginger hair and a freckled face. She was a missionary, she told him, and worked in a Christian school in a village up in the hills. She blinked a lot as she spoke. Tom noticed that she was drinking barley water.

His eyes met Millicent's as she made her way towards him. She looked stunning in a white sequinned evening dress, her neck sparkling with diamonds. She introduced Tom to her husband, Sir James.

'This is Tom Ellis, darling. He's just started working for United Rubber as an overseer, but in real life, rumour has it that he is a lawyer.'

Tom was startled. How had she found that out?

She gave him a teasing smile. She knew what he was thinking. 'News travels in mysterious ways in the East. You'll soon get used to it,' she laughed.

'A fellow lawyer? And why did you give it up?' asked Sir James.

'Well, the work was really rather dull, I'm afraid. I needed a change.'

'If you ever want to come back, we're always looking for bright young men in the Straits Legal Service, particularly in the Courts. You should give it some thought.'

'That's very kind of you, but I've never done any litigation in my life.'

'Oh, I wouldn't worry about that. You'd pick it up in no time.'

Sir James was a good twenty years older than his wife. He was running to fat, and had heavy jowls, but his thick head of dark hair and intelligent brown eyes still lent him a youthful demeanour. There was something about him, an easy charm that seemed to draw people to him.

Now, watching them together, Tom wondered whether the rumours about Millicent were really true. She had her arm through her husband's and was smiling up at him while he related an anecdote to an old lady. They appeared to be a perfectly devoted couple.

'Don't be taken in by appearances,' whispered a voice behind him, and turning round he saw Henry standing there, grinning broadly.

'Oh, hello, old man. I wasn't sure if you were coming.'

'Oh, yes. Wouldn't miss the Athertons' parties for the world. They're the toast of Penang. You'll find some crusty old relics here, but amongst them, some decent types too. Everyone is here, Tom. Anyone and everyone.'

Dinner was served in a huge galleried room on the first floor, lit by chandeliers and cooled by ceiling fans. The table was so long it had been difficult to make out the faces at the other end.

Tom's company for dinner was not so enticing however. On one side of him sat a deaf old woman, Mrs. Roberts, the mother of the chief of police in Penang. She was a redoubtable type who had spent her entire life in the East. If seemed odd to Tom that someone who appeared to be so English had only visited the mother country a couple of times in her life. She regaled him with gossip about the colony, but was unable to hear any of his replies unless she held an old-fashioned ear trumpet to her ear. On the other side of him sat a mousy little woman, the wife of another of the overseers on Tom's estate. She barely touched her food and hardly spoke; she had explained to Tom at the start of the meal that she'd had a bout of fever recently and was not feeling up to much.

Every so often, Millicent, who was sitting at the end of the table nearest to him, would catch his eye and watch him for a moment, with that same amused mocking look she always gave him.

After the meal, the guests proceeded up a flight of stairs. There was dancing to a band on the terrace overlooking the town. It was a romantic scene, with the sparkling lights from the boats moored in the harbour and the full moon shining on the water. Tom felt self-conscious. He had not danced for years, but Millicent took his arm and drew him onto the dance floor.

'I'm not sure,' he said, pulling back.

'You mustn't be a kill-joy,' she said, laughing.

'Well, I'm a bit out of practice.'

'Never mind. This one is freestyle.'

Tom had let Millicent take him in her arms, and allowed her to lead him in the first dance. She danced confidently and gracefully, and after a while he relaxed and remembered the steps. By the third dance he realised he was enjoying himself.

As he said goodbye at the end of the evening, Millicent leaned into him and whispered, 'Would you like to play tennis with me on Tuesday evening? James is out of town at a hearing in Singapore.'

Tom hesitated. Why did she feel it necessary to mention that her husband would be away? He was aware that she was waiting for a reply. And everyone on the steps behind him seemed to be waiting for him to move on. Was it simply inertia and politeness, and the fact that his driver was waiting beside his car with the door open and Tom did not want to hold everyone up any longer? Or was it that promise in her dark eyes? He didn't know what made him say yes to Millie.

'That would be very nice,' he said.

'Six o'clock. Don't be late,' she said, laughing her mocking laugh.

Now, sitting in the pit, fevered and weak, in his state of extreme hunger, Tom found himself visualising all the courses of that meal he had at High Tops. First there was salmon in aspic. He could remember the perfect delicate taste of the dish even now. This was followed by fish soup, then rare beef and new potatoes. He could actually taste the succulent meat if he closed his eyes: luscious and pink and running with juices. The dessert was Pavlova. The most delicious, melt-in-the-mouth, creamy meringue that he had ever tasted. He found himself salivating at the memory. But gradually, as the image faded, and the reality of the punishment pit returned to him with savage force, the contrast between his present predicament and that sumptuous evening was almost impossible to bear. He clenched his fists and tried to pummel the sides of his prison in his anger and frustration, but his hands were so constricted he could only manage a feeble punch or two. He slumped forward against the bamboo bars and let out an impotent roar.

15

Laura opened the trunk and the stale smell of old clothes hit her. Slowly, she began to take things out of it: a cream linen suit; some hand sewn shirts; a couple of pairs of leather shoes, stiff with age; some books; a framed photograph of a middle-aged couple posing beside some potted palms in a photographer's studio. She studied it, recognising the graceful figure of Grandma Louise, and beside her Granddad Edward, looking severe, dressed in a pin-striped suit. She found another photograph, of Dad, young and fresh-faced, standing beside the Asian woman whose photograph she had found tucked into her father's book.

'Joy de Souza,' she whispered. They were in a tropical garden, palm trees and frangipani bushes behind them. They stood together shyly, not touching. She stared into the woman's dark eyes. 'Who are you?' she asked into the silence.

At the bottom of the trunk, she found a few PG Wodehouse novels, a couple of volumes of Shakespeare plays, and a few 78 rpm gramophone records of crooners of the 1930s, Al Bowley and Bing Crosby.

Underneath all this lay a dinner jacket. She had almost missed it. It was camouflaged against the dark lining of the trunk. A card protruded from the pocket. She pulled it out: 'Sir James and Lady Millicent Atherton request the pleasure of your company at High Tops House, Georgetown.' She held the jacket up to her nose. The fabric smelt musty, but she thought she could detect the faint tang of lemon verbena. She half closed her eyes and tried to picture the function at High Tops. She could imagine her father dancing under chandeliers, with a slim woman in a sequinned dress.

She looked in vain for some clue about the war, but there was nothing else in the trunk. All she had was the jumble of bric-a-brac she'd found in the box in the study – the badge of the Straits Settlements Volunteer Force, and the one from the Northumberland Fusiliers, the signet ring, and the shrivelled flowers. What did they all mean? Would she ever find out?

She went to bed alone again, but this time her anxieties about Luke were replaced by anguished thoughts about her father and what might have happened to him during the war. Had he suffered like the men whose accounts she had read? Had he starved, been beaten by the guards?

The next day she went back to the museum. She asked the assistant to show her the records of the Northumberland Fusiliers. She looked down the lists of men. Hundreds were killed in action in Malaya or Singapore, and hundreds more had died as prisoners in camps in South East Asia. She looked down the columns for the initials IFR. Her heart stopped when she found only one: 'Ian Frances Ryan, Private. Died in captivity, Thailand, 1943. Believed executed.'

Executed? Had Dad known that? They must have been friends. Was this the IFR who had given him the signet ring? Was he buried there in Thailand?

She closed the book and sighed. What was the point of all this now? Dad had died with all this knowledge that he had kept from her all those years. Why did she need to know about it now? She wondered if she was simply trying to distract herself from her reality, from the pain of her loss, from wondering about what she should do with her life now. She thought about returning to finish her stint in the Paris office, to the tense meetings with men in suits, to the painstaking hours spent drafting documents and dictating letters, to the lunches with colleagues, and to the predictable flirtation with Adam grinding on to its inevitable conclusion in a hotel bedroom.

As she walked back towards the Lambeth North tube station, she suddenly realised that she didn't need to go back to that life. With the money Dad had left her, she now had enough to do what she wanted. Perhaps she could even make a journey to Thailand herself. The accounts she had read in the museum had awakened in her a need to find out about what had happened to Dad during the war. Perhaps there were documents or records in those museums near the Bridge on the River Kwai. Perhaps they could tell her something of the life he had lived there. She could go to the very place where her father had suffered, could see the railway first hand, find some connection with the place and with the time. She couldn't articulate it clearly to herself yet about why she had to go there and what she hoped to find there, but she knew that making such a journey would somehow bring her closer to her father. Perhaps it could help make up for the fact that she had not thought to ask him about those years properly while he was alive. Even though he was no longer with her, it did not feel too late to do that. In fact it felt as if it was the right thing to do, the only thing to do. Perhaps she could go to Malaysia too, to Penang, to follow in his footsteps and see if there was any trace of the mysterious Joy de Souza there.

There was nothing to stop her after all. She had no one to take care of in London anymore. She could just pack her bags and leave today if she wanted. She wondered fleetingly what Joy might look like now. Would she even remember Dad? If Laura could track her down, she would make sure she found a way of telling Joy about the letter, even though it might be decades too late. At least that might make up in some small way for throwing it on the fire all those years ago.

By the time she emerged from the tube station at Highbury Corner she'd made up her mind. Tomorrow she would go down to the bucket shops in Earls Court, look for a flight to Thailand, and start to plan her trip.

She was smiling as she pushed open the front gate, fishing in her bag for the front door key. When she looked up she noticed a dark figure sitting on the step. She froze in surprise. He stood up and came towards her.

'Luke. You frightened me.'

'I came here to say that I'm sorry.'

'Where have you been?'

'I went to stay with the guys at the new squat. I'm sorry. Things were getting a bit heavy around here. I just needed to be on my own for a while.'

'You could have said. I would have understood. But you didn't even phone. It's been three days.' She brushed past him and went up the steps. 'You'd better come in, I suppose.'

They sat in the back living room and she poured them a couple of cold lagers.

As she set the glass down on the coffee table beside him, he pulled her to him.

'I'm sorry, Loz. Will you have me back? I was wrong to go.'

She pulled away and sat down in the chair opposite him.

'You go away without a word. Don't even bother to get in touch for days, then come back and expect everything to be normal?'

He smiled. 'I'm not a normal guy, Loz. That's why you like me.'

It was true. She thought back to the time her friend Izzy from law school had introduced them in 1984. Luke had been with a couple of other activists in the King's Head in Islington. It was during the miners' strike, and they were collecting for the miners' families, shaking plastic buckets painted with the slogan 'Dig deep for the Miners'. On the table where they sat for a pint, they had placed miners' helmets.

Izzy, a punk with left-wing ideals whose only interest in being at law school was to be able to represent worthy causes eventually, had introduced Laura.

'This is Luke. We were at university together in Brighton.'

Laura remembered how he'd stared at her, and how she'd felt self-conscious and inadequate, as if she'd hardly lived, and that the life she had lived so far had been selfish and pampered. Here was someone who'd rejected the safe options in life for a risky impoverished existence because he believed in what he was doing.

After that first meeting, she'd often thought about him, about his striking good looks, the intense scrutiny he'd given her when Izzy introduced them, his brave and unconventional life. He'd been a stark contrast to all the other men she had known. Safe, dependable men like Matthew, who followed their pre-destined path with assurance and confidence, without looking outside the privileged existence the quirk of birth and education had handed to them.

She hadn't imagined for a moment that he might be interested in her until several months later. They'd bumped into each other again at one of Izzy's parties in her flat in Clapton. Matt had been away on business, so she went alone. Luke had approached her and with that intense look that seemed to shut out everything else around him had said, 'You're Izzy's token capitalist friend, aren't you? I remember you from the King's Head.'

'Yes, I remember you too. I'm surprised you can find it in you to even speak to me, if that's what you think.'

They had sparred like that all evening, and at the end she had offered to drop him off at his squat in her taxi. As he got out he had kissed her, full on the lips. She had felt a thrill of shock, and the memory of the kiss stayed with her for weeks afterwards. When Matt returned from Geneva, although she tried, she could never again feel the same about the way he kissed her.

She looked at Luke now, at his dark hair framing his face, at the stubble on his chin, at his deep brown eyes focused on her, at his slim creative hands. She couldn't fight her attraction to him. She was drawn to him like a moth to a bright light. She looked away.

'I'm going away for a few weeks. Let's see how we feel when I come back,' she said.

'Where are you going? Perhaps I could come along?'

She shook her head. 'I don't think so. I'm going to Thailand. Malaysia maybe. I want to go to the bridge on the River Kwai, to the railway where Dad was a prisoner. And I want to go to Penang. You know, where he worked before the war. It will be a sort of pilgrimage for me. You'd probably find it boring.'

'Don't you want some company? You might be lonely. I haven't got anything to do here at the moment.'

'I've only just started to think about it. And anyway, you don't have any money, Luke.'

Watching his face, she thought she saw a flash of irritation. He got up to go.

'I'll be getting back to the squat then.'

She stood up and walked with him to the front door. He turned the handle, but then turned around and put his arms around her, kissed her hard, pushing her up against the wall. She returned the kiss reluctantly at first and then found she couldn't stop kissing him back. His hands were inside her shirt.

'Stop,' she said. 'Ken might come downstairs.'

'Shall we go up to your room?'

They hurried upstairs and fell on the bed kissing, their hands all over each other, undoing clothes, throwing them aside.

When Laura awoke the next morning, her first thought was the memory of the night before. She turned and saw that he was still there. She felt shame creeping through her. What had happened to her resolve to forget him and make plans of her own?

She crept out of bed and went downstairs to make tea. When she came back, Luke was awake.

'I've been thinking,' he said. 'I could get the airfare. One of the guys in the squat owes me a hundred quid, and I'll get my dole this week.'

She laughed. 'The fares will be quite expensive.' Looking at him now, her resolve was beginning to weaken further. 'I suppose I could lend you the money if you really want to come.'

'Hey, that's generous of you. I'd pay you back. You know that.'

He propped the pillow behind his head, and his face relaxed into a smile. Did she really know that? Had he ever paid her a penny for the bills he'd run up at her flat, or for all the meals they had shared? Not that she begrudged paying. She was earning money, and he wasn't.

She slid into bed beside him, and he put his arms around her and kissed her hair. So it was settled. He would come with her to Thailand, and she would pay his fare. She didn't know whether to feel pleased or thwarted.

16

On the fourth day they took Archie's body out of the pit. Tom watched, his mouth dry with horror, as four guards surrounded the hole, threw aside the corrugated iron and the bamboo, and leaned in to pull Archie out. The boy's face had almost turned blue and was covered in wounds from his beatings. His body was stiff and unwieldy, and it took the guards a lot of pulling and heaving to remove him.

Tom's anger and grief spilled over. 'You bastards! You murdering bastards. He could have lived. You've murdered him in cold blood.'

He screamed and shouted until his voice was hoarse. 'Let me out! Let me out! Or I'll die too!'

One of the guards came over and pulled the metal aside. He shoved his steel-capped boot into Tom's head. The guard kicked him again and again. Tom tried to put up his hands against the blows, but the pit restricted the movement of his arms. He stopped shouting.

The lid was clamped back down. His head was pounding. He watched as four prisoners arrived with a bamboo stretcher and loaded Archie's body onto it. They had brought a large but battered Union Jack with them, which they draped over the body. Then they picked up the stretcher and carried it away towards the cemetery. They did not stagger under its weight. Archie was so emaciated that he must have weighed no more than a child.

Tom closed his eyes and imagined the scene in the cemetery. He had been to many funerals during his time in the camp. The padre would recite the words of the funeral service as men stood round in mournful little groups, watching and praying, their heads bowed. The body would be lowered into the shallow grave, and earth would be shovelled on to his body. They would be careful to remove the flag and fold it, and keep it ready for the next dead prisoner. Then the men would wander back to camp with heavy hearts.

'Goodbye, Archie, old mate,' Tom said quietly, breaking into sobs.

* * *

Tom's misery turned to despair. He was beginning to suspect they would never let him out. He was sure he would die a humiliating and pointless death in this filthy hole in the ground. He tried to think of Joy, but her memory failed to bring him any comfort. There was no point even hoping that he might see her again. He found himself weeping at this thought. He couldn't bear to think he wouldn't see her again. That would be the death of all hope for him. He would give up and surrender to his inevitable end. He slid his palm over the photograph and pressed it against his sweating chest. Closing his eyes, he tried to conjure up her face once again.

He screwed up his face with the effort, but it was not Joy's face that swam before his eyes, but Millicent Atherton's. That very English face, with the pampered pale skin and carefully applied makeup. He felt she was watching him, even here in this god-forsaken pit, with that knowing, sardonic smile.

He was back on that first Tuesday evening at the Penang Club. Millicent and Tom had met at six o'clock as arranged and played tennis as the sun set over the harbour. Millicent played competently, but Tom, who was unfit and nervous, made many mistakes, and she won the match easily. As he went inside to change she said casually, 'When you're done, come upstairs to Room 201. It's my private suite. We can have a quiet drink.'

Tom spent a long time showering and changing. He was agonising over what was inevitably about to happen between him and Millicent. He was reluctant to encourage her, but for some reason he could not explain to himself, either then or now, he felt drawn into the situation. As he walked slowly across the entrance hall and mounted the marble staircase to the private rooms, he sensed a sudden hush in the club and the eyes of every single member and servant upon him, following him, assessing him, judging him.

Room 201 was a palatial suite overlooking the harbour, furnished with soft white sofas and low Chinese tables bearing bowls of lotus blossoms. Millicent was wearing a flimsy silk bathrobe.

'Lighten up. I'm not going to eat you,' she giggled as she opened the door for him. She was smoking a slim cigarette from a tortoiseshell holder. 'Come on in and sit down. Would you like a ciggie?'

She passed him a cigarette. As she leaned forward to light it for him, she watched his face intently.

'Are you normally so nervous?' she asked.

'Normally?'

'Yes. When you are with a woman. You look like a lamb to the slaughter.'

'Well, perhaps I'm not used to being alone with a married woman, who is wearing only a bathrobe.'

'Oh, don't be so prim. And I wouldn't worry about the married bit. James doesn't mind.'

'Really? I find that hard to believe.'

'Well, you wouldn't if you knew the full story. Perhaps I'll tell you one day.'

She had a bottle of champagne standing ready in an ice bucket. It had already been opened, and she poured them each a generous glass. Then she sat down next to him. As she leaned over to pass him his glass, she allowed her robe to fall open a little at the front. Tom looked away quickly.

'Now, why don't you tell me all about your life in London, Tom?' she purred, watching him closely.

'Well, there isn't that much to tell. It was all rather dull, I'm afraid,' he said, trying not to meet her eyes.

'Oh, come on. You must have had lots of girlfriends.'

'Not really. Nothing serious, anyway.'

'Now I find *that* extremely hard to believe,' she said, edging a little closer, so that her thigh touched his momentarily. He felt a surge of desire, but inched away from her.

She ran her hand slowly along the inside of his thigh, sending shivers up his spine. She then undid a button and slipped her hand inside his shirt. It felt cool and smooth against his skin. Tom realised he needed to act quickly to stop what was happening. But he found himself frozen, partly through embarrassment and partly through indecision. A part of him didn't want her to stop, wanted her to carry on, and didn't want to think of the consequences.

He felt her lips on his. Their tongues touched. Then he was lost. He was kissing her back with the suppressed passion and stifled expression of all his dull, empty years. He felt as though he was suddenly opening up, like a bud flowering to her touch.

After that first time they met discreetly, two or three times a week, sometimes at the club, sometimes at his bungalow. Occasionally, she would turn up in Sir James's old Bentley, with a picnic hamper on the back seat. She would drive him to a deserted beach near Batu Ferringhi, where they would eat under the coconut palms and swim in the clear water. At first he felt as though every eye in the European community was on him, and that he was being judged, ridiculed. But after a while he ceased to care. No-one said anything to him, except for Henry: 'I warned you, old boy. Be careful,' he remarked with an amused glint in his eye.

Life established itself into a round of idyllic days. He was up before dawn and out on the estate when the mist was still rising from the trees and the earth was still cool. His undemanding routine was finished in the afternoon, and he would bathe, rest and then go down into Georgetown to the club most evenings. Sometimes he would play tennis with Henry. Tom's game even became passable.

It was a blissful life, one he couldn't even have imagined a few months before. He went through the days in a happy dream-like state, half expecting that one day he would wake up and be back in an office in London, poring over a contract.

On the few occasions that Tom saw Sir James at the club, the older man showed no sign of knowing anything about Tom and Millicent. He remembered who Tom was, though.

'Have you decided to come back into the legal fold yet?' he would ask each time they met.

Tom was not in love with Millie, but he felt a powerful physical attraction to her, and he enjoyed her quick wit and entertaining conversation. However, when he was with her, he found himself very aware of the feeling that she was just playing with him, amusing herself, passing the time with him until she tired of the game.

She was a good ten years older than Tom, and close up she looked her age. She was not beautiful, or even pretty, but she made the most of herself. She had arresting grey eyes and strong features.

Tom wondered why she had never had children. One day, when he felt the moment was right, he asked her. They were lying under the mosquito net in his bungalow, sharing a cigarette. The heat of the afternoon was stifling, the ceiling fan just stirring the hot air. Beads of sweat covered her naked body.

When he asked the question she turned over quickly, away from him.

'I'm sorry. Have I upset you?' he asked, instantly regretting having asked her.

'I was going to have a baby once,' she said in a low voice, still turning away from him. 'Imagine it, I was only nineteen. I was at Oxford, and James was lecturing part-time. He was a barrister then. We fell in love, and I got pregnant. Of course we got married very quickly. He had already accepted this post, and we set off to come out here. I lost the baby on the voyage. It was a girl. And since then I have never got pregnant again.'

'You were at Oxford?'

She nodded. 'I was studying History.'

'I can't really imagine you as a bluestocking.'

She laughed. 'I was never one of those.'

'Do you regret giving it all up?'

'Not in the slightest. Life out here is wonderful. It might be frivolous, but I could never leave. I could live like this forever.'

She turned onto her back again and stretched her arms out languidly. Her white breasts were flat against her chest.

'And now, of course, James and I will never have a child because we've drifted apart,' she said casually. 'I expect he amuses himself in a discreet way when he's off on trips, but certainly not with me.'

'Really?'

'Yes. For quite a number of years now.'

'So you find your pleasure elsewhere. Is that it?'

She smiled.

'And doesn't he mind?'

'He turns a blind eye. I think he is relieved in a way. It eases his guilt.'

She rolled over onto her side, and settled her head on a pillow. She began to stroke his back. 'Anyway. Let's not talk about all that. In fact, let's not talk at all,' she said.

* * *

Tom had been in Penang for a little over a year when news broke that Britain had declared war on Germany.

He was not surprised. His father's letters had alerted him to the storm clouds gathering in Europe. He was at the club with a group of ex-pats when they listened to the broadcast from the World Service on the crackly wireless in the smoking room. The news was treated with polite interest, but like a story from a far-off land, as if it had no effect upon the assembled company whatever. There was only one voice of concern.

'It'll be us next,' said Barry Cliff, propping up the bar as he had done every night since he had arrived in Penang as a rookie reporter twenty odd years ago. He was now a seasoned hack on *The Straits Times*. 'You just wait. The Japs are building up to something.'

'You've got to be joking,' jeered Douggie Chambers, one of the hard-drinking rubber planters.

'No. Not at all. Look how many troops have been drafted into Singapore over the last few months. And there are more on the way.'

'Well, that's just a precaution, surely. It's not serious. Singapore is impregnable. Everyone knows that.'

'And there are Jap spies everywhere,' Barry continued. 'Haven't you noticed? They are all over the place: in the barbers, in the tailors' shops, in the doctor's surgery. They're spying on us to get information for an invasion. You people really are naïve.'

Douggie laughed uneasily and slapped Barry's back.

'Now I know you're paranoid, Cliff, old man. My advice to you is to have a couple more whiskies and forget all about the Japs.'

And Douggie expressed the view of virtually all the ex-pats on Penang. Life went on exactly as it had for years: one long round of tennis and drinks, and dances at the club. They felt untouchable. The rubber industry was booming, supplying the war effort in the West, and the estates were all working to capacity.

They read the news of the Blitz in the papers with interest, but with a creeping feeling of guilt. Here they were, leading the Lotus Eater's life, when back at home people were dying. It seemed hardly credible, under the endless sun and in the comfort of their pampered existence. Tom was concerned about his parents, living in central London, but a letter arrived from his father, informing him that they were leaving to stay in Dorset with his sister for a while, and that Tom was not to worry.

It was a few months later that Tom first met Joy. He was still seeing Millicent then. They had slipped into a routine of meeting twice a week, more often than that if Sir James happened to be away. Tom was beginning to tire of the whole thing. It irked him that they had to be so discreet, and that the relationship was ultimately finite. He felt stifled by the constraints it imposed on him, trapped by the secrecy.

One weekday morning he happened to be in Georgetown. He had to visit one of the go-downs on the docks to find a spare part for some machinery on the estate. The man he came to see was delayed on the mainland, so he decided to kill some time by wandering around town.

It was sweltering on the main square. It was almost midday, and the sun was reaching its full height in the sky. Crossing the square, he happened to notice the museum. It was a long low building with arched windows and columns adorning its white facade. Having nothing else to do, he wandered up the flagstone steps, under the shady portico and in through the open door.

It was cool inside the vaulted hall, under the whirring fans, and he took his topee off and wandered around the displays. A portrait of Sir Stamford Raffles and a massive statue of Sir Francis Light, the founding father of Penang, dominated the room. Tom stared at the statue for a while, before walking up the wide stone staircase to the upper level.

A school party of excited Malay and Chinese children dressed in blue and white uniforms appeared at the top and started to swarm down the stairs. They were chattering and shouting, pushing each other and jostling for position. Tom stood aside and waited for them to pass. But as the last group clattered by, one of the little boys, who was holding a fountain pen, flicked it in Tom's direction. A shower of ink flecks appeared on Tom's white jacket.

'Hey! Wait a minute,' he shouted, but the boy had already run off with his friends, shouting with laughter. Tom turned round, exasperated. He was proud of that jacket. The Chinese tailor had run it up for him only the previous month, and it was cool and comfortable.

Then, suddenly, a young Eurasian woman was standing in front of him, tearful, full of apologies.

'I'm so sorry, sir. He is my pupil. He will be punished severely.'

Tom looked at her. Even in the heat of his anger, he was struck by her beauty. She was truly exquisite. Her face was delicate and fine boned, with creamy skin, full lips and slightly tilted eyes, brown and soft, now brimming with concern. Her shiny black hair was swept back from her face.

Tom tried to put her at her ease.

'No, please don't worry. It really doesn't matter.'

'Oh, but of course it matters. That jacket looks new. I know someone who will be able to remove the stain. The school will pay. Please let me take it just for a day or so. I will ensure that your jacket is as good as new.'

She spoke in a precise way, enunciating every word carefully, as if English was familiar to her, but not her first language.

She held out her hand, and automatically he slipped his jacket off his arms and gave it to her.

'If you are sure it is not too much trouble. I could easily have it cleaned myself.'

'No, no. This person is a friend of my family. I assure you, it will be very easy for me.'

He gave it to her, not because he particularly wanted her to get the jacket cleaned, but because he knew that this would be a way to ensure he got to see her again. And that was suddenly very important to him. He knew he would do anything he could to get to know this shy, delicate girl. And he also knew, with sudden clarity, that it would be impossible for him to continue seeing Millicent anymore.

17

Tom had ceased to register the passing of the hours. He no longer even knew whether it was day or night, or if he had survived another day in the pit. He had stopped bothering to watch the routines of the camp. He would open his eyes at random and see the stars twinkling above the ragged jungle skyline, or the sun burning overhead, the officers digging the latrines on the other side of the camp.

He realised he had developed a fever now, on top of all his other ailments. He alternated between periods of shivering, his teeth chattering uncontrollably, and periods of burning up, sweat pouring off him. Most of the time, he inhabited the dream world of the past that he had recreated, so he could get himself through the present. He tried to blank out the present. He knew if he dwelled on his misfortune, he would give up the struggle. He did sometimes wonder, though, how much pain and suffering a single human being was capable of withstanding. He felt as if his fragile body could give up at any moment, as if his life hung by a thread.

One day the Ripper came striding across the clearing. He tore away the corrugated iron and bamboo from the top of the pit and bent down to peer at Tom's face. Then he poked his shoulders and chest several times with a bamboo cane as if Tom were a pig being prepared for slaughter. He was obviously not pleased with what he saw. He frowned, and shouted at the guards, lashing out at them indiscriminately with his cane, jabbering orders at them. In his fevered state, Tom was confused. What did all this mean? Were they going to take him out and shoot him? Tom tried to blank out his thoughts.

As the Ripper stomped back to the guard house, Tom allowed his mind to drift again. It took him back to the day after he had first met Joy at the museum. He remembered that he had telephoned Millicent in the morning and arranged to meet her at the club.

When they met in her private suite, he had told her that their relationship was over.

At first she thought he was joking. She sat there, lounging on the white sofa, smoking her cigarette, eyeing him with scepticism.

'What on earth has brought this on?' she asked when she had begun to realise that he was serious. 'Is there someone else?'

'No,' he said, looking down at his hands. It was the truth, but not the whole truth.

'Are you sure? I think there is. Who is it? Betty Tranter? Jane Gibbons? I've seen those tarts eyeing you up. They'd love to get their hands on you.'

'No, Millie. It's nobody. I just think we should end it because … Well, because it has been wonderful, but it is going nowhere. You have to agree.'

'So what? That didn't matter to you at first,' she said, sitting forward, anxiety displacing the mocking look her face usually held.

'Look, Tom,' she went on, stubbing out her cigarette. He was surprised to see that her hand was shaking, 'I haven't told you this. Perhaps I should have done. But you mean a lot to me. You're not like the others. You know, I really think that I'm in love with you. Come on. Let's go to bed and forget all this silliness.' She moved towards him, but he stepped away.

'No, Millie. I mean it. I'm fond of you, of course, but I'm quite serious. It has got to end.'

She began to cry, to let out great shrieking sobs that racked her body. Tears streamed down her cheeks. It shocked Tom. He had not thought her capable of feeling this way. He put his arm round her shoulder and passed her a handkerchief. She cried for a long time, but eventually her sobs subsided and with an effort of will she pulled herself together.

'I'd like you to go now, Tom,' she said quietly.

He left her, but he felt uneasy. He had completely misjudged the situation. And he had a feeling that she wouldn't leave it there. But as he drove away from the club he felt a huge weight lifting from his shoulders.

The next day was the day he'd been waiting for. It was the day he had arranged to drive to Joy's house and collect his jacket. The manager of the plantation, Jones, had sold him an old Morris a few months earlier. He drove up through the town to the outskirts. The house where Joy lived with her parents was in Pulau Tikus the cramped Eurasian quarter on the edge of town, and it took him some time to navigate the maze of streets and find the right one. The shabby wooden houses were built close together on concrete piles, surrounded by patches of bare earth where grubby children played. When she saw his car drive up, she came out onto the porch to meet him. A small crowd of children followed her out to stare at him. She shooed them inside, but Tom could see that they were still watching them through the slats of the louvered doors.

She was holding his jacket, and handed it to him with a smile.

'It's all done,' she said. 'As good as new.'

'Thank you.' He smiled back at her as he took the jacket. She looked just as lovely as when he had first set eyes on her. She stood there on the shabby porch in a pure white dress, her hair pulled back as before. She seemed to Tom the picture of serenity.

'Aren't you going to look at it?' she asked with curiosity.

'Oh, yes, of course.' He made a show of inspecting the jacket. There was no sign of ink anywhere.

'Please thank your friend for me. He is very clever. He has done a wonderful job.'

He stood, staring at her still, transfixed by her. She smiled at him, puzzled.

'Was there something else?' she asked.

'Yes. I was wondering … I hope you don't mind my asking, but would you like to come for a drive with me? We could go up to Penang Hill?'

She blushed a little then looked down.

'No, I'm sorry, but I can't do that. I have to look after the children. My mother is out at work.'

'Oh, well, perhaps another time?'

This time she looked him in the eyes. She had recovered her composure. He held his breath, waiting for her reply.

'Yes, Saturday is my day off. If that would be convenient, I would like that very much.'

He said he would collect her at ten o'clock. When he drove off, she stood on the porch watching him with her steady brown eyes. And when he reached the end of the road, he glanced in the mirror and saw that she was still standing there, watching him, as he turned the corner into the next road.

He counted the days feverishly until Saturday. When at last he drove up to the house to collect her, he found her waiting for him on the porch. It was almost as if the intervening days had not occurred. She looked just the same, standing there, except she had on a different pale cotton dress with a pleated skirt, and round her neck she wore a tiny silver cross. She carried a white cardigan and a small leather bag on her arm.

They drove up the winding road out of town, and on through bright green paddy fields. Tom had been thinking about this outing constantly for the past three days, but now that it had come, he found his courage failing him. He felt tongue-tied. Joy was quiet, too, and her face was turned away from him, staring out of the window. It was a glorious day, the bright sun high in a clear blue sky, and as they climbed higher they could see the sea, perfectly blue, sparkling in the sunlight.

They reached the funicular railway station, parked the car and joined a small queue of day trippers waiting for the train. On the trip up the hill, as the tiny red and white train chugged and panted its way through the overhanging jungle, she avoided his gaze. She seemed paralysed with shyness. He began to wonder if asking her on this outing had been a mistake.

Once they arrived at the top of the hill, they found a viewing point and stood together to look out. There was a slight breeze stirring the trees, and it was a perfect scene. On one side the town stretched out beneath them, a patchwork of low white buildings interspersed with lush greenery spreading down to the harbour. On the other side, across the farms and plantations and jungle, they could see palm-fringed beaches bordering a shimmering blue sea, which melted into a perfectly blue sky at the horizon.

'It is like heaven,' she said spontaneously, turning to smile up at him, her eyes dancing with pleasure.

'It *is* heaven,' he said, relieved that she had finally spoken to him.

'Excuse me, sir? Madam?'

A tall thin Indian man in a grubby white suit approached them, carrying a huge camera and a folded tripod. His hair was heavily oiled. He smiled a toothy smile.

'You want photograph? Beautiful spot. Beautiful lady.'

'Yes,' he said, smiling at Joy. 'Why not?'

So they stood together, a little apart, afraid of touching for the first time in front of a stranger. They watched the man erect the tripod and adjust the lens. Tom glanced sideways at Joy. Should he put his arm around her after all?

At last the equipment was ready.

'Watch the birdie!' came the muffled voice from under the black cloth. They both jumped slightly as the little mechanical bird popped out and the camera clicked.

'Thank you very much, sir. I will send messenger with photograph to your home after developing process. If I could just have your name and address.'

After that their shyness seemed to evaporate. They walked around the gardens laid out on the top of the hill, admiring the tropical plants and the views from every angle. He asked her how long she had lived in Penang.

'All my life,' she answered. 'I was born here.'

They found a small café serving drinks to day-trippers, and they went in for a coffee. As they sipped their drinks, she told him about her family. Her father was half Indian, she said, born in Goa, the son of a local woman and a Portuguese officer. He had come to Penang as a young man to look for work and met her mother, the daughter of a British civil servant and a Malay seamstress. Joy was their eldest daughter, and when she was tiny, they had determined to give her a good education. Her father got a job in the offices of an import and export company, and her mother found work in a Chinese laundry.

As she told him about her life, he watched her face. Her eyes were alight with enthusiasm and intelligence. She spoke simply and with complete sincerity. He found himself admiring her self-possession and her straightforward manner, her freedom from artifice or pretence. It was so refreshing after the games that Millicent always played.

'Do you know, years later, my parents are still working at the same jobs, so my brothers and sisters can go to school? The poor things,' she said with a heartfelt sigh.

'They must be very proud of your success,' said Tom.

'Oh, I don't know. I was lucky. I had good teachers. When I finished school in Penang I went to teacher-training college in Singapore.'

'And you came back?'

'Yes. I always wanted to be with my family in Penang. I got a job in a mission infants' school.'

'And do you like it?' he asked.

She nodded, and her eyes shone.

'Yes, I love it! And I love the children. They are so rewarding, so full of surprises.'

'I agree with you there,' he smiled.

She laughed, putting her hand over her mouth shyly.

'Oh, you mean that naughty boy with the ink pen? Yes, he was punished. Made to stay inside at lunchtime and write lines.'

He drove her home and stopped outside the house. He walked her to the door, and once again the children hung on the balcony, watching them with their curious eyes. He ached to kiss her cool cheek, but felt constrained. In the end he just shook her hand stiffly.

'Perhaps next time we could go to the Penang Club,' he said.

'Well, I don't think so,' she said, an anxious look clouding her eyes.

* * *

It was the following week that Tom joined the Straits Settlements Volunteer Force. Most of the men he knew were joining up. There had been posters around the town for some weeks, calling for men to prepare to defend Malaya against the Japanese. They all went to the Civic Hall one morning, swore an oath of allegiance to the King and were then issued with uniforms and badges. They were told to report for training the following Tuesday at an old playing field on the edge of town.

Sessions were to be held on Tuesday and Thursday evenings and on Saturday mornings. In charge was a fierce sergeant-major. He was a Scot assigned to the regiment from the Indian Army. He sported a ginger beard and a handlebar moustache and did not take kindly to any light heartedness during training. He was called Charlie Bull, and the men quickly coined the nickname 'Charging Bull' because of his quick temper and bombastic manner. He was fond of swearing at the top of his voice at any man he suspected of slacking.

The Volunteers were an unlikely group to make up an army. They came from all walks of life: rubber planters, accountants, office workers, doctors, lawyers. Amongst their numbers there were also Chinese, Tamils and Malays, servants, shopkeepers and taxi drivers. None of them was used to such strenuous physical exercise, especially in the searing heat of the noon-day sun. On the first Saturday they were made to do press-ups and to run round the perimeter of the field. Tom found himself out of breath and sweating in his stiff new uniform and heavy boots.

After that they were sent round a hastily constructed obstacle course, climbing over walls and up ladders, swinging on ropes and walking along logs over a ditch. Most of the men found themselves red faced, sweating and out of breath. Tom was tired, but the hours he had spent pacing the rubber plantation and playing tennis at the club had paid off, and he was not as unfit as some of the others. He and Henry were the first to complete the course.

During the second session they were taught how to handle a rifle. They did not actually have any rifles to practice on, only broom handles, which Tom and Henry found amusing, much to the displeasure of the Bull. But they gradually moved on to handling real rifles. One day a consignment of Lee-Enfields awaited them when they arrived for training, and they were taught to clean and load them. Then they practised firing at a target pinned on a disused hut on the edge of the field.

There was usually a certain kind of bonhomie during training, but the news from Europe and the steady build-up of British forces on the Malay Peninsula tempered their sense that this was all just a jolly jape. Perhaps, they speculated over post-training drinks in a nearby hotel bar, there was an outside chance that they would actually be mobilised and would see active service. But it was scarcely believable, they assured themselves.

Life went on for Tom as before, with his days spent working on the plantation, training with the Volunteers three times a week and going on outings with Joy once or twice a week. He lived for those meetings, so that he could rest his eyes on her perfect face and listen to her gentle voice as she spoke of her childhood, her family, or of her day at school. He found her addictive, and she seemed to genuinely enjoy his company too. They did simple things together: a meal in an Indian café; a walk around the harbour to see the ships; a drive around the island to the beaches of Batu Ferringhi where they watched the sunset and took off their shoes and paddled in the warm lapping waves.

He was becoming obsessed with the thought of her. She occupied his mind all day and every day. He longed to take her in his arms and kiss her passionately, to taste those perfect lips and hold her slender body close to his. He was shy with her, though, and in about ten meetings he had only got as far as linking arms with her when they were out walking and kissing her stiffly on the cheek when they said goodbye. He was acutely aware of her strict and religious upbringing, and the importance of high standards of conduct in her community. He was terrified of putting a foot wrong, of making a false move. He dreaded her turning to him with her sweet smile and telling him that he had overstepped some invisible boundary and that it was out of the question for them to continue to see each other.

Looking back, he knew that it was that longing to be with her that was still sustaining him, here in this filthy sewer in the ground years later, when he should really have been dead months ago.

18

Laura's body was bathed in sweat. Sun slanted through the gaps in the wicker roof, making dancing patterns on the bare floor of the chalet. It was stifling; the tiny electric fan that rotated beside her made no impression on the turgid air. She stretched and glanced over at Luke who was asleep on his front on the low bed next to her. Rivulets of sweat formed on the amber skin of his back and ran down onto the mattress. Watching him, she wondered what it would have been like to slave here building the railway. Even sleeping in this heat was unbearable, let alone working.

Pulling on a T shirt and shorts, she stepped out onto the flimsy platform in front of the hut, which was lapped by the fast-flowing waters of the River Kwai.

She leaned on the wooden rail and stared out over the wide river, at the trees on the far bank and at the distant mountains, towards the Burmese border. Her body was heavy and clumsy with tiredness, but despite that she felt the thrill of anticipation. Today she would go to the museum and see if she could find any clues to who Arthur Stone was or anything about her father's time here. Looking out over the peaceful scene, the emerald rice fields shimmering in the heat beyond the river, it was hard to imagine that thousands of men had been brutalised and enslaved here just a few decades ago.

The owner of the huts came to speak to her, her two little children in tow. Laura was amazed at how the children were allowed to play right beside the bank of the fast-flowing river, while the young mother looked on with an indulgent smile.

'You want breakfast?' she asked. 'Your husband hungry?'

'He's not awake yet,' said Laura, and the woman smiled.

'He must be very tired. You come from Bangkok yesterday. The train very slow.'

It certainly had been slow. They'd sat sweating on wooden benches in third class as the train rattled through the outskirts of Bangkok and then moved west across the flat paddy fields, stopping at every outstation and tiny village on the route. They had arrived in Kanchanaburi at dusk and wandered through the streets of the little town, carrying their rucksacks, until someone had shown them the way to the river and the lines of little bamboo huts that had sprung up beside it to cater to backpackers.

They had eaten a delicious meal of pork fried rice cooked outside in a wok over a naked flame by the young woman's husband, and Laura had taken an outdoor shower in cold water. When she had returned to their hut, yawning from jet lag and ready to go to bed, she was surprised to see Luke dressed in a clean shirt and jeans, and sitting on the platform, smoking, feet dangling in the river.

'I think I'll go and check out the scene in town,' he said.

'Don't you want to go to bed? I thought we could go to the museum tomorrow morning. It would be good to make an early start.'

'Come on. Don't be a bore. It's a holiday too, Loz. Why don't we find a bar and relax over a few beers?'

'I don't think so. I'd really like to get over this jet lag. You go by yourself if you want to.'

'Suit yourself.' He jumped up, splashing river water onto the bamboo. He ruffled her hair as he walked past. 'I'll be back later.

Don't wait up.'

Despite her tiredness, sleep hadn't come to her. She had wondered where Luke was, had listened for the sound of his footsteps. The air was filled with strange sounds: the buzz of crickets and the cries of jungle creatures, wild dogs barking in the distant hills. After some time, she caught the distant thump of music, which grew louder and louder. She crawled out of her low bed, and peered through the slats of the door. She saw a huge raft chugging past on the river, pounding out disco music, lit up with revolving lights and crowded with people, drinking and dancing. After it had passed, she was just falling asleep when once again the thump-thump of drums broke the silence. This happened at regular intervals for several hours, and she had only just managed to drift off when she was awoken again by the flimsy hut wobbling as Luke opened the door and crawled into bed beside her.

'Where have you been?'

'I found a bar down the road. Got playing pool with a couple of Aussies. Sampled some of the local ganja. It's cool stuff. You should have come, Loz.'

'I'm not really into smoking dope. You know that.'

'Oh, lighten up, won't you. You're not in your solicitors' office now.'

She had lain awake for a long time after he had started snoring, mulling bitterly over what he had said.

'I'll have my breakfast, if that's OK, and then I'll go to the museum,' Laura said now to the Thai woman.

'Your husband not go with you?'

'He had a late night. I think he needs to sleep it off.'

She left the guesthouse and walked along the road beside the river. The map in her guidebook showed her that the Death Railway

Museum was on the river at the other end of town. Before she had gone ten paces, her body was bathed in sweat. There was no pavement, so she picked her way along next to a storm drain. She was forced to step out into the road at regular intervals to avoid food-stalls, parked vehicles and stray dogs lounging on the kerbside. After a while an open-backed vehicle drew up beside her, and the driver said, 'You want songtheaw?'

She looked at him puzzled, and he banged the side of the vehicle, smiling with blackened teeth.

'This songtheaw.'

'OK,' she agreed. 'Could you take me to the museum?'

There were already several other people sitting on the two wooden seats at the back of the vehicle. They smiled at her as she scrambled on board. It stopped at various places along the road to let people off and pick up others. She gathered that it was a cross between a taxi and a mini bus.

She was dropped outside the museum, and the other passengers waved as they drove off. She hesitated at the entrance. It didn't look like a museum. It consisted of several long, low huts made of bamboo. As she went towards the first one she read a sign that explained that the huts were replicas of the bamboo atap huts which the prisoners had built to house themselves whilst building the railway.

She ducked through the low door and went inside. The ticket booth was manned by a plump monk swathed in saffron robes.

Laura smiled at him as she paid ten baht for a ticket.

'I'm interested in finding out about my father. He was a prisoner on the railway,' she said.

The monk smiled broadly and waved a hand in the direction of the entrance.

'All information is here,' he said, inclining his head.

'Do you have any records about individual prisoners?'

'Only information that is here. No records,' he said, bowing again, the smile never leaving his lips.

'Thank you,' said Laura, disappointed.

A woman behind a table gave her a ticket and waved Laura forward. She moved through the hut slowly. There was a narrow walkway between two platforms made of split bamboo slats. This was where the men would have slept, she realised, without mattresses or bedding.

All along the platforms were displays showing the building of the railway and the conditions that the prisoners had to suffer. She read the startling statistic that 12,000 prisoners of those originally captured at the fall of Singapore had perished. Among the native labourers the death toll was much higher, reaching around 100,000 people. There were pictures depicting the rudimentary medical treatments. To cure the ulcerated legs of the prisoners, the limbs were soaked in the river so that the fish would come and nibble away the rotting flesh; if this didn't help, maggots were placed on the ulcers. Often the legs had to be amputated, and no anaesthetic was given to the prisoners when this was done. There were many photographs of stick-thin men wearing only loin cloths, called 'Jap Happys', sitting on the cramped beds in their huts or toiling on the railway, under the supervision of stony faced guards wielding sticks or guns. There were also many handwritten accounts pinned up on a notice board, all the more shocking for their simplicity and frank honesty. She scanned each one, searching for her father's name, or for Arthur Stone's, but found neither.

Most shocking of all were the graphic descriptions of the tortures that the Japanese guards or military police had meted out on prisoners who disobeyed the rules. One was to make the men hold a beam or railway sleeper above his head and stand for hours in the baking sun. Another was to force him to drink gallons of water, lay a board across his belly and jump on it until his stomach burst. Yet another was to tie his wrists and ankles to bamboo plants in the growing season so that as the bamboo grew upwards and outwards, the prisoner was slowly torn apart, limb from limb.

There was a gift shop beside the exit, but Laura walked straight through it and left the museum. She felt stunned and sickened. She knew from what she had read in London that the men, including her father, had suffered. But being here, in the sweltering heat, and seeing the displays, reading the accounts made it all the more shockingly real to her.

She walked to the edge of the river and sat down on the grass watching the water flow past, trying to come to terms with what she'd just seen. Luke should have been here with her. She would have had someone to talk to about all this.

When she got back to the guesthouse, as she had expected, Luke was still lying asleep in the darkened hut. She must have woken him when she opened the door because he sat up in bed, his hair tousled and falling over his face.

'Could you shut the door, Loz? I'm trying to sleep.'

'Don't you want to get up? It's almost lunch time.'

'Give it a rest, won't you? I'm on holiday.'

Laura took a deep breath. 'I've just been down to the museum,' she said in a low voice.

Luke lay down again, and turned over to face the other way.

'Was it interesting?' he asked, yawning.

'Interesting? Yes. That's one way to describe it. It was really shocking. You should have come. It explained so much about what the prisoners suffered. Illness, starvation, torture …'

'Could you tell me about that later? I'm feeling a bit fragile at the moment.'

'*You're* feeling a bit fragile? You're lying in bed, sleeping off a hangover!' she burst out. 'What about my dad? How do you think he felt? If he was sick and starving, if he had a fever, he would have been beaten in the stifling heat into doing a day's hard labour.'

Luke sat up, his face clouding over.

'Why don't you leave your preaching for another time? I'm not in the mood. You might be here on a personal crusade, to prove something to yourself, but leave me out of it, will you? I said I'd come to Thailand with you for a holiday. I'm not interested in wearing one of your hair shirts.'

Laura went out to the balcony. She leaned on the wooden rail and took deep breaths to calm herself. On the opposite bank a family of Thai children were diving off their veranda into the river, as lithe and agile as seals. How could Luke be so insensitive? He'd known that was why she had wanted to come. Surely he could show a bit more understanding?

On the other hand, she reasoned to herself, as she began to calm down, perhaps it was understandable that he wouldn't feel the same way as she did about what had happened here. Perhaps she should stop expecting him to share her interest and try to relax a bit more. That might be easier for her to do when they got to the beach. She'd promised to spend some time in Phuket before they went on to Penang, to see if there was any trace of Joy de Souza. Yes, perhaps she should give him a chance, try and see things from his point of view.

She heard a sound behind her and felt his hand caressing her shoulder. She turned to him.

'I'm sorry I was grouchy, Loz,' he said, crouching beside her. 'I think I overdid the old wacky baccy last night. I'll just have a quick shower. Then shall we go and see the famous bridge?'

She smiled at him, relieved. Perhaps it was going to be OK after all.

'Sure. I'll go and find out how to get there.'

* * *

Laura's heart turned over with emotion as the songtheaw rounded a bend in the road. There it was in front of them, the bridge on the River Kwai. It was a great and majestic steel structure, with its distinctive hooped girders spanning the wide fast-flowing river. She had seen it so many times in photographs, and in the famous movie that had given it its name, but it seemed incredible that it actually existed. It looked larger and higher than she had imagined, and as she looked at it, she thought again about all the men who had laboured and died to build it, this bridge, a symbol of all their suffering.

The area was thronging with people, and beside the bridge was a car park packed with tourist buses. Tour guides were giving little talks through mini loudspeakers to their groups, and tourists were laughing and chattering, posing for photographs next to the famous iron girders.

The area along the river was crammed with food stalls and little shops selling souvenirs: key rings in the shape of the bridge; miniature models; T shirts; handbags and post cards.

'This is pretty tacky,' said Laura.

'It's just another tourist attraction to these people,' said Luke. 'What did you expect?'

They joined the procession of sightseers walking along the railway line and towards the steel bridge. Soon, Laura was walking on it, partly on the rails and partly on wooden boards. There were gaps in the boards, and through them she could see the river rushing underneath her. As Laura walked the other people around her seemed to fade away, and she thought about how the bridge would have looked when it was being built by the prisoners. She imagined bamboo scaffolding rising from the river, flanking the sides of the bridge, and swarms of skinny half-naked men working away on the girders, using rope pulleys to lift them into place, fixing them into position and using great spanners to secure the bolts.

'I wonder if Dad was involved in building the bridge,' she said as they reached the other side and paused to look back at the precarious route they had taken.

'It would be difficult to find out,' said Luke.

'Well, I might be able to. If only I could find the account he's supposed to have left.'

'Why don't you just forget about that?' said Luke. 'It might have been something he just made up to please you. He must have known he was dying.'

'No. I'm sure there's something in what he said. I'm going to go back to Imperial War Museum when we get home. The old man who works there, the one who is an expert, might be back then. Maybe he'll know something about it.'

'I think you're clutching at straws. Why don't you give yourself a break and come along to the bar this evening. It's only just along the road from the guesthouse. It would do you good to have a beer or two and relax. You can meet those Aussie guys I was telling you about.' Reluctantly, she agreed.

Later, she sat at a wooden table outside Patpong Bar, listening to the melancholic guitars of 'Brothers in Arms' by Dire Straits, sipping Chang beer and trying to seem interested in the predictable drunken travellers' tales of the two Australians that Luke introduced her to: Jed was a prawn fisherman from Perth, his friend Dale, a builder from outside Sydney.

Laura's mind kept returning to the horrors she'd seen at the Death Railway Museum, and the recurring thought that Dad, and countless others had suffered untold miseries very near this place. To sit drinking the night away like this was somehow trivialising what had happened here.

'We're going to head down to the islands pretty soon,' said Dale. 'This place hasn't got a whole lot going for it, has it? Once you've seen the bridge and had an elephant ride along the river, that's about it.'

'Yeah,' said Jed. 'We went to the bridge today. It's not quite what it's cracked up to be, is it? And have you been to that god-awful museum along the river? Talk about depressing! I guess some folks might like that type of thing, but that ain't my idea of a holiday, walking around and looking at pictures of Jap torture treatments and pictures of fellas starving to death and the like.'

There was a silence. Luke was watching her, was waiting for her reaction.

She got up from the table. 'Look, I hope you guys don't mind if I call it a night. I'm feeling pretty tired. Not over my jet lag properly yet, I'm afraid.'

'Don't go, Loz. We've only just started,' said Luke.

'You can stay here. I'm sure you'll have a great evening without me. I'm just not feeling up to it, I'm afraid.'

She put a couple of hundred baht notes on the table and then walked away.

19

The next morning they took a taxi to the station to catch the River Kwai Train, which travelled along the track the prisoners had built and up towards the Burmese border. It arrived late at Kanchanaburi Station, and as on the journey from Bangkok the train had only third class carriages. Luke was morose as they waited on the platform. He was nursing his head.

'Jesus, that ganja was powerful stuff last night,' he said.

'I don't mind going on my own if you don't feel up to it.'

'No. I might as well see as much as I can while I'm here,' he said, but she sensed his discomfort as they climbed aboard and sat down on the wooden benches. The carriage was dingy and bare, painted brown, with old fashioned Thai advertisements for miracle toothpaste and jasmine tea stuck on its walls. The air was stifling and heavy and still as they waited for the train to move off. The tiny ceiling fans just stirred the hot air.

As soon as the train pulled out of the station and started chugging through the town, a tepid breeze began to filter through the open windows. Luke eased himself down into a lying position on the bench and covered his head with his hat.

'You're missing the view,' said Laura, but he was already asleep.

The train had left the town behind now and was rattling on an embankment between flat rice fields, following the wide river valley. After a few miles the valley narrowed, and the train slowed as it crossed a high embankment and then plunged into a cutting between giant black rocks. The train rocked and bumped over uneven track. They were so close to the rocks that Laura could make out the scars and hollows made by the tools the men had used to chip away the rock.

She consulted the map she had bought at the station.

'This is Chungkai Cutting, I think. This was all done by hand. I wonder if Dad ever worked here,' she mumbled to herself. Luke was still asleep.

After the cutting, the train ran beside the river for a while and then slowed right down to a walking pace as it eased itself along a stretch of track that ran along a trestle platform raised on stilts above the river. On one side, vertical black cliffs towered above the track; on the other, many feet below, the river flowed, fast and strong. Leaning out of the window, Laura could hear the wooden struts straining under the weight of the train. She had an image of half-naked men chopping down jungle trees for the platform with primitive pickaxes and carrying the tree trunks on their shoulders to the river bank, all the time under the watchful eyes of Japanese guards.

The train ran beside the river for several miles. It was beautiful. The lush green jungle spilled over the banks on the other side. The occasional rice barge or long tailed boat passed them in the opposite direction, moving quickly downriver with the speed of the current. Then the track parted from the river and plunged into the forest, through dense foliage where thick creepers hung over the track. The train chugged on through the craggy jungle-covered hills for miles, rattling over embankments, through cuttings, over rickety wooden bridges.

Laura began to feel annoyed again, as she watched Luke's head lolling on the seat. Why had he bothered to come along at all if he wasn't going to make any effort?

They reached the end of the line at Nam Tok, a tiny market town. The place was no more than a shanty town really, with the inevitable stalls and shops for day-trippers. Laura shook Luke awake and they got off the train.

'This is a bit of a shit-hole, isn't it?' said Luke, looking around. 'Hardly worth the trip really.'

'The trip isn't about this place. It's about the railway. Not that you saw anything,' she couldn't resist adding.

'No need to rub it in. Come on. Let's look around, now that we're here.'

They wandered around aimlessly, pursued by touts trying to sell them day-trips into the hills.

'I'm feeling like death warmed up,' said Luke. 'Let's see if we can get a drink and then get the next train back.'

They bought themselves bottles of Coca-Cola in a tiny run-down café behind the station and waited in the shade.

'Sorry, I'm a bit the worse for wear,' said Luke, sipping his drink, then lighting a cigarette.

'It doesn't matter. I can't expect you to share my interest in the place,' said Laura, looking down at the scarred table. 'We've only got one more day here anyway.'

'Yeah. Then we can hit the beach. That will be cool.'

She tried to smile. She was beginning to regret having agreed to spend a week in Phuket. If all he wanted to do was get drunk or stoned, there were bound to be even more opportunities for doing that there.

'Have you thought about what you're going to do when you get home?' he asked.

'To do?'

'Hmm. When are you due back at work?'

'I'm not sure I want to go back to work. Not that work, anyway.'

He frowned. 'What are you going to do then?'

She took a deep breath. 'Well, I thought I might do something different. Get a job in a legal aid firm or a law centre. Defending you in the magistrates' court that day gave me a bit of a taste for it.'

He was staring at her, still frowning. He drew on his cigarette and blew the smoke out in a long stream.

'You are joking.'

'No, perfectly serious. It's time I gave some thought to where I'm heading. I got a job in the city because I thought it would please Dad. But he didn't know what it was really like. I've never enjoyed it. The money's nice, obviously. But that's not everything. Why are you looking at me like that?'

'I can't really picture you in that role, that's all.'

'Well, thanks. You were happy enough for me to help you out when you needed me.'

'You're not the sort of girl who can get by on a small salary. You're used to earning loads of money. You've got expensive tastes.'

'I could get used to it. If I felt I was doing something worthwhile, the money wouldn't be so important. Anyway, what's it to you?'

He ground the fag end into the sandy floor and looked away.

'Nothing. It's your life, Loz. Look, the train's coming. Let's get out of here.'

On the way back, Laura stared out of the train window at the darkening tropical sky. She was puzzled by his attitude. Surely, considering his political views, he would support her plans. She watched him as he sipped a bottle of Chang Beer moodily and stared out of the opposite window.

She suddenly remembered the conversation they had about selling the house, about how he had been so keen to persuade her to evict Ken and Marge. Then an uncomfortable thought struck her: perhaps she was attractive to Luke precisely because of her earning capacity and prospects, rather than in spite of them. He had spent months ribbing her for her champagne lifestyle and yuppie tastes. Yet he'd been happy enough to stay in her flat and let her pay for everything they did together. And now, when she had told him that she was planning to abandon her well-paid job, he was sulking. I'm so gullible, she thought. How on earth did I not realise this before?

The more she thought about it the more angered she became by Luke's attitude, by the recurring idea that he might have been using her all this time. By the time the train squeaked and clattered back across the River Kwai on its way to Kanchanaburi Station, she had made up her mind about what she would do.

20

Tom did not have the strength or the stomach to eat the food that the guard continued to shove roughly through the bamboo bars. Every so often, with a great effort of will, he managed to lift his arm to guide the tin cup of water to his lips. They were so cracked and swollen, and his tongue and mouth so parched and sore that it was painful to force it down. He knew that he must though, if he was to have any chance of getting out of this hell.

His memories had become vivid to him, vivid and bright and real. It was his present existence that his mind rejected: the camp, the shadowy figures moving about the clearing, the Japanese guards sauntering around by the guardhouse, the other prisoners assembling for parade and dinner had ceased to be reality for him now. He was only dimly aware of movement and the colours and shapes of his surroundings. His mind found comfort in the past, and he let it.

He tried to go back to the time when he had first arrived on Penang. He wanted to find solace in the memory of those carefree, pleasure-filled days, but instead his mind carried him to the time when the atmosphere on the island had begun to change. When the war that had previously been thousands of miles away began to threaten to disrupt the life on this tropical paradise.

It was around the middle of 1941. Training with the Volunteers had previously had a recreational feel, but it now became more intense and took on a serious note. The newspapers were filled with accounts of Japanese aggression: the escalation of the war in China and the hideous atrocities that were committed there, the occupation of Northern Indo-China with the co-operation of the Vichy French, the US trade embargo on Japan. It suddenly felt as though this perfect life could really be under threat.

The Malay Peninsula was filling up with troops from India, Australia and Britain. According to reports in *The Straits Times*, the bars and fleshpots of Singapore were crawling with off-duty soldiers in the evenings, hell-bent on getting drunk and brawling the night away.

'Do you seriously think they'll need a bunch of amateurs like us, with all the trained professional manpower they've now got on tap?' Tom asked Henry as they sweated their way round the obstacle course one sultry evening under the watchful eye of the Bull.

'They need all the manpower they can get, old man. The Japs have no shortage of men, all ready and willing to die for the Emperor.'

A month or so later, they were taken for a week's training to the jungle on the mainland. It was the first time Tom had been off the island of Penang in over two years.

When he asked for leave to go, Jones, the manager of the plantation said, 'By all means take your leave, Ellis, you deserve it. Most people would have been due to go home at some point. But with the situation in Europe as it has been …'

'I haven't wanted to go home,' said Tom quickly. 'There's nothing for me there.'

The manager eyed him curiously for a moment.

'Well, off you go with the Volunteers then, lad. We can manage for a week without you. But I must say, it doesn't sound like much of a holiday to me.'

They were taken by covered army trucks deep into the jungle

in the hills behind Butterworth. There they were taught the basics of jungle warfare. They learned how to camouflage themselves so they were invisible to the enemy, how to move silently through the undergrowth in tight columns, how to use the trees and foliage to 'dig in', how to make an invisible jungle camp and how to survive on berries and plants. Once out of the jungle, they were taken to a camp on the edge of the town, where they practised with hand grenades, bayonet fighting and hand-to-hand combat.

Like the training sessions in Georgetown, this all seemed to Tom a bit like a boy-scout outing. He wasn't yet quite convinced that there might one day be some practical application for all this preparation. After a couple of days, he found that he was missing Joy with an almost physical longing. He spent his nights under the canvas thinking of her, picturing the moment that he would see her again. He could not wait to get back to her.

They met on the waterfront in Georgetown, in the early evening of the day he returned home. He took her in his arms and kissed her.

'I've missed you so much, Joy,' he murmured as they began to walk along the waterfront.

'I've missed you too,' she said, tucking her arm into his.

His heart was filled with happiness. It was a beautiful evening. The buildings on the waterfront were already lit up and the reflection of the lights danced on the darkening water. He had a sudden impulse.

'Come on, let's go and celebrate my return at the club.'

She stopped walking.

'Oh no, I don't think so,' she said. 'I don't think I'd be allowed in there.'

'Nonsense. They're not like that there.'

She took her arm out of his.

'I think that they are. Have you ever seen a coloured person in there? Apart from the servants, of course.'

'I suppose not. But I think it's probably more because the membership is very expensive than for any other reason. I'm sure it will be OK. Everyone is very friendly and relaxed. Let's give it a try.'

She dragged behind as he strode along the harbour promenade towards the elegant white building. It was a long time since Tom had been there. He was looking forward to sinking into one of the easy chairs in the lounge bar and ordering a whisky stengah.

He strolled up the front steps, across the entrance hall and into the lounge bar. It was quiet, but there were a couple of parties of older members playing bridge at the corner tables and one or two men drinking at the bar.

As they entered, the room fell silent. People turned to stare at them both.

'Tom, I don't think …' Joy began nervously, hanging back.

'Just sit down, Joy, please. We'll order a drink.'

Reluctantly she sat down on an armchair, perching on the edge uneasily. The head waiter came over, looking immaculate in his white starched uniform and gloves. He wore an awkward, apologetic expression.

'I'm sorry, Mr. Ellis, but the young lady is not a member.'

'No, she is not a member, but she is my guest. I would like to buy her a drink.'

'I'm sorry, sir, but I cannot serve her. I'm afraid it would be against club rules.'

'What rules are those? I'm not aware of any such rule'

Joy broke in, 'Tom, please, let's go. It doesn't matter.'

'Yes. It *does* matter,' said Tom, raising his voice. 'Could you please bring us the cocktail menu, Abdul?'

'I'm sorry, sir, but I cannot serve the young lady. Club rules say that only Europeans can drink in the bar.'

'Could you please ask the manager to come and speak to me?' said Tom, but the manager, an Italian with brilliantined black hair and moustache, was already bustling over.

'Mr. Ellis, I'm sorry, but I am going to have to ask you to leave. It is against the club rules to serve a non-European.' He was smiling and spoke smoothly as if he was explaining that a particular dish was not on the menu.

Tom was about to protest, but he saw that Joy had already got up and was hurrying away, pushing through the tables towards the door.

'Joy! Joy! Don't go.'

He ran after her, but as he reached the door of the bar she was disappearing out of the front entrance. As he crossed the hall after her, he caught sight of Millicent coming down the stairs. Her eyes lit up momentarily when she saw him, but then she realised that he was running after another woman and her expression changed. She narrowed her eyes and shot him a look laced with pure venom.

He caught up with Joy on the front path. He grabbed her arm, but she shook him off.

'Leave me alone,' she said. 'How could you! Are you blind? You must have known what would happen. You've lived here for over two years. And I told you.' She was furious. Her face was flushed and eyes bright with anger. It reminded him of the time she had flared up against her father in defence of Tom during dinner with her family.

'I'm sorry, Joy. I'm so sorry. I should have listened to you. Please forgive me.'

'No.' Her eyes filled with tears of humiliation. 'I've never been so insulted in all my life. And you! You made it worse. All those people staring, looking at me as if I were a piece of dirt.'

'Look, I'm sorry. I'll do anything to make it up to you. Shall I drive you home?'

'No. I'm not going anywhere with you. I'll get a rickshaw. I'll go on my own. Please don't try to contact me again, Tom. I never want to see you again.'

She shook her arm free from him and marched off down the street and towards the square where the rickshaw-wallahs hung about, waiting for passengers. He stood there helplessly and watched her go.

'What a bloody fool I am,' he said, his head in his hands. 'What a bloody, bloody fool.'

For the next fortnight, Tom saw nothing of Joy. He went about his daily routines with a heavy heart. He was up at dawn to meet the workers at the plantation headquarters, inspecting their work and the trees on his patch all morning, and then going back to his house for lunch and a bath. All the colour and pleasure seemed to have vanished from his life. Even the view from his balcony had lost its charm. The sun seemed too hot, and the landscape too vibrant, too green. For the first time since he had arrived, he thought longingly of England, the gentle rain and the soft greens and browns of the countryside, so easy on the eye.

He drove up to Joy's house in the Eurasian quarter twice to try to talk to her. Each time her mother had come out onto the porch.

'I am sorry, Mr. Ellis, but she says that she cannot see you,' Joy's mother told him, unsmilingly. He remembered how welcoming she had been the time Joy had taken him home for dinner. Her discomfort now seemed to reinforce his own unhappiness.

The second time the message was the same, and he walked back to the car, disconsolate. He sat in the driver's seat watching the little house for several minutes, waiting for the twitch of a lace curtain to show that Joy was watching him too. But there was no movement, and he drove away feeling numb and helpless.

A few days after the incident at the club he received a terse note from the chairman of the committee informing him that his membership had been withdrawn. When he went in to collect some belongings he had left in a locker, he went to see the man in his office. The chairman was immensely fat, with rolls of midriff flowing over the arms of his chair. He was perspiring profusely and kept mopping his red face with a handkerchief.

'Is it because I brought Miss de Souza here?' Tom asked.

'Well, not directly, although that was a very foolish thing to do. You should have known what would happen. It's an unwritten rule, but it is still a rule all the same, one that we are all careful to uphold. We don't want to let our standards slip. However, it wasn't entirely that, although your association with her has been noted by several members, I should mention. No, one of the members of the committee proposed a vote that your membership should be withdrawn, and I'm afraid that the vote was carried. It was generally felt that you were not quite the right material for membership.' 'Who was it?'

'I couldn't possibly tell you that. Suffice it to say that it was one of our most respected and influential members.'

As he passed the lounge on his way out, he caught a glimpse of Millie standing at the bar. She smiled at him, and it was a malicious, triumphant smile.

'James Atherton forced me out, of course,' said Tom, when he told Henry about what had happened. 'Not that I'd set foot in that damned place again after the way they treated Joy.'

'I'm frightfully sorry, old chap. It'll be Millie's doing of course.

She's never forgiven you, you know. She's never been thrown over before. I'll miss our games of tennis, I must say.'

But there were to be no more games of tennis anyway. One evening, a few days later, a Chinese boy from the post office in Georgetown brought a telegram by bicycle. Tom's heart stood still; he immediately thought of his parents, and of the bombs falling in Britain. When he opened the envelope, what it actually said shocked him as much.

Tom stared at the words in disbelief. It was from the Volunteer Force. He was to report in two days' time to the docks in Georgetown to join the Regiment. He was to wear full uniform, bring his kit and military papers. Tom stared at the words for a long time. He realised that this almost certainly spelled the end of this delicious interlude in his life. One way or another it was certain to be over for good.

His first thought was that he needed to say goodbye to Joy. He would try to meet her one last time. The next morning he scribbled a note and drove into town. He knew she would be teaching, so he went straight to the mission school. The woman in the office looked at him with suspicion.

'Could I possibly speak to Miss de Souza, please? It is urgent.'

'Well, I am afraid she is teaching at this moment, sir.'

'Please. It is very important.'

She sighed loudly, but got up from her chair and disappeared in the direction of the classrooms. He waited in the echoing corridor. The earthy smells and the sound of children chanting in the classrooms reminded him of his own school, and took him straight back to his childhood.

The receptionist came back in a few moments. She was alone.

'I'm sorry, sir, but Miss de Souza is unable to meet you,' the woman said in a firm voice, returning to her desk. 'I suggest that you leave now.'

He swallowed. 'Would you be kind enough to hand this note to her? Please.'

The woman sighed with displeasure, but nodded.

'Thank you for this.' He handed over the note to the receptionist. She turned and headed back towards the classroom. He waited for a few moments, hoping that Joy would come out, that he would see her one last time before he left Penang. When the receptionist returned alone and stared at him, he turned and went out into the blazing sunshine, feeling as though his whole world had collapsed.

Tom spent the rest of the day with a heavy heart, packing his belongings and clearing the paperwork in his office. He stowed his few possessions from the bungalow into his trunk: the dinner jacket he'd worn to the dinner at High Tops, his shirts, his precious linen suit, the photograph of his mother and father on a trip to Eastbourne, the photograph of himself and Joy they had taken on Penang Hill, on their first outing together. Staring at it, he wondered whether to take it with him, but the frame was too large to fit in the kit bag. Closing the lid, he buckled the leather strap, thinking as he did so that he might never see the contents again. He marked the trunk with the address in Gordon Square. There was nowhere else to send it.

The next morning, he went down to the workers' quarters beyond the plantation headquarters, where they lived with their families, and said goodbye to his team of tappers. He gave them each a few Malay dollars as a parting gift and felt a pang of sadness as he trudged back to the bungalow. He had grown attached to them. They had a hard existence, up before dawn and toiling day after day in the intolerable heat for a meagre wage, but they never complained. What would become of them if the Japanese did invade?

Sleep hardly came that night. He tossed and turned, his

heart filled with regret for what had happened with Joy, and with apprehension for what the future might hold for him. He didn't feel ready to go to war; he had never wanted to be a soldier. He realised, with shame, that he was afraid.

Jones, the manager, had offered to take Henry and Tom down to Georgetown in the morning. They had to be at the docks by eight in the morning. As they drew up on the quayside in his old Ford at ten to eight, crowds of men in uniform were already milling about beside the boats.

A passenger liner was moored up, and crowds of civilians were boarding it, dragging bags and trunks and all their worldly possessions with them. Panic had set in and everyone who could was taking a passage back to England or to Australia. Tom thought he spotted Sir James and Millicent elbowing their way onboard, a turbaned coolie carrying a large leather trunk behind them. He turned away.

Tom's stomach was churning with nerves. As he got out of the car and swung his pack on his back, he caught sight of Joy emerging from beside one of the go-downs. She came running towards him. 'Tom, Tom,' she cried breathlessly, 'I got your note. I found out what time you were leaving, and I came to say goodbye.'

He took her arm and they walked quickly away from the crowd, into a little alleyway beside the go-down.

'I'm so sorry I wouldn't see you before. I was so cruel to you. I've been feeling terrible about it.'

'Don't worry. You came, and that's all that matters,' he said, relief suddenly flooding through him.

'I'm so sorry about the club, Joy. I wish I had never even mentioned it. It was a terrible error of judgement. I should have known.'

'Please, don't mention it. I know now that you didn't mean to upset me. Don't waste time talking about that. Look, I have brought you something.'

She handed him a photograph of her in a studio, dressed in her best clothes, looking surprised by the flash.

'Thank you. I shall treasure this,' he said.

'I have written on the back,' she said, and he turned it over and read the words: 'To my dear Thomas. Good luck. Joy de Souza. Penang, November 1941.'

'What about you and your family?' he asked. 'What are you going to do?'

'My father has some relatives in Singapore. If there is an invasion, we can go there.'

'Well, you should be safe there at least,' he said. 'It is supposed to be a fortress, after all.'

'Yes. I'm sure we will be safe. Please don't worry about me.'

'I'll be back, Joy,' he whispered, moving closer to her. 'Whatever happens, I'll come back and find you.'

A whistle blew down on the waterfront.

'I have to go now,' he said, and took her in his arms. He felt her firm slender body close to his. She was looking up at him, tears in her eyes. He bent to kiss her, but she drew away.

'There are people watching,' she said, colouring.

'To hell with them,' and he kissed her, but he felt her resisting. It was stiff and awkward, and lacked the passion and spontaneity their kisses usually had. She drew away.

'I'll think of you, Tom. I'll pray for you,' she said, the tears spilling down her cheeks. He suppressed a sob.

'I'll think of you all the time, Joy,' he said, knowing that he had to go, but unable to tear himself away from her.

'Go! You have to go now.' Her voice caught in her throat 'Look, they are lining up.'

He brushed her cheek again, then turned and strode away. As he reached the others and fell into line, he turned and looked back. She was still standing there, watching, looking vulnerable amid the towering buildings and machinery of the quayside.

As the ferry cast off and gradually drew away from the docks, Tom stood at the rail. He could see Joy still standing there. He watched the white figure recede slowly and eventually merge into the buildings behind her. Even then he kept staring at the spot where she stood until it faded completely from sight.

When the ferry reached Butterworth, the men were crowded on to army trucks and driven through the town and out into the countryside. They did not have to go far before they reached a small airfield with a few wooden huts at one end overlooking the Straits.

From there they could still make out the buildings on the waterfront at Georgetown. They were informed that this was where they were going to stay and that they should pitch their tents on the perimeter of the base.

'This is the Butterworth Airbase,' boomed the Bull. 'We're going to be here for a few days, training and preparing defences.'

There were some antiquated looking aircraft parked at the end of the grass runway.

'Do you think those old rust buckets will actually fly?' Tom asked Henry.

Henry looked at the aircraft and shook his head slowly.

'My God ... Is that the best that the great British Empire can muster?'

Ron, one of the Volunteer planters, overheard him and said, 'Don't worry, whatever we've got will be more than a match for the

Japs. They're hopeless airmen, all of them short-sighted. Have you seen the little pebble glasses they all wear? They'd never beat our chaps in a dog-fight.'

'You're sure about that, are you, Ron?' piped up Barry Cliff, the journalist who had predicted their fates long ago at the Penang Club. 'I sincerely hope you don't have to eat your words one day.'

Soon they settled into a strict routine, closely resembling the week-long exercise in the jungle a few weeks before. Tom had difficulty believing that this time it was for real. They pitched their tents on some waste-ground behind the wooden buildings on the first evening. The next morning they were awoken at dawn. After a rudimentary breakfast they spent the day doing physical-training exercises, rifle practice and learning how to use the anti-aircraft guns that had been installed in shallow ditches around the perimeter of the airfield. After a few days the routine became boring. They spent a great deal of time playing cards and watching the old Buffalo aircraft take off for reconnaissance flights over Thailand. They began to wonder why they had been mobilised at all.

But after a couple of weeks, everything changed. One day they were awoken before dawn by the drone of aircraft overhead. From the sound of the engines Tom could make out that these were not British Buffaloes. Everyone scrambled out of their tents, dressed hurriedly and ran to their positions beside the anti-aircraft guns. Three of the aircraft on the airfield were taxiing to take off. Tom watched as they lumbered along the bumpy runway and lurched unsteadily into the sky in pursuit of the enemy.

The Bull was apoplectic, running about, shouting meaningless orders in all directions. Before the Volunteers could get to their guns, the enemy aircraft were swarming overhead. There were dozens of them. They swooped in low, engines screaming, strafing the buildings, dropping bombs on the airfield, which exploded with ear-splitting crashes, spraying mounds of grass and earth in all directions and leaving jagged craters. Tom fired as hard and as fast as he could. A thrill went through him; one of his rounds had hit a low flying aircraft. The plane began to stutter and list sideways, eventually diving off in the direction of the sea.

His whole body was shaking as he fired the great gun. It was shaking with adrenalin though, not fear. His heart was pumping fast, and his mind was clear and fully focused. He glanced around at the other men at his station. They were all concentrating hard, sweat standing out on their brows, their eyes shining.

Soon all the wooden airbase buildings were on fire and some of the platoon were trying to douse the flames with a hose. The flames leapt up into the blue of the morning sky, black smoke billowing. Three aircraft on the ground had all been hit by incendiary bombs, their fuel tanks exploding in flames, their fabric burning in a bright yellow flourish until all that remained were the blackened metal frames.

Most of the enemy aircraft had disappeared by now, having inflicted maximum damage on the airfield in a matter of minutes, but there was still a dogfight going on in the sky above them. The lumbering RAF Buffalo seemed to be no match for the more manoeuvrable Japanese aircraft, but the British pilot was persistent, circling back repeatedly, looping around and firing round upon round at the other plane. Eventually the British plane was forced to come limping back onto land, its engine spluttering, its fuel pouring out from a hole on its side.

When the raid was over, the men were ordered to repair the airfield so that it could be used to land other aircraft. A wire came through that airfields further north were being evacuated and their aircraft relocated to Butterworth.

'And that's not the end of it,' said the Bull. 'I've just been informed that the Japs have landed in the north, in Kota Bharu. Our lads put up a fight but they got through anyway. They've taken the airfield there, and they are now on their way south. They bombed Singapore last night too. There was a lot of damage. There are rumours that they bombed the US base at Pearl Harbour. The Japs really mean business.'

The men exchanged looks. So this was it. No more boy-scout exercises.

They repaired the airfield as best they could. Soon after they had finished, they heard the drone of aircraft once again. This time, a fleet of British planes started to land, coming to a stop near the burned out buildings.

The next three days saw repeats of what had happened on the first day. The British planes were refuelled and took off each morning in search of enemy aircraft. This was closely followed by an attack by Japanese bombers on the airfield, bombing and strafing the field and the men on the ground. Some soldiers were hit, some killed. They were whisked away by lorry to a nearby field hospital.

On the fourth day, after their usual morning attack on the airfield, the Japanese aircraft turned on Georgetown. From his position behind the gun Tom watched in horror as swarms of aircraft flew in and dropped bombs onto the city. Some of the planes even dived in and flew low as if to fire on the ground. Smoke was soon billowing from some buildings, while others tottered and collapsed in clouds of white dust. Tom thought of Joy and her family. She had said they were going to Singapore. Had they already left? He hoped they had. He was stunned by the sight of the burning city, the city he had made his home and loved.

The next day they were ordered to abandon the airfield and were taken south by truck. The coast road took them through endless fields and plantations interspersed with patches of wild jungle. Through the trees they got occasional glimpses of the shimmering sea.

Morale was low on that journey south. The men hardly spoke, musing on the bad news that was delivered to them daily by the Bull. For the past few days, all they had heard from the north of Malaya was a litany of defeats, with the Japanese advancing virtually unchecked down the peninsula. They had taken Jitra and Penang. They had also sunk two seemingly invincible battleships, the Prince of Wales and the Repulse. It seemed scarcely believable to the Volunteers that this army of puny Asians was inflicting cruel defeats daily on the army of the great British Empire.

The men were dropped on the sandy banks of Selangor Estuary and told to pitch their tents. It had been raining, and there was nowhere dry to do this, so they pitched them on the wet scrubby grass at the top of the sand.

They were here to support a battalion of Jats from the Indian Army, manning pillboxes and defences in case of invasion by the Japanese.

'I thought the Japanese were coming down by land,' Tom said to Henry.

'Yes, by bicycle according to some accounts,' said Henry. 'But I don't think that anyone knows exactly what they're up to. Judging by our disastrous form against them so far, we're probably here to be on the safe side.'

The banks of the estuary were well defended, though. The Jats had already installed lethal-looking coils of barbed wire along the beach, and concrete pill-boxes had been constructed every hundred yards or so. Tom's section was detailed to defend one of these pillboxes; twelve of them were needed to man it and its two Bren guns. They spent long hours watching the calm blue sea and the mouth of the river. It felt as though they had been consigned to a backwater. Occasionally a vessel would pass, usually a ferry or cargo boat bound for Singapore.

Tom spent his hours on watch in anguish, thinking about Joy and Penang. He had a recurring vision of her family fleeing through the pandemonium on the streets of Georgetown as buildings burned and collapsed around them. Is this what had happened? He tried to focus on the memory he had of her at the docks, when they had said goodbye to each other, and he clung to that image instead.

Henry was on watch when he spotted a Japanese vessel. It was early evening, and the sun was dipping towards the western horizon.

'Enemy craft!' Henry bellowed. The rest of the section sprang to their positions. Tom grabbed his rifle and peered out through the slit in the pillbox. It was not what he had expected. What he saw was a battered old ferry, listing slightly to one side, lumbering past at a few knots. It was towing a flotilla of ungainly small vessels. They looked like-flat bottomed barges.

'Landing craft,' whispered the Bull, his rifle cocked and ready to fire through the slit. 'They're going to try to come up the river and land.'

He waited until the craft was exactly parallel with the pill box then gave the order.

'Fire!'

The entire section opened fire on the vessel simultaneously. There was a lot of shouting and screaming on board as the fire was returned by machine guns on the deck. It was the first experience Tom had of being fired at directly. Bullets pinged off the pill box. As soon as he had finished firing, he ducked beneath the slit to reload. One of the men next to him was shot in the eye. Blood spurted in every direction, spattering Tom's face and uniform. Tom watched aghast as the man fell screaming to the floor, both hands clamped over his eye.

'Concentrate, Ellis, or you'll be next. Keep your bloody head down, boy!' shouted the sergeant. So Tom ducked, reloaded, then aimed and fired.

The old boat lumbered on, moving towards the mouth of the river. Through the slit they could see bodies slumped dead or injured on the deck. Someone from the next section started throwing hand grenades. A couple of them hit the landing craft, causing them to buckle and list and eventually dip beneath the water. A great cheer went up from the British and Indian lines as this happened.

Then, from far away, they heard the familiar drone of aircraft. Within seconds the planes were upon them, diving low and firing directly at the pill-boxes. Tom and the others carried on shooting at the vessel. Tom was focused on this moment; firing and surviving, that was all he could think about. It was as if nothing else existed. The pillbox was full of acrid smoke from the guns, and Tom's eyes were smarting, but he kept firing, his jaw rigid with concentration. The planes went over again and again, gunning straight at the slit. Each time they came near, Tom crouched down to avoid the bullets, but as one aircraft passed, machine guns clattering, he heard a squeal of pain next to him. Henry was squirming on the floor of the pillbox, shouting. He had been hit in the head, his skull shattered on one side.

Tom looked down and saw his friend lying there, blood and soft tissue oozing from the wound on his head. He felt vomit rise to his mouth and his knees went weak and almost gave way.

'Keep at it, Ellis,' shouted the Bull. 'He's gone. There's nothing you can do. The medics will take him out. Don't worry.'

Henry's limbs were twitching now, but he had stopped shouting. All that came from his lips was a thin moan. Two medical volunteers rushed in with a stretcher and heaved Henry on to it. Tom turned back to his gun, but the image of Henry's shattered skull kept coming back to him. After about an hour of constant bombardment the Japanese vessel gave up trying to get into the mouth of the river and turned round to go back up the coast. A great cheer went up as the Volunteers sensed victory. When the boat was a safe distance away they came out of their pill-boxes and ditches and watched it make its clumsy progress northwards along the shore. There was an atmosphere of celebration. Men hung about on the beach to watch and jeer, but Tom just sat on the sand, his head in his hands. He was thinking of Henry, his cheerful unassuming friendship, and the kindness he had shown Tom over the past years. He could not find it in him to celebrate with the others.

21

Tom was awoken from his reverie by the corrugated iron cover being ripped from above him and the shocking glare of the sun hitting him like a physical blow. Then two pairs of rough hands reached into the pit and dragged him upwards. He looked up bewildered. The blank closed faces of the two Japanese guards gave away nothing. They didn't meet his eye. Behind them he could hear the Ripper's voice jabbering away at them.

Were they taking him to his death? Racked with pain and fever, he would almost welcome a bullet now, to put an end to it all. He felt less than human, stinking and filthy, stuck to his clothes with his own excrement and vomit.

The guards dragged him out and tried to stand him up. When they left him on his feet he immediately collapsed to the ground. His legs, weakened by days of stooping and crouching and staying in the same position, refused to hold his body weight.

The Ripper shrieked something to the guards, and they left him there, sprawled on the dirt beside the stinking hole, his cheek pressed into the rough soil. He closed his eyes to blot out the savage glare of the sun. He did not know how long he'd been lying there when he heard footsteps. He opened his eyes to see two of the medical orderlies from the hospital hut kneeling beside him. One of them was slapping his cheek.

'Are you still with us, mate?' he was asking tentatively.

Tom opened his mouth and tried to answer, but no words would come. In the end he just nodded his head wearily and closed his eyes again.

He felt the orderlies gently manoeuvring his broken body onto the bamboo stretcher they'd set on the ground beside him, then picking him up and carrying him quickly across the clearing.

'We really thought you were gone, Ellis,' the doctor said cheerfully in the hospital hut, leaning over him. 'I sent the chaps over to collect a corpse, but amazingly you're still hanging on. You've got malaria. And dysentery, too, by the looks of it. And you're more than half starved. It's unbelievable that you're still alive. Now these men will clean you up, and we'll give you some food. You'll soon be on the road to recovery.'

Tom felt tears stinging his eyes at the sound of the doctor's reassuring voice. All he had heard since the death of his friends was the abuse of the guards.

'Now, Ellis, luckily you've got what we call "gate fever". Something to live for. It doesn't matter what it is – could be a woman, kids, some sort of ambition. Whatever it is, it sees people through. And that's the reason you kept going when you were in the pit.'

He closed his eyes and let the men cut his filthy shorts from his legs and wash his body with rags dipped in a bucket of cold water. But when they came to take his shirt he grabbed it back.

'What's the matter, mate?' asked the orderly gently.

Tom was still unable to speak. He pointed to the breast pocket of the shirt, his eyes pleading.

'Something in there, mate?'

The orderly drew out the picture of Joy and stole a glance at it.

'Is this what kept you going in there?' he asked softly. Tom nodded, swallowing the lump that was rising in his throat.

'I can see why. Now I'll just put it under your pillow so you'll know it's there.' The orderly slipped the photograph under the folded rice sack that served as Tom's pillow. Once again, his eyes filled with tears at this act of kindness.

They brought him boiled water and a small bowl of rice flavoured with fish. One of them spooned it into his mouth, and he managed to force it down his swollen throat. Then he lay back on the rice sack, panting with exhaustion. His back and torso still ached painfully from the beatings, and his whole frame was protesting at being crammed into the same position for all those days.

He felt the fever coming on him again. He began to shiver and his head throbbed, feeling as if it would explode. The men brought more rice sacks to put over him, but he still lay there, shivering, his teeth chattering uncontrollably, sweat pouring from his brow.

His mind wandered again to his past. He was back in Singapore with the rest of his depleted platoon. They were marching defiantly over Johor Causeway to the sound of shells and gunfire and explosions as the Japanese bombarded the mainland defences. Smoke billowed from the naval base to the east, and a cloud of dense black smoke from the oil depots that had been set on fire during the shelling hung over the island.

The whole army had withdrawn from the peninsula to the island, and after the last troops had crossed, the causeway had been blown. Places that had previously just been points on a map now gave their names to notorious defeats. The sound of these names struck fear in the hearts of the Volunteers. They knew all about the brave fighting by the British and Indian Divisions at Kampar and the Slim River. They had heard all about the battle of Johor, where the Australian Eighth Division had put up a stubborn defence, and of the defeats at Muar and Gemas. The Japanese had been wily and fearless in battle, cutting off divisions by going behind them. And they had superior equipment. They had tanks, whereas the British had none. Japanese planes dominated the air. But at least there was some hope, the Volunteers had been told, of holding Singapore.

Tom felt filthy and dog-tired. He had not had a shower or a proper night's sleep for weeks. It was either steamy and hot under the canvas or, if it was raining, the tents leaked and the soldiers were soaked to the skin. They were permanently wet, either soaked in rainwater or bathed in their own sweat. They had been camping for several days in a rubber plantation on the edge of the city, listening to the shelling on the north coast, waiting for the Japanese to cross the narrow stretch of water and make their final bid for the island.

The plantation ran along the edge of one of the main roads into the city. Opposite was a line of buildings that had been bombed during an air raid. The roofs had caved in, the front walls were crumbling and the insides were blackened with smoke. The road was strewn with smashed-up vehicles, abandoned rickshaws and, worst of all, the putrefying bodies of several Malays and Chinese who had been struck down by the blasts. From where Tom sat on the edge of a storm drain that ran round the perimeter of the plantation, he could see the clouds of flies buzzing around the bodies in the heat of the day. He stared in horror. He could hardly believe that these stiff shapes were human bodies.

His eyes smarted constantly from the black cloud of smoke that was ever present. When it rained, black soot from the cloud poured down on them, staining their uniforms and streaking their skin. Tom felt strangely calm now. Having seen the horrors of the raids on the air base and the battle at Selangor River, he realised that it was possible to survive. He might just come through this alive.

Now they were waiting for orders. Which part of the city

would they have to defend against the invaders? Every so often a formation of Japanese planes would scream overhead, dropping bombs indiscriminately, swooping in low to strafe people on the ground. The tension was palpable. The crash and rumble of the guns was moving closer by the day. The soldiers around him were growing increasingly nervous. Several of the Chinese and Malay Volunteers started pleading with the Bull to let them go. If they were not in uniform, they said, they could slip away into the city and find relatives, and the Japanese might leave them alone.

'I can't let you go. You've sworn an oath of allegiance to the King. But I understand how you feel. When I'm in my tent at night, I sleep pretty soundly,' he added quietly.

That night, the rain dripped off the trees and on to the canvas above Tom. Unable to sleep, and while listening nervously to the bombardment on the edge of town, he heard rustling, and through the thin canvas of his tent saw a few shadowy forms creep away from the camp and lose themselves among the rubber trees. In the morning they found that a few of the Chinese and Malay Volunteers had taken the Bull's hint and abandoned their posts.

The section was now severely depleted. There were only about ten men left. As dawn broke they heard the sound of vehicles roaring towards them down the road, swerving to avoid the bodies and wrecked cars. The Volunteers drew their rifles and crouched in the storm drain, ready to fire. Tom's nerves tingled; his finger felt taut on the trigger. The vehicles rounded the bend and came into view, and they saw that they were full of Australian troops withdrawing from the battle. As they belted past, the men were leaning out of the trucks and shouting, 'Move boys. You want to move. You want to get out of here as quick as you can. The Japs are coming. Move!'

'Take no notice of them,' said the Bull firmly. 'HQ has ordered us to stay at our posts and wait for the enemy.'

After that Tom's nerves increased. Every sound on the road seemed to signal the forward march of the Japanese. The men around him became jumpy, too, ready to fire at anything.

It was about an hour later that they came. As he crouched in the storm drain, he watched, incredulous, as a convoy of hulking green tanks bore down on them, firing from the turrets. Tom had never seen a tank before. His mouth went dry, and he could not swallow. He tightened his finger on the trigger, but as he did so wondered what a rifle could do against the great guns on the tanks. The guns were blasting in every direction, at the buildings, into the rubber trees. They were soon upon them.

'Fire for all you are worth, boys,' yelled the Bull, and they all fired in unison at the first tank, but their bullets just pinged off the metal. The great gun swung round and faced them, blasting at them, round after round. The Japanese were also firing machine guns at them from inside the tank. The Bull went down with the first hit, then one by one the others were struck by bullets, screaming out in pain and falling back into the drain like rag dolls.

Tom felt his breath coming in uneven gulps. He gave up firing and crouched down low behind the Bull's body, trying to hide himself from the enemy. A sob of fear rose in Tom's throat. The tanks went rumbling past him on their great caterpillar tracks, churning up the tarmac, brushing obstacles aside, moving on relentlessly like great voracious insects. When the last of the tanks were gone, he could hear troops marching past. Wave after wave of feet pounded the road, only a few yards from his ear. He was shaking all over. It would take only one of them to notice he was alive.

A whole battalion must have gone by while he lay there stock still, trying to hold his breath. Even after the sound of their boots on the tarmac had long died away, he stayed there, immobile, afraid of being seen. Eventually he opened his eyes, and then lifted his head. All around him lay the bodies of his fellow Volunteers. They had fallen at odd angles, lying on top of one another. It chilled him to think that he was the only one alive in the whole area. He went to each one of the men in turn, slapped each face, put his ear to each chest and listened for a heartbeat. Blood stained their uniforms and trickled from their wounds. It was hard to think that only an hour before each of these men had been full of life.

They were all dead now. There was nothing he could do. He scrambled to his feet and looking about warily, began to run back through the rubber trees. He did not dare walk on the road, and he thought that there might be the possibility of meeting another British unit if he doubled back. He soon reached the other side of the deserted estate, crossed another storm drain and emerged onto a residential street. It had been bombed, too, and its houses were in ruins. He walked in the direction of the city centre, keeping close to the buildings, his breath coming out in rapid pants, unsure about what to do.

Emerging onto another street, he felt a wave of relief when he saw a group of British soldiers marching there. He jogged to the front of the column and spoke to the commanding officer.

'Sir, I'm from the Straits Settlements Volunteer Force. My whole section was killed by tanks on the edge of the city. I'm the only one alive.'

The lieutenant gave him a grim look.

'Don't you know, Private? We've surrendered. We've been ordered to lay down our arms and march into the centre of the city. I suggest you put down your rifle before a Jap sees you.'

Tom was shocked. Why hadn't the Bull been informed of this?

But he obeyed the lieutenant. He cast his rifle into the front garden of one of the bombed-out houses.

'That's better. Now fall in with my men and you can march with us.'

* * *

For days Tom lay there in the hospital hut, racked with pain and fever, ministered to patiently by the two orderlies, George and Alan, who had picked him up when he had been dragged out of the pit. They were both Plymouth Argylls and spoke with a soft West Country lilt, which often made him long for the gentle rain and emerald green hills of Devon that he remembered from his childhood holidays.

There were other medical orderlies working in the hospital hut under the supervision of Colonel Bell and Captain Strang, and amongst them was Jim Leech. Tom remembered the rumours about Leech's ruthless entrepreneurial activities at camp, robbing the bodies of dead patients and selling their possessions, trading goods from the locals to the prisoners at inflated prices and bribing men to give him food in return for cigarettes.

When Tom was conscious and well enough to bother about what was going on around him, he watched Jim Leech out of the corner of his eye. He noticed that Leech never came near him. He seemed to make every effort to avoid ever being allocated work that involved being in Tom's area of the hut. Tom thought back to the times when Leech had tried to trade with him and Ian and Harry, and the bitter arguments that had broken out when they had refused to go along with him. Perhaps that was the reason Leech was avoiding him now. In any case, Tom was happy with the arrangement; Leech's presence made Tom uneasy. He found the stealthy way that the man went about his tasks unnerving. Also, the fact that he was always dressed in a clean shirt and pair of shorts, when everyone else went round in rags and even the doctors had only Jap Happys to cover their loins, made Tom all the more suspicious of Leech, made him dislike the man all the more.

Gradually, when the worst of his fever had passed, men from Tom's hut began to pay him visits. They stood staring silently at him, seeming to wonder at his survival against the odds. One of the first to visit was Roddy, the man who had slept next to Tom in their hut. He was a Volunteer from another unit who had survived the battle and ended up in Changi. He had been a mining engineer in Malaya. He was hardy and strong, and usually full of witticisms. But even he appeared humbled by Tom's appearance.

'Are you OK, Tom lad? You sure look a sight ... How on earth did you stay alive?'

Tom could only mumble feeble responses, but tried to show in his eyes that he was glad Roddy had come to visit him. .

'You were lucky to get out, lad. You know why they let you free, don't you? Some big shot colonel's arriving to inspect the progress on the railway. The interpreter got wind of it, and it's been all round the camp for days. The Japs have been preparing for it. They're even more brutal than usual, making everyone work longer hours, beating up sick men who can't work fast. The Ripper's been running around like a headless chicken, shouting his head off. Yes, that's why they let you out, my lad. They didn't want to get any stick from this colonel fellow for cruelty to prisoners.'

Tom nodded. That was probably why the Ripper had come and prodded him a couple of days before he was set free.

'Anyway, I'd best be going for my chow now. There's been a bit more space on the bunk since you were away, lad. I was kinda hoping you might not make it.'

Tom's face cracked into a smile.

'You should be so lucky …' he managed to croak.

Before he went Roddy put his hand on Tom's arm and said, 'I'm so sorry about your pals, Tom. We all are. They said they'd been shot.'

Tom nodded, his eyes filling with tears.

'They were brave men. The best,' said Roddy.

It was the first time anyone had mentioned the loss of his friends to Tom. But after Roddy's visit many men came to his bedside to wish him well and express sadness for his loss. Although each conversation brought back painful memories for Tom, he was touched by the concern, and this provided him with at least some comfort from his grief.

The padre came to see him after a few days. By this time Tom was beginning to recover. His wounds were healing and his bouts of fever subsiding.

'Ellis, I'm so pleased to see you on the mend,' he said. 'I wanted to come and offer my condolences for your poor friends.'

'Thank you, padre.'

'We held a service for them, you know, whilst you were … you were away. We wanted to thank God for their lives. And for their bravery.'

Tom looked away bitterly. What difference would a service make? They were still gone.

'Everyone in the camp turned out, you know, to pray for them.'

'Thank you, padre,' he repeated mechanically.

'Now, I know that you are not a churchgoer, Ellis, and that you generally don't come to our little services here in the camp, but if you should ever change your mind, or if you would ever like to pray alone with me, you only have to say the word.'

'Of course, padre. It's very … thoughtful of you. Thank you.'

The padre left. Tom thought of all the times he had lain on his bunk while other prisoners had trooped to the corner of the camp where the padre had a makeshift altar and listened to his sermon and sang a hymn and prayed. Tom had been disgusted at their foolishness. If there was a God, where was he? What was he doing when men were beaten and starved and worked to death? He thought of Ian and Harry. Of his friends standing against the pomelo trees as the death squad had opened fire on them, of their bodies jumping grotesquely at the impact of the bullets, then collapsing on the freshly dug earth like puppets cut from their strings. And he thought of Archie, of his blue and emaciated body as it was pulled out of the pit, of it lying there, stiff and lifeless. Tears of anger sprang to his eyes.

'Where was your God then, padre?' Tom whispered, and he wept again for his lost friends.

22

Luke's snores came loud and regular from his side of the bed. Laura crept about, so as not to waken him. The first rays of the morning sun were beginning to penetrate the gaps in the wickerwork roof. She glanced at her watch, aware that she needed to move quickly. She folded her few clothes and slipped them into the backpack, along with her flip-flops and wash bag and the guide books she had previously unpacked.

She pulled a notebook from her rucksack and scribbled a few lines:

'Dear Luke, I've been doing a lot of thinking over the past few days and I've decided to go straight on to Penang alone instead of coming to Phuket. You'll have a far better time without me. I'm sure Jed and Dale will be great travelling companions. I'm sorry things haven't worked out between us. I'm sorry, too, that I dragged you here on a quest after my father's past. I know it's been very dull for you, but it was something I needed to do. I'm going to get the early train back to Bangkok and then a night train down to Malaysia. You look as though you need some sleep, so I'm not going to wake you.'

She wrote 'Love Laura' at the end, but then hesitated, and scribbled it out quickly. She had loved him, but she couldn't feel any trace of it now. She propped the note against his water bottle and crept towards the door. She paused as she opened the door and the sunlight flooded into the room, afraid that it would wake him, but glancing back, she saw that he slumbered on. She stared at his sleeping form, the half open mouth, the mass of dark hair spread out on the pillow. He was still beautiful, she observed, even if all her desire for him had vanished. So this was it. There was no going back now. If she left, it would be the end. She felt an odd thrill of excitement at what she was about to do. With one last look, she hoisted her rucksack onto her shoulder and walked away.

The owner of the guesthouse was already up and bright-eyed, frying rice for breakfast in the outdoor kitchen behind her own hut, the toddlers playing around her on the floor. She looked at Laura with frank curiosity when she said that she was checking out but that her friend was staying on. She smiled, put her hands together in the traditional Thai greeting of 'Wai', wished her well as she paid the bill, then walked out onto the dusty road.

When she arrived at the station, breathless and sweaty from the walk, she was told that the Bangkok train was not due for another hour. She bought a ticket, deposited her rucksack at the left-luggage counter and set off for the museum again.

It was just opening. The monk on the door, setting out his tickets and money tray for the day, greeted her with a smile and a deep bow: 'Welcome back. You are my first customer today, madam.'

This time she didn't pause to look at the exhibits. Instead, she walked quickly through the museum area and made straight for the shop that was set up in the last of the bamboo huts.

She looked around at the disappointing display. There were a few cheap trinkets on show, similar to the ones sold on the stalls beside the bridge – little metal models of the bridge, key-rings, pencils. There were a few postcards showing the bridge, the railway and various scenes from the surrounding countryside, and one or two books wrapped in yellowing cellophane. She picked them up and examined them. One was about the filming of *The Bridge on the River Kwai*, and the other was written in Thai script. The only thing that looked worth buying was an illustrated pamphlet written by the Buddhist monk who had founded the museum. Laura flicked through it. It summarised the history of the railway in simple terms. She bought it and a couple of postcards to send to Ken and Marge.

Smiling her thanks to the monk, she wandered out onto the road, feeling deflated, and started to head back towards the station. She walked past a row of stalls set up at the side of the road, mostly selling local produce. The stallholders shouted out greetings and waved to her as she passed. Tucked amongst the food vendors, a little way along the line, she was surprised to find a tiny stall selling a few dusty second-hand books.

She paused and looked at the books with idle curiosity. There were a lot of dated, heavily-thumbed paperback thrillers and Mills & Boon romances. An old man who had been gossiping with the stallholder next door ambled over and smiled at her.

'Good morning, madam. Can I help you?'

'I'm not sure. I'm looking for a book about the building of the railway.'

'Oh, I only have one or two here. I don't often get them. They are very difficult to find. Very rare.'

His head disappeared behind the stall. Laura could hear him rummaging under the table. He re-emerged a few minutes later with a wooden crate. He carried it round to the front of the stall and heaved it onto the table in front of Laura.

She peered inside. There were one or two old histories by military historians, titles that she remembered noticing on the shelves at Imperial War Museum. She sorted through them and took out a couple that she thought might be worth buying. She knew that she would have to bargain hard with the old man; his protestations about the books' rarity were obviously his opening gambit. She was beginning to learn that this was the way things were done here. She thanked the old man and set off again.

Along the road to the station there were two or three other second-hand stalls that had a few old books amongst the bric-a-brac. She flicked through them, but most were old novels discarded by people passing through. At the last stall though, Laura noticed a thin volume tucked inside another book. It was covered in brown paper, like a school exercise book. She pulled it out, curious. There was no title on the front cover, so she opened it up and looked at the front page: 'A Short History of the Thai-Burma Railway.'

'How much is this?' she asked the stallholder, who eyed her shrewdly, clearly assessing how much she might be persuaded to pay. Once again, she paid well over the odds for the pamphlet.

Later, as she sat on a wooden seat in the cramped third class carriage she opened the little book. Curious about what might be on the cover, she ripped off the brown paper. There was a crude photograph of the bridge, the title in capitals and underneath that the author's name: Dr. Arthur Stone.

Her heart stood still. Arthur Stone. She couldn't believe her luck. It was really no more than a pamphlet, printed in courier script like a draft manuscript. Holding her breath, she turned to the back cover: 'Arthur Stone read Military History at Oxford University and has researched and charted the history of many conflicts. He is currently curator of records at Imperial War Museum, London.'

She flipped back to look at the date. 1965. That was a long time ago. She wondered if he was still alive.

She flicked through the pages and read the preface written by the author:

'This work is the culmination of several years of study of the conditions endured by Allied prisoners-of-war in the Far East at the hands of the Japanese. I spent a long time interviewing surviving prisoners-of-war in the late 1940s and early 1950s. All had been profoundly affected by their experiences. Many felt shame that they had survived when their comrades did not. Many had been discouraged from speaking about it. Most did not want their identities revealed, which is why these accounts are unattributed.'

She read on. By the time the train started to rattle through the outskirts of Bangkok, she had finished. She slipped it back into her backpack, disappointed. It was no more than a summary of interviews given by several prisoners: details of conditions in the camps, the lack of medical supplies, the harsh treatment by the Japanese and Korean guards, the malnutrition and disease, the camaraderie between the men that got them through their ordeal. It told her nothing new, and certainly no more than the diaries she had read in the museums and the few books she had been able to find on the subject.

She stared out the window at the suburbs of Bangkok. Sprawling and ramshackle, built along canals and dirt tracks, wooden stilted houses set amongst lush vegetation and the occasional shining modern block flashed past her. Her thoughts returned to Luke. She imagined him waking up, bleary-eyed and hung-over, and discovering her note. What had he felt when he read it? Would he try to follow her? She doubted it. He would take up with those two Australians and find a suitable beach bar to hang out at until his funds ran dry. It occurred to her suddenly that they had return tickets booked for the same flight in a fortnight's time. She resolved to go to the airline office in Bangkok and try to change hers. Even if she had to pay a fee, that was preferable to the pain and embarrassment of spending twelve hours in a cramped airline seat next to him.

When the train arrived at Thonburi Station in Bangkok, she took a taxi to Kao San Road, where she and Luke had stayed the first night they had arrived from London. She avoided the guesthouse, where the friendly Chinese owner was bound to ask awkward questions, and found a quieter place at the other end of the road, where she rented a single room for one night.

She ate her evening meal at a food-stall, sitting at a plastic table in the steamy street, watching the owner rustle up delicious concoctions in a fast-moving wok over a gas flame. She sipped a bottle of Singha Beer and enjoyed the feeling of being alone in a busy place, free to do what she wanted and go where she wanted without having to negotiate, persuade or compromise. She wondered why she had ever agreed to Luke coming along in the first place. It felt so right to be alone here.

The next day she got up early and went out onto the street while the saffron clad monks were making their daily procession for alms before morning prayer. She took a tuk-tuk to the airline office located in a modern shopping centre and changed her ticket for a day in the week after Luke's flight. Later she went to Hualamphong, the main train station, and booked a sleeper train to Butterworth in Malaysia, which would leave that evening.

Before she left the guesthouse, she went to the lobby and dialled the number of the house in Highbury New Park from the phone behind the reception counter. She wanted to tell somebody that she was setting off to another country. The faint distant tone rang for a long time.

Ken's voice was obscured by buzzing and crackling. It sounded thousands of miles away.

'I thought I'd just let you know, there's been a change of plan,' she had to shout. 'I'm going to Malaysia early.'

There was a long delay before he said.

'Where's laughing boy?'

'It's finished, Ken.'

'I'm sorry to hear that.' There was a pause. She wasn't expecting words of comfort. He was obviously struggling to find the right words. Finally he said, 'Have you had any luck with your search?'

'Not much. I'm hoping for more luck in Penang.'

'Oh, by the way, someone's been trying to get in touch with you. He's called a couple of times. A boy called Rory.'

'That's strange. He's a friend of Luke's.'

'He seemed a bit agitated.'

'He's a bit odd. Tell him I'll call when I get back if he phones again. I'll let you know when I get to Penang.'

'Good luck, lassie.'

The night train to Butterworth raced across the flat rice fields of the Central Plain of Thailand as the huge red sun dipped beneath the western horizon. Laura sat at her table in the first class compartment and was served supper by a smiling waiter. She stared out at the tropical landscape, the sun streaking the paddies red. For the first time since she had left home, she felt content.

She thought about Dad and his words to her about Luke: 'If he makes you happy, that's all that matters.' What an idiot she'd been. She knew now why those words had troubled her so. Dad had known that Luke could never make her happy. But it had taken this trip for her to work that out for herself.

23

Tom quickly got used to the routines of the hospital hut. The patients would be woken early, before the bugle sounded outside for roll call. They were given a similar breakfast as the rest of the men in the camp, but only about half the quantity. One of the orderlies told Tom that the Japanese would not provide rations for those who were too sick to work. Everyone's rations were reduced accordingly, and the officers had to beg and bargain with the Thais outside the camp for eggs and chickens to supplement the sick men's food and give them at least a fighting chance of getting better.

During morning roll call all the sick men in the hut listened anxiously to what was going on outside. Often the doctor was called out, and a fierce argument would ensue when he was asked to explain why there were so many sick men. The Ripper would then order him to produce some sick men to make up the work parties. The doctor always refused to do this and was invariably beaten up. The men in the hut could hear the dull thuds as the doctor was kicked and punched. They winced as they listened to his groans and shouts of pain. But after it was over he would stagger back in to the hut, his face swollen and bloody. The doctor would dab his wounds with a cloth, straighten himself up, and carry on caring for the sick men as if nothing had happened.

More than once during roll call, a group of guards burst into the hut and pulled out sick men from their beds, forcing them to their feet and shoving them outside into the glare of the sun at the point of a bayonet. Some of these poor wretches could barely walk. They made a pitiful sight, staggering out through the doorway, their skeletal frames unfit for any manual labour. Tom was secretly relieved that he was never picked. Perhaps he just looked too sick and wasted, even by the standards of the camp.

Every day new patients were brought in: victims of tropical ulcers, dysentery, beri-beri, malaria. The ulcer cases were confined to one end of the hut, yet their odours of putrefaction, the sickly stench of rotting flesh still permeated the whole place. The orderlies did their best to ease the suffering of these men. They brought them water, fed them by hand, bathed the sweat from their brows and helped them to the latrine. But they had no medicines to give to them, and many men died every day. They died quietly, without fuss or complaint. Each evening the bodies were taken out of the hut on bamboo stretchers and carried to the cemetery on the edge of the camp to be buried.

Tom found living so close to death terrifying. He knew how near he had been to succumbing. It made him all the more determined to pull through. He was getting better and stronger by the day. The welts and bruises from his beatings were healing gradually, and his fever seemed to have peaked and was on the wane.

'We'll soon have you up and out working that cutting again, my boy,' said Captain Strang one day, with a twinkle in his eye. 'By all accounts, it is almost finished now. They're nearly through to the other side.'

Tom groaned.

'Please don't send me back there, Doc.'

'I'd dearly love to spare you, Ellis, but if it isn't you, it would be someone even sicker than you. And that's hardly fair, is it?'

'No, Doc, I suppose not,' Tom said, looking around the hut at the sick and suffering men.

Tom continued to watch Jim Leech whenever the orderly was in the hut. Leech still avoided Tom and his area of the hut. He would cast a furtive glance in Tom's direction and then look away quickly if he saw that Tom was also watching him. Tom was becoming increasingly curious and suspicious about the man's behaviour.

One day when he was chatting to George, Tom stumbled upon something that might explain Leech's strange behaviour towards him.

'It's rotten about your young friend,' said George to Tom as he was cleaning the wounds on Tom's back. He was a wiry little man, burnt copper by the sun, and although he was skinny like everyone else, he looked fit and healthy. He was working away energetically at Tom's back, clearing away the pus so that the wounds would have a chance of healing.

'It's terrible … Terrible,' said Tom. 'I knew he would never survive in there. He already had malaria. It was murder to put him in that pit. He was done for.'

'He was in here a good few days before it all happened,' said George.

'Yes, of course. I came in a few times to see him. He was in a really bad way.'

'He was fevered most of the time. He was delirious, you know, mumbling something or the other.'

Tom turned and looked at George. 'What do you mean by that?'

'Well, he was ranting and raving about this escape attempt of yours. When you were going to go, who was involved, and he was worried about if you all had enough money, if you would get lost in the jungle, if you would get caught by the Japs. You know, when a man is delirious all his worst fears surface. And Archie must have been really worried about what was planned, because it all came out. Was the Thai to be trusted? Would he bring the map? Oh, there was nothing he didn't say about it.'

'Dear God! So you all knew?'

George shrugged. 'Of course. But you needn't worry, Tom. Your secret was safe with us. We hear a lot of odd things in here when a man pours his heart out in delirium.'

Tom was silent. It had suddenly occurred to him why Jim Leech had been avoiding him, why he would not work in his area of the hut, why he would not even meet his gaze. This was why. He had overheard Archie's delirious ramblings, and had used the information to betray them all to the Japanese for a reward. That was how they knew so quickly about their plan, and about where to find Ian and Harry. How else had Leech managed to get new shorts and boots, to keep himself so well-fed and healthy all the time? He even had flesh on his bones and colour in his cheeks. He looked positively chubby compared to most of the men.

Tom felt his muscles flex and his fists clench involuntarily. He vowed that when he was well enough he would find some proof and challenge Leech. And if his suspicions were confirmed, he would kill the filthy little traitor.

* * *

Captain Strang came to examine Tom one morning. When he had finished he said, 'I can't keep you here much longer, Ellis, I'm afraid. I suggest over the next couple of days you try and walk around the hut a bit. If you go outside, don't go anywhere near the guardhouse or they'll punish you for not working. My guess is you've had enough punishment for a lifetime.'

'You bet,' said Tom grimly.

When he returned to his old quarters the men in his hut treated him like a long-lost brother. Roddy even moved up and made a space for him on the slats. The first thing Tom did was to check that his pack under the bed was still there. The badge that Harry had given him before he left was still there, and into the bag he slipped the flowers from the pomelo tree, which were now shrivelled and brown, and the photograph of Joy.

He found it odd sleeping back amongst his old companions. The bed bugs and mosquitoes were worse here than in the hospital hut, and the men slept closer together. The foetid air was stifling. Tom could not sleep. He lay awake, listening to the heavy breathing and snores of the others and reflecting on what he had been through over the past few weeks.

The next morning, he was up at dawn for roll call, marching through the jungle to the cutting under the scowling supervision of Fat-so once again. Tom was astonished to see the progress that had been made on the cutting. It was fifty yards long now, he reckoned, two great towering slabs of rock flanking the railway bed.

Tom had a new partner for the hammer and tap: Frankie Pace, whose previous companion had died of septicaemia in the hospital the week before. Frankie was silent and brooding, never smiled, and hardly exchanged a word with Tom all day. The time dragged. Tom missed Harry and his ceaseless banter. In his weakened state, the physical challenge of wielding a heavy hammer became almost too much to bear. His muscles and limbs soon ached as before, and all the pains from his previous ailments resurfaced. Sweat poured from his body as he worked. But he was determined not to collapse and give Fat-so the pleasure of beating him.

In the evening, Tom decided to seek out Jim Leech. As soon as he had finished his ration of rice flavoured with greasy soup, he went straight to the hut where the medical orderlies slept.

There was no sign of Leech inside the hut, and nobody seemed to know where he was. They all shook their heads and looked away when his name was mentioned. Like most men in the camp, they were probably afraid of him. Tom walked outside and around the edge of the hut. He found Leech in a little clearing on the side of the hut that bordered the jungle. He was sitting on the stump of a palm tree, a sliced ripe pineapple on another stump in front of him, set beside a flickering candle. He was tucking into one of the slices, juice glistening on his chin. Tom's breathing quickened with anger, but he stayed where he was, watching. After a few minutes Leech fished inside his shirt and pulled something out. He held it up and peered at it. It was a long silver object that glinted in the moonlight.

'Leech,' said Tom, bearing down on him. 'I want a word with you.'

Leech jumped and looked up at Tom. He tried to shove the object back inside his shirt, but it fell on the ground between them. He stopped chewing, a piece of pineapple poking out from the side of his mouth. He would have made a comical sight if Tom had not been so angry. Leech bent down to pick it up, but Tom was there first. His heart missed a beat as he felt on his fingers the familiar steel strap of the watch his father had given him. He snatched it up and stared at it. The watch was tarnished and dirty, and the back was dented, but it was unmistakable. The last time he had held it, he had handed it to Harry as a parting gift. He needed no more proof of Leech's guilt.

'Get up!' Tom dragged him to his feet, knocking the candle and the rest of the pineapple slices to the ground angrily.

'You've got some explaining to do, Leech. Your little game is up. I know what you've been up to.'

Leech was quivering all over. The pineapple fell from his mouth onto the dirt.

'I don't know what you mean,' he spluttered.

'Oh, I think you do know what I mean. I think you know very well what I mean. This proves what you've been up to.'

He held the watch up to Leech's face.

'The Japs gave it to you, didn't they? As a reward for the information you gave them about my friends.'

Leech shook his head, meeting Tom's eyes. The man was brazen.

'I found it yesterday. Out on the parade ground.'

'You're a liar,' Tom shouted, his face only a couple of inches from Leech's. 'Why else did you avoid coming near me when I was in the hospital? You wouldn't even look at me, would you? Guilt. There's guilt written all over your face. And with damned good cause.'

Tom shoved the watch in his pocket and held Leech by the neck, pushing him up against the bamboo wall of the hut. He had his hands around the man's throat. He realised how easy it would be to apply pressure to his wind pipe and stop his breath.

'Please.' Leech's eyes were bulging, terrified. His face had turned bright red. Sweat poured from his forehead. Tom eased the pressure a little.

'I just want you to admit it to me, and then I'll leave you be. I need to know. It was you, wasn't it? You betrayed us to the Japs, didn't you?'

Leech shook his head.

'Don't lie to me, Leech, you little bastard. You overheard the lad, Archie, ranting and raving about the escape attempt, didn't you?'

'No ... No,' he panted.

'Everyone in the hospital heard it, so you must have too. You're a liar.'

'I don't know what you're on about. Let me go.'

Tom ignored his plea.

'Well, knowing what you're like, you couldn't resist using the information for your own ends. So you went to the Japs with it, didn't you?

'No ... I would never do such a thing.'

'Then, how do you explain this watch? I gave it to Harry just before he left. They must have taken it off him and given it to you. And what about your new clothes, and all the food you have. You're well fed, aren't you? Not like the rest of us poor wretches in this camp.'

'Trading,' he said trembling. 'You know that. I trade in the camp, and I trade with the natives. I take risks for that money.'

Tom brought his knee forward sharply and slammed it into Leech's groin. Leech let out a moan.

'Be quiet, for god's sake,' hissed Tom. 'Or I'll put it about the camp that you are a traitor. They'll tear you apart limb from limb.'

Tom tightened his fingers around Leech's throat again.

'You can't prove anything,' croaked Leech.

'I don't need to prove anything. You're going to tell me the truth, aren't you?'

He squeezed even tighter.

'Please, please don't kill me,' Leech was whimpering now.

'Well, you're going to tell me the truth then. Or I'm not going to let you go. I'm strong, you know. I survived the pit, didn't I? Survived being beaten by those bastards.'

Tom dragged him forward and threw him on the ground. For a well-built man, Leech was surprisingly weak. He hardly put up any resistance.

'You've never had a beating from them, have you?'

Tom began to kick him in the ribs.

'Now, I want you to see what it feels like. It's not good, is it?'

Leech writhed on the ground, trying to shield himself with his hands.

'Stop … Stop, please. OK, I did it. I'm sorry. I did it. I sold them out for money. But I had no idea they would be killed. I didn't think they would die.'

'You didn't think they would die? You lying bastard. You were at Changi, weren't you? You saw those men bayoneted in cold blood because one of them tried to escape from a work party. Did you think things had changed? That the Ripper had mellowed in his old age? What a load of bullshit. You just didn't give a damn what happened to them.'

Then Tom let his anger loose. He kicked and pummelled the man on the ground as hard as he could. And as he did it he relived the grief that he had suffered for his friends and all the days he had spent in the pit, all the beatings he had taken himself. He took out all his anger and terror and pain and grief onto Leech. He lost control of himself in a frenzy of violence, gave into it. When he had finished, he stood there panting, staring down at Leech. The man was barely conscious, his face swollen and puffy. His body was covered in ugly bruises.

Tom dragged him back to the end of the hut where he knew that someone would stumble on him when they visited the latrines. He bent over Leech.

'Now, if I find that you have been exploiting people again, making money out of starving men, I really will kill you. I mean it, Leech.'

24

There were no repercussions for Tom over Jim Leech's injuries. From the looks that people gave him and from the odd comment they dropped here and there, Tom formed the impression that the whole camp knew about what had happened and understood his reasons for hurting Leech.

Tom often went back to the hospital hut after work to visit the orderlies who had helped him recover. Jim Leech was always there, pottering about, his arm in a sling made from a ragged pair of shorts and his face bruised and puffy. Tom made a point of staring boldly straight at him. Leech would meet his gaze shiftily, and quickly look away.

One evening George took Tom aside as he was leaving the hut. He pulled him into the shadows.

'We understand what you did to Leech, Ellis. I realise now what he did. He betrayed you and your friends to the Japs, didn't he?'

Tom nodded. He felt ashamed to admit his outburst of violence to this kind, mild-mannered man.

'You were right not to go to the officers about it, though. He's got so much on most of them. They'd all done dodgy deals with him at some time or another. You wouldn't have got anywhere with them.' George pursed his lips together. 'He had it coming to him. Many's the time that I've stood in that hut watching him and feeling helpless, when he's half-inched a sick man's belongings to trade, or even taken things from a dead body. I wanted to stop him, but couldn't. And that racket he had going with the food – rice today for rice and soup tomorrow – I've seen so many men brought down sick because of that. Wicked that was.'

'Yes, well, he won't be doing any of it again in a hurry,' said Tom.

'You've done the whole camp a favour then,' said George, patting his shoulder.

The days wore on in the same old back-breaking routine, with Tom and Frankie working the hammer and tap in heavy and tiring silence. Tom found himself desperately weak and exhausted. Sometimes he barely had the strength to wield the sledgehammer. His stomach constantly gnawed with hunger, but at least he was not sick, and he felt grateful for that.

At last the day came when the last of the great black rock had been cleared away, and the cutting was finally finished. Engineers arrived in the middle of the afternoon and inspected the work, their faces wreathed in smiles. The men stood and watched, bemused as the engineers and officers strutted about, congratulating themselves. The prisoners felt no sense of achievement. This just meant that the Japanese were one step closer to finishing their railway and being able to supply their troops on the front line in Burma. The men just wondered what awaited them next, as they walked back to camp, released early as a reward for the progress.

They didn't have to wait long to find out. The next morning, after roll call, the Ripper addressed them and told them that their work here was finished, but that other important work for the Emperor awaited them elsewhere. They were told to pack their things quickly and assemble beside the river.

The same flat-bottomed barges that had brought them here

came to collect them and take them down to Kanchanaburi. The men crowded on, uncomfortably aware that their numbers were now severely depleted. As the barge cast off into the current and began its journey downriver, Tom whispered a quiet goodbye to Harry, Ian and Archie, and all the others whose bodies or ashes would remain here in this remote spot in the jungle. Looking around at the sombre faces of his companions, he guessed they were all doing the same.

The camp would soon be abandoned, would rot back into the ground, and the ground would be gradually reclaimed by the voracious creepers and bamboo of the jungle. He imagined future generations coming past on the river, admiring the savage beauty of the place, unaware of the cruelty that had been meted out on this spot and of the lives that had been lost here.

A convoy of army trucks awaited them at Kanchanaburi, and the men were all loaded on to them immediately, hurried on with sticks and bayonets by the jabbering guards. A crowd of bemused locals stood and watched them silently. Some of them even dared to wave as the trucks drew away.

At Ban Pong, they were loaded straight onto trains, the baking hot cattle trucks waiting in the sidings. They were crammed on just as before, thirty to a truck. There was barely enough room to stand. The train stood there in the searing heat for over an hour before setting off. Sweat was pouring off the men, and they were shouting for water. They had not eaten since breakfast, eight hours before, but they were used to hunger. It was thirst that terrified them.

The five-day long journey was a repeat of the ordeal they had endured coming up from Singapore. The train stopped twice a day for the men to be fed rice and slop from buckets. The men had to stand up most of the time because there was simply not enough room to sit down. At night, they took turns to lie down, but it was too uncomfortable for any sleep. The metal truck, which in the daytime burned to the touch, became a freezing ice-box at night, and without warm clothes they shivered. On this journey, though, the train had to make several unscheduled stops to bury the men who had died along the route. These men had survived the starvation and beatings and slavery of the railway, but for them the conditions of the journey had proved too much. Shallow graves were dug quickly beside the tracks. A few hasty words were said by the padre, while the others bowed their heads at the thought of losing another of their own, then the men were bundled back on the train to continue the journey.

As the train rattled south, they watched the countryside through the open door. The rice paddies of Southern Thailand gave way to the plantations and jungle-covered hills of Malaya. This would be beautiful, Tom thought, if only their circumstances were different.

When they felt they could endure no more, the train finally drew into Singapore Station. They were unloaded and forced at the point of rifle and bayonet to march several miles through bombed-out streets to a dilapidated prison camp. In contrast to the jungle camps, this was gated and surrounded with a high fence, topped with coils of barbed wire. The men were herded inside and told to find somewhere to sleep.

The camp was already over-crowded. Tom managed to find a space on the bare earth next to one of the huts, where someone had stretched out a shabby tarpaulin for shelter.

Talking to some of the men already there, mostly Australians who had also been working on the railway, he discovered that the place was called 'River Valley Road Camp'. Although some people had been there for some time, it functioned as a sort of transit camp.

'Transit?' asked Tom. 'For what?'

'The Japs are shipping prisoners to the motherland to work

in mines and factories there,' said one of the Australians. 'I don't suppose you lads are going to be here for too long. We're supposed to be out of here tomorrow. There's a ship waiting for us in the harbour. Then you might be able to find somewhere to sleep.'

In fact, they were there for over a month. During that time Tom and the others were taken out daily on work parties to the docks and ordered to unload food and equipment from cargo ships. It was back-breaking work and, as on the railway, the guards urged them on all day, with sticks and rifle butts, beating up anyone who appeared to be slacking.

On the first morning, Tom had watched as the prisoners lined up on the dock. They were in a pitiful state, bone-thin and unshaven, naked but for their Jap Happys. But strangely they all carried packs that appeared to have just been issued.

The vessel was an ancient cargo ship that looked as though it had recently been transporting coal. It was black and filthy. It took hours to load the prisoners onto it; there seemed to be thousands waiting on the quayside. Tom could not believe how many were crammed onboard. They just kept on loading them. Hundreds and hundreds of them walked unsteadily up the gang-plank and were forced below through hatches. When they were all aboard, Tom watched as the guards battened down the hatches. A chill went through him.

That will be us one day, Tom thought to himself.

* * *

Soon it was indeed their turn to march down to the docks and assemble in the heat of the midday sun with what was left of their belongings. They had their first glimpse of the ship that was to take them to Japan. It was a rusty old tub, a cargo ship, with no name painted on the side. To Tom, it looked impossibly small to carry all the prisoners crowded before it. Like the other groups that Tom had watched before, they were each issued with a pack containing a set of thick clothes for the colder climate they were bound for.

They began to be loaded on board. There must have been over a thousand of them, Tom thought as he looked at the press of bodies on the quayside. The crowd pressed forward, and one by one the prisoners walked the rickety gang-plank onto the deck. They were then driven across the deck to a hatch, where a ladder descended forty feet into the bowels of the ship. As Tom crossed the deck, he overheard one of the senior officers arguing with the Japanese commandant.

'You can't expect all these men to travel on this ship. There simply isn't enough room. The holds are already full to bursting, and you're still loading. Do you want them all to die before they get to Japan?'

'They are lucky they did not die in battle,' was the only response from the stony-faced Japanese officer.

'At least tell me you won't batten the hatches. The men will suffocate. I've heard on some ships the hatches have been nailed down. I give you my word that no-one will try to escape.'

'Get below with your men, Colonel. All will be well.'

Tom hesitated as he stood at the top of the hatch and looked down. The hot air and stench of the hold hit him as he leaned over and looked down. The idea of being trapped down there in the heat and the dark with hundreds of other men appalled him.

He felt a sharp jab between the kidneys.

'No wait! You get down,' scowled the guard. 'Hurry!'

He had no choice. He slowly lowered himself onto the ladder and began climbing down, rung by rung, into the darkness. As he descended, the clammy heat of the stinking hold enveloped him. He climbed down past two decks full of men, crammed in so tightly they could barely move. At each level stood a guard holding a bayonet, barring his entrance.

'Go down, go down,' they shouted, and he was forced to descend right to the bottom level. The filthy boards were already half full with nearly naked men, sitting there miserably in their own sweat. Tom found a small space for himself not too far from a tiny porthole; although inadequate, it might at least let in some air once the ship started moving.

Tom did not know how he was going to survive this.

It was hours before the ship was loaded, and the temperature must have reached a hundred degrees inside by then. Men were shouting for water and air. Some fainted in the heat, collapsing onto their neighbours. They could hear officers pleading with the guards for water, but none came until the ship had cast off and moved out onto the open sea. Then a bucket was passed around and men dipped their metal cups into it. The temptation was to gulp it straight down, but experience had taught Tom that it would be a very long time before any more water was given to them. He sipped his as slowly as he could.

Later the latrine bucket was passed round, preceded by shouts of 'Honey-bucket on the way!' Men had to stand and pee where they were. Some did not have a very good aim, and soon the boards were awash with urine. Another option was to go up on to deck and use one of the *benjos*, a wooden box suspended over the side of the ship with a hole cut out from its middle.

Tom went up later, glad to have an excuse to get out of the foul and stuffy atmosphere of the hold and have a chance to move his arms and legs.

On the deck, he found George looking after a few sick men. His patients were stretched out on the boards in the full glare of the sun. Most of them looked near to death.

'What's the matter with them, George?' Tom asked.

'Dysentery,' sighed George. 'Most of them won't pull through. I wouldn't be surprised if the whole ship went down with it with the disgusting conditions on board. Either that, or we'll be torpedoed by the Yanks.'

'Torpedoed?'

'Yes. They're trying to sink all Jap ships going to Japan. There are no markings on any of them to show that they're carrying prisoners. Loads of POW ships have already gone down. That's why we're travelling in a convoy.'

Tom looked out to sea, and sure enough he could see that they were part of a line of ships stretching as far as the eye could see. The ship in front was a bulky cargo ship, but the one behind looked like a destroyer, with long guns protruding from its deck.

'But there would be no way to get out of the hold if that did happen. We're right at the bottom,' said Tom.

'Yes, it's murder. Cold-blooded murder.'

A guard doing his rounds saw Tom speaking to the orderly, and came and poked him in the stomach with a bayonet.

'Go back. Go down. No stop here!'

Tom descended the ladder reluctantly. As the sun went down, he and the others watched through the tiny porthole as two great sacks were thrown from the deck into the sea.

'What the hell are they?' asked someone.

'Bodies probably,' Tom murmured. 'There were some men on deck with dysentery. They looked as though they weren't going to last long.'

The sacks bobbed on the surface for a few minutes, and then the water around them became choppy.

'Sharks.'

They watched as the sacks were quickly pulled apart, and then disappeared into the water. The sea around them turned a foamy red.

Later that evening a bucket of rice and watery fish stew was lowered, and although it smelled foul, the men once again dipped their tin cups into it gratefully. When night came they had to stay in the same crouched positions they had been sitting in all day. The temperature, although a little cooler, was still unbearably hot. It was impossible to sleep.

Tom spent a little time making sure that his treasured possessions were on his body rather than in the pack, in case George's predictions came true. He checked that the picture of Joy was in the pocket of his shirt; his clothes were so tattered and torn now that it was almost pointless wearing them. He hung Ian's ring, Harry's badge and his own Volunteers' badge around his neck then slipped the brown pomelo flowers, which he had wrapped in some rice sacking in the camp, into his shorts pocket. All night he sat there, cramped and sweating on the bare boards, listening anxiously for the sound of aircraft or submarines. All he heard, however, was the chug-chug-chug of the engines turning below as the ancient ship made its laborious progress across the South China Sea.

The days wore on in exactly the same routine. Three times a day the buckets were lowered to the prisoners: latrine, water and food. In the cramped and filthy conditions, men began to get sick. Many developed dysentery. Too weak to get up the ladder, they soiled themselves, and then sat there, pictures of misery in their own filth. Others succumbed to the roll of the ocean and got seasick, retching onto the floor, so that soon the boards were slippery with vomit and shit. The smell was unbearable. Tom spent as much time on deck as he could, trying his best not to arouse the attention of the guards. At least out there he could get away from the stench of the holds.

He noticed that the amount of food in the food buckets was dwindling. More than once there was not enough left in the bucket for him to fill his cup.

'Someone here's taking too much food out of the bucket,' Tom said, looking at the desperate faces that surrounded him.

A man near the ladder shook his head. 'It's someone on the next deck up. I saw him do it,' he said. 'He's got two cups. He fills one for himself and keeps the other one to sell to whoever's hungry later.'

'Why the hell do they let him do it?'

The man shrugged. 'You know what it's like. He's a bully.'

Tom had an uneasy feeling. He was almost sure he knew who this bully was. He decided to confirm his suspicions for himself. The next time he heard the food bucket being passed around on the floor above, he climbed the first few rungs of the ladder. He looked around at the sea of faces, some familiar, some not. They all wore the same hollow-eyed look of hopelessness. As he looked around he spotted one face that didn't look hungry or desolate.

'Jim Leech,' he shouted. 'I knew it was you. You're taking extra food, you bastard.'

Leech stared back at him. This time he did not flinch or look away. There was a look of defiance on his face.

'So what? There's plenty to go round.'

'There's not enough down here. Everyone's falling sick.'

'Well, what are you going to do about it?'

Tom sprang forward and lunged towards Leech, but he could not get at him through the press of the bodies. The men around them held him back.

'Cool down, mate. Leave it. There's no use fighting here.'

They kept pushing him away, and Tom had no choice but to step back down the ladder onto his deck. He sat there brooding. He thought about Harry and Ian, about their faces full of hope as they had set out from the camp, about their brutal execution only two days later. The scene played over and over in his mind: the two of them standing under the pomelo tree, then their bodies dancing grotesquely as the bullets hit them. He thought of Archie being dragged to the pit, of his body lying on the ground stone dead a few days later. He thought of how he had beaten Leech. He could have killed him. He wished now that he had done. If they ever got off this ship alive, he would have his revenge.

The next morning, after another dreadful night of near-suffocation on the filthy boards, Tom was desperate to get out on deck. He used the pretext of needing to use the *benjo*, but after having sat there for a few minutes, his backside hanging over the side of the ship, he got off and lingered on deck for as long as he could, trying to keep out of sight of the guards. He found a quiet place beside the rail and watched the waves for a while, gulping in the clean sea air. He could just make out the grey smudge of land on the far horizon, and wondered which islands they were sailing past.

He listened to the rhythmic drone of the ship's engines, and as he listened he realised they were getting louder. Did the ship have engine trouble? A chill went through him as the drone became a deafening roar. The planes were upon them. Swarms of them, like great black birds, filled the sky, blotting out the sun. As they came over the convoy of ships, they began to dive, one after another, almost vertically, engines screaming. They dropped so fast that it looked as though they would hit the deck. As they pulled out of the dive, Tom watched in horror as one by one the bombs detached from their undersides and plummeted towards the ship.

He threw himself down and scrambled to take cover under a tarpaulin, knowing as he did so that it would give him no protection. There was a series of deafening crashes around him, the cracking of beams and splintering of wood, the yells and screams of men below. The planes returned and dropped another series of bombs, blasting the funnel in two and making more great craters in the deck.

He could hear the Japanese crew and guards running about, screaming in terror. The sound of the aircraft receded and all that was left in the silence was the cracking and splintering of the stricken ship and the groans and yells of injured men below.

Tom was shaking all over. He could barely control his limbs. He forced himself out of his hiding place and stumbled over to where the top of the hatch had been. There was now a gaping hole there, with a jagged splintering edge. A great metal joist had fallen in, and some men had been crushed and mangled under the weight of it. The ladder had disappeared, and men were desperately trying to haul themselves onto the deck, clambering up on the broken beams, trampling on others in their panic. Tom put his hand out and with supreme effort pulled up one man.

'Thanks, mate,' said the man, and scuttled off towards the rail.

'Hey, wait,' yelled Tom. But the man was gone. Tom put his hands down and pulled up another man. This one stayed and helped him to heave the others on to the deck. Some helped pull their mates up, but most were anxious to get off the boat as quickly as they could.

Tom felt his strength slipping away from him. Pulling each man up was a massive effort. It was sapping his energy. There was no alternative, though. The deck was already listing badly. The ship was on its way down, and anyone left in the hold would go with it. So he carried on pulling up desperate men. His hands were wet and slippery with sweat, yet he didn't give up. A couple of others had stayed to help him, but they weren't working fast enough.

Tom put his hand out for the next man, and then froze.

It was Jim Leech. He was looking up at Tom with pleading eyes. Tom took his hand away and extended it to the next man.

'Please!' screamed Leech. 'Please don't leave me to die … I'll make amends. I promise.'

Tom looked away. His wish had come true. All he had to do was to ignore Leech's screams, and when the ship went down he would be trapped under the deck and be drowned.

He pulled up several other men, shutting his ears to Leech's pleas. None of the other men on the deck seemed to hear him either. They were engrossed in helping others. Perhaps, like Tom, they had good reason to ignore him.

Soon all the men had been helped out of the holds. Leech was the last man alive down there. Tom stood up. His heart hardened. He would leave Leech here to die.

Tom began to walk across the deck. It was listing dangerously now. It could only be a matter of minutes. Leech's sobs came to him from beneath the splintered deck. He hesitated. He thought of all the men that he'd seen die in the last three years: of the Bull and his mates cut down in the storm drain, of the pitiful wrecks dying in the hospital hut, of Harry and Ian, of Archie, and of the men lying crushed and bleeding beneath the beams in the hold. Suddenly, he stopped and turned. He couldn't do it. How would he be able to face himself if he let a man die? He could not bear the thought of it. How could he go back to Joy, so sweet and good, and ask for her love with this on his conscience?

He scrambled back towards the edge of the hole, slipping and stumbling as he went. When he put his hand over, he felt Leech's slippery grip on his fingers. Tom pulled and heaved. Leech was heavier than the rest of the men, and Tom had to summon extra strength to help him out. Soon Leech was sprawling on the deck beside him.

'God bless you, Ellis,' he said. 'I won't forget this. God bless you.'

* * *

The old ship shuddered and lurched, listing to one side. Prisoners who had fought their way out of the hold hurtled along the deck and landed in a heap against the rail. Tom shouldered his way between the sweating bodies and struggled over the slippery bars. Like dozens of others he flung himself clear as the ship pitched. For a few seconds, as he fell, everything was a blur. Then he smacked down on the waves and was instantly sucked under with the drag of the vessel as it slipped beneath the surface. His ears were filled with the rush and pressure of the sea and the metallic creaks and groans of the huge collapsing hull.

The force of the sinking ship dragged Tom down deeper and deeper. Powerless, he held his breath until his lungs were bursting. He began to panic and struggle.

This is it, he thought. This is the end.

He opened his mouth and gulped a belly-full of salt water. Then, suddenly, the downward pressure eased, and he found himself shooting upwards. He kicked furiously, sensing a chance to save himself. Peering up, he searched for the light, but nothing was visible through the shadowy water apart from the flailing legs of other prisoners.

He finally burst clear of the surface, gasping and spluttering for air, choking up salty bile. As he rubbed the water from his eyes, the blurred images of other men came into view. Some were beating around in panic, others yelling for help. He scanned the sea around him and caught a glimpse of George, only a few yards away, clinging to a broken beam. Tom gathered his strength and swam towards him with clumsy strokes. George's face was sickly pale. His skin was almost transparent, the white bones of his cheeks and nose visible. Tom stared at George's eyes. That expression. He'd seen it on so many faces, especially on the faces of the sick men in the hospital hut. A look of hopelessness. A look of surrender.

'I can't bloody swim, mate,' George said, his teeth chattering.

'Just hang on. We're going to be all right. We can't be far from the shore.'

Above the yells of the prisoners and the lapping of the waves came the buzz of an aircraft. It circled the area. As it banked overhead, Tom caught sight of the stars and stripes on the tailfin. Then suddenly the aircraft dived, swooping towards them from the clear blue sky. The hammering of machine gun fire filled the air. Bullets slapped the water like tropical rain. Men screamed as they were hit.

'What the hell are they doing?' yelled George.

'Duck,' Tom shouted.

Tom took a gulp of air and forced his head back underwater. Again he held his breath until his chest was nearly collapsing. When he returned, choking and sputtering to the surface, he saw that the plane was still circling above them but had stopped firing.

The water frothed and eddied where the ship had gone down. All around, bodies floated on the surface amongst debris from the wreckage, shattered planks of wood, hatch covers, rubber life-preservers, a cooking pot, a few broken latrines. Desperate prisoners clung to some of these things. Other men thrashed around, looking for something to grab onto, shouting in vain for the help that would not come.

The aircraft moved on to join a swarm of planes attacking the next ship in the convoy. As Tom struggled to keep afloat, treading water next to George's beam, he had a clear view of dozens of planes strafing the bulky vessel, their fuselages flashing in the sun as they dived. Anti-aircraft guns blazed from the deck. Within seconds the horizon lit up with the orange shock of an explosion as the fuel tanks caught. The ship blew up in a ball of fire. A giant wall of flame coursed over the water, raging towards the survivors. Oil drums bobbing on the surface caught and started to burn. Amid the chaos of the explosions came the agonised screams of burning men.

A lifeboat from Tom's ship nosed its way through the fires and the wreckage. Perilously low in the water and lopsided, the lifeboat was crammed with Japanese guards and soldiers from the ship. Some prisoners swam towards it, pleading to be taken on board. Tom watched in horror as one by one they were pushed back into the water; their knuckles beaten off the side with oars and bamboo poles. One man clung to the bow of the boat, refusing to let go. A guard stood up and opened fire with his machine gun. The prisoner fell into the water, a pool of his blood spreading through the waves.

'Bastards,' choked George. Tom's teeth were chattering despite the tropical sun overhead. He knew he needed to find a way of getting George to shore. He tried dragging the beam with one hand and swimming with the other, but he was too weak to make any progress.

'Just go, Tom. You might make it without me,' George gasped.

'Go now, mate.'

'Don't be stupid. I'm not leaving you.'

Tom searched around for something to float on. He couldn't tread water any more. There was plenty of debris from the ship floating his way, and when a sizeable plank came by he grabbed it with both hands. He hoisted his body onto it front first, forcing splinters from the rough wood into his stomach and thighs. It was then he realised his left leg was throbbing. Looking down he saw there was an open gash on his shin. The flesh had peeled right back to the bone.

He lay on the plank, panting, trying to regain some strength. The sea was rougher now, and it was taking all his energy to keep afloat. His stomach gnawed from the lack of food, and every bone and muscle in his body felt weak. Would he have the strength to paddle both floats? He glanced around. In those few moments George's beam had drifted several yards away.

'Hold on, George, hold on!'

No reply. Tom paddled back towards him. The beam was moving up and down with the swell, and George's head with it. As he got closer the beam disappeared from view behind a wave. It reappeared after a second or two, but George was no longer on it.

'George!' he screamed, taking frantic strokes towards the spot. He slid off his own plank and dived under the surface, beating around in the cloudy water. He could see nothing. He came up for air and dived again.

It was hopeless. Tears of anger and pity pricked his eyes. He had seen so many men die that it had become commonplace, but with each death he experienced a fresh surge of rage and frustration. He dragged himself back onto the plank and shut his eyes, trying to blank it out, to gather enough strength to save himself.

He lost track of time. Each time he lifted his head there were fewer and fewer men around him. After a while he couldn't hear anyone shouting for help. He would have to push himself to the edge to get out of this. He wasn't going to be one of those who slipped silently beneath the waves.

Each time he rose on the swell, he could just about see the dark smudge of land on the horizon, but there was no way of telling how far away it was. He made an effort to paddle in that direction, but for every yard he struggled to advance, he was washed back another by the tow. The cramp in his arms sometimes made it impossible to keep going. This forced him to lie still on the plank until he could move again, his jaws clamped together, rigid with cold, even though the skin on his arms and legs was scorching and peeling in the tropical sun.

More than once he drifted out of consciousness. The last time he came round the sky was growing dark and the sun was dipping beneath the western horizon. Tom was now so thirsty he could barely swallow. His mouth and blistered lips were coated in crusted sea salt.

With the sun gone, a breeze got up and it was icy cold on the water. He paddled on when he could find the strength, but without the sun to guide him he couldn't tell whether he was heading further out to sea or towards the land.

He must have been paddling and drifting for hours. Suddenly he felt a sharp pain as his injured leg brushed against a rock. He made a last supreme effort to haul himself forward, and after a few more strokes the plank ground to a halt on gritty sand. Tom lay there panting, face pressed down on the breakers, allowing his body to be dragged back and forth by the waves. He could not muster the energy to haul himself onto the beach.

He heard a shout. Then the splash of footsteps in the shallow water. Tom struggled to sit up. About a dozen men in shabby uniforms surrounded him on the moonlit beach. Several of them were holding guns. One of them yelled something at him, his rifle pointed at Tom's head. Slowly, Tom raised his hands in surrender and waited for the shot that would end it all.

25

The ferry lumbered across the flat waters of the Malacca Straits towards Georgetown. Laura leaned on the rail, welcoming the salt breeze on her face, a respite from the fierce sun. She watched the other vessels ply to and fro between the island and the mainland, and the deep green hills of Penang drawing closer and closer.

She was tired. Her limbs ached from the twenty-four-hour journey on the train. Even though she'd managed to get some fitful sleep, the steward had woken her at six in the morning, wanting to get the bunks stowed away and set up the carriage for breakfast. She was served with rubbery bacon and eggs, and as she ate she watched her fellow passengers with interest. There were two Malaysian businessmen deep in discussion over charts and graphs, a Thai family with two perfectly behaved little girls, and a German family whose children noisily refused to touch the food. Across the aisle, a couple of backpackers, dressed in shorts and flip flops, were so wrapped up in each other that they hardly looked out of the window or noticed anyone else around them. She thought about Luke, and looked away.

The landscape rolled past her: the craggy limestone outcrops of Southern Thailand, occasional glimpses of a turquoise sea between the jungle-covered hills, the little towns where locals waited for slow trains on crowded platforms with their bundles of wares and luggage tied up with string.

When night fell she stretched out on the bunk. Lying on top of the linen sheets the steward had put on, she read the books she had bought in Kanchanaburi. She stared at the artefacts she had brought from home: the photograph of Joy de Souza, the invitation to High Tops. She felt thwarted by having found out so little in Kanchanaburi. Even finding the book by Arthur Stone had been a false dawn. Perhaps she would discover more in Malaysia? She glanced again at the picture of Joy, at the enigmatic expression in those dark eyes. 'Are you still there, Joy? Will I find you?' she whispered.

She scribbled postcards to Ken and Marge, and one to Adam. It was difficult to think of anything meaningful to say to him, and she just trotted out the usual hackneyed phrases. 'Having a wonderful time in Thailand. Incredibly interesting. Beautiful country, wonderful people, lovely food. Now on night train to Malaysia. See you in a few weeks' time, Laura.' She did not want to offer him any encouragement, but she felt a glow of warmth when she thought about his kindness in suggesting she should take time off. This was tinged with a creeping guilt that she was going to repay it by handing in her notice.

The ferry docked in Georgetown, and as the passengers descended the metal ramp onto the quayside, they were surrounded by a clamouring mob of rickshaw drivers, touts and guides. One grabbed Laura's arm and pulled her aside.

'You want hotel? I show you good hotel.'

The sun was beginning to dip behind the buildings. She was suddenly apprehensive about being alone.

'Is it far?'

'Not far from here, madam. Two streets away only.'

She climbed on board the rickshaw and stowed her rucksack on the seat beside her. The man jumped on the bicycle in front, and for the first time she experienced the odd sensation of being pulled along by another human being. It felt precarious and somehow wrong. She noticed his calf muscles bulge as he strained on the pedals.

'I'm too heavy,' she protested. But he flashed a reassuring smile over his shoulder and pulled out into the slow-moving traffic. The hotel was only a couple of blocks from the waterfront, a faded Portuguese-style mansion, its crumbling façade painted pale yellow. Its shuttered windows, grand pillared entrance and an elaborate fountain on the drive proclaimed past glories. 'Cathay Hotel' a shabby notice by the front door said.

'Very good hotel. Very cheap,' said the rickshaw driver.

This would do for tonight, Laura thought. She paid the man more than he asked and went inside. An old Chinese man behind the counter, dressed in a faded blue tunic, greeted her with a wide smile and a bow. He showed her up the sweeping staircase to a high-ceilinged room on the first floor.

'Number one room,' the man announced proudly, switching on the ceiling fan and flinging open louvered shutters and windows with a flourish. Mosquito nets covered the openings.

She looked around. 'Very nice. Thank you.' He hovered in the doorway, waiting for a tip. She hastily handed him the few coins she had in her pocket, and he shuffled away.

Laura explored the room. It was huge, with a bare wooden floor and heavy antique furniture. The bathroom was almost as large, with a Victorian bathtub with claws for feet and a constantly dripping tap that ploughed a rusty furrow in the discoloured enamel. She leaned out of the open window. Between the buildings she glimpsed moonshine dancing on the waters of the straits. Exotic smells floated on the steamy air, spices and musk mingling with open drains. The voices of the rickshaw-wallahs waiting for passengers at the gate rose and fell on the evening air.

She felt excited at the thought that tomorrow she would begin her search for Joy. She lay down on the bed. Exhausted from the journey, she fell asleep straight away.

As she walked into the reception the next morning, the Chinese man greeted her with a warm smile.

'You want rickshaw? You want tour of city?'

'I'm looking for someone,' she said tentatively. 'Someone who lived in Penang during the war. Do you know how I might find her?'

The old man shrugged.

'Many, many people in Penang,' he said. 'She Chinese?'

'Wait. I have a picture.' She showed him Joy's photograph. He put on a pair of thick glasses and peered at it.

'Pretty lady. She Eurasian. Many Eurasian families lived in Farquhar Street area before war. Many died. Many vanished or move away.'

'Died?'

'Killed. In bombing raids. Many people die. My uncle and cousin die in bombings at dock.'

'I'm sorry. You were here then?"

The old man nodded, and for the first time he wasn't smiling. He hung his head in sorrow. The folds of his old face sagged, and the shadows of memories crossed his eyes.

'Let me look again.' The man took the photograph, turned it over and peered at the writing on the back.

'De Souza. Many, many people have that name. Very common. Look.' He produced a telephone directory from under the desk and thumped it on the counter. It was battered and grubby and was dated 1979. Laura thumbed through to the page showing 'de Souza'. There were several columns of that name. Her heart sank.

'Is there somewhere I could find out more? A public records office perhaps?'

'Record?' he peered at her, frowning.

'You know? Where they keep details of people, lists of residents.'

The old man shrugged again. 'There is post office. Maybe they know. There is also museum. You go there. Rickshaw-wallah take you. I tell him what you want. He speak good English.'

The rickshaw-wallah pedalled her through steamy streets lined with Chinese shop houses and food stalls, buzzing with colour and life. At the general post office she waited for a long time in a slow moving queue. When she reached the front she could not make the friendly woman behind the grille understand what she was looking for.

The woman just shook her head and said, 'No information here. You go to Kuala Lumpur. You try there.'

She returned to the rickshaw; the man was waiting under a tree, dozing, his feet propped up on the rickshaw's handle bars.

'No find lady?' he asked, waking up and seeing her face. She shook her head.

At Central Museum the woman behind the reception desk took the photograph and studied it carefully.

'I'm sorry, I do not know this lady,' she said smiling, handing the photo back to Laura.

'No, but do you have any records of residents in the town that I could look at.'

She shook her head. 'Public records in Kuala Lumpur. The lady must be very old now. Maybe dead?'

'I hope not,' said Laura, a shudder passing through her.

She wandered around, looking at the displays. A statue of Sir Francis Light dominated the lower hall. Sketches of the history of the island were displayed on the walls, charting the rise and decline of British rule. There was even a section devoted to the bombing raids and the Japanese Occupation in the war. She stared at pictures of civilians running for their lives, their faces masks of terror, as buildings around them crumbled and burned.

It was late afternoon as the rickshaw made its way back through the streets to Cathay Hotel. Laura closed her eyes and absorbed the sounds and smells of this exotic town as it wound down for the evening: the cries of street hawkers, the aroma of cooking over open fires, the salty tang of the sea floating on the breeze.

She stopped at a small café near the hotel and ordered some satay. It was a canteen-style establishment crowded with locals taking an early evening meal. She sat alone at a table on the pavement. Next to her, a couple of men in suits conferred with each other. Each time she glanced at them, she noticed them staring at her. They were leering openly, and then conferring together, clearly discussing her. She suddenly felt uncomfortable, being the lone female in the place. She quickly paid the bill and left.

The old man at the reception desk handed her the key and asked, 'You find lady?'

'Not yet. I'll try again tomorrow.'

'Maybe tomorrow you go sight-seeing instead. You must see Penang Hill, all the temples. Very beautiful. Look, take map. I arrange tour for you.'

He thrust an old, folded map into her hands. It was printed with garish adverts for restaurants, clubs and tourist attractions. Back in her room, as she sat on the bed, a mouse scuttled out and ran across the floorboards. She stifled a scream.

Opening the map on the bed, she studied the streets, hoping that there might be something that would lead her to Joy de Souza.

She searched the map for clues. On the outskirts of the town she noticed a building marked 'High Tops Hotel'. She stared at it. Was this the place from Dad's invitation? She looked closely at the map. There was a crude sketch of a grand house, with pillars and tall windows.

As she settled down for the night there was a soft knock at the door. She pulled on a shirt and opened it a fraction. A middle-aged man stood outside, short and stout and dressed in a suit. She recognised him as one of the businessmen at the restaurant where she had eaten her supper.

He said something to her in Malay.

'I don't understand,' she said, moving to shut the door.

He stuck his foot in the gap before the door and tried to grab her arm. She pulled away and slammed the door in his face, then rammed the bolt across it.

She sat down on the bed, shaking all over, waiting for his footsteps to go away, but there was no sound. The shadow of his shoes remained under the crack of the door, motionless; she stayed frozen on the bed, still shivering in shock, her eyes fixed on them. Her breathing seemed noisy in the silence. After a few minutes, there was movement under the door and the footsteps finally retreated. She heard him walk down the stairs. Still rooted to the spot, she couldn't get up and go to the window, but she heard his footsteps on the front steps and crossing the drive.

She lay down on the bed and stared at the ceiling, still shaking.

'What am I doing here alone? I must be mad.'

In the sunshine of the morning, it seemed hard to believe this had happened. Even so, she packed her bag and asked the old man to give her the bill and call her a taxi. He was perturbed, wringing his hands.

'You not leave Penang?'

'Oh, I thought I'd explore the island. Perhaps stay on the beach for a couple of nights.'

But as soon as they had turned out on to the street she asked the taxi driver to take her to High Tops Hotel.

The driver shook his head and said, 'I not know that hotel. Not famous. You go my brother hotel. Very close.'

'Pull over. I'll show you the map.'

The battered taxi squealed to a halt. The driver scrutinised the map she passed him. Then with much tutting and sighing, he set off again.

'That bad place. That not good like other hotel in Penang.'

She ignored him and stared out of the window at the shops and houses flashing past her.

He drove recklessly, blasting his horn at rickshaws and taking bends too quickly.

As they got further out from the town centre, the buildings began to thin out. The road began to rise into the hills. They squealed round a bend in the road, and the taxi turned in between some scabbed white pillars and moved on to a wide drive, spraying gravel as it came to a halt. The grand porticoed entrance to the house lay at the top of a flight of sweeping steps.

Laura paid the taxi and walked up the steps. A couple of large dogs of indeterminate breed got up and came up to her, sniffing her legs and wagging their tails in greeting. Like the Cathay Hotel, this place was fading. But more gracefully somehow, and it looked cared for. There were potted plants on the terrace, and the lawns were mowed in perfect stripes.

The reception area was in a tiled hallway, with a grand staircase leading up to a galleried area and panelled doors opening off it.

An immaculately dressed young Malaysian woman greeted Laura at the hotel's reception desk. Laura enquired about rooms, feeling self-conscious in her creased clothes.

'Many rooms available, madam,' said the young woman 'We only have three other guests, and one of them is leaving today. The price is all-inclusive. Breakfast, lunch and dinner, at seven o'clock.'

As the receptionist handed her the large metal key to her room, Laura asked, 'I was wondering if you know anything about the history of this house?'

The receptionist shook her head with an apologetic smile.

'I'm sorry. But you could ask the owner. He will be back later today. He has been away in Kuala Lumpur for a business meeting. I'll let him know you asked.'

The room was on the first floor, at the front of the house, overlooking the town. It was larger than the one at Cathay Hotel, and more welcoming, with an old-fashioned wooden dressing table, floral bedcovers and curtains, and flowers placed on a marble washstand. It looked like a down-at-heel country-house hotel in England. It felt safe here, away from the town. She lifted the Bakelite telephone receiver and asked the receptionist for an international line. Ken answered after several rings.

'I thought I'd let you know that I'm in Penang now.'

'Well, that's a relief. I've been worried about you.'

'I stayed at a dodgy hotel for a couple of nights. But I've moved now. I'll probably be here for a few days. It's called "High Tops Hotel" if you need to get in touch. In fact, I think Dad might have been to a party here before the war. How are things with you?'

'Not too bad. Oh, by the way, that boy came round yesterday.'

'Boy?'

'Yes, the one who's been trying to get hold of you. Rory, with the curly blond hair. He seemed pretty agitated. Asked when you'd be back.'

'How long ago was this?'

'The day after you called from Bangkok.'

'Did he leave a message or anything?'

'No, nothing. Left a bit abruptly when I told him I didn't know how to get in touch with you.'

'Well, if he comes round again, try and get him to leave a number or something, so I can give him a call.'

She replaced the receiver, wondering what could be so important. Was it something to do with her flat? It was strange the way he had left so suddenly with his parents when he'd seemed so committed to the protest. Her mind wandered to Luke, and she surprised herself with a pang of regret at the way she'd walked out on him. Perhaps she'd been too hasty running away from him in Thailand? Perhaps she should have given him a bit more of a chance. She stared out of the window at the lush garden bathed in sunlight.. The sun was almost directly overhead. It would soon be time to go down for lunch.

The peace outside was broken by the sound of an engine, and a car appeared on the road, swung in between the gateposts. An old Bentley drew up on the gravel drive with the blast of its horn. The dogs that had been lazing on the top step bounded down to greet the car, barking, their tails wagging. The receptionist appeared at the top of the steps, smiling. An old Sikh man in a turban got out of the driver's side and went round to open the other door. But before he could do so, the door swung open and a tall man dressed in a crumpled white suit clambered out. The dogs bounded to him, and he greeted them as they jumped up to lick his face.

'Get down, you silly idiots,' he said in an English accent. He then turned to the driver, 'Don't worry about that bag, Adesh. I can carry that.'

'Oh, I'm so pleased you're back,' the receptionist began.

'Me too. The bloody train from KL was murder.'

They went inside, followed by the dogs.

Laura turned back into the bedroom. She'd been drawn in by the scene. She wondered what it must be like to live here in these beautiful surroundings, in this place so far from home, to own this great shambling mansion. What sort of man was the owner?

Lunch was served in a great sunlit dining room. Laura was waited on by Adesh. She was starting on her first course when a voice surprised her.

'Miss Ellis?'

She looked up. The owner was standing beside the table. He had changed out of his white suit for another pair of crumpled trousers and a white short-sleeved shirt. He was tanned, and close up she could see that his face bore the lines of age.

She stood up and shook his hand.

'David Atherton. Welcome to High Tops. They told me you were asking about the house. If you come along to the reception after you've finished, I'll show you around.'

'That's very kind of you. There's no hurry, though.' Where had she heard that name before?

'I'd be delighted. It's not often I get the chance to show off the old place.'

After she'd finished she went up to her room to fetch the invitation she had found in her father's trunk and then returned to the desk. The owner was poring over some columns of figures. As he looked up, she caught a glimpse of anxiety in his expression before a smile banished it.

'Great. Let's make a start on our tour.' He came out from behind the desk.

'Have you lived here long?' she asked. Then she glanced down at the invitation and realised where she had seen the name.

'All my life, practically. I grew up here.'

'Really? You see, I have this. It was in my father's belongings. He died recently.'

She showed him the invitation.

'I'm so sorry to hear about your father,' he said. Then he took the printed card and smiled. 'How interesting. This must have been an invitation to one of my parents' house parties. I know they used to give a lot of them before the war. My mother was quite a socialite. Did your father live in Penang?'

'Yes. He worked for United Rubber for a few years. I've been trying to find out a bit about his time in the Far East.'

'I've got a collection of photos from around that time in the ballroom. If you'd like to come along I'll show you. I had them framed and hung on the wall after my mother died.'

He showed her upstairs and down a dimly lit corridor at the front of the house. It smelt of polish and citronella. He proudly opened door after door off a long corridor on the first floor. The large rooms must once have been grand. Now they had a forlorn look, smelled of moth-balls, had their furniture covered in dust sheets.

'These rooms only get used in high season,' he explained, slightly apologetic.

Then he threw open a set of double doors at the end of the corridor and took her into a vast empty room, with a double height ceiling and dusty chandeliers hanging from the rafters.

On the walls were dozens of framed photographs of groups of people in evening wear, holding up glasses, or in fancy dress, standing under the chandeliers. There was something eerie about all these faces frozen in time, people who had once lived here and danced in this empty room and filled it with laughter and life.

'Take your time. I know there are lots of them.'

The guests were not named, but the year in which they were taken was printed beneath each photograph.

She came to a photograph dated 1938 and stopped. She looked closely, and her heart missed a beat. There he was in the back row, standing between a stout lady with a pince-nez and a burly man with a jocular smile. He was smiling and holding up his glass, looking handsome in a bow tie and starched white shirt, his dark hair swept back from his face.

She turned to her host. She pointed to the photograph with tears in her eyes.

'This is him,' she smiled. 'This is my father!'

26

Tom stood at the rail as the ship sailed up the straits between the mainland and Penang and into Georgetown harbour. The smell of frangipani and lotus blossom drifted on the air, and he felt a tingle of anticipation as the vessel eased into the dock on the Georgetown wharf.

It amazed him that he was finally returning to the place he had longed for throughout his captivity. He thought about how many times he had been close to death, had been convinced he would never make it back here.

When he had been washed up on that beach and surrounded by all those men with guns, he thought he had only a few seconds to live. To his astonishment the men had put down their guns and helped him up out of the sea, had virtually carried him to their camp deep within the jungle. He was greeted by six other exhausted and emaciated prisoners in the camp, who, like him, had managed to make it to shore from the shipwreck. They told him that this was the Philippines, the island of Luzon, and that the men helping them were Filipino guerrillas, who were fighting to drive the Japanese from their islands.

Tom and the others had stayed there for weeks, being fed and cared for by the guerrillas. Some of the men were very ill and spent the time recovering from malaria and other fevers. Tom, who had broken his leg escaping the sinking ship, simply lay in his tent the first few days, unable to move. When the pain in his leg subsided, he began to walk around camp, hobbling about with a stick made of thick bamboo, talking to his fellow soldiers and attempting to hold conversations with the guerrillas with simple words and hand gestures. When his wounds began to heal, he was able to help them prepare meals and maintain and clean the camp. Gradually all of them began to grow healthier, to put on a little weight. News of the progress of the war was brought to the camp regularly by the locals who brought them food and supplies.

Tom's heart had filled with hope when he observed that the tide of the war was beginning to turn, and that it might all be over very soon. One day the whole camp had erupted in jubilation with the news that the US Army had landed on the island and that the Philippines had been liberated.

Soon after, a US Army truck had arrived at camp. It was to take Tom and the other prisoners to Manila. From there they were assigned to ships to take them home. Tom and the other soldiers had wept with joy and relief. They were finally free.

The journey from the Philippines to Penang had taken eight days. The transport officer at US Command in Manila had wanted to send him home on one of the troop ships bound for the United Kingdom, but Tom had insisted that he needed to report to his regiment in Malaya. So they had paid for his passage, issued him with some civilian clothes, and sent him on his way with twenty US dollars.

He could still feel it there now in his jacket pocket as the ship drew closer to the shore. It was an odd sensation to know that he was now a free man, that he could go into a shop and spend his money as he liked. As they tied up at the dock he was shocked to see the destruction on the waterfront, the bombed out go-downs and warehouses, and behind them the burned out shells of Chinese shop-houses flattened by the air raids. Where once had been bustle and commerce, there was now an air of hopeless devastation.

Tom didn't have enough money to check into the Eastern and Oriental, so he found a small Chinese guesthouse a few blocks back from the waterfront, where rooms were cheap and clean. When he'd washed and changed his clothes, he went out onto the street and hailed a rickshaw. It carried him slowly through the backstreets of the town and up towards the Eurasian quarter. He stared about him, shocked at how many buildings had been bombed or burnt to the ground. Yet there was now an air of industry in this part of town, he noticed. Everywhere there was the sound of hammers and drills at work. Buildings were being rebuilt or replaced, bomb sites cleared of rubble and debris.

He held his breath as they turned the corner into Joy's road. To his relief all the wooden houses were still standing. The scene was exactly like the one that had greeted him the first time he had driven along here. Grubby children played amongst the chickens and pigs, underneath the wooden houses.

The house came into view and the rickshaw pulled up outside. Tom stood there, staring at Joy's home for a long time. From a distance it had looked unchanged, but now he saw that all the windows were boarded up, and the potted plants on the veranda had withered and died. He paced around the house. In the overgrown back garden were a few broken toys and an empty washing line. Over the fence he spotted an old Indian woman, watering plants.

'Excuse me,' he asked her in Malay. 'Do you know what happened to the de Souza family? They used to live here.'

The woman shrugged. 'I do not know. I am new here. No-one has ever lived there since I came.'

He returned to the street and asked some children playing in the opposite garden, but they just giggled and stared at him. He knocked on a couple of doors. None of the occupants seemed to know what had happened to the family.

One old man said, 'One day they left. The whole family. Carrying suitcases. I do not know where they were going. It was the day of the raid.'

Tom thanked him and returned to the rickshaw. He paid off the driver and said he would walk back to the hotel. He needed some time to think.

He walked slowly back through the old quarter, barely noticing his surroundings. Why had he assumed that she would still be here? All the time he'd been a prisoner, he'd imagined that Joy might have been to Singapore for a short while but would have returned to Penang. He'd thought that her life would have gone on as before, that she'd be waiting for him on the porch wearing a simple white dress just like in the old days. How deluded he'd been. How naïve. He wandered on and eventually joined a wider road. He wasn't sure of the way the rickshaw had brought him out of town, and he soon realised that the buildings were thinning out and that he must be going the wrong way. So much had changed since he was last here. Buildings had been flattened, and new ones stood half-built on muddy plots where the undergrowth had been slashed away. He turned around and began to walk back down the hill.

Rounding a curve in the road, he noticed the back of a familiar building. He stopped and stared. It was High Tops. It looked odd from behind, surrounded by trees. He'd never approached it from this side before. He walked on, and as he drew nearer the sound of voices and the strains of a jazz band floated up to him. Stopping at the gate he held the bars and peered through. On the lawn in front of the house, a garden party was in progress. Women stood around dressed in bright colours, men chatted in groups. There was a burst of laughter as someone cracked a joke. A trestle table was set up, loaded with sandwiches, and servants in uniform walked amongst the guests with trays of drinks. He realised the music was coming from a gramophone set up beside the table.

Was Millie still there? He remembered the glimpse he'd had of her and Sir James pushing their way up the gang-plank on the crowded liner the day he'd left Georgetown with the Volunteers. He scanned the guests, but couldn't see her amongst them. Perhaps the house had been sold. He was about to turn away when he did catch sight of her. She was sitting at the edge of the lawn in a deck chair, surrounded by a group of children. She was reading from a book. She must have changed dramatically from the woman he'd known before the war.

He turned away, feeling more wretched than before. The sight of all those healthy and sociable people reminded him more than ever of his own isolation and of what he'd lost in the war. He knew he could never open the gate and join them. He looked down at his bony frame, and the cheap clothes he'd bought from a market in Manila. He moved away from the gate before anyone noticed him, and began to walk back towards the town.

* * *

The next day he found the little office that now served as the Penang headquarters of the Straits Settlements Volunteer Force; it was on the main street, above a bank. The man behind the desk looked down at his list when Tom stated his name.

'Ah ... Private Thomas Ellis. Missing in shipwreck, June 1945.

Believed drowned.'

He looked up at Tom with an air of finality.

'Well, I'm obviously not drowned. I'm here, alive and well.'

The man eyed him sceptically.

'Do you have any proof of ID?'

Tom produced a chit of paper signed by the US Quartermaster, verifying his identity. He then placed his regimental badge on the counter. The man pushed the badge back towards Tom.

'I don't need that, Private. Your little unit has been disbanded now the war is over. Keep it as a souvenir. I suppose you will be wanting your back pay? Quite a tidy sum you've made ... Three years and seven months to the day.'

So that was it. He was out of the army, without ceremony and without thanks for his loyalty, without apology for his captivity. He stood on the pavement outside the office, clutching his envelope stuffed with dollars, contemplating the situation. He felt numb, deflated. Slowly, he walked away towards his hotel, staring at the ground.

He spent the evening in a little Chinese café near the guesthouse. He sat at a table beside the window, eating noodles and watching the streets for Joy. Once, his heart leapt when he thought he had caught sight of her, a slim girl with shiny black hair, walking and chatting with a group of friends. But then she turned and laughed at something one of them said, and he saw that it was not Joy. He turned away, disappointed.

Penang did not feel like home any more. The place had changed, and he guessed he had too. There was no longer an air of ease and colonial languor on the streets. There was a feeling of industry. It was filled with new people rushing everywhere, with engine noise, activity. It was not the place he had known before the war.

He toyed with his food and wondered how he would go about finding Joy if she had gone to Singapore. She could be living anywhere. He had his back pay now though, so perhaps he could afford a trip down the coast to look for her.

He looked up and suddenly caught sight of a familiar figure coming down the street. It was the manager from the rubber estate.

'Mr. Jones!' shouted Tom, getting up from the table and waving to get his attention. The manager did not notice him.

Tom put enough money on the table to cover the meal and a tip, and then dashed out onto the street. He ran after the man and put his hand on his shoulder.

'Ellis!' The man was astonished. 'We all thought you were dead. You are looking a bit skinny, I must say, but you seem to be alive at least.' He patted Tom on the back, smiling brightly. 'Come on, I'll buy you a drink.'

He took Tom to a bar a few doors down from the café. It was dark and steamy, with loud music being played on a gramophone. It was packed with men. The bar girls, heavily made up and scantily dressed, were making a great deal of fuss over the customers, sitting down beside them, draping their arms around them, flattering them with dreamy looks.

They were shown to a table. They ordered whisky stengahs.

'So, what brings you back to Penang?' asked Jones.

'I'm looking for a friend.'

'Your lady friend? The one you were seeing before the war?'

'Yes. I went to her house today. It was boarded up. No-one seems to know where the family went.'

'There was a hell of a lot of chaos during the air raids, Tom.' Jones sighed. 'People went out onto the streets to watch. They thought they were going to see a dog-fight in the sky, but they were bombed or mown down by bullets.'

Tom looked at him in alarm.

'She said they were going to Singapore.'

'Perhaps they did. Is there anyone else you could ask about her whereabouts?'

Tom sipped his stengah and thought about it.

'I suppose I could go to the school where she worked. I don't know why I didn't think about that before. I'll go first thing in the morning'

Jones looked at him steadily.

'Would you like to come back to United Rubber when you've found her? We're really short of manpower. We could do with someone experienced like you, Tom.'

Tom looked into his drink for a moment, considering the offer.

'I'm intending to marry Joy, if she'll have me. Would that be a problem?'

Jones leaned back on his chair and laughed.

'You mean because she's Eurasian? Things are changing here, Tom. The old pre-war prejudices are a thing of the past. As far as I'm concerned it wouldn't be a problem in the slightest.'

They held their glasses up and drank to the future, then two bar girls brought them more drinks and squeezed in to the seats next to them.

The one next to Tom put her arm around his shoulders and started stroking his face. She was heavily made up and could not have been more than sixteen.

'You so handsome,' she purred.

Tom felt uncomfortable. He only wanted Joy, not this little Chinese girl who would go with any man for the price of a meal.

Jones was obviously enjoying the attentions of his own girl, who had now progressed to sitting on his lap and running her hands through his hair. His eyes were fixed on her breasts, bulging with lust, his face flushed with the pleasure of anticipation.

Tom finished his drink and stood up.

'I'll leave you to it, Mr. Jones. I think I'll get an early night. Maybe see you tomorrow.'

His bar girl pulled a face and grabbed on to his sleeve to try to stop him, but he shook himself free from her grasp and walked quickly out of the bar, and back to the guesthouse.

* * *

The school had not been touched by the air raids. Tom walked into the front hall the next morning, when he knew that lessons would be in full swing. It looked and smelled exactly as it had done that morning in 1941 when he had last come looking for Joy. There was even the same grey-haired woman on the desk.

She looked up. Tom thought he saw a flash of recognition cross her face.

'Can I help you, sir?'

'I'm looking for Miss Joy de Souza. She was a teacher here. I was wondering if you knew her whereabouts.'

The woman looked flustered. She got up from her seat.

'Could you step this way, please, sir?'

She beckoned him towards the office and left him at the door while she slipped inside and whispered something to a woman seated behind a desk.

'The headmistress will see you, sir,' she said, coming out and sidling back behind her desk.

Tom stepped inside the office. It was painted white and was

very bare, with a picture of the crucifixion above the desk. The headmistress, a tall thin woman, stood up and shook his hand.

'Are you a relative of Miss de Souza?' she asked.

'No, a friend. I've been a prisoner of war. I haven't seen her since 1941.'

'I'm so sorry.'

She hesitated for a moment, watching his face. Then she looked directly at him and said, 'I'm afraid I have some very bad news. Miss de Souza and the whole of her family were killed in an air raid. They were walking to the harbour to catch a boat to Singapore. She had told us that she was going the day before. They are buried in the graveyard along the road with all the other victims of the raid. The school paid for the headstone.'

The blood drained from Tom's face. His mouth went dry, and he thought he was going to be sick, or collapse. The room became a blur.

'Would you like to sit down? Shall I get you some water?'

She guided him to a chair and handed him a glass. He slumped down; his head was swimming. He put his face in his hands.

'I can't believe it. I just can't ...'

In all his dreams, in all his nightmares and deliriums he had never considered that this could happen. It had always been him who might die and never come back here. It had never been Joy, not once, not even for a second. He had never let that thought enter his consciousness. Even after he had arrived back in Penang and seen her house boarded up and neglected, he had not thought she might be dead. He had simply assumed that she and her family had gone to Singapore as they had planned to do.

He fought back the tears. He didn't want to cry here, in front of this woman he didn't know.

'It must be a dreadful shock for you. I'm so sorry. Miss de Souza was a wonderful teacher. We all miss her terribly here at the school.'

When he felt able to walk, he muttered his goodbyes and went outside. The sudden force of the sun made his head throb. He walked as if in a dream, hardly noticing where he was going, crossing roads without looking, zigzagging between people on the pavement. He reached the cemetery.

There was a mass of new graves on a separate piece of ground at the back under the trees. It looked as though it had been cleared especially for all these new bodies. There must have been hundreds of people buried there. Most were marked with simple wooden crosses, but one or two had proper carved headstones. He wound his way through them, reading the names. It was heart-breaking. Whole families were buried together. Eventually he found it. A white marble cross embossed with gold lettering: 'Here lie Joseph de Souza, his wife Bertha, and their children: Joy, born 1916, Grace, born 1922, Hope, born 1928, Paul, born 1932, Luke, born 1934, and Elijah, born 1936. All died on December 11, 1941. They are sadly missed.'

Tom sank to his knees and wept. He wept for the countless times that he had taken out her photo for a glimpse of the face that had given him the hope and the will to survive. He wept for all the plans he had made for his life with her. He wept because now he could never take her in his arms and ask her to marry him. He wept for her lost life and his lost future.

'You got me through it all, didn't you,' he asked her, tears streaming down his face. 'You weren't here, but your spirit got me through, Joy. Because of you, I survived.'

27

Laura stretched out on a sun-lounger beside the pool. When she closed her eyes all she could hear was the chattering of birds in the lush vegetation, and the swish and splash of the waters as the Malay boy cleared fallen leaves from the pool. She was on the terrace of High Tops Hotel. The sun warmed her face, burning red through her eyelids. If she opened them she would see the view over the tree tops to the town shimmering in the heat of the morning and the blue of the straits beyond, melting into the sky. She was beginning to understand why Dad had left London for the lure of this beautiful island, had been seduced into staying here.

She thought about the previous evening. After she'd found the photograph of Dad in the ballroom, her host had taken her on an extended tour of the house and grounds.

He had shown her the terraced garden, full of exotic shrubs and trees, and the garage, formerly a stable block, in which a pre-war Morris and an ancient Bentley were stored. He had then taken her up to the flat he occupied on the top floor. It was untidy but comfortable, full of old books and antiques. Beside a casement window overlooking the town stood a writing desk, scattered with papers and holding a portable typewriter. In the kitchen, a slim Malay woman sang softly as she peeled vegetables.

'Don't worry about me tonight, Suria,' he said, 'I'll probably eat downstairs in the dining room. If it's OK with you?' he asked, turning to Laura, 'I thought I might join you.'

'That would be very nice,' Laura had answered.

She caught a brief exchange of glances between the two and wondered fleetingly if the woman was his lover.

They ate in the long panelled dining room at the front of the house. The tables were set with linen tablecloths and silver, and lit by candles. The old Indian waiter brought dish after dish of deliciously spicy Malay food. Only one other table was occupied, by an elderly American couple who kept the waiters dancing attendance.

David poured wine.

'It's so nice to have someone to talk to in English. I can speak Malay and do have lots of friends here, but sometimes it's nice to chat away in English to someone who understands.'

She watched his face as he told her about his life. He wasn't handsome, she decided, but his strong features were attractive, and he had unusual pale-grey eyes that held your gaze. He told her that he'd been born in Australia after his parents had fled the Japanese invasion of the island, and that they had returned to reclaim the house soon after the war.

'Pa wanted to go back to England. There was some rioting here in the Malayan Emergency, but Ma wouldn't hear of it. I remember her saying, "What's there for us there, James, retirement in a bungalow in Tunbridge Wells? Ration books and bombsites? At least the sun shines here, and it's beautiful. I wouldn't give this up for the world." So we stayed. She usually got her way. Pa died of dengue fever when I was ten. He was a lot older than my mother.'

'Do you remember him?'

'Yes, very well in fact. He used to read to me in the study and take me around the island in the Bentley. That was his pride and joy.'

'Did you ever go to England?'

'We visited occasionally. Ma had to go back for a few months for medical treatment just before she died, and I went with her. That was in 1975. We rented a flat in London and saw all the sights. She was really frail by then. She had cancer, you see.'

'You must have been very close.'

'Yes, I suppose we were in a way. But she could be difficult. She was a strong personality, and got more demanding as she got older. We had our tricky times.'

'A bit like me and Dad,' Laura said wistfully, thinking of the precious moments wasted on needless confrontations and misunderstandings.

She realised that she was comfortable with this man, even though she'd only met him that morning. With him she felt able to talk about things that she would not have been able to say to any of her friends. It must be the security of knowing that she was just passing through and would probably never see him again, she told herself.

'What made you decide to turn the house into a hotel?' she asked after a pause. He laughed and Laura detected a trace of bitterness.

'Desperation, I suppose. I didn't go to university or anything. Ma and Pa didn't want me to go away to boarding school, and I just had tutors here. Hopeless, most of them. So I'm not really qualified to do very much. After Ma died and the money dried up I hadn't a clue what to do. I was on the point of selling up. It was my wife's idea to have a hotel, but when the hard work started she upped and left. Back to Australia.'

'Don't you get many guests here?'

'Not really. If you're not in the Lonely Planet you don't get a look in. I've never really gone all out to compete with the Georgetown hotels, though. I just want to cover the cost of maintaining the house, pay the staff a living and myself a subsistence salary.'

'This is a beautiful house.'

'I'm glad you think so.' He sipped his wine. 'Have you explored the island yet?'

'Not really. I only arrived the day before yesterday, and I've only been in Georgetown so far.'

'Perhaps I could take you on a bit of a tour? I could drive you around tomorrow, if you would like that. There aren't many other guests anyway, and Suria can take care of the place for a day.'

'That's very kind, but I really came to Penang to see if I could trace someone.'

She told him about the photograph of Joy, and how she had tried to find some trace of her in Penang, but had so far drawn a blank.

'You might have to go to the public-records office in KL. That's where most of that information is kept. If you don't mind me asking though, why do you want to find her so badly?'

Laura took a deep breath and told him about the letter with the Penang postmark.

'I think it was from a woman. It opened with the words "My Dear Thomas". I only got as far as the first paragraph, which went something like, "I know it's been a long time since we were in touch …" Then Dad came in through the front door, and in an impulse I threw it in the fire, so he wouldn't catch me reading his post. I tried to tell him about it before he died, but he didn't want to know. I know he was close to Joy, from what she wrote on the back of the photograph and from another photo I found of them together. I suppose I'd really like to find her to say I'm sorry for what I did with the letter, and to find out what she was like, and what Dad meant to her.'

David swirled the wine round in his glass, his eyes not meeting hers. After a while he spoke.

'Have you considered the possibility that she might not be here anymore. She might have left the island. She might even be dead?'

'Not really, but I suppose I should face the fact that it is possible.'

'Why don't I take you to the graveyard in Georgetown tomorrow? It would be a start. At least you could eliminate that possibility before you search any further.'

'That sounds a bit of a macabre way to start looking for someone.'

'Yes, but since the other way involves a trip to KL, which would take you a day and a night on the train from here, it does seem the most sensible thing to do.'

She had agreed. Now, sitting by the pool in the bright sunshine, she wasn't too sure.

David emerged from the patio doors and came towards her, shading his eyes. He was wearing a pale blue shirt and linen trousers. Perhaps he could even be described as attractive, she thought, reminding herself quickly that he was forty-something and she only twenty-six.

'Are you ready for our trip? I've got the car ready and waiting on the drive.'

He drove her out towards Batu Ferringhi in a battered jeep. She wound the window down and let the warm wind blow her hair. The bright scenery flashed by: rubber plantations, patches of untamed jungle, settlements of wooden houses on stilts with long thatched roofs. It was beautiful. The road wound up through the hills. It did not take long to reach the other side of the island. Laura glimpsed the sea through the trees as the road ran parallel to the coast. After a couple of miles, David pulled the jeep off the road and brought it to a halt on the soft verge. He jumped out.

'Come on. I'll show you somewhere special.'

Beckoning for Laura to follow, he plunged into the undergrowth on a tiny path, barely visible between the trees. It wound its way through the thick vegetation, almost obscured in places by hanging creepers and overgrown bushes. Laura looked around anxiously for tree snakes as she walked behind David. She supposed it must be safe; he was a native after all. After about five minutes the forest thinned out and the bright blue sea came into view between the palm trees.

'Tourists don't know about this place,' he said, leaning against a palm and staring out to sea. Laura followed his gaze. The crescent of white sand was punctuated by smooth round boulders. Huge coconut palms leaned gracefully over the beach in a perfect curve. Shallow waves lapped at the sand. It was perfectly clean and unspoilt.

'This was my mother's favourite spot,' said David. 'She used to come down here and just sit on that rock there, staring out to sea. Especially towards the end when she was ill. She seemed drawn to it.'

'I can see why,' murmured Laura.

'Luckily, it's escaped development so far. The road's too narrow here. But it will come.'

Then he drove her up to the car park at the base of the Penang Hill where they caught the funicular railway train to the top. They strolled round the gardens and stood at the view point, where David pointed out the landmarks of the town, and over the misty water to Butterworth on the mainland. To Laura the gardens looked strangely familiar. As she turned away from the viewpoint, with a shiver of recognition she realised that this was the place where Dad and Joy had posed together, that the palm tree and the bushes were the backdrop of the photograph she had found in her father's trunk.

They went into the little café and ordered coffee. David asked her about her work.

When she told him what she did, he said, 'That sounds pretty impressive. Do you enjoy it?'

'No. That's the trouble. I find it really unfulfilling. Dad encouraged me to do it. He only wanted the best for me, I suppose, and I never had the heart to tell him that I loathed the work. The money never really made up for that.'

'Have you thought about doing something different?'

'I've been thinking about looking for a job in another branch of the law, something a bit more worthwhile, work in a law centre maybe. That's what my Dad did himself. But these last couple of days I've had my doubts about that too.'

'Why don't you have a complete break? Take a year off or something. You could stay here and help me build up the business. I'm trying to persuade the bank in KL to give me a loan, but it would make all the difference to have someone else on board. I've been looking for someone to help out for some time.'

She stared at him.

'But you barely know me.'

'I know enough.'

She smiled. 'That's very flattering. I'll certainly give it some thought.'

They drove back to Georgetown, and as they neared the centre, David stopped the car beside a little church. It was stone built, with a spire and stained glass windows and a neat churchyard. It looked like a church one would find in any English town or village.

'All the British used to come here before the war. It was where everyone came to be seen. This church was as much of an institution as the club.'

Laura bit her lip. Dad wouldn't have come here, she knew that. He was a committed atheist. Or perhaps that was just after the war, after what he had been through.

'Shall we go and have a look?'

She wandered between the graves and saw English names engraved on the headstones. She was astonished by how young these people had died. There were many tiny graves, too, of children, buried beside their parents. She lingered beside them, touched by the sadness.

'You see that corner,' said David, pointing to the back of the graveyard behind a wall, where the graves were closer together. 'That's where all the Christian victims of the Georgetown bombings in the war were buried.'

Her heart beat faster. She left David by the church and walked along the gravel path to the place he had pointed to. She made her way along the lines of graves, staring at the headstones, holding her breath, dreading what she might find. There were many British names here too, amongst the Indian and Portuguese. Again, she saw the graves of many children, of whole families buried side by side.

She nearly missed it. It was at the end of a line almost in the very corner of the graveyard.

'Here lie Joseph de Souza, his wife Bertha, and their children: Joy, born 1916, Grace, born 1922, Hope, born 1928, Paul, born 1932, Luke, born 1934, and Elijah, born 1936. All died on December 11, 1941. They are sadly missed.'

She stared. Could this be *the* Joy de Souza? Could there be another one? It was a common name. She remembered the columns of de Souzas she had seen in the phone book at Cathay Hotel. She peered at Joy's date of birth. Joy would have been twenty-six in 1942

– the same age as Laura was now. She turned away, overwhelmed.

She felt David's hand on her arm.

'I'm so sorry,' he said softly. 'I take it that's the person you were looking for. Are you OK?'

She nodded and turned away, and with an effort of will suppressed her tears.

'Come on. Let's go back to the hotel.' He guided her back along the path, a firm hand on her arm.

Suria looked up from the desk as they entered the hotel lobby.

'There is a message for Miss Ellis,' she said smiling. 'Could you please call Ken at home,' she read from the note.

Laura dialled Ken from the telephone in her room.

'Laura. Glad you called. It's six in the morning here.' His voice sounded distorted, as though he was shouting from the end of a long tube.

'I'm sorry. But they said it was urgent.'

'Yes. Laughing boy's in a spot of trouble.'

'Laughing boy?'

'Your friend Luke.'

'But he's in Thailand still, isn't he?'

'Phuket. Somewhere called Patong, to be precise. Sounds pretty seedy. He called here yesterday. Said he was calling from a police station. He's in the clink apparently. Some misunderstanding. He wants you to go and see if you can bail him out. Well, not bail, strictly. Probably a bribe, reading between the lines.'

Laura swallowed. She could barely take it all in.

'Why did he phone you?'

'Said he was desperate, that there wasn't anyone else he could turn to. He knows you're in Malaysia. Suppose it was a long shot. I'd leave him to rot if I were you.'

When she said goodbye and replaced the receiver, she sat silent for a long time on the edge of the bed, thinking about Luke, weighing up the options, wondering whether to respond to the call, or to take Ken's advice and simply ignore it.

28

The frenetic sights and sounds of Patong Bay assaulted Laura's senses as she made her way along the waterfront. Her clothes stuck to her in the intense heat. Under the rucksack, her back was running with sweat. She shaded her eyes and looked around. On one side jet skis buzzed about on the gleaming ocean. On the other, across the busy street, a strip of bars and cafés pumped Western music and flashed neon signs proclaiming delights such as 'Fish n' Chips', 'German Beerkeller' and 'Go Go bar'. She could smell chips frying from where she stood.

'You want hotel?' A tuk-tuk drew up beside her, its engine putt-putting noisily.

'Later, maybe. Can you take me to the police station first?'

The driver peered at her and spat his betel nut onto the pavement, the red stain darkening instantly in the heat.

'Sure. One hundred baht.'

She knew it was expensive but was too tired to haggle. The twenty-four-hour journey from Penang by ferry, train and minibus had left her reeling with exhaustion. She slid onto the hot plastic seat gratefully and held onto the bar, breathing in neat diesel fumes as the tuk-tuk careered off the main drag and down a side street, past more girlie-bars, night clubs and fast food outlets.

The police station was a squat concrete building sandwiched between a lady-boy cabaret and a Muay Thai boxing school.

The officer at the desk showed her through a back door into a yard. As she followed him she noticed the gun and truncheon swinging from his belt. He waved her in the direction of a cell crowded with half-naked men, some sitting on the floor, others squashed together on a narrow bench against the wall. With a start she recognised Luke; he was dozing against the wall, his hair dishevelled and his feet shackled with irons. He was the only foreigner in the cell.

'Hey farang!' the policeman yelled, and Luke's eyes flickered open. He struggled upright and approached the bars.

'Laura, thank god, you've come. I've been rotting in here for days. Lost count of how long it's been.'

His face was deeply tanned under the dirt and showed the beginnings of a beard. He wore a filthy T shirt and shorts.

'This is becoming a bit of a habit,' she said dryly. 'What on earth happened to you?'

He gripped the bars and brought his face close to hers. She could smell his rotten breath.

'Why did you leave me, Laura? I wouldn't have got into this trouble if you'd been with me.'

'Don't blame me. You were determined to party. What happened anyway?'

He lowered his voice, and his eyes darted around the yard.

'The Aussies and I were just having a sun downer in a beach café, rolling up a couple of spliffs when there was a fucking raid. The police must have had a tip off.'

'What happened to the others?'

'The bastards scarpered. Managed to run out the back way, but I was on the other side of the table, stuck in the corner. No way out. Arrested for possession, of course. Been in here ever since. They said I could phone one person, so I phoned your house in London.

Thought you might have gone home.'

'What's going to happen to you?'

'The guy from the consulate came down yesterday. Said if I could raise five hundred quid I'd probably be okay – the bastards probably wouldn't charge me. The whole thing stinks, Laura. If you think it's bad at home, you've no idea.'

'And what if you can't?' she cut in.

'Can't what? Laura. Don't do that to me. You can raise the money. It's hell in here. There's no proper law and order. You can see what it's like.' He lowered his voice. 'These guys are animals. Murderers, some of them.'

'What if they prosecute you?'

'I'll be in for a stretch. The word is that Phuket jail is rough as hell. Think about it, Laura. All you've got to do is go to the bank.'

'I'll try. But I can't promise. It's not that easy to get a bank transfer so quickly.'

'Please try. Please. And Laura, can't we patch things up between us? I've really missed you. I don't blame you for leaving like you did. I was behaving like an arsehole, I know. I really don't blame you. But I still love you.'

She avoided his gaze. 'It wouldn't work.'

'Come on. Just give it a chance. We were great together.'

'Just leave it, Luke,' she snapped, turning away. 'I'll see what I can do about the money.'

She left the police station and found a bar across the street. She ordered a beer and sat at a table on the pavement. With fascinated disgust she watched a few skimpily dressed girls in a next-door bar drape themselves over some overweight tourists. She thought about High Tops and longed to be back in the peace and beauty of the garden. She remembered David's words as they had said goodbye on the drive: 'I meant what I said, Laura. There's an opening here for you if you decide you want to come back. Just give me a call.'

The tuk-tuk man took her to a hotel on the waterfront. She checked in and left her backpack in the tiny stifling room, then went down to the reception area. She had promised Ken she would call him when she arrived in Patong.

He sounded relieved to hear her voice.

'I've been worried about you, lassie. Marge is too. Have you found laughing boy?'

'Yes. He's in the cells.'

'And?'

'I'm going to try and get him out.'

'You really are a soft touch, lassie. When are you coming home?'

'When I've got this sorted out. I'm about to go to the bank and get an advance on my credit card.'

'Are you sure that's wise? Why don't you just let him sweat it out in there. It might do him good.'

'He only smoked a bit of dope. He's been unlucky, that's all.'

'You're too soft-hearted, Laura. Oh, by the way, Rory came round again. Yesterday.'

'Did he leave a message this time?'

'Yes, he left a note for you.'

'Why don't you read it to me?'

'If you're sure.' She heard the rustle of paper at the other end of the line. 'OK, here goes,' Ken said:

'Dear Laura, I've been meaning to tell you this since February, but I didn't have the courage. It's the reason I quit the protest and went back to live with my parents. I'm sure you'll think badly of me, and I do feel guilty. So guilty, that I can't keep it to myself any longer. I was telling the truth when I said I saw the police officer beat up a protester. But what I didn't tell you was that I saw Luke throw the breeze block at the windscreen. He'd crossed the road and gone round the other side of the lorry. I followed him, but he didn't see me there. I tried to tell you this when you phoned from court but you were in too much of a hurry. It's hard to believe, I know. He was a hero to me, and he let us all down. I can hardly believe it happened, but I saw it with my own eyes. I know it is too late now to do anything about it, but I think you should know.'

Laura swallowed hard and stared out at the sea before her. A lone windsurfer wove to and fro on the crest of a breaker. She followed him with her eyes.

'Laura, are you there?'

'Yes, I don't know what to say.'

'You're not going to bail him out after this, are you?'

'I don't know. I've got to think.'

She went straight back to the police station. Luke was waiting for her, a look of relief in his eyes. Somehow, he'd combed his hair.

'That was quick. Did you get the cash?'

She grabbed the bars and hissed at him.

'You lied to me.'

'What are you talking about?'

'You know what I mean, about the lorry at Wapping. It was you. You lied to me.'

The smug expression vanished.

'Just get me out of here, Laura. We can talk about this later.'

'You let me go into court and peddle a whole load of rubbish. How could you?'

Anger and panic flashed in his eyes.

'So, what if I lied? The whole of News International's game and the police game was built on lies. You didn't expect me to play fair with them, did you?'

'You promised me.'

'You're so naïve, Laura. What did you expect?'

'And what about that poor man, the lorry driver? He could have died.'

'He took the risk. He was a scab.'

She stared at him.

'I'm not getting the money,' she said, suddenly calm.

'Laura? Now, come on. That's not fair. I can't stay here.'

'Why not? You should have been sent down for what you did in Wapping. You won't be in for long. It's a minor offence, possession of cannabis.'

'Don't be a child, Laura. You can't mete out some screwed-up type of rough justice like that. Stop being melodramatic. It doesn't suit you.'

'I'll tell you what doesn't suit me, Luke Goddard – You. You don't suit me. You've used me from the start. Naïve little Laura. Pull the wool over her eyes. She'll pay for me. She'll let me stay in her flat, pay for my booze, pay for my trips.'

'It wasn't like that, Laura. I love you. Truly, I do. Look, get me out of here, and I'll prove it to you. We can go somewhere else, just the two of us. One of the little islands, find a beach hut.'

She looked him long and hard in the eyes. 'Forget it, Luke,' she muttered. 'Look, I'll get the money and give it to the man at the desk. I couldn't have it on my conscience, even though I would really like to leave you here to rot. But after that I'm leaving straight away, so don't try and find out where I am.'

She walked back through the police station, her whole body shaking. She went straight out past the front desk and turned towards the seafront without looking back.

29

There was a stack of post on the hall table when Laura returned home that chilly April morning. She picked up the pile and shuffled half-heartedly through a couple of letters.

There were the usual bills and credit card statements. But there was one official-looking letter addressed to her that made her stop and examine the envelope: it was expensive looking stationery, and the postmark was West London. She ripped the letter open.

It was from a firm of solicitors in Kensington:

'Dear Miss Ellis,

We act for the estate of Mr. James Edward Leech, who sadly died on March 15, 1986. We are writing to you because Mr. Leech left you a bequest in his will of the sum of £10,000 pounds. We would be grateful if you would telephone and arrange an appointment to collect this sum from our offices either by banker's draft or cheque.'

She stared at the letter. She thought about Jim Leech, that diffident, sorrowful old man, and she felt sad at the thought that he had died alone and unloved. She wondered about what dreadful wrong he'd done to Dad. Whatever it was, he had not been able to bring himself to reveal it to her when she visited him that day at Albert Hall Mansions. Perhaps she would never know.

The door to the study opened, and Ken put his head round. She stuffed the letter back in the envelope.

'Hello, stranger,' he said, coming into the room and giving her a hug. 'My God, you do look brown.'

'Yes, it was incredibly hot. By the way, I brought you something from duty-free.'

She went to her backpack in the hall and came back with a bottle of whisky and a long packet of a hundred Marlboro cigarettes.

Ken's face lit up.

'Thank you very much, Laura. That is very kind indeed. Would you like a snifter now?'

'It's a bit early for me, thanks, Ken,' she said.

'I cleared out your Da's room while you were away,' said Ken. 'Took most of the things to the charity shop.'

'That must have been difficult.'

'Yes, it was. Most of his stuff was old. He never did care about clothes much, did he?'

'No,' she said, smiling, remembering the socks full of holes in the drawer.

'Did you find anything else?'

'Anything else?'

'Letters, for example?'

'No, nothing like that. There were a few old slips from the bookies. I threw them out, I'm afraid. Why? Were you looking for something?'

'No, nothing really.'

She looked down at the letter from Jim Leech's solicitor. 'A really strange thing has happened. You remember that old guy, the one you saw Dad shouting at when he had his fall?'

Ken nodded. 'The one your Da wouldn't talk to?'

'He wouldn't talk to him, and he wouldn't tell me about any of it.'

'But he never would, would he? He must have made a conscious decision at some point not to talk about it.'

'Yes, and I'm not much nearer to finding out anything about it. But the strange thing is that Jim Leech died while I was away, and he's left me some money in his will.'

'Why would he do that?'

'No idea. But he did seem to want to repay Dad for saving his life in the war. I don't think he had any family. Or even any friends by the sound of it.'

'Well, you are a lucky girl!'

On an impulse, she said, 'How about selling me Betty? I could hang the painting in my flat.'

Ken gave her a sideways look. 'I was looking for five hundred for her,' he said slowly.

'Five hundred wouldn't be a problem.'

'You're a gem, Laura. That'll keep me in oil paints and whisky for a good few months. Come here and give me a hug. I'm so glad you've come home.'

Later, she went down to the basement to visit Marge. It had been years since she'd been down there. She remembered that she'd promised to go down and visit the day she'd come back from Paris. But she never had.

Now she sat nursing a strong cup of tea in the old armchair in the corner. Marge had a colour television now, but apart from that the little flat had hardly changed. It even smelled the same. Coming down here always brought back the feelings of her childhood: the grief for the death of her mother, the loneliness and boredom of waiting for Dad to come home from work.

Marge was bustling about purposefully. There were bright daffodils in a vase on the windowsill, and the cats lazed on the mat in the glow of the gas fire. She had made a fruit cake as a welcome gift for Laura.

'Did you find what you wanted on your trip, love?' she asked, putting a slice of cake on the table next to Laura.

'I went to the museums in Thailand, and saw the railway where Dad was a prisoner during the war. But I didn't find out much else. It was a bit disappointing on that front. What I really wanted to do was to find his friend, Joy de Souza. I found a photo of her tucked into one of his books just before he died. I wanted to find out a bit about her.'

'Joy de Souza. I've never heard that name before. Did you find out anything about her, my love?'

'Yes,' she said, looking away. 'I found out that she died in the war.'

'Well, that is sad.'

'I had a feeling she might still be alive. I think she'd written to Dad once about ten or eleven years ago. I saw a letter, you see … From Penang. But it couldn't have been from her, after all.'

Marge looked at her sharply. 'Then it must have been from someone else.'

'Do you know anything? Did he ever tell you about anyone from Penang?'

Marge stared at her hands. Then she put down her teacloth and came to sit beside Laura.

'There *was* someone who came to the house once around that time. She wasn't a foreigner, but I know she lived abroad. Had that air about her, looked like one of those colonial types. Thin as a lollipop stick she was, had dyed black hair and makeup like Polyfilla. All done up in furs. She left a box of matches on the sideboard, came from the Penang Club or someplace like that. Stunk of French perfume.'

'Where was I?'

'You must have been at school. He'd taken the afternoon off work. All very secretive he was about it. Never mentioned it once, not to me or to Ken.'

'Do you know who she was?'

'No idea. But she looked like trouble. Had that air about her. Like Wallis Simpson. Sort of stuck up but lacking in class, all at the same time.'

Laura laughed. 'How could you tell? You only saw her from the window, Marge.'

'I could tell. You mark my words, girl. I know these things.'

'Did she come again?'

'No, never saw her again. But I know she wrote to him.'

'Really?'

'A letter arrived a few weeks later. I saw it on the hall floor. Knew it was from her. Same perfume, same Penang postmark. I put two and two together.'

Laura felt sense of relief creeping over her. All these years she'd agonised about ruining his happiness, when perhaps what she had done had made no difference at all. He'd seen the woman who had written the letter, and she'd written to him again.

'Perhaps there was someone else then,' she said slowly. 'He never told me anything about his life before the war. Did he ever say anything to you?'

'Never. As far as I was concerned, his life before he met your mother was a closed book.'

'Do you think he kept the letter?'

Marge shrugged. 'You went through all his papers, didn't you?'

'Only official stuff in his desk. I didn't have the heart to go through his bedroom. Couldn't face it. I asked Ken to clear it out while I was away. You know, take the old clothes to the charity shop. I asked him if he found anything, but he didn't.'

'You could always have another look. You know what men are like. They often miss important things.'

Tentatively, she opened the door to her father's room. All the memories came flooding back. Memories of her mother sitting up in bed and holding her arms open in the morning as Laura jumped on the bed between them. She remembered the warm glow of happiness she had felt as she snuggled down in the hollow between her mother and father. They would read her Beatrix Potter stories together: her father would do the voices of the male characters and her mother the female ones. She remembered how she would sit at the dressing table and try on her mother's jewellery and make-up, smearing red lipstick onto her lips and pouting in the mirror just as her she had seen her mother do. Sometimes her mother would let her try on her high-heeled shoes, and she would stagger around the room, while her mother sat on the bed and watched her, laughing.

She stopped, swallowed hard and banished the ghosts. The room was bare and tidy; it smelled clean and fresh. The bed had been made, and the furniture polished.

She opened the drawers, one by one, but they were all empty. She felt round in the bottom of the wardrobe, found nothing, then stood on a chair and ran her hand along the top of it. She looked under the carpet, even checked the floor for loose boards.

She was leaving the room as she noticed the musical box. A memory surfaced of her mother lifting the lid and a display of toy fairies dancing on a mirror as it lifted. The box was locked.

She ran down to the kitchen and found an old screwdriver Dad had kept in the drawer for odd jobs. She knew it might ruin the box, but she had to find what was in there. She began to try and prise the lid open. She didn't have to apply much pressure. It clicked open easily. Sure enough the dancing fairies sprang into life and moved to the tinny tune of the 'Nutcracker Suite'.

She eased out the upper layer, and the music stopped.

There it was, nestled in the blue velvet lining. An envelope with a Penang post mark, dated February 1975.

She started when she saw the address: 'High Tops House'. Her hands shook as she opened it. When she unfolded the letter, a lock of brown fluff fell out onto the bed. She read on:

'My Dearest Tom,

It was wonderful to meet you last month and talk about the old times, after almost half a lifetime. I couldn't have come to London and not looked you up. I'm glad I persisted even though my first letter went astray.

I had to tell you about the baby, although I knew it would sadden you to know that she died so soon after she was born. I'm sending you a lock of her hair as I promised I would. The treatment I had in London was good, but not good enough I'm afraid. I was keen to get back here to High Tops for my last days.

The lock of hair should be with you when I'm gone. Our baby was a little miracle. She brought James and me closer than ever before, close enough to conceive our own son who has been such joy and strength to me.

If you ever go to Penang, her ashes are scattered off the little bay where you and I used to walk. I brought them back from Australia when James and I returned to High Tops after the war. I often go there still and think of her, and think of you and the good times we had together.

Take care, Tom, and remember me.

Forever yours,
Millie.'

Stunned, Laura put the letter down and sat on the bed for a long time, thinking. She thought about the remote beach where David had taken her. He had said his mother had loved to go there. But he hadn't mentioned a baby. She wondered if he knew.

She suddenly thought of the money that Jim Leech had left her. It could be just the injection of cash David would need to get the business on its feet. She had no real need of it for herself. She thought about telephoning David to tell him about the letter from Millie, and about the baby, but quickly decided it would be too difficult to explain over a crackly phone line. No, she would write instead. She could explain properly in a letter and at the same time mention the bequest.

* * *

The next morning, Laura went back to the Imperial War Museum to see if she could find out anything about Arthur Stone. The girl with glasses who had helped her before was sitting at the desk. She looked up and smiled at Laura.

'Peter,' said the girl and turned to the elderly man who sat next to her, wearing a pince-nez and an old colourless cardigan. 'This is the person I told you about. She was looking for something about … What was it now? I've forgotten exactly.'

'I wanted to find out about Arthur Stone,' said Laura. 'Oh, and I found a second-hand book by him.' She delved in her bag and produced the pamphlet she had bought in Thailand.

The old man took it eagerly. His eyes lit up, and he examined it with a sort of reverential wonder.

'Arthur's thesis! I haven't seen a copy of this for a good many years. How wonderful.'

He flicked through it eagerly.

'I didn't know there were any copies left. May I ask where you found this?'

'In Thailand, actually. Kanchanaburi. At a little second-hand book stall near the museum.'

He carried on reading.

'I was wondering if you could help me?' she asked. 'Before he died, my father told me that he had told someone about his experiences as a prisoner of war. He told me to ask Arthur Stone about it.'

'Arthur's very old now, you know. He's been retired a good many years. But he knows more about the Burma-Thailand railway than anyone else. He interviewed dozens of prisoners for his research in the 1940s and 1950s. Your father must have been one of them.'

'Could I speak to him, perhaps? Do you know where I can find him?'

'Well, I suppose you could go and see him. He loves visitors. He's in a residential home in Surrey. I've got the address here somewhere.'

He rummaged in the desk drawer and produced a battered address book. He flicked through the pages and scribbled something on a piece of paper.

'There you are. It is in Rushmoor, near Farnham. Trains go every half hour from Waterloo, I believe. Give him my best regards. I should warn you though, he is in his nineties and rather deaf.'

Laura caught a bus to Waterloo and took a train to Surrey. She stared out of the window as it rumbled through the outskirts of south-west London and out into the countryside. It seemed to stop at every station along the way. Soon the suburbs gave way to pine forests and heath land. How different this was to the lush beauty of Malaysia and Thailand. How dark and oppressive this landscape seemed.

At Farnham Station she got a taxi to Rushmoor. The Pines was a rambling old Edwardian house, surrounded by forest on three sides and overlooking a lake on the other.

A formidable looking woman opened the door.

'Are you a relative?' she asked peering at Laura when she asked to see Arthur Stone.

'No, I'm here to see him about some historical research.'

The woman raised her eyebrows.

'We normally ask visitors to phone first, but Arthur is usually happy to see people. Please don't tire him. He's very old, and his health is failing.'

She was shown into a bright airy dayroom with picture windows overlooking the lake. A huge television was on at full blast on one wall. The residents sat staring at it or were slumped asleep in upright armchairs. But the woman bustled past them and guided Laura to the other side of the room.

An old man in a wheelchair was sitting by the window. His knees were covered by a tartan blanket, but he wore a three-piece suit.

'Arthur? Arthur?' said the woman sharply. 'There's a young lady here to see you. It is about some historical matter, she says.'

He turned round, and on seeing Laura, he held out a frail hand. Laura took it. He looked very old and very pale. He had a wispy covering of white hair on his head, and behind his thick glasses his face was deeply lined. He looked immeasurably older than either Tom or Jim Leech.

'Well, I'll leave you to it,' said the woman.

'Do you think you could turn that infernal TV down a bit, Mabel?' he asked.

'Of course,' she said, and she bustled away.

'Hello, I'm Laura Ellis,' said Laura taking his hand. 'I think you might have known my father.'

'Really? What is this all about? Pull up a chair and sit down.'

She did as he suggested.

'Dad was in Singapore in the war. He was a prisoner on the Thai-Burma railway. He died recently and just before he died, he said that he had told someone about his experiences during the war. He said that I should ask Arthur Stone. I have read your book.'

She handed him the slim volume.

'Oh, marvellous, marvellous!' he said, almost jumping up in his chair. 'I had almost forgotten about it. The toil that went into this, you can't imagine.'

Like the man in the museum he went into a reverie, flicking through the book, scanning paragraphs, sometimes exclaiming out loud, gasping over certain passages.

Laura waited. In the end he looked up and saw her sitting there. He frowned as if he had forgotten who she was. Then he said, 'So how was it you said I might know your father?'

'Well, as I said, he was a prisoner on the Thailand-Burma railway. Just before he died he mentioned that he'd told someone about his experiences and that I should ask Arthur Stone.'

'Hmm, I interviewed lots of prisoners for my thesis. Some of them wrote accounts for me. I put little advertisements in the daily newspapers, and there were a lot of responses. I think many of them felt the need to unburden themselves. What was his name?'

'He was Tom. Thomas Ellis.'

'And what was his battalion?'

'The Straits Settlements Volunteer Force.'

The old man closed his eyes again and put his fingertips together. He bowed his head as if in deep meditation. After this had gone on for a few minutes, Laura began to worry that he had fallen asleep. She wondered whether to try and wake him.

Then he shook his head.

'No. I'm sorry. I simply can't remember any of their names. There were so many. What did he look like?'

'I've got a photo.' She showed him the photo of her father that she always carried in her purse. It had been snapped in a photo booth for a passport, but rejected for that purpose because he was smiling.

She waited breathlessly, watching the old man's face as he studied it. But again, he shook his head and handed the photo back to her.

'I'm sorry, my dear. It's so long ago, you see.'

Laura stared out over the lake. The sun was dipping behind the line of black pines, streaking the lake with reds and golds.

'I'll tell what I can do. I'm not promising anything though,' Arthur said. 'What happened was that men wrote me accounts under pseudonyms. Most of them didn't want to reveal their identities. They wanted to remain anonymous, to protect their families from what they had suffered. They were ashamed, a lot of them, strange though it may seem. The accounts were typed up and archived in Imperial War Museum under the pseudonyms. That's why you didn't find his account there. But that's not to say it isn't there. I kept a list of who they were and what names they went under. It's in my old desk at my daughter's house. She's coming to visit me tomorrow. I could ask her to dig it out and give you a call if she finds anything.'

'Oh, would you? That would be fantastic.'

'I'm not promising that your father's account will be amongst them. Some of them gave very sketchy ones, and I didn't keep those. Also, I might not have kept a full record of those who only spoke to me and didn't write anything down. It all depended on the quality of the material, you see. Was your father an educated man?'

She nodded.

'Then I would probably have asked him to write it down for me. You'll have to wait and see. I'll ask Margaret tomorrow and get her to give you a call.'

30

London was even more drab and grey than he remembered it. As the train chugged in through the East End he could see that whole streets had been flattened here as well. Terraces were blown away, and houses stood with their inside walls exposed, their furniture balanced on sagging floors. Other buildings were boarded up. Rubble was piled high on the streets.

He had sent a cable to his mother and father in Gordon Square from the ship a few days before reaching England. But he hadn't received a reply.

The ship had docked at Tilbury, and he had then taken a train to Liverpool Street Station. He stared out at the monotonous landscape. The patchwork of grey-green fields was dull compared to the lush colours of the East. Would he ever get used to it again?

At Liverpool Street he took the underground to Russell Square. He looked around at his fellow travellers, bundled up in dark coats and hats. Their pale unhealthy faces looked closed, furtive. Nothing had changed.

Part of Russell Square had been bombed, and there was a gap in the buildings on the north side, but otherwise it was much the same as when he had last seen it in 1938. As he crossed the gardens in the middle of the square he remembered the day he had walked out of his job in the city. He hardly recognised himself in that confused youth who had sat on a bench, eating an ice cream, wondering what to do with his life. He felt immeasurably older now, physically and mentally, as if his experiences had wrought a permanent change in him. He was also much thinner, his skin permanently sallow through years of exposure to the sun, and he walked with a limp.

People gave him strange looks as he passed. They stared and then looked away, shocked and embarrassed as if there was something shameful about his appearance. He wondered if they knew anything about the war in the Far East and about the plight of the prisoners there.

The house in Gordon Square was still standing. It looked exactly the same as he remembered it. The door was painted blue, just as it had always been. With an odd feeling in the pit of his stomach, he walked up the steps and knocked firmly with the brass knocker.

His mother opened the door. He hardly recognised her. She appeared diminished in every way. Her hair was streaked with grey, and her face and body seemed to sag with age.

She peered at him for a moment. Then her face registered astonishment and joy.

'Tom.' She stepped forward and flung her arms around his neck.

'I sent a telegram, Mother. Didn't you get it?'

'Yes, but it only arrived yesterday. I guessed you would be almost home so I didn't send a reply. You look so different, Tom,' she said as she ushered him into the house. 'Come on in! Don't stand out there in the cold.'

He stepped into the hall. There was a bicycle propped against the hat-stand, and several overcoats hung from the hooks.

'How's Father? Is he home?'

Her face suddenly wore an anguished expression, and her eyes filled with tears.

'He died in 1943, Tom. A heart attack. I would have let you

know, but I had no way of contacting you. All I had was a postcard from the Volunteers to say you'd been taken prisoner by the Japanese at Singapore.'

'Oh, Mother.'

He put his arms round her and held her, but he had no words of comfort to offer her. He felt nothing himself. It was as if the shock of Joy's death had robbed him of the capacity to feel grief.

He followed his mother into the kitchen, where once a cook and scullery maid would have been hard at work preparing the evening meal. It was empty and shabby now. She put a kettle on the gas hob.

She turned around as someone clattered down the stairs behind her and with a shout of 'See you later, Mrs. E,' went out, slamming shut the front door.

'Times have been very hard, Tom,' his mother explained. 'Since your father passed away. I've had to take in lodgers.'

'Do you mind if I stay here a while? I need to look for a job.'

'Of course. You must stay, Tom. It's your home. Have you thought about what you might do now?'

'I might go back into the law. Not in the city, of course, but in a small way, helping ordinary people with their legal problems. It's not well paid, but I should be able to give you something when I start.'

She took his hand on the table.

'How wonderful to have you back,' she said, looking into his eyes. 'I sometimes wondered if you were dead, but something inside always told me you were still alive. A mother's instinct, I suppose.'

He smiled. 'I did come close to death a few times,' he said.

'You must have been through some dreadful times.'

He nodded, but remained silent.

'And I couldn't help noticing that you're limping. You must go to see Dr. Harvey. He might be able to help you.'

'Is he still around? He must be very old now.'

'Yes. He's still going strong though. Promise me you'll go? You look as if you are in a lot of pain.'

'All right, Mother, I'll go tomorrow.'

Later, as they sipped their tea, she asked softly, 'You have forgiven me, Tom, haven't you?'

He was confused by her question. He then realised that she was referring to that moment in 1938 when he had opened the drawing room door and had seen her with that man. The moment had not crossed his mind for years.

He patted her hand.

'There's nothing to forgive, Mother. Don't mention it ever again.'

* * *

Dr. Harvey had a small surgery in Bernard Street. He'd been their family doctor since Tom was a child. He made Tom lie on the couch and examined him thoroughly.

'Your body's been tested to the extreme. That's surely obvious, Tom. The malaria will probably keep returning to trouble you every so often. But otherwise you are in fairly good shape, considering your ordeal. Your leg looks as though it might benefit from being pinned. I think I'll refer you to the hospital for an X-ray.' He scribbled on a piece of paper then told Tom that they would write to him from University College Hospital with an appointment.

'That's with Dr. Roberts, the radiographer there. He's first class, Tom.'

As Tom got up to go, the doctor cleared his throat and said, 'Your incarceration will have had an effect on you that is not just physical, Tom. Lots of people won't realise that, and you may have some difficulties relating to the world again. You might want to bottle it up, but in my experience that would not be very wise. You may want to talk it through with someone. If you do ever need to talk about it, I'm always here.'

'Thank you, Doctor. That's very kind. I'll bear that in mind.'

'You could also try this, if you'd prefer to talk to someone you don't know,' the doctor smiled and handed him a copy of *The Times*. He pointed to an advertisement in the classifieds: 'PhD History student looking for Far East POWs to interview for research into conflict – contact Arthur Stone.'

Tom considered the advertisement. At that moment he had no desire to speak to anyone about what he had suffered. But so as not to offend the doctor, he tore out the advertisement and put it in his pocket.

In the weeks that followed, he thought about the doctor's words. It was true. As he wandered through the streets of Central London, trying to acclimatise himself to the changed city that was once again his home, the well-fed people who pushed past him on the pavements and in the underground, whose hostile eyes occasionally lingered on his bony frame, seemed to come from another world. He felt that no-one would understand what he had been through, and even in his own mind his ordeal took on an air of unreality, an almost dream-like quality.

Back at home, alone in his room, he sat on the bed and took out the objects he had managed to bring back. His father's watch (whose hands had remained frozen at twelve noon, the time the ship went down), the brown leaves from the pomelo tree, Ian's ring and Harry's medal. He turned each over in his hands, remembering. He sniffed the dried-out leaves, but they had no odour now.

He wrote to the Regimental Headquarters of the Northumberland

Fusiliers, asking for the names and addresses of Ian and Harry's relatives. He intended to catch a train up to Alnwick and take the objects to them as a last gesture of respect. But after a week or so he received a letter informing him that Ian had no next of kin, and Harry's wife and child had been killed in an air raid. He put the medal and ring, along with his own from the Straits Settlements Volunteers, in an old wooden box, then stowed it all away under the bed.

He spent long hours staring at Joy's photograph, trying to remember the tone of her voice, the sound of her laugh. The fact that they were slowly slipping away from him tore at his heart. Even looking at the photo now didn't give him the same comfort that it had when he was a prisoner. It reminded him sharply of his loss, of how her life had been so cruelly cut short. Yet it also reminded him of how her image had stayed with him, throughout those years of hell. She had always been there for him. And even though she herself had perished, she had kept his hopes alive.

31

Laura ordered a coffee and waited at a corner table. He was prompt, of course, and as he made his way towards her, weaving between the tables, she noticed the eyes of several other women follow him.

'Laura. I'm so glad I could meet you while I'm in London. It's great you're back from your trip,' Adam said as he leaned forward to kiss her on the cheek. She caught a waft of expensive aftershave. He sat down and the waitress bustled over.

After he'd ordered, he said, 'So why the secrecy? Why didn't you want to come into the office to meet?'

'It's not secrecy, really. I just didn't want to bump into everyone at the firm. I wouldn't know what to say.'

'I'm sorry. How crass of me. I wasn't thinking. You must still be feeling dreadful about your father.'

'It's not that. It's that … Well, Adam, I don't think I'll be coming back.'

He gulped and stared at her.

'Can I ask why?'

'Of course, I'll come back and work out my notice if you really need me to, but you said to take a few weeks off, so I figured that could be my notice period.'

The coffee arrived, and he stared at it, shaking his head.

'But why, Laura? Just tell me why.'

'I've done a lot of thinking since Dad died. You know, Adam,

I've never really felt this job was right for me.'

'But you have such a promising career ahead of you. You are so committed.'

'Not really. I was there for someone else.'

'Someone else?'

'Yes. My father. I was trying to please him.'

He stared at her. Poor Adam. He was so straightforward. He would never understand.

'You've changed, Laura.'

'Maybe. Losing someone you love does that to people sometimes.'

'And what about us?'

She looked him in the eye and said gently, 'There was no *us*, really, was there? Just a fumble at an office party. I'm really sorry if I led you to think otherwise. I shouldn't have done that.'

He blushed. 'I thought there was something between us. We always got on really well. But I suppose you were always hooked on that down-and-out you used to hang about with.'

'Luke? Not anymore. We split up in Thailand.'

Adam was silent while he digested the news. Then he looked up at her and said, 'So what are you going to do?'

'Not sure yet. I'm going to think about it for a bit. Go back to the drawing board. I thought I might like to work in a law centre. But that's just one of the options.'

He blinked. 'You're joking! After what you've been used to?' She thought about the plush office, the smooth running machinery of the administration, the chrome and modern art pieces, the potted palms.

'Some of us have a social conscience, believe it or not.'

'Touché,' he said. 'What else? What else do you think you might do?'

'It sounds mad, but I might go back to the Far East.'

'That does sound mad.'

* * *

The girl at the museum desk looked up and smiled as Laura approached.

'How did you get on last week? Did you meet Arthur Stone?'

'Yes, he was really helpful. He couldn't remember my dad, but he got his daughter to dig up the records he kept.'

'Did she find anything?'

'She called me this morning. She'd managed to find the pseudonym listed beside Dad's name. A partial anagram, apparently: Sam Lisle. She thought that whatever he wrote for Dr. Stone would be filed here in the museum under that name. Would you be able to look for me and see if it's there?'

Laura watched, her stomach tightening as the girl quickly selected a drawer in the chest behind her and thumbed through an index. She was frowning with concentration. At last she pulled out a typewritten card. She looked up and smiled.

'You're in luck. There is something here under that name.'

She went to a box file on a shelf. Laura watched again as she took out a pile of brown files and examined each one.

Why was she taking so long? Laura could hardly breathe with anticipation. Let it be here, she prayed.

At last, the girl looked up and held out a battered folder.

'Here you are. It's quite bulky.'

Laura took it from her, her hands shaking. From the weight of it, it felt as though it was several pages thick.

She held the folder carefully as she crossed the room and sat down at one of the reading tables. 'Memoirs of Sam Lisle. Far East Prisoner of War. 1946,' was typed on a faded label on its front cover. Her heart was beating fast. She put it on the table and stared at it for a few moments. Then she took a deep breath and opened it.

Her father's account had been typed on paper as thin as tracing paper, using an old fashioned typewriter in courier font. She began to read:

'My name is Sam Lisle. I am thirty-three years of age. In the autumn of 1945 I returned from the Far East where I spent over three years as a prisoner of war in Japanese hands. I am going to write about my treatment as a prisoner for several reasons. First, because I would like the world to know what happened to us prisoners, for it never to be forgotten, and in the hope that it may never happen again. Second, because I would like to preserve these memories while they are still fresh in my mind. I am also doing this for a selfish reason. Because I hope that in setting down my memories on paper it will help to free my mind from the nightmare that I live with every day, so that perhaps I can begin to live something approaching a normal life.

On February 15, 1942, I watched as every other man in my division of the Straits Settlements Volunteers was mown down by the guns of Japanese tanks that entered the city of Singapore. I walked alone through a rubber plantation and through deserted city streets until I found another group of soldiers. They were the Northumberland Fusiliers, and their colonel told me to lay down my rifle because the British had surrendered.

We were marched out of the city at gunpoint, past jeering crowds of locals waving Japanese flags. We marched fifteen miles with our packs in the sweltering heat of the day, through the rubber plantations and farmlands to the other side of the island. In the distance we could see the forbidding walls of the Changi gaol and barracks – this would become our prison and home for the next six months. This was where our living nightmare of incarceration and slavery would begin.'

Laura found herself crying softly. It was as if her father's voice was speaking to her directly from the page. She read on.

EPILOGUE

Tom sat propped up against the pillows, watching the activity on the busy ward from his hospital bed. The nurses bustled about in their starched white uniforms, moving efficiently from patient to patient, dressing wounds, taking temperatures, checking pulses. He observed their quiet efficiency, and how the equipment they used was shiny, clinically clean. They worked under the watchful eye of the sister, a stern woman who patrolled the ward inspecting for specks of dirt and any sign of laxness on the part of the nurses. She clearly struck fear into their hearts.

His newly pinned leg still throbbed from the operation and the stitches were sore. He was grateful for the painkillers the nurses doled out to him at regular intervals.

Lying in this spotless, echoing room with white walls, high ceilings and enormous windows, Tom couldn't help but compare the ward to the makeshift hospital hut in the jungle at Chungkai, constructed of bamboo and thatched with atap palm leaves. There, sick and dying men had to lie on hard cane platforms without pillows or blankets, and the doctors and orderlies went about barefoot and half-naked on the bare earth floor, caring with warmth and compassion, with improvised equipment and virtually no medicine, for men who had little hope of recovery.

He forced himself to stop thinking about it. He knew he must stop dwelling on those memories. A few months ago, when he had first met Arthur Stone, he had made a pact with himself that he would stop his mind from wandering back there, that he would write down everything that had happened to him and that would be the end of it.

It had taken him nearly two years to take the step of contacting Arthur Stone. He had carried the advertisement the doctor had given him in his wallet, sometimes taking it out and reading it, thinking about acting on it, but never really getting around to it. He wanted to wait until he felt ready to speak about what he had been through.

He had met Arthur Stone in an old fashioned spit-and-sawdust pub near King's Cross. Arthur was an amiable and slightly eccentric academic. He explained to Tom that it would help his research enormously if Tom would write down his memories. Tom had been worried about revealing his identity, so they had worked out an alias together, and he had left the pub resolving to start writing straight away.

But his life was busy now and he was left with little spare time. He had found a job at a small legal practice in Hackney that provided low-cost advice to poor and destitute people. He loved the work. The knowledge that what he did every day made a difference to someone's life gave him great comfort. The pay was dismal, but he had saved enough to rent a studio flat above a shop in Islington so that he could move out of home and become independent.

He had promised himself that he would start writing his account for Arthur Stone while he was in hospital, but since he had come round from the anaesthetic he had received a steady stream of visitors.

Two of his colleagues, Peter and Steven, had visited the day before, bringing him a basket of fresh fruit. His old friend David Lambert had visited, and his sister Elsie had come along too. She was now happily married to a stockbroker and expecting her first child. They had stayed for a long time, chatting about the old days. Watching Elsie's plump, contented face as she sat beside his bed gossiping away, he had been struck by how dull her company was. He wondered how she had inspired so much passion in him all those years ago.

This morning his mother had appeared carrying an enormous bunch of white roses. She bent over and kissed him, and the delicate scent of the roses had wafted towards him.

'That's very sweet of you,' he said.

'I saw them at the flower stall by the tube station. I couldn't resist them. I thought it would cheer you up on such a gloomy day' she said, glancing at the grey sky out of the window. 'Aren't they beautiful?'

'They're lovely. Thank you. I don't think anyone has ever bought me flowers before.'

'Well there's a first time for everything, Tom. And besides, you haven't been in hospital before either, have you?'

He smiled at her, blotting out the image of the hospital hut in the camp. His mother knew nothing of that. He wanted to keep it that way.

His mother had stayed for a couple of hours, holding his hand, chatting. Then she had kissed him again and left.

Now there was no excuse anymore. He leaned over and took the pad and pencil from the shelf beside the bed. He had to start writing. He nibbled the pencil. How could he begin to tell that extraordinary story? The memories came flooding back to him, crowding in on one another. He decided he would start with February 15, 1942. The day he was taken prisoner in Singapore.

He opened the pad and scribbled down a couple of paragraphs.

It all came quite easily to him until he came to the part about the march to Changi and remembered that it was the first time he had seen Harry and Ian. His hand began to tremble, and he dropped the pencil. Suddenly he wasn't so sure he could do this. The heat and noise and confusion of that day came back to him, and he was there again, marching alongside his old friends, feeling confused and lost and terrified.

'Penny for them?'

He looked up, momentarily confused to be back in the present. A nurse was standing there in front of him, smiling. He had not seen her before. He would have remembered if he had. She was young and petite, fine-boned with blue eyes and delicate features. Her blonde hair was tucked up into her starched cap, but a lock or two had escaped and fell around her face.

'A penny for your thoughts,' she repeated. 'You looked miles away.'

'I was,' he said. 'About seven thousand to be precise.'

'That sounds adventurous,' she said. 'Sorry to bring you back down to earth, but I've got your painkillers here, Mr. Ellis. It's that time of day again.'

He took the tablets and the glass of water from her, and gulped them down obediently.

'Are you writing something?' she asked, her eyes lighting on the notebook.

'Oh, it's nothing really,' he said quickly. He closed the book and put it on the shelf beside him. 'Just a few meaningless scribbles, that's all.'

She went to the end of the bed and picked up the clipboard that held his notes.

'How's the leg faring today?'

'A bit better today, thank you. It will be fine.'

The nurse nodded, writing something on the notes. She began to move around the bed, tucking in the sheets, tidying the covers. She moved deftly and neatly, and as she came close and leaned over him to fold the sheet back over the blankets, he noticed that she wore a tiny silver cross around her neck. It stirred a memory buried deep inside him.

'How did you injure it? I hope you don't mind my asking. Is it a war injury?' she asked as she straightened up.

'Yes. I got it when I was a prisoner of war in the Far East. I was jumping off a sinking ship.'

Her face was suddenly serious. She looked at him with her blue eyes, now brimming over with sympathy and sorrow. She put her hand on his arm.

'I'm so sorry,' she said. 'You must have had a dreadful time. I've heard a bit about it from other patients, but it's hard to imagine what you must have been through.'

He swallowed and was silent, but he was grateful for her frank acknowledgement of his experience. Many people did not know how to react when he'd told them that he'd been a prisoner of the Japanese. They would avoid his gaze, shuffle uncomfortably or change the subject.

She moved to the bedside table to refill the water jug. She stopped.

'What beautiful roses!' she exclaimed.

'Yes, they're lovely, aren't they? My mother brought them this morning.'

'White roses are my favourite,' she said and she leaned forward impulsively and buried her face in the petals, drawing in a long deep breath.

'What a lovely scent,' she said. 'Your mother has perfect taste.'

She looked at him with smiling eyes, and at that moment the sun emerged from behind a cloud and filled the ward with pale sunlight, lighting up the stray strands of her hair in shades of white and gold. Tom smiled back, and as he looked at her, his heart suddenly filled with hope.

ACKNOWLEDGEMENTS

I would like to thank the following people for their help and encouragement:

Members of YouWriteOn, the peer review website, especially Siobhan Daiko, and my sisters Mary and Dot for their comments on my early drafts.

Special thanks go to Sujatha Sevellimedu for her inspirational, patient and tireless editing.

The following organisations helped enormously with my research:

The Thai-Burma Railway Centre at Kanchanaburi, especially Terry Mantann who drove me to the sites of some of the camps near Kanchanaburi in August 2010 and helped piece together the details of my father's wartime experience; Michael Hurst MBE, Director of the Taiwan POW Camps Memorial Society, who first provided me with information about the sinking of the Hofuku Maru and Dad's time in Shirikawa camp in Taiwan, and his wife Tina who kindly translated Dad's record cards from Japanese; also members of the Far East Prisoner of War Association who first pointed me in the direction of the records of POWs in the National Archives at Kew.

The following books have been sources of inspiration and information:

Peter Thomson *The Battle for Singapore*

Brian P Farrell *The Defence and Fall of Singapore 1940-1942*

Colin Smith *Singapore Burning*

Brian MacArthur *Surviving the Sword*

Sir Clifford Kinvig *River Kwai Railway*

Rod Beattie *The Death Railway: A Brief History*

Geoffrey Pharoah Adams *The Thailand to Burma Railway*

Paul Gibbs Pancheri *Volunteer!*

Richard Kandler *The Prisoner List*

Alistair Urquhart *The Forgotten Highlander*

James Clavell *King Rat*

Charles McCormac *You'll Die in Singapore*

Gregory Michno *Death on the Hellships*